Even So

Even So

Lauren B. Davis

Publisher: Scott Fraser | Acquiring editor: Rachel Spence | Editor: Shannon Whibbs
Cover designer: Sophie Paas-Lang
Cover image: istock.com/andipantz
Printer: Marquis Book Printing Inc.

Library and Archives Canada Cataloguing in Publication

Title: Even so / Lauren B. Davis.
Names: Davis, Lauren B., 1955- author.
Identifiers: Canadiana (print) 20200359444 | Canadiana (ebook) 20200359452 | ISBN 9781459747647 (softcover) | ISBN 9781459747654 (PDF) | ISBN 9781459747661 (EPUB)
Classification: LCC PS8557.A8384 E94 2021 | DDC C813/.6—dc23

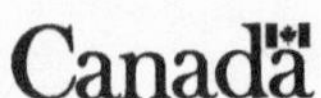

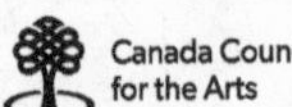

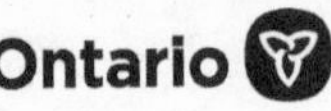

We acknowledge the support of the Canada Council for the Arts and the Ontario Arts Council for our publishing program. We also acknowledge the financial support of the Government of Ontario, through the Ontario Book Publishing Tax Credit and Ontario Creates, and the Government of Canada.

Printed and bound in Canada.

Dundurn Press
1382 Queen Street East
Toronto, Ontario, Canada M4L 1C9
dundurn.com, @dundurnpress

To Sister Rita Woehlcke, who knows so many things, including why.

And did you get what you wanted from this life, even so?
I did.
And what did you want?
To call myself beloved, to feel myself beloved on the earth.

— Raymond Carver, "Late Fragment"

Angela

Angela sat on the side of the bed, lacing up her running shoes, and watched her husband standing at one of the two sinks in their ensuite. Philip was shirtless, a towel wrapped around his waist. It was early spring, predawn, and the overhead light cast unflattering shadows. The bathroom was so very white and cool. Philip leaned in toward the mirror as he shaved. His belly, a hairy fold of flesh, rested on the top of the sink. His legs were ham-pink, and a purple varicose vein wriggled like a worm at the back of his right knee. Angela watched him in the silver-framed mirror. He squooshed his face up, lips pursed. There was a considerable amount of loose skin and so he used his left hand to pull it taut. *Scrape, scrape, scrape.* Rinse the razor. *Tap, tap, tap* on the sink. Repeat. Wipe face with towel, wipe the sink with the same towel, and deposit towel in hamper. No towel was ever used twice. He turned back to view himself in the mirror. He posed to the side, and slapped his gut three times, as though in congratulations, and grinned at his big, meaty reflection. He noticed Angela staring. He unwrapped the towel at his waist and waggled his dangling bits in her direction, raising his eyebrows.

"I've got ten minutes." He waggled again, the grin and the heavy eyebrows working in tandem.

While it was true Philip's bits were impressive, the last thing Angela wanted was to have sex with him. In fact, the extent of her distaste for the man to whom she was married came as a bit of a shock. She could just about manage sex after a bottle of burgundy on a Saturday night had put a little Vaseline on the lens, but, in the full-on glare of morning's bathroom light? No. No, she very much did not want to have sex with Philip. It had been, what, three months since there'd been one of those Saturday nights? She tried not to let her aversion show and walked to the closet to grab her jacket so he wouldn't see her face. *Oh*, she thought, *let me just get out of this now. Don't make a fuss, Philip*. The image of his belly slapping against her ass popped into her head and she winced.

No wife should be thinking this about her husband. But there it was. The little toad hopped in, with no promise of turning into a prince. When had this happened? Slowly, she supposed, over time. They hadn't always been so distant, so much at odds. When Connor was little there had been parties, and dancing, BBQs in the back yard. Business-related events, mostly, but she'd liked some of the wives, even if all they really talked about were kids. That was okay. She'd only wanted to talk about Connor, anyway. The perfection of him. The joy of him. And with the parties had been champagne, and martinis, and yes, there had been sex, quite a bit of it, to be truthful.

Had her desire for Philip fallen away because of the way his body had changed over the years, or was it more than that?

It was puzzling, she thought, the way someone so persnickety about household perfection — no dust, no clutter, nothing out of place — could care so little about his own body, and equally baffling that he thought his wife would find it attractive. Philip had never boasted a six-pack. He'd always been slightly on the heavy side, but at least it had been firm flesh back when they'd met. And he'd smelled of some woodsy cologne she liked. What was it about men, wanting their women to be sylph-like and flawless while they went the way of all flesh? For her part she was still slim, not five pounds over what she had been twenty years ago when they married. Her auburn hair shone from expensive conditioners and was kept in the softly curling bob Philip said made her look like Audrey Hepburn. Her hazel eyes were framed by perfectly arched brows and thick lashes. Not a single line hovered over her full lips. All this was expected of her, while just look at Philip there, in all his self-satisfied glory.

Those waggling eyebrows. That grin. Those dangling bits, now slightly tumescent.

"Can't," she said, keeping her voice cheerful. "Got to get this run in. I'm at the Pantry this morning."

Philip rewrapped the towel, his grin disappearing. "Again?"

"Yes, again."

"I don't get it, Angela."

"I know you don't." She zipped up her windbreaker. "You've made that clear."

"Like emptying the sea with a slotted spoon," Philip said as he applied deodorant.

Angela had begun volunteering at the Our Daily Bread Food Pantry a little over six months ago. One of those frequent fundraising letters had come in the mail, asking for donations. She had written a cheque, of course, but then had begun thinking. She had time on her hands, too much time, in fact. Connor, off at the Lawrenceville boarding school, was home infrequently, and at his age was hardly interested in hanging out with his mother, more was the pity. She had no job outside the home, which was mostly managed by Irina, the twice-a-week cleaning lady, anyway. She had few friends, since she was uninterested in things such as golf or bridge or shopping-and-lunch. She had joined a book club, briefly, but the women (no men) seemed more interested in gossip and wine than Balzac or Morrison. Her greenhouse and beloved orchids were important, a sort of meditation on the solace of beauty, but they didn't contribute much to the world at large.

Ever since Connor had moved to the Lawrenceville boarding school, the restlessness Angela had felt creeping up on her for so long had become impossible to ignore. Running helped, but she couldn't run all day every day, could she? When she felt that tinge of possibility looking down at the cheque she'd written for the Pantry, she felt perhaps this was what she was being called to do. She telephoned them. Spoke to the nun, Sister Eileen, who ran the place and asked if she could pop in with a cheque and for a chat about volunteering.

This is the way it had started. She went once a week, more or less, and the place now mattered to her. Perhaps not as much as her orchids, but still. It was a bone of contention between her and Philip. He didn't like her heading into what he called The Wilds of Trenton. For some as yet unexplored reason, that made her want to be part of it even more.

She looked at Philip again, stepping into his pants now, heaving them up over that belly.

"See you tonight. You going to be late?" She shoved her hands in her pockets and jogged down the stairs.

"Home by eight. Hey," he called after her.

"Yeah?"

"Langs' for dinner tomorrow night, remember? Can you pick up some gift? She cooks."

"I'll find something."

"Love you," he called again.

"Love you, too."

Her hand was on the doorknob. Love him? Did she? She had once, she thought.

An odd memory flashed through her mind of the two of them, dressed in white linen, playing croquet at a fundraiser for the Princeton Hospital. They drank Pimm's with mint and cucumber. She wore a fetching wide-brimmed straw hat with silk flowers on it and a slip dress with a drop waist, all very 1930s. He hit his ball into hers with a hard *clack* and then prepared, as the rules gave him permission to do, to smash hers into the deep wilds. But he didn't. He looked sideways at her, smiled, and tapped it ever so lightly. Then he stood and touched the rim of his boater, bowing gently. She had loved him in that moment, looking, as he did, like some English lord, so sturdy, a country man, but elegant in his whites, and so gallant. She had loved him then, she was sure.

Love. Did she even have the faintest notion of what that word meant? She shook her head and set out into the brightening spring day. It was too early for all this.

HER FEET WERE LIGHT on the pavement as she ran. She could see her breath in light puffs as she passed the fancy mansions. How beautiful these houses were. Solid and immoveable. Testament to prosperity, security … what she'd always wanted.

She stretched her shoulders as she waited at the traffic light, jogging in place.

Almost no one was out at this hour. A man walking an ancient golden retriever. A few cars. The houses were waking up. Lights coming on. When she and Philip first moved here, she'd been thrilled to be living in one of these houses. And now? It was what she had wanted, right? But that "wanted." *Oh, dear. Past tense.*

Something was changing. Something *had* changed in Angela over the twenty years she and Philip had been together. Angela understood he was all the things she had been raised to want: steady, well-off, honest, faithful, and kind — at least to his family, although outside his immediate circle he stood solidly in the no-welfare-for-deadbeats camp. Angela thought she would be safe with him.

She was a twenty-five-year-old administrative assistant at a stock brokerage firm in New York when they met. Philip was a thirty-two-year-old analyst on the way up. They had lunches with wine. That first lunch at the Gramercy Tavern Angela ordered a Chardonnay. She knew it wasn't the usual quick business lunch. The beamed ceiling, the well-heeled diners, the tablecloths and hovering waiters, lots of glasses and cutlery at each place. She wanted him to see her as a bit of a thrill. She'd seen a woman pick him up at the end of the day now and then. Nice enough, Angela was sure, but the woman wore loafers and Bermuda shorts. If Philip's girlfriend was sensible shoes, Angela would be red-soled high-heeled Louboutins. Not that she could have afforded shoes like that, but a girl could dream.

She wasn't interested in Philip, at least not at first. Angela dated musicians and actors and guys with Celtic armband tattoos. Philip wore Brooks Brothers and his pants were ever so slightly too short. She could make him want her. A game like that took some of the boredom out of her menial job.

So, she ordered wine and he grinned and said, "I'll have one, too."

She saw it in his eyes, how he looked at her and what he thought. She was the little wild one. She was going to add spice to the bland old business stew. She saw how it puffed him up, how he liked the idea that a man like him — with prospects, with cash, with a BMW, with a loft in Tribeca — deserved a girl like her. It was one of the perks of Wall Street. *She* was one of the perks. Angela played with the buttons on her blouse and licked her lips.

It was all just supposed to be fun.

She liked it. Liked the power. It turned her on. Women had little enough power, after all. Men made more money, got the promotions and the respect. She had taken her power where she could. She was so young, then. She knew so little.

She'd been running for a couple of miles now, and she felt the sweat on her back, under her windbreaker. She rounded the corner and slowed to a walk as she neared home. That house. Was it hers or Philip's? The cars? That security she had longed for?

Maybe Philip did hold all the power. Maybe all she really did was fit in around his life. Maybe she'd taken the only option available to her. Was that true? Was she a victim of the patriarchy? She chuckled as she opened the door. What she was, was a woman in her midforties, indistinguishable from the other Princeton matrons, although never had she fallen to the level of loafers and Bermuda shorts. Connor, her son, her love, had given her purpose. Maybe nothing else mattered. Maybe she could martyr herself on the pillar of motherhood. Maybe. But Connor wasn't here anymore, was he? Not really.

DINNER THE NEXT NIGHT was with Philip's business associates, Ellen and Bill Lang. A French provincial house in the horsey part of New Jersey, outside of Princeton. Grey stone. Gilt-framed mirrors. A candlelit dining table, Moroccan chicken tagine and an excellent white wine, with smooth jazz wafting in the background. The orchid Angela had brought, in a silver pot, decorated the centre of the table, and the pomegranate oil, which was the second part of her offering, was now in a small glass pitcher, being passed around to add a certain piquancy to the tagine. When it came around to Philip, he winked at her, letting her know she had done well.

The conversation had turned, as it often did, to how high taxes were in New Jersey. A woman, Paula Camini, said she didn't see how it could keep on going that way, with them forced to support so many people who didn't even pay taxes. She smoothed her seemingly effortless upswept brown hair. Her short fingernails were painted plum.

"It's the schools," said Angela. "They're so good around here. Compared to places like Newark and Camden and Trenton. At least we get that in return."

"Do your children go to public schools?" asked Bill Lang, a tall, trim man with dark hair Angela suspected he touched up, and a waistline that spoke of many hours in the gym.

Philip answered, "We just have the one son. And no, he doesn't go to public schools. Lawrenceville."

"Oh," said Ellen, dabbing at her red lipstick with her napkin. Angela was sure she was trying to raise her eyebrows but found herself unable to. "Our niece goes there. I wonder if they know each other. Her name is Cynthia."

"I'll ask Connor," said Angela. She paused, unsure of exactly why she didn't want to let this go. "Taxes or not, though, we're all doing pretty well. We can afford them, and others really struggle."

"There'd be fewer problems if more of those people had jobs," said Philip.

Ellen Lang, silver glasses glinting in the candlelight, chuckled softly. "Oh, come now, Philip. It's more complicated than that, surely."

"I'll say it is," said Angela.

Philip snorted. "Our Lady of the Needy. Salvation of Trenton."

She felt herself bristle, just as she felt the room go ever-so-slightly tense at the tone of derision in Philip's voice. She was glad she wasn't seated next to her husband, as she might have been tempted to accidently spill her wine in his lap.

"You mean the work I do at the food pantry in Trenton. At least I do something."

Paula gazed at her wide-eyed while Anthony, her husband, the sort of just-beyond-middle-aged man who looked as though he'd walked out of a magazine ad for expensive Scotch, pressed his lips between his teeth to try and camouflage his sneer.

"Trenton?" Paula tilted her head as though speaking to a child. Her dangling earrings danced. "How interesting. I don't think I'd have the courage."

"You wouldn't, honey," said Anthony. "You don't even like to talk to the lawn guys."

The men at the table chuckled.

"Tony! That's not true. Not at all."

"Well, I can't say I see the point," said Philip. "I mean, what sort of a difference is it going to make? Some people just have the right ambition, the strength of character to get out of these shitholes, and others don't. Most don't. Then I'm expected to pay for health care for people who eat crap all day and take drugs and drink themselves to death? Pay welfare for them when they won't work? That's the problem, right there. There's no work ethic."

Angela flushed. She put her fork down. "So, Philip, you don't think blind luck has anything to do with good fortune. Fortune like yours, like ours?"

Oh, she didn't want to have this conversation, especially not in front of other people, but she couldn't stop.

"I do not," said Philip. "Hard work, smarts, focus, and not hanging out in the streets selling dope has more to do with it than luck."

"You don't call inheriting the family money 'luck'? Having your college paid for? Daddy's contacts on Wall Street? Let me tell you, there are things people go through you can't imagine."

"Like what?" Paula asked. "I'd really like to know."

"Well, okay," said Angela. "Listen, I didn't think I'd like going to the food bank. I didn't. And I'm sort of surprised it's grown on me so much. The people … they're troubled lots of the time, sure, but they're also amazing. I, don't know …" A woman's face popped into her head. "Right. Let me tell you about Yvette. She wrote poetry. Not a great poet, I admit, but still, she had this passion, you know? Anyway, when she was fourteen, she served a short stint in juvenile detention after getting stopped by the police with a little bit of weed. The sort of 'crime' that results in rich white kids from Princeton being driven home by the police and reprimanded."

"Oh, come on, Angela," said Philip. He drained his glass.

"You know it's true …"

"She has a point about that," said Ellen.

Angela thought Ellen might have said more, save for the look her husband shot her.

"So," Angela continued, "the day of her release she was waiting for her mother, but her mother never showed. Why? Because she'd fallen down icy steps at her apartment and died. After that, Yvette lived with her older brother, or cousins, or friends. She got a part-time job at Target as a cashier."

"Did she finish school? High school, I mean?" asked Paula.

"I don't know. Maybe. Probably not."

"Well, she was hardly going to get anywhere without even a high school diploma. I mean, that's a big problem, right? These kids dropping out of school," said David.

"Sure, sure, it is, but that's not what I'm getting at here."

Paula sipped her wine and then put the glass down. "Let Angela finish," she said.

"Thanks. Okay. So. A couple of years ago her face started to hurt and she went to the emergency room. They said she had a sinus infection and should see her regular doctor. A bit of a joke, of course. She didn't have a regular doctor. People in her neighbourhood can't afford regular doctors and since she wasn't full-time at her job, you know … no benefits."

Angela put up her hand to silence Philip, who she could see was about to interrupt her. He shrugged, and she went on.

"A week later it got worse. She went to a clinic. They gave her antibiotics, which did exactly nothing. Six months later someone thought to send her for X-rays, but by then the cancer — yes, *cancer* — was so far advanced all they could do was hack off parts of her jaw and ear and cheekbone."

"Oh, good lord," said Ellen, as she passed the couscous to David.

"Right? I knew her for three months, and then she died, but right up to the end she was writing poetry, and drawing, and laughing. Even when she looked like something out of *The Walking Dead*, she always had a joke. That *Walking Dead* line, for example, that was hers. Thirty-two years old. There's a picture of her hanging on the wall at the Pantry. She's holding one of her little poetry books, the ones she made herself at a copy shop."

There was silence at the table and then Paula said, "Well, I think what you're doing is really admirable."

"Why don't you come down with me sometime?" Angela picked up her wineglass and drank, hoping the blush she now felt rising on her skin wouldn't be too noticeable in the low lighting.

Paula's hand went to her throat. "Oh, I would, but I work, I'm afraid."

"Uh-huh, like I told you," said her husband.

THE ONLY THING PHILIP SAID to her on the way home was, "You sure know how to kill a party. Remember next time, these people are the ones who help you pay for that greenhouse of yours, okay?"

Sister Eileen

Eileen sat at one of the two chairs beside the tiny Formica table pushed up against the kitchen wall. It was seven-thirty in the morning and, not having slept well the night before, she was grateful for the strong coffee in the cup around which she warmed her hands. Anne leaned against the counter, absurdly upbeat and energized for someone of her advanced years. Anne was seventy-four, thirty-four years older than Eileen, and was alarmingly chipper in the morning. The cabinets were once a jolly yellow, but now they were dull and chipped. One of the doors was gone completely, and the dishes on the shelves were mismatched. Anne's hair was tied up in a messy knot atop her head, and she was dressed in what Eileen had come to think of as the Nun Uniform: sensible shoes, loose-fitting pants, a blouse and light jacket. What Eileen was, in fact, wearing herself.

"Test today," said Anne. "We'll see how well I've done teaching algebraic word problems. Scares them. Don't know why. It's all about breaking it down and turning it into an equation. Anne tipped her coffee cup to her lips and drained the dregs, with what looked like regret. She shrugged. "I have to run."

"See you later." Eileen, who had been scared of algebraic word problems herself, thought it was way too early for mathematics of any kind.

Anne ducked out the door just as Caroline appeared, slipping her arms into a pale blue cardigan. She strode to the coffee pot.

"Want some more?" Caroline held the pot up and tilted her head. She tucked a strand of the curly black hair that had escaped her ponytail behind her ears.

Eileen rubbed her eyes with the heels of her hands. "I didn't get much sleep last night with all the noise. So, yes, please, even though it's my second. Did you sleep?"

"Sort of. Anne said she did, but I think that's because she turns her hearing aid off. I don't see how anyone can sleep with the sirens and I'm sure those were gunshots I heard. Do you think it was?"

"Probably. Not uncommon, I'm sorry to say."

Caroline filled Eileen's cup and then fiddled with one of the dials on the stove. "We really should see if someone can fix this."

The appliances were old, but serviceable — although one of the burners on the stove had stopped working the week before.

Caroline looked around at the room. "Maybe we could get a couple of gallons of paint. Yellow, maybe, something cheerful and clean."

Eileen chuckled. "That would be pretty. If you've got time to paint. Do you?"

"Yes, I think so."

"I envy you your energy," said Eileen as Caroline sat down beside her. "At the end of the day I'm exhausted." She blew on her coffee and then sipped it, sighed, and leaned back in the chair. "You're with me today, I think, right?"

"Yup, all this week."

As part of her mission year, prior to taking her first vows, Sister Caroline was discovering where her talents might best be employed, shifting her time between working alongside Eileen at the Our Daily Bread Food Pantry, and with Anne at the school.

Caroline got herself a bowl of cereal and returned to the table. She said, "Maybe we could get someone to tear up that concrete out front. We could put in a garden. You've got that gardener guy coming to the Pantry today, don't you? We could ask him, maybe."

"It would be nice to have a garden. We'll see. Does the house bother you?"

"No, I mean, not for me. But you know, it might be nice for the street. It might set an example and would certainly be more welcoming than that slab of grey." Caroline paused. "I'm not a snob; at least I don't think I am."

"I don't think you are, either. And you're right. It would be good to spruce the place up a bit, as we can."

"A coat of paint. A few flowers. Sort of a bare minimum, I think."

Eileen smiled but said nothing more. Caroline had been raised in Greenwich, Connecticut, in a Nantucket-style shore colonial worth five million dollars. She had once said to Eileen that she had imagined a house full of nuns in an urban neighbourhood like this would stand out, be a beacon of cleanliness, calm, and serenity in a jumble of chaos, when in fact this plain-fronted, almost tumbledown place bought at foreclosure auction looked like every other building on the street. Theirs was grey siding, some of the others were brick, and most were duplexes, while this one wasn't, and it did boast an ash tree in front, and a tiny porch with latticework from which, in the summer, the sisters hung potted plants and set out chairs. Eileen wondered what Caroline would think if she knew where Eileen had grown up — over a bar on the Jersey Shore, amidst the drunks; the fights; the motorcycles; the stolen cars; the shit-faced, fist-happy father; the narcissistic, martyred mother. It must surely be a sign of God's great plan that women from such different backgrounds would both find their way here.

Caroline was tall, with big wrists and wide shoulders, strong-looking, suited to soccer and field hockey. Now, she fingered her necklace. All the Sisters wore one. It bore the symbol of the Sisters of Saint Joseph, a silver globe with a cross to the side. One of the cross's arms was elongated, as was the downward portion. The symbol represented the Order's vision of embracing the whole world: downward toward earth, upward toward the cosmos, outward to humanity, creating lines of communion and union with God, with each other, and with the "dear neighbour without distinction."

Eileen got up, wiped the counter, frowned, and said, not unkindly, "I do wonder if you'll be comfortable here in Trenton. I find it challenging enough and I've been here for a long time."

"I'm glad I'm not the only one, at least," said Caroline. "I like a lot of the people, but it's kind of shocking to see some of them working two minimum-wage jobs and still not able to make it through to the end of the month."

Eileen rinsed out the cloth she'd been using on the counter. "Having the electricity turned off. Kids doing homework by candlelight." She sighed. "Ah, the 'deserving' poor, right? They're easy to love, but it's harder to love those not only to whom harm has been done, but who have done harm in return."

"That's where I am. I know Christ calls on us to love everyone, to see Him in everyone, but the guy who beats up his wife and kids? The ones who fight dogs?"

Eileen could see Caroline was about to continue with what she suspected was a long list. "Yes, Caroline, even them. Hard as it is. Listen, I try. Often fail. I try again. But it's not for everyone, and that's no shame. It's what you're here to find out: how best to serve God, being exactly who you are."

Caroline bowed her head and took the medallion in her mouth like a child. "It just seems so dangerous."

Just then Ruth, lean, with wiry salt-and-pepper hair and the air of an eager, bounding wolfhound, stuck her head in the door. "I'm off! Have a good day, everyone!" She waved and disappeared again, off to her job as chaplain in the New Jersey State Prison. "Oh, Eileen," she called, "can you take the lasagna out of the freezer? Tonight's dinner!"

"Will do."

"Bye, Sister Ruth! Have a blessed day!" called Caroline.

Eileen reached into the freezer and produced a large tray of frozen lasagna. "Ruth cooks enough for a dozen," she said. She put it on top of the stove and peeled off the plastic wrap covering the top. She glanced at Caroline. "You know, I was raised on the Jersey Shore. Bars and blue-collar families, the hardscrabble church-centred life where everyone knew everyone's family and every family had its troubles. Domestic violence. Drunks. Car crashes in stolen vehicles. Rape, sometimes by members of the clergy. Oh, don't look like that, you know it happened … happens. Abused kids. Drug abuse. It wasn't the sort of community that could hide its bags of bones. I grew up understanding life is both as messy as the beach after a hurricane and as indescribably beautiful as moonrise over still water."

"So, you think I shouldn't be here?"

"I didn't say that. You've only been here a few weeks. Give it a chance. But look at Anne. She adores teaching. It's what she's made for. You have a master's in English literature. You won't use that much here. You might be better suited to a more suburban posting, maybe a teaching post. You're wonderful with children. Just something to consider. Time will tell, and you and your spiritual director will work it all out."

"You never wanted to teach?"

"Me? Nope. Not my thing. Not great with kids, at least not for any period of time."

Eileen did not tell Caroline about the time she was twelve, babysitting her little eighteen-month-old cousin, and when the child would *not* stop crying Eileen had slapped him, hard, across the mouth. Oh, that terrible moment when, in shock, he'd stopped crying, his mouth and eyes wide and wild, and then, a wrenching moment later, the screaming had begun. Crying of an entirely different order, a wordless protest to the world's cruelty and injustice and horror, having been betrayed by love for the first time. She'd done that, destroyed a child's innocence, just like that, as her own had been destroyed by her mother with a similar slap. Teach? No. She was not made for children. Her great shame.

"I'm just saying I found it difficult when I first arrived, and I still have my moments."

"Was it always like this?"

"Trenton? Oh, it goes through ups and downs, but it's been a sad place ever since the late sixties, I guess, when most of the industry left. Always trying to get back on its feet, to be the great city it once was. Hard, though, when there's nothing much for people to do."

"You don't get scared? Ever? Come on." Caroline snorted.

"I've been scared, of course. A couple of times. But after a while I began to see it as an opportunity to rely more fully on God. And we're not in danger, you know. Not really. Other than some random incidents that could happen anywhere, the violence is self-contained. Gangs. Young people against each other. I think of the parents, how difficult it is on them."

Caroline hunched over her mug and put three heaping spoons of sugar from the blue-and-white bowl into her coffee. "I don't know how anyone gets used to gangs and guns."

Eileen shook her head. "You're right. Getting used to something like that would be awful. It would be a kind of heartlessness."

Eileen walked over and hugged Caroline with an arm around her broad shoulders. "Keep praying. Bring your fears to God. The way will become clear, I promise. And what a gift it is, to be able to feel the fear other people feel. Think how you'll be able to help them, should the need arise."

Caroline nodded. "I know I'm not alone. I feel it more all the time."

"That's a very good start. Thank God."

Eileen did not say that what she felt more and more was the great silence of God. When she had been Caroline's age, she, too, had felt God's loving embrace, God's clear presence, leading her, protecting her, guiding her. When had it left? She didn't know. She only knew that now when she prayed, she felt the words were going out into some great void. She felt as though she was dying of thirst sometimes, her soul cracked and parched as old leather. She felt like King David crying out, *My God, my God, why have you forsaken me? Why are you so far from saving me, from the words of my groaning? O my God, I cry by day, but you do not answer, and by night, but I find no rest.* She understood she should see this as a call to trust the promise of God more than the perception, and that wasn't really indifferent, or absent, or silent … but where once there had been a garden perfumed with God's presence, for the past number of years there was nothing but an arid wind across a blasted landscape of unrelenting darkness.

She hoped Caroline would never experience this dark night of the soul.

Eileen shook her head to scatter the bleak thoughts. *No time for this. There is work to be done. Blessed is the day the Lord has made.*

Angela

Angela and Deedee sat in the cozy book-lined room next to the kitchen of Deedee's farmhouse a few miles outside of Princeton.

Angela said, "I think I might be entering menopause."

"Hardly, sweetie. A few years in the old girl yet."

"Well, something's going on."

"Such as?"

"I am so … I don't know. Discontent."

"The winter of your discontent?"

"Made *not* glorious by this son of York."

Deedee giggled. "Philip?"

"Yup."

"He does not caper nimbly in a lady's chamber?"

"Pardon?"

"Sorry. Just more of that speech by Old Will. What's going on?"

"Nothing. Everything. I don't know. Philip and I have nothing in common. He has no passion for life, only for making money. I want more, and I think it's too late."

Deedee was Angela's only real confidante. Whom else could she be honest with and not fear her complaints would end up rattling in the ear of every woman at the golf club, at the bridge games, at the ladies' dinners? The year she moved to Princeton, a woman had invited her to a "girls'" dinner when the men were all off at Hilton Head playing golf. They had spent the entire dinner complaining about a woman who hadn't been invited. No, not complaining … *eviscerating*. Angela had tried, with as much subtlety as she could manage, to make them see they were behaving like the mean girls of high school, but doubted she got through to any of them. She was the odd one out. They thought her strange indeed. And so, Angela avoided such gatherings as if they were held in a viper's den, but no matter, the gossip slithered out with distressing rapidity whether she was present or not.

Photographic portraits of Deedee's grandparents as small children in frilly christening gowns stared out wide-eyed from the walls. Angela thought there was an alarming amount of chintz. For all that Deedee had been raised in Tennessee, her taste ran decidedly to English Country, complete with a tumble of three large, shaggy dogs of indeterminate breed sleeping in the corner. The wildish Victorian garden beyond the mullioned window was ragged this time of year, but amidst the brown leaves and stalks, the purple butterfly bush, burgundy chrysanthemums, pink toad lily, and yellow helenium offered hope of better days. Angela was something more than an amateur gardener, and the women had met ten years earlier when a mutual friend introduced them, and Angela had helped Deedee design her garden. She considered it now with a critical eye and found it adequate. She made a mental note that it would be improved come spring by some lavender, maybe even a kitchen herb garden.

The two women sat at the round, claw-foot oak table, drinking tea from blue-and-white cups, on which were depicted pastoral scenes. Angela held hers in both hands and gazed into the fawn-coloured liquid. She remembered her grandmother, whom everyone called Gypsy despite her name being Edith, because although her brothers and sisters were blond-haired, blue-eyed and so pale they were nearly translucent, Gypsy's hair was raven, her skin a light brown, and her eyes the colour of topaz. Family secrets, no doubt. So much of who one was in the present was predetermined by those who cradled our genes before us. Gypsy read tea leaves. When Angela was twelve, her grandmother stared into the cup and showed Angela a large clump near the handle, surrounded by long stalks. "Trouble of your own making," she said, "and much having to do with men." Even then, Angela considered having to live under a prediction like that unfair.

As the words of Angela's discontent floated on the air between them, Angela wondered whether Deedee would understand what she was feeling. Deedee's husband, Ed, played golf with Philip. Both women deplored the game — ruined a perfectly good walk, as someone once said. Deedee and her husband seemed to live independent lives, she with her animals, he with whatever amused him. Ed was a long-legged, slow-talking man with a sly sense of humour who'd inherited his money. Deedee jokingly called him her real-stone cowboy. Angela thought they looked hilarious together — Ed was a good six foot five and Deedee hardly topped five-two and couldn't possibly weigh more than a hundred and five pounds even with her pockets full of horseshoes. Of course, Deedee had never said a word about not loving Ed.

"Huh," said Deedee. "Going to be that kind of conversation, is it? Well then, break out the bourbon."

"It's after four, right?" Angela smiled, pulled a tissue out of her jeans pocket, and blew her nose.

"Honey, where I come from the old ladies keep a bottle of bourbon in their purses for moments such as these, no matter the time of day. Always a porch party going on somewhere."

Deedee disappeared into the kitchen, her thin blond ponytail bouncing behind her, and returned with a bottle of Blanton's Bourbon and two cut-crystal glasses. The ornate bottle, with the silver racehorse stopper, looked more like a perfume than a liquor bottle. *Eau de Stables, perhaps,* thought Angela. Deedee poured two healthy shots and they clinked glasses. The bourbon's scent was tinged with orange and tasted of caramel and cloves.

Deedee sipped. "So, you have a little passion problem."

"It's not just about sex. It's an attitude to life. He's a barnacle. I want to be a …"

"Great white shark?" Deedee chuckled.

"No, Deedee. Not a shark. I want to be the waves, the wind, maybe even the goddamned storm." This sounded faintly ridiculous, melodramatic, even, to Angela's ears. She glanced at Deedee and was relieved to see only concern in her expression.

"When did all this start?"

"Damned if I know. But it's here now."

"You want a passionate life." Deedee held the glass to her nose and breathed in, her eyes on Angela.

Angela felt her neck redden. "You make it sound silly. I wish you wouldn't." She took a gulp of the bourbon. The warmth spread through her like warm honey. Belly and arms and legs. Sweet warmth.

Deedee leaned forward. "I don't want to sound like some agony aunt larding on the wisdom, but, well, I think the thing is, you must decide, honey. You must ask yourself if you want to live a compassionate life or a passionate one."

Angela's face tightened, and she knew her annoyance was evident. She put her glass down and folded her arms. Her mother had always laughed at what she called her "Chief Thundercloud face" and said she should never play poker. How she'd hated that, although only later did she realize how racist it was.

"Can't you be passionate *and* compassionate? Passionate about compassion? Passionate about love, about art, about justice, about equality, and do so with a compassionate heart?"

"Of course," Deedee said. "I like to think I'm both about animals, for example, although the compassion there led to the passion, do you see? When it comes to love, however, I believe there are two ways of loving: passionately and compassionately. Not my idea. A psychologist about twenty-five years ago, Elaine Hatfield, opened the discussion on the kinds of love, although you might say C.S. Lewis did it earlier, and I don't know, probably Socrates or Aristotle before that … but, any old way, Hatfield talked specifically about passionate and compassionate love. Compassionate love, she said, involves feelings of mutual respect, trust, and affection, while passionate love involves intense longing of union with the other, and sexual attraction."

"What if I want both?"

"I'm not sure passionate love lasts, and then all you end up with are a series of wild affairs, going from one to the next. Does that sound satisfying? Sustaining?"

Angela shook her head, for who would admit a life of wild affairs sounded exceptionally enticing?

In the garden, a frantic squirrel ran about looking for a safe place to bury a hickory nut it carried in its mouth. It began to dig in the garden near the toad lily, then dashed across the lawn and up a fir tree with the nut still in its mouth. The ragged, slightly malodorous heap of dogs slept on.

"With great luck," Deedee said, "a passionate love grows into a compassionate love. Passion is a peak experience, if you know what I mean. I might even be so bold as to say it's an undeveloped sort of love." She smiled and rolled the glass in her palms. "From the look on your face, I see you don't like that. Well, let me put it this way: it's the sort of experience that can create a good deal of drama in one's life. Lots of slapped faces and slammed doors, a bit like a French film. Do you want all that drama?"

Angela spoke into her glass. "The alternative sounds, well, *beige*. Just a vast landscape of beige."

"Does it? How sad." She looked at Angela with something like pity on her pale, nearly eyebrow-less face.

"Tell me about the donkeys," Angela said. "How are they getting on with the goats?"

Deedee didn't skip a beat. With her impeccable, if sometimes inscrutable, Southern manners she said, "Why, like old friends. Like they were just made to be together. It's one big frolic out there in the pasture — goats and horses and donkeys, oh my!" Her chuckle was so deep and full, it seemed to come from another body entirely.

ANGELA DROVE HOME two hours later, only slightly sleepy from the bourbon, and since the highway didn't seem prudent with a couple of shots under her belt, she took the side streets. Mothers picked their kids up at school bus stops along the route while Angela waited, almost patiently, for the stop sign attached to the metal arm to click back into place on the side of the bus so she could safely continue. Crossing guards guided children through the dangers of four-way stops. People walked their Labradors and Jack Russells and golden retrievers. *Simple lives*, she thought. Tidy, freshly painted clapboard lives. Had they all chosen these lives, or had they washed up, drifted, eddy-flung into them the way she had?

Her conversation with Deedee lingered. Angela pulled a bit of chapped skin off her lower lip with her teeth. She wanted to be good, to do good, to be a kind and compassionate person, and she considered herself such, but these days … oh … she longed for passion's fizz and bubble in the blood. She missed passion's *power*. As the street scenes flicked by, they brought flashing images up from the basement of memory, and she pondered if there was some key to the discontent of the present down there in her past. *Mothers. Well, if it wasn't one thing, it was your mother.* She chuckled.

Daddy disappeared before she had any clear memories of him. Being raised by a single mother who thought she was Stevie Nicks contributed to Angela's aversion to flowy scarves and perhaps to her shaky self-esteem. That boy on the corner, tall and slouching, with a flop of blond hair over his eyes, reminded her of Daniel, her cousin. She had lost her virginity to Daniel when she was thirteen and he eighteen. Statutory rape is what it would have been called if she'd ever told anyone. It hadn't seemed like that at the time, though, only deeply erotic, perhaps more so because of the taboo. Key to her discontented present? Probably not, just a mundane set of occurrences and environmental factors, which, along with that ancestral soup of genetic code embodied in her odd-duck Nana Gypsy, had mixed together to create Angela, just as she was.

The small bungalows and split-levels ended at an intersection, and beyond that stood Lawrenceville, where Connor boarded, a private school with its own golf course and a bevy of diplomats' kids; and now she coasted along the leafy streets of Princeton. Prosperous Princeton. Town of professors and pharmaceutical executives and high mucky-mucks of banking and finance like Philip, whose financial acumen paid for their six-bedroom faux-Tudor with the marble bath and kitchen, the linen sheets on the king-size bed, the Persian carpets, the espresso maker, the many flat-screen TVs, the twice-a-week cleaning lady and the conservatory full of Angela's orchids.

Mulling over the life she'd led as a girl and sticking her family under a microscope was pointless. She was now a woman in her forties, living this life; old enough to have broken free of all those sticky predictable membranes. She sighed. Why was she suddenly trying to rip through? She had wanted all these things she had, had wanted exactly this way of life, and she had it. So now, having accomplished so much, she thought with a snort, what was she to do with this one life — with the years to come?

Sister Eileen

Eileen and Caroline walked through the early-morning streets of Trenton. Eileen was, as always, struck by the contrasts. She tried to take in everything, a kind of practice in loving all the world. Large shiny SUVs dotted the streets, probably owned by the more successful drug dealers, next to rundown, dented old junkers with mismatched paint jobs and side mirrors held on with duct tape. The streets were potholed, the sidewalks cracked and weed-riddled, blotched with trash. The sky on this March morning was a smooth blue egg overhead, but the walls on the boarded-up and derelict buildings were scarred with gang tags: black, red, gold, and blue. Sometimes the sound of rap music drifted from an apartment building, and someone sang along. Now and again, a young boy was visible near a window on the second floor of that building right there, learning to "spit rhymes" as the kids said, practising, no doubt, to be a rapper himself. He was skinny as a fox, wearing a white undershirt, hands punctuating the air with his syllables. A poetic shadow boxer. Not this morning, though. The window was a blind eye. A clump of grass grew next to a telephone pole on which fluttered a remnant of yellow police tape left over from a recent shooting. A stunted tree stood in front of Poppi's, a tiny shop selling nearly-out-of-date milk, soft drinks, junk food, Mexican spices and canned goods, a few dusty magazines, and cigarettes. Poppi, a large Hispanic man wearing an apron under his puffy jacket, sat on a folding chair in front of the shop, his head tilted back, welcoming the sun's appearance.

"Hey, Sisters. How you doing this morning? You doing good?"

"Doing great, Poppi," said Eileen. "How's your daughter? She need anything for the new baby?"

Poppi reached up his jacket sleeve and scratched, revealing a faded five-point crown tattoo on his forearm. He had once been a member of the Latin Kings but had left the gang after doing time for aggravated assault. When he came out of prison, he was older, tired. He tried to keep the kids on the street out of gangs now. He and Doug, one of the program coordinators at the Pantry, along with a few other men, teamed up to patrol the streets at night, herding what kids they could back inside and out of harm's way.

"Naw, we doing all right," he said. "Man, she a sweet little baby, that one. Don't hardly cry at all. Sleeps through the night, like six hours at a time. She gonna be a beauty."

Caroline said, "I'll come round to see them, if that's okay. Maybe this weekend?"

"You always welcome, Sister. Bless you."

"And you, Poppi."

As they turned the corner, a brindled pit bull rushed the fence surrounding a tiny house and threw its weight against the chain links, barking, making the fence bulge and shiver.

"Caesar! You scared me!" Eileen laughed, while Caroline stepped back.

The dog stopped barking and seemed to laugh, its wide jaws open, tongue lolling.

"Every day! Do we have to go through this every single day?" Eileen reached over the fence and petted the dog's massive head. He licked her hand. "Come on, Caroline, give him a pet. He's just a big baby." She pulled a dog biscuit from the tote she carried and offered it to the younger sister, who took it, her eyebrow raised skeptically.

"I'm not wonderful with dogs," said Caroline.

Caesar danced in anticipation.

"Go on, "said Eileen. "Hold your palm flat and don't pull away or he might snap and nip you without meaning to. Just trying to catch the treat, you know?"

"Not really," said Caroline, but she did what she was told, and Caesar gently took the biscuit and trotted off to eat it.

"You see?"

Caroline grinned widely. "He is rather sweet, isn't he?"

Caesar was relentlessly optimistic, thought Eileen. The yard was dirt and his shelter nothing more than a makeshift plywood box with a filthy pillow and what looked like a towel in it. A battered blue plastic bowl, the edges chewed, served as a water dish, although there often was no water in it and Eileen always made sure she had some in case Caesar was thirsty, especially in summer. It wasn't that the old woman who owned him was cruel or didn't care about the dog, but Caesar wasn't a pet; Caesar was a security system. He was treated much the same way a car would be. Minimum maintenance. Eileen thought she might bring him a ball to play with. The sheet tacked over the bungalow's front window moved, a hand pulling it aside. Eileen waved, and the sheet fell back into place.

"I'm not sure his owner is happy with you taming him," said Caroline.

"Oh, he's a smart dog," said Eileen. "He knows friend from foe."

There weren't many people on the streets in this part of Trenton, away from the government offices, and the ones who were out sat on the stoops or shuffled off to get morning coffee and breakfast from one of the local fast food spots. The only real business left in the state capital was that of government. Everything else had moved out years ago and what was once a shining city by the river was now a poverty-eaten mess. Drugs and violence and lots of funerals. Not today, though. As they walked, Eileen talked again about how excited she was about the man coming to help plan the vegetable garden the Pantry was starting in the vacant lot next door.

"I'm so glad," said Eileen, "that you're here today. The end of the month, you know, so it'll be busy."

So many cupboards were bare this time of month. Food stamps didn't go far enough. Money ran out. The Pantry would probably serve seventy families before they closed for the day.

Birdy and her sister, Carmen, with Carmen's two grandbabies, Tyler and Tyko, walked toward the nuns. The babies were twins, not quite two, with snotty noses. Tyler sat in a battered stroller and Tyko tottered alongside, trying to climb in. Eileen could see the screaming was about to begin. Carmen, her hair in a turban, her enormous arms straining the denim jacket she wore, pushed Tyko down.

"Not yet, you. You wait your turn," she said.

Eileen was wondering if she should pick Tyko up when Birdy, who looked enough like her sister to be her twin, scooped the child off the sidewalk and balanced him on her hip. She dangled her keys in front of him and he quieted. Birdy wiped the mucous off his lip with her hand and then wiped her hand on the back of her jeans. Eileen sighed.

"Good morning," she said. "Got your hands full there."

Tyko stared at them as they approached, his big, brown eyes liquid and open, his cheeks chubby and his hair softly curling. Caroline waggled her fingers and he took the keys out of his mouth and smiled at her. She took his face in her hands and kissed his forehead, making him giggle.

Eileen asked after the women's families. Carmen's son had been in prison in Bordentown but had recently been transferred to the evaluation centre in Trenton, which meant he was one step closer to release. Might be home in a couple of months. He'd be looking for work when he got out and was, Carmen assured her, a good boy who just made a stupid mistake. Eileen seemed to remember it was more like three stupid mistakes.

"Tell him to call me when he gets home," she said. "He did tile work, didn't he? I might know someone. There might be space for him in the Work Development Program, although that's only an intern position."

"Construction, you know," said Carmen, "something that pays. Boy's got to start feeding these babies."

"I'll keep an eye out."

"Thanks, Sister. God bless you."

"I can't promise anything, but I'll do my best. You coming by later?"

"Yup."

As the women walked off, Eileen said to Caroline, "Babies are so much easier to love when in someone else's arms."

"Sister Eileen!"

"Does that shock you? Well, God forgive me. I know. It's hard to admit I don't like children all that much; no, I shouldn't say that. I don't *dis*like them. I do, however, find them exhausting, and so very messy. Perhaps being the oldest of six children and having been expected to care for the youngers before I was old enough to do so has made me defensive around children. They need so much, and make so much noise, and leak from everywhere."

Caroline laughed, her face betraying disbelief. "I'm not buying this act of yours. You're good with kids."

Eileen arched a brow. "My clever disguise is working, I see."

"Wow, I'm not sure I'd admit that." Caroline didn't look so disbelieving now.

Eileen smiled. "I'm just not meant to be around kids. I always knew I wasn't cut out to be a mother. Just not mother material."

The women walked along quietly for a moment, and then Eileen said, "So, thank God the Sisters of Saint Joseph recognized I wouldn't make a good teacher. Administration and organization, that's my strength. Put me up against a committee of planning department bureaucrats and I'm a tiger; put me in a room full of crying five-year-olds and I'm a panicked alley cat."

"Are you trying to tell me something?"

"Only that there's no shame in recognizing what you can and cannot do." They had arrived at the Pantry, and Eileen fished the keys out of her tote. "I'm telling you that so you understand you aren't going to be asked to do something you're not made for. You'll find the right path, with God's help."

She unlocked the Pantry door, stepped in, and Caroline flipped on the lights. Everything looked in order. They hung their jackets in a locker and Caroline set about straightening the tins on the shelves, while Eileen put the coffee machine on. Over it hung a small glass cabinet with some of the more unusual articles people had donated over the years. A tin of haggis. A small (empty) blue vial that purported to be for toothaches and whose ingredients included laudanum. A can of Spam from the 1960s, which Eileen thought might or might not still be edible, given the nature of Spam. People had good intentions, of course, but often donations came from those clearing out the homes of dead relatives, and they got overwhelmed and just piled everything into boxes and dropped them off. The haggis was her personal favourite. She could just imagine what Carmen would think if she suggested she try it.

Doug, the coordinator for the food program, arrived. He was, as usual, half asleep, and looked like a great fifty-year-old bear disturbed mid-hibernation. He ambled to the coffee machine and stared at it until the gurgle indicated it was ready. He poured a cup and stood drinking it. When done, he poured another and then greeted Eileen and Caroline. Claire arrived, plump as a miller's sparrow, a giggler in her late thirties, although she looked closer to twenty, Claire oversaw communications and fundraising. People found her optimism irresistible, as they did her assumption that everyone was generous at heart. Claire turned and said hi to Diane as she stepped in. Diane, motherly, with floury cheeks and dimpled hands, was another program coordinator, deceptively soft-spoken, but practical and efficient, who worked with clients in need of emergency funding for utilities and rent.

Eileen checked the volunteer roster for the day. Six volunteers.

> Chuck Davis, Nancy Davis, Tristan Lewis: personal shoppers
> Angela Morrison: intake
> Karen Martin, Susan Wells: greeters

Roxie, the volunteer coordinator, came up behind Eileen. "Hey, good group this morning."

Caroline looked up. Roxie was a good foot taller than she. "I didn't see you come in. How are you?"

Roxie made a noise with her teeth, which Caroline had learned was a staple of Jamaican conversation. "Daniel, he working early shift at Whole Foods, you know, unloading deliveries and like that, and so he leave the house around about two-thirty and you know me I don't be getting back to sleep no way. It's a five-cups-of-coffee morning."

"I'm sorry. It's so hard not to sleep."

Roxie pushed her thick dreadlocks off her shoulders. "Not the worst thing, is it? Least he working. And maybe he get a promotion soon, you know he want to be a butcher, eh?" She pointed at a name on the list. "Ah, man, she better be on time today. Stand on my last nerve that one."

Angela Morrison. Roxie was right. Eileen liked Angela, but she did have an unfortunate habit of tardiness and Eileen was something of a stickler for punctuality. It was a courtesy thing. If people depended on you, you didn't keep them waiting. Of course, if something urgent came up, something that couldn't be helped, that was a different matter, and although Angela always had some excuse — traffic, something she had to do at her son's school, her husband needing something — it annoyed Eileen, although she tried not to let it show. What could one do with volunteers? They were so much more difficult to manage than paid employees. But thank God for Roxie. Equal measures of no-nonsense and jocularity. She wrangled them.

"I want to talk to Angela about helping with the garden," said Eileen.

"Got a greenhouse and all, she tell me." Roxie waggled her head, rolling her eyes, to indicate that Lady Angela thought she was posh.

Eileen ignored it. "I want to introduce her to the landscaper coming in today to start the garden project. I met him at a planning committee meeting with the city. He's putting a bid in for work around city hall."

"And you went and nabbed him, huh?" Roxie laughed.

"I might have mentioned that doing some volunteer work wouldn't hurt his profile with the city."

"Uh-huh. Wise old owl."

"At any rate, we'll need someone who knows plants and gardening and such on-site. I can count on the landscaper to get the beds in and so forth, but more day to day, you know."

"You think she going to want to get them pretty hands dirty?"

"Oh, Roxie." Eileen hugged the tall woman. "I think she'll be great at it, if she's interested."

"Well, you know best. Oops, the volunteers at the door, I think. Got to go. My money on Angela getting here last, though."

Later, Eileen checked her watch when she saw Angela at the door. Roxie had been right. Fifteen minutes late.

Angela

Princeton was mowed lawns and cocktails on the terrace and fundraisers for the library. It was, for want of a better word, *pleasant*, that white-bread word. Trenton had a wild beat. It had a pulse. It was hot-blooded. It mattered. It was street art and sirens and all the insistent urgency of survival on the edge of a falling knife. Philip had asked her once why she was so fascinated with Trenton. But it wasn't the place; it was the people, the difference between Princetonians who rolled through life on golden wheels, and Trentonians who clambered up mountains, cursing sharp stones. The untamed *necessity* of life in Trenton, opposed to the complacent luxury of Princeton, was what drew her.

Princeton wasn't all bad. So many smart people from the university, not that they had much to do with people outside academia. It was beautiful, too, in the spring when the pear trees on Witherspoon were in bloom. Labyrinth was a good bookstore. The library was terrific. Nassau Street sported an independent movie theatre, and she couldn't discount all those lectures one could attend at the university. The restaurants were fine. McCarter Theatre Center had good plays and music and dance. When she'd first moved there, it had seemed like a kind of movie set for small-town life, and in fact, movies were filmed there, like that one about Einstein starring Meg Ryan and Walter Matthau. A not-quite-true but entertaining film, just like Princeton was ersatz in some way she couldn't define, but entertaining. Nice. She thought of it as the Brigadoon of New Jersey, from that old British movie about the magical Scottish town that rose mysteriously out of the mists once every hundred years.

Trenton, on the other hand, had no facade at all. That had been torn down years ago. It put on no airs. It didn't bother dressing up. Angela liked herself there. She felt that throb in her veins when she welcomed the poor and the hungry into the Pantry and filled their bags with nourishment. She was twenty-three again, scrabbling on the streets of New York, drinking ice-cold vodka shots for a dollar in a Polish basement bar. The rough men made much of her in that bar. Pretty girl. Like a hothouse flower. Their cheeks were stubbly, their hands calloused, with dark dirt moons under their nails. The Stenographer, they called her, teasing her about her business suit, her high heels. The few women in the place, Russian and Polish, hard, leather-skinned women with ice-pick glares, said dreadful things about her in languages she didn't speak. She didn't need to know what they said to catch the drift. She didn't care. She gleamed. They glowered. She fancied she smelled only of Coco Chanel, while they smelled of cigarettes and cabbages. She liked the power she believed she had over their men.

Now she thinks: *How those women must have hated me. And they had every right.*

The Pantry doors opened at 9:30 a.m. It was closer to ten by the time she parked the car and headed for the door. The March wind blew sharp and smelled of gasoline and garbage. By then a few early people had been and gone. A small group of women stood gossiping by the door. None of their jackets looked warm enough. Inside, Roxie greeted her.

"I'm so sorry I'm a little late. Accident on Route 1."

"Was there? Oh, dear," said Roxie. "I guess the others got here before it happened. Lucky them." She turned to greet a new shopper at the door.

A young nun sat behind the intake desk by the door. Angela walked over and apologized again for her tardiness and explained about the accident.

"Well, I'm glad you're here now. Can you take over?"

Angela slipped out of her coat, hung it over the chair, and held her purse out. "Sister Caroline — it is Caroline, yes? — Can you pop this in the office for me? Thanks."

Three people were already shopping. Sister Eileen stood chatting with them, laughing at something. Like many nuns, judging her exact age was difficult. What was it about nuns? The fact they wore no makeup? That they seemed to smile more than they frowned? That they spent so much time in prayer and meditation? Was that what kept them ageless until suddenly they were very old indeed? Or was Angela simplifying, romanticizing? Possibly. Sister Eileen looked about Angela's age. Well, whatever age, she was a whirlwind of energy in a pastel cardigan and comfortable shoes. Sister Eileen was stout with hair starting to turn grey, and her voice held the rhythms and nasal honk of the Jersey Shore, but she radiated a kind of calm, no matter what the circumstance. Angela often had the impression she was one of those people who might actually have experienced God somehow. She seemed to exist in two worlds at once, and always saw the bigger picture. One felt both humbled and hopeful around Sister Eileen. She smiled at Angela and gave her a little salute before turning back to the shoppers.

The clients each represented a household. At intake, they got a card that noted how many items per food group they could take, depending on the number of people in the home. They "shopped," complete with a small cart, for canned vegetables, pasta, rice, soup, bread, dairy, and whatever fresh fruit and vegetables were on hand. Most things were bought in bulk at reduced prices, thanks to a generous Princeton grocery store. Today the "specials" board announced bananas, apples, broccoli, onions, butternut squash, and green beans, all pre-packed in baggies.

The room was set up to look as much as possible like a small market. Metal shelving ran against both walls and one up the middle, creating aisles. The intake desk, where Angela sat, was the first stop for clients. She took down their particulars for the database: name, address, income, number of people in the household, ages. She tried to get a sense of other needs — counselling, medical care, computer education, social services of various sorts. She preferred this task, since she liked talking to people and was curious about them: the eighty-three-year-old woman who lived on six hundred dollars a month social security and whatever her daughter could give her; the father of four who'd been laid off his job as maintenance worker at one of the pharmaceutical companies and hadn't been able to find anything else yet; the grandmother raising three of her grandchildren.

She patted hands and gave out hugs. She dandled kids on her knee and didn't care about sticky fingers on her old jeans. She left her jewellery at home, even her wedding band, for it would have been unkind to flaunt those diamonds. She saw herself as the gracious girl with the soft hands, soothing, listening, saving, brightening people's lives with her sympathy, her concern, and occasionally a little harmless flirting. She was making a difference in the lives of the marginalized. Rewarded with smiles and being known by name. *Hey, Miss Angela! How you doing?* She was, unironically, Lady Bountiful. If she was aware of her self-regard, her self-concern, her self-congratulation, well, she rationalized this didn't lessen the good she was doing.

Darryl was twenty-two. Tall and gangly, he wore low-slung jeans, a white T-shirt, and a track-suit jacket with black stripes up the sleeves. Angela was filling out the usual information. His clothes included no colour, so he wasn't identifying with a gang. She checked colours and tattoos out of habit. Bloods wore red. Crips blue. Latin Kings were black and gold. Netas were red, white, and blue.

"How many in the family, Darryl?"

"I'm here for my grandmother, right? You know her, Leonetta West? She said you know her."

"Yes, sure. Miss West. Is she all right?" Miss West cared for a few children. Four, five, sometimes six.

"Her diabetes kicking up. Legs all swollen, so she can't walk good."

"It's nice of you to help. Are you living with her now?"

"For a little while. Until I get my own place."

Reading between the lines, it was probable Darryl had been recently released from a halfway house or from prison. The percentage of young men from Trenton who had done time was obscene, but Angela had long ago learned that simply because someone had been to jail didn't make them a bad person. In fact, most of the time, almost *all* the time, their moral centre was no different than hers, or anyone else's she knew. It was just that the rules were different here. Kids grew up with a set of street rules foreign to her experience, but a code of conduct, nonetheless. Living up to that code made moral sense for the people who grew up with it. There were all kinds of criminals, and she'd met some supposedly upstanding members of financial society who had committed crimes with considerably more far-reaching effects than those committed on these streets.

"I'm sure Miss West is grateful to have you with her. She can certainly use the help."

Darryl pushed up the sleeves on his jacket, revealing a home-made tattoo on his forearm that read $ BEFORE BITCHES. She couldn't help but laugh.

He jerked his chin. "What?"

She tapped his arm. "How's your love life?"

He looked puzzled for a second and then broke out in a sheepish grin.

"Yeah, young and stupid, right? Got that when I was, like, fourteen and thought I knew everything. I'm saving up. Gonna have it lasered off."

"Forgive me, but I know a dermatologist who removes gang tats for free."

Darryl dropped his eyes. "Nope."

"Wrong of me to ask. But I just thought —"

"Sure." He shuffled in his seat, put his hands on his knees, about to stand. "We good?"

"Absolutely." The flush rose in Angela's cheeks. She handed him his shopping card.

Darryl smirked and strolled off, wrapped in his eloquent silence.

Angela's impulse was to run after him, to tell him he was wrong about her, to persuade him she was without judgment. But Darryl's insight pricked her. It was a flashbulb, revealing all sorts of flaws.

The next client was waiting, a haggard, grey, overweight woman in a jacket with HOLLYWOOD emblazoned across her ample bosom in gold. She plunked down in the seat. Angela's smile widened and she willed it up to her eyes.

"Hey, Sophia, how you doing today?" She would charm Sophia. She would make her day better.

Sophia told Angela how her seven-year-old had taken the scissors to her own hair. "I caught her in the bathroom doing it."

"What did you do?"

"Filmed that thing and stuck it up on YouTube. Bet it goes viral."

She pulled out her phone to show Angela. There was the child, scissors in hand, snipping great chunks out of her shoulder-length brown curls. The tiny bathroom was a riot of plastic bottles and makeup. One of the drawers was missing and the mirror over the sink was cracked. Most of the front of the little girl's hair was gone. She looked like a tiny tonsured Druid.

"Whatcha doing, sweetie?" Sophia's voice came from off-camera.

"I'm at the hairdresser." A handful of hair from the side drifted to the bathroom floor.

"How come?"

"I want my hair like Miley."

"Miley Cyrus?"

"Uh-huh. Snip, snip, snip."

"Good job, Cassie."

Angela laughed. Sophia said since most of the hair was already gone, there wasn't much point in getting angry.

"You gotta love that kid," she said.

"You're a good mother."

"Excuse me, Angela." Sister Caroline's hand on her shoulder. "When you're done, Sister Eileen wants to introduce you to someone. Come outside, okay?"

"Be right there."

She finished up with Sophia. Another client stepped up. A woman with two children. "Can you wait a sec? I'll be right back."

The woman sighed and rolled her eyes. "I guess."

"Sister Caroline? Can you take over for a second while I see Sister Eileen?" Angela slipped on her jacket and made her way into the street, wondering what was up and why outside?

The day had warmed up a little and in the sun against the wall it was almost spring-like. Roland, the security man, was talking to a couple of guys in front of Sammy's Liquors and Bar next door. He towered over the other men. His Trenton Thunder jacket with the blue storm cloud throwing a lightning bolt strained across his back. He had pitched with the Thunder team for a couple of seasons, but a rotator cuff injury had ended his hopes for a chance at the big leagues, and then came a stint of trouble with drugs and an assault charge.

"Roland, where's Sister Eileen? She wanted to see me."

He pointed right. "In the lot, with some gardener guy."

Angela rounded the corner and saw Sister Eileen in the vacant lot talking to a tall man. He had a slightly receding hairline with a high widow's peak. The blond hair above was tousled and revealed a gleam of gel. His face was square, sun-lined, with deep-set blue eyes. He held a wide stance, his legs set firmly, and his arms were crossed, fingers tucked beneath his biceps, thumbs tapping his chest. His eyes darted toward Angela. He smiled.

Sister Eileen turned. "Oh, good. Angela, come here — I want to introduce you. This is Carsten Pilgaard. He's a master gardener, owns a nursery, and he's generously agreed to donate his time and materials so we can build the community garden."

He took Angela's hand in both of his. They were calloused, strong, warm. "I am very happy to meet you, Angela. Sister tells me you are a wonderful gardener. We will do some great things here, ja?"

His spoke as though there were a small cave in his mouth; he moved his lips very little, his tone steady, nearly monotone, but deep and full of hollows. He half-swallowed the *r*'s. Swedish?

"Sister Eileen exaggerates," said Angela. "I volunteer at the land trust, and at the governor's mansion, and I fuss with orchids. I like to putter in my garden. A few flowers, some lettuce. Herbs."

"A kitchen garden. Everyone should have a kitchen garden. But you like to do this?"

"Yes. I do. Good to get out and dig in the dirt sometimes. Good for the soul."

"The soul." His grin slightly mocking. "Also, the belly."

Sister Eileen looped her arm through Angela's. "Think of it. We'll turn this no man's land into our own tiny farm. Maybe just the first. All these zombie houses gone, and the lots turned into vegetable gardens." She radiated delight. "I just knew God would answer our prayers. He sent Carsten."

"Sister tells me it is hard for people to get good vegetables."

"They're expensive, and if you don't have a car you're not going off to a farmer's market. Fast food is cheaper and more filling, even if it's only *technically* food. Part of the initiative is education." Sister Eileen looked up at Angela. "You'll help Carsten with this, won't you?"

"Anything I can do."

"I hope you are good with a hammer and nails. We must build raised boxes. This soil here must be not good, maybe even very bad. We will get good organic soil and pumice for the bottom of the beds and some screening to keep out squirrels."

Sister Eileen said, "I'd like to put you in charge of this project, Angela. Anyone can do intake, but you have a way with people and can get volunteers to help with the heavy work, and I know you aren't afraid of work yourself, and you have a green thumb, and, oh, it's so wonderful!"

Angela let Sister Eileen's enthusiasm sweep her up. Sister Eileen saw the whole world as evidence of God's love, saw God in every face, even the most filthy, toothless, battered, and raving street person. It was a force to be reckoned with, that love. Best to just let the wave carry you.

Besides, working for a few months with this man? *Oh, all right, if you insist.*

"Of course." Angela smiled up at Carsten and he smiled back.

Did their eyes lock for that slight moment that signalled mutual interest? They did. Was she glad she'd visited the salon the day before and had her hair coloured and shaped to frame her face in soft curls? She was. That she wore the teal sweater that suited her skin tone so well? Indeed. That she'd applied her favourite lip gloss? You bet.

She licked her lower lip. "It's going to be great," she said.

That fizzy feeling sparkled up through her belly, the old feeling, signalling the game was on. She told herself that's all it was. *A game. A little fun. Nothing more.*

How reckless she was with all the fragile things she held.

Sister Eileen

It was stuffy in the prison, and more so in the blue-walled classroom where Eileen was trying to help Taruk with his GED. It had been a difficult month. Overcrowding, no air conditioning, and an incident that resulted in the death of a young man who had unfortunately sported an Aryan Nation tattoo had put everyone on edge. Tempers flared. There were taunts and insults and tensions in the dorms and the gym and the chow hall. As a result, most of the usual volunteers had failed to show up the last couple of weeks, and so Eileen had, at Ruth's request, stepped in. She leaned over Taruk and tried not to wrinkle her nose at the stench of sweat coming off him. He'd probably run out of money and couldn't afford the overpriced deodorant in the commissary.

"Okay," she said, "let me explain it again. You'll get it."

At a nearby table sat another inmate, talking with a girl about his age, a college student from Princeton who wore a green T-shirt with the name PETEY GREENE stenciled on it. The Petey Greene program was a volunteer organization that brought college students into the facility to help tutor the inmates. She was the only other volunteer who'd come in today.

Taruk shuffled his feet and cracked his knuckles. M.O.B. was tattooed across the back of one hand. R.R.R. across the other. M.O.B. meant either "Member of Bloods" or "Money over Bitches," and R.R.R. meant "Respect, Reputation, Revenge."

"Bullshit, man," he said. "It's all bullshit. When am I gonna use this crap?"

"I don't know. But if you want to pass your GED you have to learn it. Okay?"

"Whatever." He slumped.

"Okay." She put her finger to the spot on the Xeroxed page to which she wanted, desperately, to direct his attention. Voices were raised in the hall for a moment, but no bells rang, and the voices subsided. "All prime numbers can be divided only by one and itself. This means that the number has exactly two factors," she read.

"What's a factor?"

She knew this, of course she did, but … blank. Eileen scanned the page, looking for the explanation. It had to be there, didn't it? *For example, 13 is a prime number because 13 can only be divided evenly by 1 and 13. If the number has more than two factors, we say that the number is composite.* "Um, I think, yes, factors are numbers we can multiply together to get a number. So, if you multiply two times three, you get six, right? So, two and three are factors of six."

"They're just numbers, then. So why don't they call them that?"

"I don't know," she said. "I'm a math idiot."

Taruk twisted his head around to look at her. "Why are you the one teaching me, then?"

In his eyes, Eileen saw a series of emotions, much like an old flip-card animation, surprise, amusement, fuck-you, and dismissal.

No, she thought, *no, don't. Stupid old white woman*. How could she be anything but a stupid old white woman?

"Your regular tutor will be back next week, I'm sure. But for now, ya got me. Not ideal, I agree. Listen, don't you have a passion? I mean, my passion is literature, okay? I'd read all day long if I could. In fact, we should probably switch to the English section if I'm going to be in any way useful here, but come on, tell me, what's your thing?"

"My *thing*?" He laughed, looking away from her.

"Yes. Something that, when you do it, it just feels right, down in your bones." And, she prayed, *Friend, make me better than I am*. And in the praying came that hollow feeling again, the place where God was not.

"My kid. That's my *thing*." He said the last word with mockery.

"Your kid."

"Yeah, my kid."

"Girl? Boy?"

"Daughter. She five."

"What's her name?"

He side-eyed her. "Daniella."

She moved around the small, metal desk and pulled up a chair. "Tell me about her."

"Nothing to tell. She's five." Taruk leaned away from her, took the hem of his scrub shirt and wiped his face with it. He stretched out his legs, crossed his ankles.

"But, when you're with her, how do you feel?"

He looked up at her. Narrowed his eyes. "She's everything, right? She's my light, she and her mother."

"Who's her mom?"

"Roxane. Known her all my life. Lived next door to me, so we, like, got no secrets, you know."

She did know, because that's what she had always wanted God to feel like for her. The one from whom she had no secrets, who knew her flawed self, and loved her anyway. In principle, she believed this. In experience? Like Taruk, whose beloved seemed so far away, so did hers. That silence, it could deafen you. She said, "And you love each other, knowing everything."

The inmate behind Taruk slammed his hand on the desk and laughed loudly. Taruk jumped and spun around. "The fuck?"

The man held up both his hands. "Sorry, man. Sorry."

He turned back to Eileen. "Yeah. Like that. I guess. I just want to go home and take care of them like they deserve, you know?"

"You need a GED for that, yes?"

"I need money."

"Then you need a college degree."

"I need to take care of business."

"There are programs that can get you into college. Get a degree and a decent job."

He shook his head and laughed. "Sister, what world you live in?" His voice has softened, as though he had just realized he was talking to someone who couldn't, given her apparent brain injury, be held responsible for her idiocy.

"I'm serious. The NJ-Step Program. Scholarship and Transformative Education in Prisons Consortium. They have higher education courses for all students in prison while you're here, and then assist you in making the transition to college life when you're released. Sister Ruth knows all about it. Do you want me to get you some of the information?"

"I don't know. I guess."

"You can do it, Taruk. You can get out, get a job, take care of Roxane and Daniella."

"I'm gonna do that in any case. No doubt."

"I believe you."

Did she? She believed he would try. She believed he would put every bit of effort he had into it; she could see that determination in his face, but she also understood that his chances were awful. A convicted felon? Who would hire him, without even a degree, unless a group like NJ-STEP, who boasted journalists and activists and college professors among their ranks, helped him? He'd be back on the corner, with a gun in his belt, a return to prison almost inevitable, if not a radically shortened lifespan.

"And if you end up back here, what then?"

"I'm not coming back here. I'm out, I'm out." He chewed the inside of his lip.

"Let's just say whatever activity that got you in here isn't what you want to spend the rest of your life doing. What, I mean other than being with your daughter, what do you like doing?"

"I don't know. Like what?" He paused. "I got some rhymes."

"You write?"

"Maybe."

"Let's start there."

"Nothing you'd like."

"Maybe, maybe not. I don't have to like it. But if you want to write it, well, at least that gives us an excuse to move from math to English, right?"

"Yeah, well." He looked up at the wall clock. "I'm gonna go take a shower. Thanks for coming in, Sister. Appreciate it."

"Hey!"

Officer McIntyre, a lanky ginger-haired man with a long moustache and watery blue eyes, opened the door and walked into the classroom. Usually the guard, posted at the end of the education corridor, stayed behind his desk, only venturing into the classrooms if summoned by a teacher. He pointed at the young female tutor.

"You, you're done. Come with me."

The girl turned bright red and stood up. She looked at the inmate she'd been helping and said, "What's going on?"

"Officer?" Eileen stayed in her seat. "Is something wrong?"

Taruk kept his eyes on the pages in front of him, tapping his pencil rapidly on the paper.

"No physical contact," said Officer McIntyre.

"What? I just touched his arm. You know, like …" and she reached out to touch him again. The young man moved his shoulder away.

"Kevin, get back to your dorm. I'll deal with you in a minute. Miss, you'll be leaving. Come with me." McIntyre held his arm out, making come-here gestures with his fingers.

Eileen was about to say something, but a small *em-em* from Taruk stopped her. She would talk to the administrator later. It was ridiculous.

The girl gathered her possessions and left the room with McIntyre without another word, the student trailing behind them.

"Really?" said Eileen. "What's going to happen now?"

"Yeah, that's why I don't get tutored by no girl who don't know nothing, right?"

Eileen was glad of her age at that moment.

"Why?"

"Because these girls, they come up in here and be all nice and touchy like they our friends and shit and look, okay, they mean well, no doubt, and we appreciate it and all, but we the ones get in trouble. Kevin going to be in seg for a couple of days now. She breaks the rules, but what they going to do to her 'cept tell her she can't come back? No big deal, right. We the ones got to pay."

RUTH'S OFFICE WAS IN THE administrative corridor. It was a small cinder-block space, with a desk, two chairs, a filing cabinet, and a bookshelf; the sort of office a low-level bureaucrat in the

1950s Soviet Union might have enjoyed, the point of which was to reinforce the fact that whomever occupied the space was a lesser creature, there due only to the beneficence of those truly in power. Ruth had told Eileen that the point the administration wanted to make was that although God might be a good influence, *they* were the ultimate authority, and oversaw everything and everyone within these walls, even God's handmaids. The air gave one the impression of a tepid petri dish.

Eileen slumped, facing Ruth, who, phone to her ear, sat behind the desk.

"I do understand you think he's properly medicated, I do," Ruth said to whomever was on the other end of the line, "and I don't mean to be a buttinsky, but I'm telling you his depression is worsening. He needs to be reassessed." She looked at Eileen and rolled her eyes.

On the wall behind Ruth hung an icon of Saint Maximilian Kolbe. He was portrayed holding a scroll that said, in French, "Be a man. Do not be ashamed of your convictions." *Sois homme. Ne rougis pas de tes convictions.* A blue-and-white-striped Auschwitz prison's uniform was draped over his left shoulder, the red triangle identifying him as a political prisoner, and his identification number lay over his heart. Saint Maximilian, patron saint of, among others, drug addicts, journalists, and prisoners. He had been a Polish Franciscan friar sent to Auschwitz for hiding Jews during the Second World War. When the Nazi guards selected ten people to be starved to death in an underground bunker as punishment for one thing or another, Saint Maximillian volunteered to die in place of a man he didn't know, who had called out for the sake of his wife and children. *Imagine that*, Eileen thought. The moment. One hears a man cry out and doesn't hesitate but to step forward. Would she have done it? She doesn't know. Kolbe hadn't died fast enough to please the Nazi guards.

He was, in fact, the last of the ten alive. Two weeks. Everyone else died as they ought to have. It annoyed the guards, and so they injected carbolic acid into his veins, which did the trick, albeit in grisly fashion. He was said to have raised his arm calmly to meet the needle. *Well,* she thought, *I might have done that. Two weeks without food or water in an underground bunker. Just kill me.* A dreadful thought. She imagined the burning, the convulsions, the foaming … no … she was no martyr.

She had asked Ruth once why she had chosen St. Maximilian. Ruth told her that although the saint hadn't been imprisoned for doing anything criminal, but was an innocent, as in fact some of the men here might well be, given what plea-bargaining and an ill-named justice system led to these days, what was most significant was the way St. Maximilian had comported himself while held in Auschwitz. Right up to the end, regardless of how the Nazis tried to dehumanize him, he held on to those things that made him human — his kindness, his sense of justice and of mercy, and his faith. It was an example she hoped the men who lived here could learn from. Like Viktor Frankl, whose book *Man's Search for Meaning* she handed out willy-nilly, Kolbe's life was testament to the fact one need not be defined by one's surroundings.

Ruth was still on the phone. "Do you think maybe he doesn't talk to you the way he talks to me? I'm not breeching any confidentiality when I tell you he exhibits signs of suicidal ideation and if anything happens to him, I am going to wonder if you won't consider yourself at least partially responsible." A pause, and then. "Oh, I don't think it will come to that. Not at all. Why would I talk to his family about this when I'm sure you'll do the right thing? What's the big deal? Just change the script." Another pause. "Well, actually, I *am* a trained psychologist, you know, the PhD kind." She chuckled. "You can call me Doctor if it makes you feel better. We shouldn't quibble, being colleagues, am I right? You have such a good heart, Doctor, and I know how difficult it is for you to spend the amount of time you'd like to with all your patients. Can't you believe I'm merely trying to be of assistance and to save everyone, including Derek, from having something awful happen, something that, apart from possibly causing Derek harm, would reflect *so* badly on us all? You will? Oh, I knew I could count on you. Do you think you'll be able to do that soon? I'm going to see Derek this afternoon and I'd like to give him some hope." She listened. "Hello? Dr. Barnes? Hello?" She put the phone back in its cradle. "Pompous power-mad old poop." She lay her hands flat on the desk, spreading out her fingers, and smiled at Eileen. "How's *your* day going?"

Eileen told her what had happened in the classroom. "I don't know how you manage not to be furious all the time," she said.

"Oh, you know how we are. I get plenty mad, and when I do, I wrap that anger up in a big red bow and I bring it to God and I tell God to hold it while I get on with the job he's given me to do, and then, at the end of the day, sometimes I go home and I chop up all the onions and carrots and potatoes we have in the house. It does wonders, I find, for getting the mad out. When I was younger, I played tennis. Then my knees gave out." She chuckled. "If I'd been less angry, maybe I'd have better knees now. Mind you, sometimes I wonder if Sister Brigid's gig at Edna Mahan," she said, meaning the only prison for women in New Jersey, "doesn't have it easier."

"What makes you think women would be easier to deal with than men?"

"I suppose. If anyone should know how difficult women can be, it's nuns, right?"

"Ruth!" Eileen laughed, but it was true.

Ruth tilted her head. "What about you? I get the feeling you're dealing with some challenges. Anger? How are you going to get rid of it?"

"I'll join you at the chopping block. We'll make enough food to feed the multitudes." A little laughter felt good. "Taruk wants to know about the NJ-STEP program."

"Does he?"

"He wants to take care of his family when he gets out. I said he'd need a degree."

"Or a marketable skill, yes. I'll talk to him. Keep in mind, though, not everyone is cut out for university. Taruk has impulse-control issues. No patience. And his reading is awful. It would take a lot of work and dedication for him to handle the courses. However, he's a whiz with engines. He would be a first-rate mechanic. Auto mechanic technology. Master mechanic. He's expressed interest in airplane mechanics. Once he gets out of his head and into his hands, he's a magician."

"Ah."

"He didn't tell you we'd been talking about that?"

"No." Eileen jiggled her leg and then stopped. "Why wouldn't he tell me? Bit of a waste of time, then, today."

"He's got nothing *but* time, and he might have thought you'd respect him more if he showed interest in college."

Bells went off in the hallways. Time for inmate movement again, for the first tier to head to the chow hall. She imagined the plastic trays, the brown unidentifiable mush (or the greenish unidentifiable mush), the slice of white bread. Apparently, there had been a time when the food was, if not good, then at least better, but since food services had been privatized it was wretched and the inmates complained they were hungry all the time, since who would eat that slop? Only those who had no one on the outside putting money in their account for canteen food, especially since sometimes the food made the men sick. There were reports of maggots. None of this helped morale. It was all just so unrelentingly grim.

Someone knocked on the door. One of the guards with an inmate to see Ruth. Ruth opened the door and thanked the guard, ushering the man in. He looked young, and his hair was matted, sticking up in nodules all over his head. Eileen had no idea if this was a new fashion. He wore the thick-rimmed black plastic frames all inmates who needed glasses were issued, the kind that had become so fashionable with hipsters who had no idea where the trend originated.

"Carl, have you met Sister Eileen?"

"Hey," he said, barely looking at her. "We gonna talk? I made an appointment, right?"

"I was just leaving," said Eileen. "Nice to meet you."

EILEEN AND RUTH SAT with bowed heads, praying. It was nearly nine at night. Anne and Caroline had retired to their rooms. The Himalayan rock salt lamp on the bookshelf gave Eileen's small room an orange glow, and other than the crook-necked bedside reading lamp, was the only illumination. The room smelled faintly of the roast chicken they had eaten for dinner, and from outside came the occasional whoosh of car tires. The women were praying for the inmates at the prison.

Eileen raised her head and opened her eyes, waiting to speak until Ruth had done the same. How tired Ruth looked. She ran three miles daily and had the leathery, almost stringy physique of a marathoner. There was no fat on her to blur the edges of distress. The relationship between the two women was deep. When Eileen had returned from a retreat, years ago, at which she'd first confronted the demons of her past, first faced the sexual abuse and trauma, she had known she was skinless and fragile and that the Sisters with whom she lived would have to be told, so they would know how to help her and live with her as she healed. Ruth had been the one she told first, knowing that Ruth had a difficult past herself, one that involved not sexual abuse, but violent physical abuse from a brother who was eventually jailed for life after killing a man in a fit of rage over a parking space. Since that time, Ruth had been the Sister of her heart, which was not perhaps a friendship such as those outside the religious life shared, but rather a relationship focused on their mutual love of God and desire to please God. They felt safe with each other, which is not to say she didn't feel safe with the other Sisters, but there were bonds with Ruth, born of their mutual understanding of the other's traumas.

When Ruth ended her prayer, her smile didn't reach her eyes. "So many stories to break your heart," she said.

"Who are you thinking about?"

"Morgan."

"He's the one who came in so young."

Ruth nodded. "Fifteen, transferred to the adult jail two years ago. Another four years to go before he's eligible for parole."

"A long sentence for someone so young."

"He says it wasn't really his fault. He was only trying to rob someone, but the man chased him, and they fought. Morgan had an ice pick. Says he was fighting for his life. Stabbed the man in the ear. He says the man would have lived except his family pulled him off life-support, wanting him dead for some shadowy reason."

"What do you think?"

Ruth leaned back in the plaid-upholstered rocker and said with a shrug, "I think unless he comes to terms with what happened, really happened, and how he's responsible, he'll continue to be a mess." She shook her head and pressed her lips in a sort of smile. "At fifteen, no parents to speak of, raised by his grandmother or his cousins or a stepfather at one point, briefly … and all this over what? There was less than a hundred dollars in the till. There wasn't anyone to pay for a defence, so he pled down. They almost all do. Remember Randall?"

Eileen did. She'd met Randall a couple of years earlier when he participated in a writing class she taught. A born-in member of the Bloods, without a single tattoo, for if your family was in the Bloods for generations, you didn't need them. A high-ranking member, running a large and profitable crew, he was caught up in a sweep. Randall knew he was, at least technically, innocent of the charges, since he was smart enough never to carry either drugs or guns on his person, or in his car, save for a legally obtained handgun he kept close to hand at home if he was alone. He had money. He had prestige. He knew a thing or two, and so Randall decided he would do what the rich white kids do and hire himself an expensive lawyer. Let the other guys plead out; not him. And there, alas, his smarts ran out. A Black twenty-one-year-old from Camden walks into court with a high-priced lawyer. The prosecution, annoyed as hell at having to try the case, couldn't stop laughing. The rest of his crew received two, three- and four-year sentences. Randall got eighteen years.

Eileen also remembered how charismatic he was, how the intelligence just shone out from his eyes. The first time she'd met him, he'd handed her an essay he'd written. "Universal Justice: Does It Exist or Not?" It wasn't a perfect essay, but Eileen couldn't deny how well-argued his position was.

"I guess he wishes he'd pled down," she said.

"Yes, probably. He'll be under forty when he gets out, providing he survives it. Who knows, but he may still do something wonderful with his life. Not impossible." Ruth bowed her head for a moment, and then breathed in deeply. When she raised her eyes, her expression had softened. She asked, "And your day? What about you?"

Eileen noticed a stink bug crawling on the inside of the pink plastic shade on the lamp beside her bed. The bug bumbled about for a moment and then settled. They were terrible flyers. One could so easily scoop them up and toss them outside. They were such ordinary insects. Mundane. Okay, they smelled like acrid slime, but what kind of a superpower was that?

"I'm fine," she said.

There was no point in burdening Ruth, who had so many people leaning on her already, with her problems. She'd talk to her spiritual director, Felida, soon.

Angela

It was a Saturday, Connor's seventeenth birthday. He was home at the end of spring break, having spent a week in Bermuda at a friend's beach house.

He stumbled downstairs into the kitchen shortly after nine. His feet too big for the stair treads, he reached out for the railing before he fell. In sports he had an almost balletic grace, but coming down the stairs, or even walking down a hallway, turned him into a clumsy galoot. Angela had learned not to shriek at his missteps. His dark hair stuck up every which way. He'd thrown on sweatpants, sneakers (untied, of course), and a ratty old sweatshirt, but he obviously hadn't taken a shower. Philip sat staring into his cellphone and Angela was reading the paper at the other end of the old refectory table.

"Hey, birthday boy," said Philip.

Angela got up, kissed Connor, which he allowed, and wished him a happy birthday. He smelled of boy, that goatish scent of hormones and sports equipment. She went to the fridge to get the pancake batter. A tradition: blueberry pancakes on birthday mornings.

"Hungry?"

"Sure," he grunted. Not one of nature's morning folk.

Angela put a cast-iron frying pan on the huge, six-burner-plus-grill stove that would have been better suited to a restaurant. It always made her feel guilty, that stove. She felt she should be taking in the homeless, foster kids, refugees. She should be feeding the world with that stove. The gas whooshed on.

"So, plans for the day?" Philip asked.

Angela ladled the batter into the pan. "We're having dinner tonight, yes? I made a reservation at Mistral."

Connor poured himself a cup of coffee. He'd started drinking it last summer and Angela found his affectation at adulthood rather sweet. When he was home, she mixed in half decaf.

He scratched the back of his head and shrugged. "Do we have to?"

It pinched Angela's heart. "You don't want to?"

He'd be off at college next year, studying law and political science. He'd been accepted at Princeton but didn't want to go to school so close to home, which Angela could almost understand. He'd wanted to go to Stanford. They'd settled on Harvard, where Philip had gone. Lawrenceville was, after all, the alma mater of several governors, senators, two chiefs of the Cherokee Nation, ambassadors, congressmen, and at least one president of a foreign country. Big things were expected.

She said, "This might be our last birthday dinner."

"No, of course it won't!" said Philip. He stood up and stuffed his hands in his pockets, jingling coins, something he did when irritated, impatient, or excited. "Boys his age don't want to hang out with their parents, and besides, he might want to drive his friends down to the shore or something."

Connor's head came up. "You gonna loan me the bimmer?"

"Nope." Philip grinned. "Better."

"Better?" Connor's grin matched his father's.

Philip pulled his hand out of his pocket. He dangled a key chain. "Much better."

"Get out!" Connor yelled. "For real?" He reached for the keys.

It didn't quite register with Angela until Connor made a dash for the front door.

"You didn't," she said.

"Hell, yes."

Philip followed Connor, and, because Angela felt she had no choice, she turned off the flame under the frying pan and went, as well.

Parked in the circular driveway was a large red beast of a vehicle with a black roof. The silver plaque on the grille read LAND ROVER.

"Where did that come from?" Angela was sure it hadn't been there earlier.

"I had a guy from the dealership drive it over this morning. He'll mail me the second set of keys." Philip was so puffed up one would have thought he'd built it in the garage from a kit. "Hey, Connor," he called to his son, who was already behind the wheel, touching the dashboard, running his hands over the leather seats. "Connor! Double overhead cam, V6, 8-speed shiftable automatic, GPS, of course, Meridian premium stereo with eight speakers —"

"You got the upgraded speakers? Wow, Dad, this is great. I mean, really great!"

The engine roared to life. Connor fiddled with dials. Country music blasted.

Angela's hands flew to her ears. "Connor!"

He turned it down. "Sorry."

He pulled his phone out of the pouch on the front of his sweatshirt. Philip leaned in the window and showed him how to connect it. A moment later, rap music flooded the cab. Angela poked her head in the passenger side.

"I don't want you on that phone when you're driving. I'm serious."

She might as well have been talking to the squirrel chattering from the poplar at the side of the driveway.

"I'm gonna drive over and show Jake, maybe pick up Meghan and Emily." Connor was texting furiously. "Okay?"

"What about breakfast?" Before the words were halfway out of Angela's mouth, she knew how idiotic they sounded. Pancakes, blueberry or otherwise, could not compete with a double cam overhead whatever.

"Yeah, of course, go on. Hey, wait! You got your licence?" asked Philip.

"Sure, yeah." Connor pulled his card-holder out of his pocket and waved it.

"All right, then." Philip saluted him.

"Wow. This is really amazing. Thanks. Thanks so much."

Angela had to step back; the beast was already moving. "For God's sake," she called after him, "be careful."

He waved without turning around, the way you do to a stranger who has let you into their lane.

A dinner they'd been to at the Morrisseys' a few years earlier popped into Angela's head. One of Lynne and Walt Morrisey's beautiful daughters was home from Vassar. Sybil, a round-faced freckled girl with a habit of twirling a lock of her red hair around her finger when she was thinking, was talking about what a pain the traffic was driving from Poughkeepsie. Angela mentioned she hadn't even learned to drive until she and Philip moved to Princeton from the city, when she was nearly thirty. Sybil looked as though Angela had just coughed up a hairball onto the salad plate. "Oh my God," she said, "you didn't have a car? How did you get by?" Angela told her that until she met Philip, she couldn't afford a car, let alone gas, insurance, and all that.

"Really?" Sybil had looked sincerely puzzled. She picked up a spear of asparagus and nibbled it, then cocked her head. "Well, I guess if my parents hadn't bought me mine, I wouldn't have been able to afford it, either."

Had this just occurred to her?

"But you know," she said, "it's just a Honda. SUV, sure, but just a Honda. A lot of the kids at Vassar have a Lexus or Mazda."

Angela had vowed Connor would never talk like that. By this she meant he would never take such luxury and plenty for granted, not that she wouldn't want him to have a fine car. When had this shift happened? The idea of being able to give her beautiful boy everything he wanted and more had once been a hope, a dream, an aspiration. Now, she watched her son disappear around the corner onto Stockton, a street Angela thought far too busy. She felt scooped out inside, not as though a dream had been fulfilled, but rather that some greater hope for Connor had just died.

"I wish you'd talked to me about this first." She shivered in the chilly wind.

Philip put his arm around her. "Come on, every kid his age needs a car. He's got his licence."

"That doesn't mean he shouldn't have to work for his first car; that he shouldn't have to earn it."

Philip's face set in that way it did when he disapproved of her, of her ideas, of her opinions. Disapproval wrapped in disappointment. He dropped his arm from her shoulder.

"Connor's job is to go to school and get good grades, and he's performing well. That's how he earned his birthday gift, if you want a rationale."

"I want to be consulted."

"Like you consulted me about taking on yet another good-works project?"

Angela had come home from the Pantry excited about the community garden and had foolishly thought Philip would be enthused, as well.

"Oh, for Christ's sake." She turned and stalked back into the house.

Philip followed her in, through the hall, past the portraits of his parents and grandparents and great-grandparents — robber barons and debutantes and at least one rum-runner.

Angela poured a cup of coffee and put the remainder of the pancake batter back in the fridge, thinking maybe it would keep until tomorrow morning. She sensed Philip behind her, seething. It had been a bad week for them; lots of sniping, several instances of turning him down for sex, a smart remark or two about his cigar-smoking, a dig here and there about her drinking.

Let him seethe, she thought. She kept her back to him, staring out the window into the garden. The statue of the girl holding a lotus flower was leaning slightly, made unstable by winter's earth-heave. She made a mental note to call the gardening service and have them fix it. Philip slammed a cupboard and she jumped.

"Stop behaving like a spoiled child," she said.

"That's rich, pardon the pun, coming from you." He rattled the coffee pot, stomped to the fridge for cream, and stirred his coffee as if he hated the cup.

Angela turned and leaned against the counter. Philip stood on the other side of the island, leaning on his hands, the fingers splayed out against the granite. He looked every inch the boss man in the boardroom about to dress down an employee or launch a hostile takeover.

He pointed a finger at her. "You better get yourself in line, Angela."

"In line? Are you kidding me? What are you, my drill sergeant? Well, yes, sir!" She saluted in a mockery of the one he had given to Connor.

"Sarcasm. Is that supposed to be an intelligent comment?"

"I wouldn't waste an intelligent comment."

Philip pulled back his head. "Wow, you've been real nasty lately, and I don't like it one bit, and I'm not sure how much more of it I'm going to take. What is it? Hangover? Hormones?"

"Piss off."

"Snap out of it, for Christ's sake."

"You just miss the little girl who fucked you whenever you wanted it."

He laughed, mirthlessly, and then his face fell, just for a second. He said, "No, that's not it, Angela. I miss my wife."

A good person would have responded to the pain in that.

"Is this your way of not talking about Connor? Because it's a cheap trick, if it is."

Philip's eyes glazed over with a fine veil that struck Angela as something like hate, and she wondered if it mirrored her own expression.

"Fine." He folded his arms. "What do you want to say about Connor? Let's get that out of the way."

She put the cup down on the counter and folded her own arms over her chest. "You gave him that beast of a car without giving a thought to anything except your own ego. You want all the neighbours to be impressed. But did you talk to him about not texting and driving? Did you talk to him about not drinking and driving? Did you talk to him about speeding and how many kids he could have in the car? Any of that? Anything?"

"I thought I'd leave the nagging to you, since you're mother of the year."

"What do you mean by that?"

"How much time have you spent with your precious son over the past few years? You missed how many of his games? And he's the goddamn quarterback!"

"You make it sound like I'm neglecting him, like I'm an absentee mother, and you know that's not true. I'm just not into sports. We do other things together. We talk. He talks to me. We go for walks, go to the movies. Besides, I made the playoffs. I made the championship."

"Bully for you. Did you know he has a girlfriend?"

That made Angela open and close her mouth a couple of times. "Who is she? Is it serious?"

"Mother of the goddamn year."

"You can be a real bastard, you know that?"

"And you can be a real bitch, a real ice bitch."

"So, we're back to sex, are we?"

"I want to know what's going on with you. I'm thinking maybe we should see someone." His tone had dropped. His eyes darted, and he hefted up his khaki pants.

Someone? A therapist? Who had put that in his head? God, he looked like he'd just proposed a threesome, something Angela might have found more interesting once upon a time. "Let me get this straight, you want to see a marriage counsellor?"

"Might be a good idea."

"No."

The colour rose on his cheeks. "Just like that?"

"I don't see the point."

"Of what? Getting help, or our marriage in general?"

"Oh my God, you're making a mountain out of a dust pile. There's nothing going on with me, except, oh, I don't know, hormones or boredom or something."

Philip came around the island that had stood so decisively, so solidly, between them. Angela willed herself not to stiffen. He opened his arms and she let him hug her, even returned it. His back was soft under his golf shirt; her nose was mashed into his shoulder. Why did they never seem to fit? Had it always been like that? She remembered him picking her up and making love to her as she perched on the edge of a sink in some hotel, in Berlin, she thought it was, on one of his business trips, before Connor was born. It was a black sink, black shower, huge silver bath. Orchids in silver vases, a mass of them, making the bathroom vanity like a kind of altar. She wore a black bustier and black thigh-high stockings. The memory of the actual sex was fuzzy, because she'd been drunk. They'd both been drunk. It hadn't felt particularly great, but she remembered liking the idea of it, of being taken that way, of being the girl a man took like that. A man. Not necessarily Philip.

Now, he began to nuzzle her neck. "It was good once, wasn't it? We can get back there again, I know we can," he murmured. "If you need more excitement, I can give that to you."

She pushed him away. The harsh March light shone full on his face. He was overexposed, full of vulnerability. His eyes were begging. His slightly open mouth (that coffee breath), pleading without speaking. Exactly what she did not want.

Angela had never done well with wet puppies. *Don't need me. WANT me.* There was no point trying to present herself as the sweet and nurturing type. She did not want anyone expecting her soft hands to soothe their troubled brow. She once had a therapist tell her that because her mother was such a mess it was natural for her to feel repelled by need, that it was the way she was hardwired.

Behind Philip the kitchen gleamed. The counters shone. She had picked out the hanging light fixtures, imported from France, the palest celadon ceramic, with a weighted system allowing one to lower them or raise them at will. The dishes in the antique cabinet were Astier de Villatte. She had her own orchids now, better than the ones in the Berlin bathroom. She could see them through the French doors leading to the attached greenhouse. And not just the common moth orchids, but the Brassavola, which emitted a citrusy smell at night (she kept two in the bedroom); the Oncidium, with its sprays of little yellow dancing ladies; Vanda, with its extravagant burgundy flowers; and the Miltoniopsis, the sweetest of all, the little pansy orchid. The flowers made her think of someone … Carsten … only for a moment, but in such sharp relief. She cultivated the flowers as she did her life, her house. She had decorated it, filled it with objects she thought would make her happy.

And so, *Let me be happy*, she prayed to the God she wasn't sure even liked her. Let her love Philip the way a wife should love her husband, who was a good provider and a good father, and who loved his wife. Philip did love her, she never doubted that. Maybe, she reasoned, that would be enough. Maybe it was the first bread crumb leading them back to where he thought they'd once been. She didn't have to tell him she didn't think she'd ever been there, did she?

Oh, but his complacency, that lack of passion, of engagement with the larger world. A passionate life was, she knew, waiting … all ripe and ready to be picked. She wanted to bite into the flesh of life, to feel the juice run down her chin. She wanted Philip to be as hungry as she, but had learned it was best not to begin with what she wanted from him.

She said, "I want you to know I appreciate what you do. This house, this life, I only have it because of you and how hard you work."

"I want you to have nice things," he said, running his fingers through her hair. "You deserve them. I like giving you things, but I want us to be close."

"I feel dead inside all the time, Philip." She had her hands on his shoulders, hoping not to sense him stiffening as she had. "I want us to be closer, I do. But women aren't like men. We're not all just physical without any emotional component."

There it was — the twitch under the muscle. She dropped her hands.

"I can see why you don't want to go to a therapist. You already talk like one."

"I don't mean to. What I'm saying is that there are all sorts of ways to turn me on, not just, well, pawing me." His eyes flashed. "I don't mean … look, excitement is contagious, okay? You never seem to care much about things, you know, things out in the world. The environment, hunger, poverty, literature, music, the theatre, animal abuse, human trafficking … something! All you talk about are finances, and I'm sorry, but I just can't get turned on by stock market reports and Dow Jones averages."

He disengaged, walked back around the island, and picked up his coffee cup. He saluted Angela with it. "You don't have any trouble spending the money I make from it though, do you?"

"I'm not the one who bought a Land Rover for a seventeen-year-old."

"Is that it? You're pissed because I spent money on someone other than you?"

"Jesus Christ, Philip! It's not about the money!"

"Well, there's a first. Have you seen the credit card bills? Oh, please, you're a real saint, but let me tell you, Our Lady of Trenton, I wonder what your friends down there would think if they knew how much you spend on clothes and crap for the house and days at the spa. You want to know what would turn *me* on, not that you've ever asked, but what would turn me on is to have you maybe contribute a bit to our finances instead of just being a big sink hole, a fucking black hole for cash."

"You're kidding, right?" She was genuinely taken aback. She couldn't remember Philip ever complaining about how much money she spent. In fact, he'd always seemed rather proud of it, a perverse way of showing off their bulging bank account. "Do we have money problems?"

"It's not about that. It's about respect. Nobody wants to be nothing more than a money machine." He leaned his elbows on the granite and clasped his hands in front of his face. "Look, you don't seem to want me to touch you. You're out of the house more than you're in it. When you're home in the evening you're halfway down a bottle of wine." He put his fist up to his mouth, made a strangled sound. "We used to laugh. We had parties. We made love. I miss it. I miss the fun."

"And what if it wasn't fun for me?" She said it as softly as she could. She couldn't look at him.

"Ah. You don't mean the parties. You mean the sex." His nostrils flared and his mouth set. "You never complained. Never said you didn't like it. Quite the contrary, as I recall."

"Why do you think I'm always halfway down a bottle of wine, as you put it?"

He paled. She was afraid he was going to cry. "Why the fuck did you marry me, then?" He blinked and then put his hands up. "No, wait, don't tell me … money, money, money."

"Philip, no, it's not like that."

"Fuck you," he said, as he walked out.

She couldn't blame him. Angela was crying now.

THEY DIDN'T GO OUT for dinner that night. Connor came home in the afternoon, electric with automotive excitement, and showered. Angela made him a bacon, lettuce, and tomato sandwich, toasted the way he liked it, with plenty of mayonnaise. She sipped a glass of Chablis and watched him as he stood at the sink eating it.

"Can you please take the plate and sit like a human being?"

He plunked the plate on the island and threw a leg over a stool. "At least I eat over the sink, right? Emily's mother says she'd be happy if people ate over the sink instead of leaving a trail of crumbs around the house."

"Emily? Your girlfriend?"

He shrugged; his mouth full. "I guess. Nobody really has girlfriends or boyfriends anymore. We're not like you were. We don't," he made a face, "date or anything." His phone dinged. He picked it up and began furiously texting.

Emily Patton? They lived around the corner. Emily's mother, Deirdre, and Angela had occasional boozy lunches together.

Texting. Eyes down.

"What do you mean you don't date?"

Connor stopped texting. "What?"

"You said nobody dates, so what do you do?"

The phone dinged. He picked it up. Grinned. Texted.

"Connor, I asked you a question."

"I don't know. We hang out. Like in a group." Thumbs flying.

He'd have arthritic joints by the time he was thirty, Angela thought. They all would. A generation of finger-crippled techno-zombies.

Angela's phone dinged just then. Fine. Two could play at that game.

Can we have coffee and talk about plans for the garden?

Carsten.

Angela's universe whirled and twirled and was shot through with a black hole of desire. Did she flush? Did something happen between her legs? Yes. And, just as quickly, in the same instant, she told herself she wasn't that kind of woman, whatever that meant. The text was a message from a man with a justifiable reason to contact her. They were people who cared about the "under-served," as Sister Eileen called them. They were devoted to a greater purpose. It wasn't personal.

But of course, it was. Like electricity through a faulty socket, it singed her.

Sure. When? Where? Send.

Instant regret. Shouldn't she have let the message sit for a day? Shouldn't she show more professional distance?

Connor and she were in their own spheres of reality. Technologically separated while standing just feet from each other. If she truly wanted a relationship with her son, shouldn't she have ignored the phone? She didn't even glace up at him, all the while aware she wasn't looking at him.

"So," Connor said, "is it okay if we skip dinner? Tomorrow, we can do it, if you want, okay? But I just thought, you know ..."

Oh, to be seventeen again, and to think everything hinged on what happened in one night.

"It's okay, Connor. If you want to hang out with your friends, you go on." He stood and she held up her hand. "But wait, listen, I need to know if you're ... if you and Emily are ..." She had sworn, before she had a child, that she would never be this uncomfortable, never this awkward idiot. "If you're sexually active, and that if you are, you're taking precautions, being careful. You need to use —"

"Oh my God, Mom. Stop talking!" He was laughing. "I'm not thirteen!"

Thirteen? "You've already had a girlfriend?" As soon as the words were out of her mouth it was clear, even to Angela, that she was not only an idiot, but an anachronism. A virgin at seventeen? Even she hadn't been a virgin at seventeen. *Are we all doomed to turn into our parents? To repeat the mistakes of the past? Apparently. Maybe that is our greatest sin. We forget.*

Her son was looking at her as though she were an embarrassing stranger; or perhaps more accurately, a homeless, toothless wreck on the street, suddenly revealed to be his long-lost mother, the sort of person who initially horrifies you, and whom you then ignore.

He held his hand up and stepped back. "It's all good, Mom. Okay? Everything's good." He spoke slowly, in the way one does to old people. "We'll have dinner tomorrow, is that okay? I'm gonna go, right?"

Angela thought it best not to laugh. But still … "So, if I offered you condoms, you wouldn't take them?"

"Man, you are the weirdest mother I know," he said.

He did make a noise that might be interpreted as a laugh, if one was generous.

"Yes. Fine. I'm weird. I love you. Go!"

He leapt up and kissed her. His lips on her cheek were so soft, and so quick, like the kiss of an angel, she thought, impossible to hold, a kiss that left only questions: What if you believed? What if you really knew angels existed and you'd just met one? Wouldn't that change the way you lived your whole life?

"We can do it tomorrow, okay? I love you, Mom." His back was already to her.

"I love you, too," she called after him. "Be careful, okay? Drive careful. No texting!"

He hadn't even asked after his father, the purchaser of magical chariots, which was fine with Angela.

Ding. *Monday? Maybe lunch? Do you know Acacia?*

Acacia was a restaurant in Lawrenceville. Across from Connor's school.

What about Witherspoon Grill? I have to be in Princeton on Monday.

Witherspoon Grill. Faux French bistro in the centre of Princeton. Steak and frites. Oysters. Huh. There she was again. The first lunch she'd had with Philip in a fancy place, the certainly-not-just-lunch place, the jeans and black turtleneck with high-heeled boots she'd wear on Monday. It occurred to her she might run into someone she knew at the Witherspoon Grill. It was next to the library. Philip and she donated a significant amount of money to the library. Princeton was an absurdly small town when it came right down to it. Still, it was the sort of pseudo-professional place one could go and not be accused of having anything other than a business lunch. Which is what they would be having, right? A business lunch. Bottom line? It wasn't the sort of place you'd go if you were afraid of being seen.

That's perfect. 12:30?

Angela stared at her phone. Waited. Nothing. Why did she think he'd text her right back? What was she, a teenager? She picked up the plate Connor had left on the counter. She swept the crumbs off the granite onto it. She dumped the crumbs into the garbage. She rinsed the plate.

Maybe she shouldn't have said *perfect.* Was *perfect* too eager?

Ding. Philip. *I understand dinner's off.*

Where are you?

Ding. Carsten. *See you then. I will bring plans.*

Ding. Philip. *Springdale.*

The golf club. Golf. Angela's idea of existential despair.

Ding. *Steve and Lynne want to have dinner. You up for it?*

See you then. From Angela. A tilt in the world and a flush. She'd sent that to…? Crap. No, it was all right. She'd sent it to Carsten. Breathe. It wouldn't have mattered, though. Innocuous wording. She could not deny, however, that it didn't feel innocuous, and this slight shiver up her spine wasn't simply not innocent, it was delightful. A twig-thin, brittle old biddy in the back of her mind rapped her knuckle on the inside of Angela's forehead and advised caution, signalled a warning. She noted it, snapped the finger off the old biddy's hand and tossed it in the tiny, smouldering fire starting to burn in her belly. She knew what she was doing. Knew it fully and ran to it, telling herself she could make it all work, somehow, that maybe, even, Carsten's appearance in her life was a sign that this hollow she'd been experiencing, this alienation from hearth and home, didn't need to be. Of course, she told herself, nothing would come of it. Nothing at all. But allowing the possibility of passion, just the possibility of it, could only be a good thing. She had been dead inside for so long.

Did she want to go to dinner with Philip, Steve, and Lynne? She did not. She texted, *Sure. Sounds like fun. What time and where?*

AND AFTER A PLEASANT enough dinner, during which she'd enjoyed a vodka martini and several glasses of wine, Philip and Angela came home and he followed her into the shower, and she didn't protest. His breath stank of Scotch and wine. She turned around and put her palms against the tile and wanted him to take her from behind, but he took her hand and led her to the bed, and she let him. She told herself the physical response she had was, like dinner, pleasant enough, was an assurance from the universe that awakened passion regardless of the source was a good thing for her marriage.

Everyone fantasized. She was sure Philip did. In fact, early on in their relationship he once started talking dirty to her, but his fantasy was about Angela as a naughty schoolteacher with himself as a student she'd kept after class to satisfy her insatiable needs, and it appalled her. She told him to stop, and he never shared a fantasy with her again. She believed that what went on in his head was his business, and now, if she closed her eyes and turned her head away, imagining the hands of a Viking raider claiming her body, what was the harm?

She rationalized that the good thing about her fantasies was that, no matter how embarrassing, no one would ever know. It was something just for her, something to help her cope, not unlike the vodka that relaxed her. It changed her perspective. She was nicer to Philip when a little buzzed. How could that be a problem?

Sister Eileen

Eileen walked along the sand, watching the waves crest and roll and the spray drape a lace veil over the seawall. A pair of dolphins rose and dove just past the breakers. Dawn was beginning to send its rays east, toward the distant horizon. The only other people on the beach were a couple of fishermen standing at the end of the jetty.

The Sisters of Saint Joseph had a retreat house here on Cape May called St. Mary's-by-the-Sea, a great rambling U-shaped building facing the ocean, with a red roof, 150 rooms, and twelve hundred feet of covered porches scattered with rocking chairs. The place had been built in 1889 as the Shoreham, once named as one of America's foremost hotels. Ten years later, when the hotel failed, it was sold and became the Home for Aged and Infirm Colored People, a venture that also failed in 1909, which is when the Sisters bought it. The ballroom became the chapel. Since then it had weathered a number of brutal storms, set out on the point as it was, as well as occupation by the U.S. Army during the Second World War. This latter set of "visitors" left the property at least as damaged as any storm. But through it all, the time and terrible tides, the erosion and occupation, the will and hard work of the Sisters prevailed. Families came for vacation. Nuns came for retreat and rest and these days they led those same retreats for people of any and all faiths, or none at all.

There had never been a time when St. Mary's wasn't a part of Eileen's life. She had come as a child with her mother and siblings as volunteers during the summer. They lived not far away in Wildwood, over Dead Davy's, the bar her father owned, named for the previous owner, Davy Culligan. For Eileen's mother, this was a time of both work and contemplation, and the work itself — preparing meals, gardening, doing laundry, etc. — was a sort of contemplation. The nuns didn't usually take in young volunteers but, knowing the family situation, they understood the need and so welcomed them. They made salads and set the tables and gathered the dirty dishes from the dining hall and, during their downtime, they swam in the sea and walked the beach, while their mother sat in a rocking chair on the second-floor veranda, gazing out at the water and sky. Rooms at St. Mary's were furnished with a single bed, a chair, a bureau, and a coat stand. Bathrooms were shared. No phones in the rooms, no televisions. Bare bones it might be, but it was quiet, and there was no booze, no brawls, no bad language, and Eileen's father did not join them. And there, just yards away, was the sea, the shining, ever-moving, ever-changing, life-affirming miracle of the sea.

Now, Eileen carried her shoes in her left hand, delighting in the feel of warm sand on her square, callous-heeled feet. She glanced back at St. Mary's. Though her mother had now passed on, she imagined she could still see her there, sitting on the farthest corner of the southeastern arm of the building, second floor, rocking away, rosary in hand, fingers moving. She was, as always it seemed, praying for her husband, for him to put down the bottle, for him to stop tossing all their money into the wind, or into the hands of other women, or bookies … she was praying for guidance, and for patience.

Eileen kept walking, praying for the same things. Well, not for her father, who was long in the grave, his liver finally giving out, and no surprise there. But she prayed for patience, for the ability to see Christ in the face of every human, even the messy ones, even the highly annoying ones. And she prayed for guidance. How to help? How to heal? How to stay faithful in times when God seemed to go silent? Like now. Only the seagulls sang; God remained mute.

Caroline came to mind. Eileen doubted she'd make it as a nun. Rich girl. No Catholic background. Eileen could tell the young nun was less than thrilled with her accommodations, the old furniture, the handoffs, the grubbiness of it all. Eileen suspected she had grown up on a diet of movies featuring whatever the contemporary version of Loretta Young/Ingrid Bergman nuns were — Whoopi Goldberg? Didn't Eric Idle play a nun once? Killer nuns, sexy nuns, mean nuns, funny nuns, crazy nuns, sainted nuns, where did one go to find portrayals of real nuns? Just women, trying to deal with life on God's terms, full of questions, joys, fears, weaknesses, strengths, doubts — yes, that, for what kind of faith would not stand up to questions — anger and moral agency? And so, she walked, and prayed for Caroline, that she might find the path God wished for her.

As the sun rose, Eileen turned back. She was at St. Mary's to lead a weekend retreat on centring prayer for all those in twelve-step programs. There were eighteen participants this weekend, including her sister, Alice. Eileen knew Alice would want to speak to her this morning; knew the conversation would be difficult, in spite of the fact they'd had it more than once, heck, more than a dozen times over the years. Eileen sighed. She said a prayer. *Come on, Jesus, help me find the right words. Let me be a servant to the greatest good. Hello? Hello?*

She followed the path up through the beach grass, past the wild rose bushes toward the lookout on the top of the dune. Alice sat on one of the benches, her long brown hair braided down her back. A plump woman in her early forties, she had inherited their father's love of drink, and only been sober for the past two years. The long history of cigarettes and whisky, of late nights and broken hearts, had left its mark in the deep lines on her leathery skin and in the shadows under her eyes. Her hands moved nervously, pulling her T-shirt down over the swath of skin between it and the waistband of her shorts. She crossed and uncrossed and crossed her ankles again, then brushed invisible sand off her thighs.

"Hey," Alice said. "I thought I'd find you here. I was going to join you on your walk, but you were gone so early and then, when I saw you out there, I figured you were praying or something, so I didn't want to disturb you."

"How did you sleep?" asked Eileen.

"Okay. You know. It can get pretty hot in those rooms on the third floor."

"I thought you wanted to be up there, away from everyone. Do you want to move? There's a second-floor room open, I think, one with a breeze."

Alice looked toward the sea and paused before speaking. "I was surprised you said what you did in the meeting last night."

"Were you?"

Alice snapped her head back to look at Eileen. Her eyes sparkled. Tears coming. "Of course I was. How can you talk about something like that in front of all these people?"

"How did it make you feel?"

"How do you think? People looking at me now, wondering if Father Devlin went after me as well."

"You've said he didn't."

"He didn't."

Eileen let the silence sit between them. Her abuse at the hands of the neighbourhood priest was no secret, nor was the abuse of her siblings Monica, David, and Peter. And so why, now, was Alice so upset by Eileen's not-very-new revelation? Alice kept looking out at the ocean, at the light dancing there now the sun was up. In profile she looked very much like a pouting child, mad that she hadn't been invited to something. This was, if not an old conversation between them, at least not a new one.

"Alice, I've come to terms with all this."

Eileen thought about that day, so many years ago, when she'd finally been willing to let it go. She had sat in the sand, not far from this very place, and written the names of the priests who had abused her on pieces of paper. She wrapped the paper around rocks she found. And then, she stood, walked to the water's edge and, with a prayer that her fury and brokenness might go with them, she flung them far out into the waves.

"Good for you," said Alice.

"What is it that still upsets you so?"

"Someone should have done something. Mom and Dad, they should have."

"Is it the injustice, then?"

"Yes, sure. No." She raked her fingers through her hair. "I don't know. It just makes me so fucking mad."

"Our parents were pretty wrapped up in their own lives. Dad's drinking and all."

"Like that's an excuse."

"Not an excuse. Maybe just an explanation. Mom was so busy covering up for Dad during those years, I don't think she really knew what was going on. Having Aunt Toni take us off her hands for a few hours was a godsend, I expect. Things were different by the time you came along. Dad was more or less dry by then."

"Great. Rage instead of booze."

Eileen looked out across the sand at the fishermen far out on the jetties. No one was catching anything this morning. "I didn't say sober, Alice. That's something else entirely, as you and I both know. Are you still going to meetings?"

Adult Children of Alcoholics for Eileen, and Alcoholics Anonymous for Alice. Eileen, like her sister Mary, didn't seem to have inherited the alcoholic gene, not the way Peter, Alice, and Anne had. Paul, too, although his drug of choice was much harder stuff. Off the needle fifteen years now, but every day was a struggle.

Alice was crying now. Fat, oily tears slipping down her cheeks, dripping onto her T-shirt. "It's too hard," she said, "all of this. It's too fucking hard."

Ordinarily this might have been the moment when Eileen would ask, what's the invitation? Here, in this pain and darkness, what's the invitation? To release? To forgive? But how did you ask these things of your own sister? This is why Freud should never have analyzed his own daughter. He knew too much, he projected too much. He knew so little.

Eileen took her sister's hand, and Alice allowed it. "It's all right," she said. "I promise, all shall be well …"

Alice smiled, "And all shall be well, and all manner of things shall be well, right?"

"And this too shall pass," said Eileen. "Eventually."

There was laughter then, against the blinding light of the glittering sea, with all that depth and turbulence, unseen, unexpected, and oh so dangerous.

The two women walked back to the retreat house, arm in arm. The storm had passed, and Alice was chattering about her new job with the Department of Children and Families and how difficult it was to see what really went on in people's houses, how impossible it was to believe the terrible things people could do to their children. "Careless," she said, "they're all just so involved in their own dramas, they never see what they're doing to other people."

And Eileen thought, with a snottiness she recognized, *Right, it must be so hard to take care of other people, to keep cleaning up their messes.* Silence, though. She kept her silence and prayed for patience and release.

LATER THAT AFTERNOON, Eileen and Felida, her spiritual director, sat in the corner room of the retreat house that was set aside for conversations between directors and directees. Felida, grounded as an oak stump, with the air of a pioneer wife, someone who would be as comfortable behind a mule team as leading a chapel service, wore a long denim skirt and a white short-sleeved blouse. On her feet she sported Birkenstocks and socks, which made her bunions less painful.

"And yet?" asked Felida, in response to her inquiry into Eileen's prayer life.

Eileen shrugged. "It is, as it has been for so long, a one-way conversation." She sighed and lay her palm over the Sisters of Saint Joseph's medallion at her throat. "It's not getting any better."

"What's that like for you?"

"It's damn hard. Miserably hard. I'm getting pretty annoyed at God."

"She can take it." Felida chuckled. "Anyone else you're annoyed at?"

She thought about Angela Morrison. Eileen was drawn to the vivacious woman while at the same time she was vexed by her, a reaction that shamed her. There was a kind of glow about her, an energy, a glamour, with her chic bobbed hair, her quick smile, and the easy way she had with people. Charm, Eileen supposed it was. Something she had never had. "Yes. There is, as it happens."

She looked at Felida with her Buddha-placid face, slightly sunburned, her skin etched with tiny lines. A peaceful face. A face with no strain in it. A surrendered face. It was the face Eileen wanted for herself, plain but kind, unadorned and open.

"I think," she said, "I have trouble seeing God in careless people."

"The dear neighbour." Felida raised an eyebrow to encourage Eileen to keep going.

"Although God has been distant for a long time, I can still almost see Her in ordinary things, just a glimmer, and it disappears the second I try to look directly at it, which makes it feel like a sort of hide-and-seek God's playing, but sure, there, in the everyday stuff — the dish soap, the tea towel, and the recycling bin. In the ordinary activities, in the cleaning of a toilet, the scraping of a plate, the making of a bed, the scrubbing of a floor.

"No! You know what it is? It's like a piano. I can feel the tap on the keys, I can feel the hammer move on the string, but there's no music."

"Wow."

The two women sat quietly, allowing that image to resonate.

Then, Felida said, "I hear you talking about things you do alone."

"I know it. It's people who are the problem. And not all people. I don't find myself annoyed with the clients at the Pantry, no matter how often they seem to make the same mistakes over and over again. I see how the Sacred works in their lives, even if She's not obvious in my own at the moment, but it's people who are careless in that *Great Gatsby* sort of way, running after their own desires, knocking other people down to get them, expecting other people to clean up after them."

"In what way careless?" asked Felida. "Like who else?"

Eileen snorted. "Damn. Well, it always goes back to the old wounds, doesn't it? Yes, my father was a careless man. Careless with booze, with his fists, with his money, with his wife, with his kids. And Mom, well, that was another kind of careless. Narcissistic. Dramatic."

"So, as the oldest, you were left to clean up after everyone."

"I've had enough of that crap."

Felida laughed. "I'm sure you have."

"There's someone at the Pantry, a volunteer, and I don't know why she reminds me of all that, but she does. She was flirting with someone today and it was all I could do not to smack her hand and say, 'No! Not for you!'" Eileen chuckled. "That little voice is telling me, well, my dear, there's trouble. You know, sometimes I think I should have gone into a cloistered order and spent my life praying and making cheese or something."

Eileen said it as a joke, but part of her yearned for stained glass and gothic arches, for wide, fragrant meadows and star-encrusted nights. The Great Silence that was not in fact silent at all, but rather filled with the breath of God. The swish of long skirts. The sound of bread being kneaded on a wooden table. Soft footsteps on stone stairs.

Felida said, "And here we are stuck with the God of the daily mess. God of the salt and pepper shakers. You know, Eileen, that's the God who gets me through, silly as it may sound. We all want the visions and the glory; we hope for it. We want to be Hildegard of Bingen or Julian of Norwich or St. Joan — well, except for the burning bit — but we end up being more like the Buddhists with their 'before enlightenment, chop wood and carry water; after enlightenment, chop wood and carry water.'"

Eileen raised an eyebrow. "So, is it wrong that I want the pillar of mercy and light right there next to the salt shaker?"

"Not wrong, Eileen, but imagine with me, the pillar of salt. That's what comes to my mind when you say that."

"I hadn't thought of that." She paused. "Lot's wife looked back, didn't she?"

"Exactly. Although she was saved, and her family with her, she didn't look forward to God's grace, but behind her, to a place that offered her nothing."

Eileen made a face, wrinkling her nose. "She did, however, become a lesson for others. What a damn cost, though."

Felida folded her hands in her lap. "I wonder if this great distance you feel from God, Her apparent refusal to draw you near, isn't in some way linked to the carelessness you felt at the hands of your father, at the hands of the priest who so horribly harmed you, and now, is perhaps mirrored in the behaviour of this woman? What does it feel like in you when I say that?"

"Yuck."

"Something to meditate on, then, yes?"

The old novitiate maxim, "Resistance is the edge of growth," came to mind, and for sure she felt that resistance, like she was about to undergo a spiritual root canal, and it confirmed to Eileen it was precisely what she needed to do. Another reluctant yes, but yes nonetheless to this mysterious God, *because* of the resistance, not in spite of it.

"Yes."

"Good. And more shall be revealed."

Eileen didn't say so aloud, but in her head a small voice said, *That's what I'm afraid of.*

Oh, dear.

Angela

The Witherspoon Grill faced onto the Albert E. Hinds Plaza, a small square with the library on one side and some retail spots on the other. A few people, bundled up in sweaters and scarves and jackets, sat at the scattered metal tables and chairs, drinking coffee and eating their lunches. The weather had been rainy, icy and cold that winter, and people were starving for any bit of sunshine.

Angela had parked behind the library. She'd arrived a few minutes early but sat in the car reading Facebook posts about cats and loudmouth politicians until twelve thirty-five. She checked her face in the rear-view mirror. Hair softly gamine, with the short curls in the right place along her cheekbones. Red on lips and not on teeth. Liner accentuating almond-shaped brown eyes. As planned, she wore a black turtleneck, leather jacket just battered enough to be chic without trying too hard; jeans with the small, precisely placed and delicately shredded hole just above the knee;

boots with just-high-enough heels. A silver heart on a long chain rested on her breasts. Her nails were shiny, painted a burgundy shade called Embarca Dare Ya! She'd dabbed a little Coco behind her ears, on her wrists, and throat.

A young woman smiled at her from behind the reception podium. She wore a black-and-white gingham blouse, had long, dark hair, blood-red lips, and an alarming number of teeth. "Table for one?" she asked.

"I'm meeting someone. He's probably already here." Angela scanned the room but didn't see Carsten. A tall, upholstered divider separated the bar from the restaurant proper. It was possible he was sitting on the other side, where she couldn't see him, or perhaps in one of the booths. She glanced at her watch. Twelve-forty.

"Do you have a reservation?"

"I don't know. Maybe. Under Pilgaard?"

A cold draft behind her. "Oh, so sorry. There was car accident and I was stuck behind. You have not been waiting long, I hope."

Blue cashmere scarf around his neck, knotted in that European way that looked as though he wasn't trying at all. It made his eyes look like glacier water. He, too, wore a leather jacket, although Angela suspected the distress showing on his was authentic wear and tear. He had a roll of paper tucked under his arm.

"No, it's fine. I was a bit late myself."

"So, you have a nice booth for us?" he asked over her head to the hostess. "I need a little space to show off my drawings, okay?"

He smiled at the woman and Angela noted its effect. If the hostess had to move people around to make a place for him, she was likely to do so.

They followed her to a booth at the end of the row, nearest the window. Angela felt Carsten's hand gently on her elbow.

"Is this all right?" the hostess asked him.

"Thank you very much."

She placed menus before them as they settled. She walked off and Carsten picked up a small card in a silver holder on which the oyster menu was written. "I very much like oysters. It is much of why I come here. Do you like oysters?"

"What's not to like?"

Angela remembered Carol, one of the popular girls in her high school, holding court in the bathroom while sneaking a cigarette. Curvy and full-lipped, Carol was an expert on sex, or so everyone believed. She told her acolytes that a man who likes oysters also likes women, since there were certain similarities in taste and texture. She had wiggled her eyebrows and Angela hadn't understood, for a moment, what she meant … and then she did and was mortified by the flaming red that flashed on her cheeks and caused everyone to point and laugh.

Carsten put the menu card down. "But perhaps oysters are inappropriate for a business lunch, do you think?"

"Inappropriate?"

"I knew a woman once who would not order spaghetti for a first meal with someone. She said it was very difficult to eat pasta and one might make the wrong impression." He looked terribly serious. "How does one eat oysters without the occasional slurp? Is this, we must ask ourselves, professional?"

"I see your point. Also, a little indulgent, I would think, especially juxtaposed against the cause we're here to discuss."

"So, you see the dilemma." He folded his arms and leaned forward, looking from side to side as though they were spies.

"Of course." She mirrored his posture. "And yet, oysters are brain food …"

"And we are going to be thinking hard."

"Exactly."

"Well then," Carsten leaned back and spread his arms wide, "we should treat ourselves and have them, yes?"

"Why not?"

"And perhaps a bottle of something crisp and white to celebrate this new and wonderful endeavour?"

"At lunch? How naughty."

"Only in America, you will forgive me for saying. In Denmark you cannot have oysters without wine, or *akvavit*, but you don't get that here." He waved to the waiter.

"You're Danish?"

"Oh, yes, from Skagen, way at the top of Denmark. The place of the meeting of the seas. Very beautiful. I still have a small cottage there. I go back when I can."

"How long have you been here?

"Eleven years. I like it. America is a very alive place."

The waiter came and they ordered. Oysters and salad. He insisted on a dozen each. They are just mouthfuls, he said. And wine. While they waited for the food, she learned Carsten came to America after he married a woman named Nancy from Hoboken. They met while she was vacationing in Skagen. She was a cyclist, he said, and had thighs like polished wood. He laughed when he said that, a big round sound that made a woman at a table behind him turn around and smile.

"Do you have children?" Angela asked.

"Ah, no."

His "no" was a long, nasal word, as though he were mimicking an animal noise. Angela found it endearing.

"And you?" He glanced down at the wedding ring on her finger. "You have children?"

"I do. A boy. Connor. He's off to university in a few months."

"It is impossible!" He flung his arms up. "You cannot be old enough to have a grown son."

Neither of them, she noticed, had mentioned the husband that went along with rings and sons. She said, "Do you regret not having children?"

He shrugged. "The marriage did not last. This happens, I think. Someone looks very romantic in a distant country, and many impressions come from books or television."

Misapprehensions on his part or hers? Angela couldn't tell.

The waiter arrived with the carafe of Chablis and filled their glasses. The wine smelled richly of minerals. He said that the slight iodine finish would be perfect with the oysters. Angela thought how desire was such a marriage of flesh and imagination.

"I'm sorry it didn't work out," she said, referring to his broken marriage.

He puckered his lips and raised his eyebrows. A kind of facial shrug. She noted how animated his face was, the expressions slightly exaggerated, although he didn't open his mouth as wide as Americans did when speaking. She wondered if all Scandinavians did this, or if it was just a trait of people using a language not their mother tongue, relying on expression in case their words weren't exact enough.

"One does not see clearly," Carsten said. "In Denmark, she saw me as something that perhaps I am not, and ..." he shrugged again, "... she was a girl from Hoboken. What did I know of Hoboken?"

"What does anyone?"

That laugh again. Angela laughed, too. It felt good to laugh. Oysters arrived in their bed of ice, with lemons, dill, and a raspberry mignonette.

Carsten clapped his hands. *"Vindunderlig!"*

The oysters, two dozen, lay there, shiny, grey and bluish, slick and fleshy. This was a bad choice, thought Angela. The game had hardly begun and yet she felt as though she had somehow lost control of it. He was grinning, reaching for an oyster, smelling it first, squeezing a little lemon, tipping the wide end of the shell to his lips, letting the flesh slide into his mouth, closing his eyes, rolling the oyster on his tongue, and finally swallowing.

Angela chose one, dribbled mignonette on it, and put it to her mouth. It was everything an oyster ought to be, briny, then creamy, with sweetness at the end. The sea on a shell.

"The oyster leads a dreadful but exciting life," said Carsten.

Angela started. "Did you just quote M.F.K. Fisher?"

He drank, savouring the wine the way he did the oyster, then wagged his head, meaning, she assumed, that it was passable. "You know Fisher? Unfortunate. I thought I could impress you with my originality." He chuckled.

Angela sipped her wine. A splash of red beyond the window caught her attention. Janet, a woman she knew from PTA meetings, walked past in her signature crimson coat. Angela prayed she wouldn't come in. Carsten was flirting — she couldn't deny that's what it was — and this lunch, and the way she looked, with her red lipstick and perfume; Angela realized that whatever was happening was quickly moving into territory at once exciting and disquieting. She watched Janet walk past the restaurant toward the parking garage and her shoulders returned from where they had hovered around her ears.

She glanced at Carsten, downing another oyster. She considered whether she was reading too much into the shellfish and the twinkle in his eyes. Was she projecting her own yearning on to him? It was just a game, after all, and she was out of practice. He clearly wasn't. She decided this was merely his way, that he would relish those oysters with the same delight were he sitting at the table with any woman. Okay, maybe not Sister Eileen, but …

"I'm still impressed," she said. "I don't know many men who read Fisher."

"I am a bit of a gourmand, you see, and I like to read. The nights in a small town on the northernmost tip of Denmark are very long in the winter. We Danes have something we call *hygge*. It is the comfort of the cold, with coffee and books and thick socks and a roaring fire and good friends. Here, you hide from bad weather. Where I am from, we make an art of it."

"Do you eat a lot of oysters in Denmark?" Her turn for another. This one required a little nudge with the small silver fork to detach. Her fingertips were gritty from the shell.

"Mostly we eat pork, a lot of liver paste, when we are not eating herring. Oysters we hardly eat, even though oysters from Limfjorden are maybe the best in the world. I know this is ridiculous. We are a ridiculous people, maybe. There is no word for 'please' in Danish. We leave babies outside in carriages to get sun and do not think they will be stolen. People say we sound like Germans if Germans held a potato in their mouths, and maybe we do because we eat potato with everything, even sandwich — *smørrebrød* — and then we forget the top piece of bread. We have picnics in cemeteries — Danes ponder death a good deal, plus, we like to lie on grass. We never walk across the street unless we see the little green light man, even if no one is driving."

"Well, now I know everything there is to know about Danes, I suppose."

"Ah, no. We are a complex people. Much lies beneath the surface. Danes are like the dark waters of the North Sea. Very mysterious. Very deep."

"Very cold, too?"

"One gets used to it. Good for the health. But one must dive in quickly. No daddle-daddling."

"You mean shilly-shallying? Or dawdling?"

"I mean no messing about. Quick dive." In went another oyster.

"That sounds like a challenge."

Carsten smacked his lips and then winked. "What is life without a challenge?"

The image of water, of diving, must have been in Angela's head, because as she looked across the table at this man she hardly knew, she felt it surge in her chest, in her lungs, in the way the very air entered her, as though she had broken through an icy surface under which she'd been swimming, looking for an escape. Life without challenge? She couldn't imagine. She couldn't, in fact, imagine what she'd been doing with her life up until just then. Where had the challenge been for her, Princeton wife and mother, gardening hobbyist? Everything seemed as though it had been preparation for something, for the next thing, the next big thing.

And after that initial gulp of air came the understanding she had broken free of some restraint. Carsten looked different to her, or rather, the way she saw him was different. He was revealed, no longer hiding behind a scrim, a veil. She could see the golden hairs on his forearms and noticed that although his upper lip was considerably thinner than his lower lip, it was curved, well-formed. He tilted his head down and three lines marked his brow. A half-smile made his cheekbones stand out.

Angela knew then what she had known before but hadn't wanted to admit. Regardless of what would or would not happen between them, she had been arranging her life — all those volunteer opportunities she sucked up like a vacuum cleaner — sorting books for the annual Bryn Mawr sale, putting meals together for the people who lived in the welfare motels on Route 1, sorting donations for the homeless at HomeFront, helping out with the reading series at the library — in the hopes of one day finding herself sitting across the table from an attractive man, just as she was now. She might have told herself she volunteered at the Pantry, at the land trust, as a gardener at the governor's mansion, because she was giving back to the community … but … but she couldn't deny any longer that there had always been a part of her hoping to meet someone interesting, someone who would lead her out of the life of fundraising galas, dinner parties with Philip's business associates, school meetings, grocery shopping, and hair salon appointments.

Angela was attracted to the glimmer at the end of the alley. Adventure, mystery, a little danger. The *beige* of her life strangled her. Some people were made for the quiet, she thought, meant for a contemplative, civic life. She was not. In that moment, right there, with her mouth full of sea and salt and flesh, she gave herself permission to explore the life she thought was made for her.

"Yes. Yes," she said.

It was like the feeling she'd had as a girl, waiting for the bus to take her to school. Out in the cold, wet wind for what felt like hours, and sure she'd freeze to death, and then, at last, it came around the corner, and although she wasn't warm and dry yet, she soon would be, and her body responded in anticipation and all the world was brighter and she thought she might just make it after all. In her imagination, she read the name of the bus … or a streetcar now … of course, of course, a streetcar named …

What relief. Having recognized her destination, it was easy to take control of the game again.

"And our next challenge," she patted her lips with the napkin, "is a spectacular garden in Trenton."

Carsten nodded. "I see it as one of many, yes? It cannot be too difficult to get permission to turn more empty lots into gardens. The city does not like empty lots, we do not like empty lots, the neighbourhoods are not good for having them. Too many kids with too little to do. We will build an army of gardeners in the city. I have been talking to someone in Detroit. They have had success. And the Trenton soup kitchen, too, they are also working with urban farming."

They finished the oysters, the salad, and the bottle of wine. They talked about the principles of urban farming, toxicity remediation, and Carsten's vision for several urban farms that could be used to train young people, to educate about food, to improve neighbourhoods …

The table cleared of plates, they ordered coffee and Carsten unrolled his plans. Raised boxes of vegetables, an irrigation system, a sitting area with a pretty fountain and a shade tree. He said they must have food not only for the body, but for the soul. Angela suggested they might even have one of those little library booths where people could leave books and take books, sit for a moment under the tree and read. He whacked the table with his hand and the cups shook. He said it was a brilliant idea and what a team they were going to be.

Angela pictured herself with her hair tied up in a scarf, wearing a T-shirt and shorts. Her legs were still good. The shorts could be quite short. She could wear a tank top with a linen pinafore over it, to give the air of casual chic. A tendril would escape the scarf. It would curl against her sun-kissed cheek. She would need no makeup. She would be laughing, with a sheen of perspiration across her clavicle.

They planned to meet in two days at the site, with Sister Eileen, and Angela would spend the next week rounding up volunteers to clean the ground, begin building the boxes, hauling in earth.

And so they began.

Angela

Angela knew Philip to be the sort of man who believed if he managed every aspect of life in the correct way, nothing bad would happen, or, if the unthinkable did occur, that he would be exempt from the embarrassing pain and consequences. Five years earlier, when his father Douglas died, for example, he thought because he had paid for the best care, had visited the old man's bedside often enough, and told him he loved him, and had ensured his mother, Evelyn, would be taken care of, that he — Philip — would avoid all the ragged and ambivalent feelings death engenders. At eighty-three, Douglas, who had retired with Evelyn to Florida, was diagnosed with colon cancer and had undergone surgery in a Tampa hospital. Philip had been by his side. His sister, Lesley, who had moved to Florida when her marriage ended ten years earlier, had held their father's hands, while Evelyn caressed his brow, and the three reassured Douglas of their respect and affection. Philp then left the hospital, confident his father would recover to enjoy a few more good years — after all, Philip had paid for the best doctors — but even if his father passed, there was nothing to be more than moderately sad about. Angela was the one Lesley called when Douglas died two days later. A complication of the surgery. Quick. He wasn't in pain. Angela called Philip at his office in the city, told him the bad news, and suggested he come home.

"Ah. Well. Not unexpected," he mumbled. "I have some things to finish up. I'll be home." And then he gave instructions for lawyers and funeral homes and people who needed to be notified.

"I think Lesley has most of that in hand."

"Damn it, Angela, just do it, all right?"

"Okay. And I'll book flights, shall I?"

"Flights. Yes. Jesus."

"Honey, are you okay?"

For a moment, there was just dead air and then choking.

"Philip? Do you want me to come and get you?"

"I'm fine," he said. "I'll be home soon. I love you."

"I love you, too," she said, and meant it.

When Philip came home, he was ashen. It was January and snowing. He stumbled into the house like a victim of shell shock. She had to tell him to let go of his briefcase and help him out of his coat. She put him by the fire, brought him a cup of hot tea laced with brandy, and wrapped him in a blanket. She sat next to him and he said nothing for a long time, and then began to weep. The tears fell, silent and accusatory. She held his hand. She put her arm around him, and he turned to her, burying his face in her shoulder, sobbing.

"I can't come to terms with the fact he's just gone. Disappeared. Like a hand out of a bucket of water. Like he was never even there. How can that be?" His voice was full of shock, his eyes wide with disbelief.

"What is it that frightens you so much? Everyone dies. It's the way of things."

But it was obvious what frightened him: all the things he didn't know; all the things he couldn't control; all the things that might be lost.

When Angela told her friend Deedee about it, Deedee said Philip was afraid of losing himself.

APRIL NOW. Seven weeks since she'd first met Carsten. It was late afternoon and Angela had been home from the garden site for about an hour, just enough time for a shower. She went into the kitchen and put the kettle on. She was looking forward to a cup of tea in the garden before dinner. A truck pulled up and Deedee got out. She was such a tiny thing, the sight of her next to the great big truck always made Angela smile. The first time she'd seen her, across the lawn at the golf club during an end-of-season barbeque, Angela had thought she was someone's child.

"Hey, hey!" She stepped into the kitchen through the back door. "How you doing, darling? Hope you don't mind me dropping in, but I was on my way back from dealing with the farrier and I thought to myself, 'I haven't seen Angela in just too darn long.'"

Deedee brought with her the scent of horses. She wore running shoes, her riding breeches with the knee pads, and a lightweight quilted jacket.

"I just put the kettle on. You want some?"

"Honey, hot tea? Have we met? You got any sweet tea? Lemonade? If not, I'll just take a sparkling water and a slice of lemon if you've got it."

"Sparkling water it is."

She sat at one of the stools at the island and ran her fingers through her fine blond hair. "I hate wearing that damn riding hat. Makes my hair look like seaweed on a rock."

Angela poured the water, without ice cubes, as Deedee preferred, added the lemon, and handed it to her friend. "How's Bruno?" The horse had come up lame a month back.

"He's doing much better, although that little bugger sure did have me worried. It was an abscess in the hoof, was all, and that's one of the reasons I wanted the farrier to see him. Make sure it was draining all right. I'm going to leave him up there for a few more weeks. Delicate creatures for all their size. Thanks, hon." She sipped her water. "What's up with Connor? All set for the fall?"

Angela sat next to her. She rather liked the earthy, rich, equine scent. "As much as we can be, I suppose. I can't believe I've got a kid who's going to study international law at Harvard. How did that happen?"

"I know! And what is he now, nearly seven feet?"

"Not quite. He has the feet of a seven-footer, though."

"Still growing then, I bet. "She patted Angela's knee. "Just be thankful he's so dang smart. I mean, Ed and I would love it if either Harper or Spenser were smart enough to get into Harvard. Spenser will do all right, I'm sure, all this tech whatchamacallit stuff he's into. Probably be a billionaire before he's thirty. But Harper? Harper is convinced she's going to be the next, I don't know, Coco Chanel or something. And here I was hoping for literature. Bit too obvious, the name thing? Anyway, I think we've finally got her talked into going to Parsons, but that has its own risks. I mean New York? Harper? She's going to come back with more piercings than a pin cushion. I tell you she got a tattoo? Something she says is in Arabic in solidarity with Muslims. On her shoulder for the love of Jesus. Can you imagine the conniption fit if I send her down to Mama for a vacation with that?"

One of the nice things about Deedee was that you could wind her up and just let her go. It's not that she wasn't interested in other people, or your life or troubles, it was just that to her talking was like singing, something best done loud and long.

Angela's phone dinged. She knew she ought to ignore it. She kept her eyes on Deedee while she chattered on about Harper and her new boyfriend, an Iranian kid named Foad, who Deedee's mother was sure was part of a terrorist cell, never mind that he was Jewish. Angela heard about half of what she was saying, because she was sure she knew who the text was from. It dinged again. She picked it up and peeked. Carsten.

It is not fair you look so attractive with dirt smear on your face. And also, you smell good. I am sure it is not the fertilizer.

Carsten had trouble with the past tense. Angela found it adorable. She also thought it was quite possibly a spiritual message that one should live in the moment. It was easy to see signs like that, ones that justified her decisions.

"What are you smiling about?" Deedee stared at her.

Angela realized she was tapping her teeth with her thumb like a teenaged girl.

"Oh my lord, and now you're blushing. Has Philip taken to sending you pictures of his privates?"

There was a horrible thought. "No, of course not. Not in Philip's repertoire."

Deedee frowned, her pale brows like feathers. She put her glass down and folded her hands. "You cannot fool me, Miss Angela. I know that kind of grin. I've seen it on Harper's face often enough."

"It's nothing."

"It's not nothing."

"It's just a man I'm collaborating with on the gardening project in Trenton."

Deedee tucked her chin in, raised an eyebrow, and gave Angela a look that might best be described as disbelieving-librarian. "What man? And since when does collaborating produce red flag danger blushes?"

This was one of those crossroads moments, and Angela understood it to be such. Turn right — let's assume the moral right — and she would tell Deedee the facts. Carsten was a gardener with a sense of humour Angela quite liked, with whom she had a working relationship and nothing more. This was technically true. The past few weeks, as much fun, as enlivening as they had been, contained no behaviour she couldn't admit with a clear conscience. There had been a few lunches. And yes, perhaps Angela had gone to a bar with him so he could have a beer (she joined him) after a long afternoon at the site. But they hadn't even kissed, apart from a peck on the cheek upon greeting each other and another upon parting. That was the right turn. But the road less travelled, the one on which she so longed to set off, meant confiding in Deedee. She would tell her. God knew, she wanted to tell someone. Not that anything would come of it.

"It's not what you're thinking."

"So, what is it?"

"He's just interesting and fun, in a way I've missed." Angela told Deedee his name. She told her about the project. "I'm just enjoying a bit of a flirtation. We were introduced by a nun, for crying out loud."

"Darling, I am not going to judge you. And you and I both know you haven't been happy for a while. But I must ask you to consider the fact you might just be playing with a smouldering flame that could easily turn into a dangerous conflagration with the teeniest, tiniest, puff of encouragement."

"Oh, come on. You're the biggest flirt I know, and you don't burn anything down."

"That's because the bland, boring, bourgeois truth is that I adore Ed and I am as committed to him as he is to me and we both know it. We made that decision a long time ago."

"I'm committed to my marriage, to my family." Her phone dinged. She picked it up. "Sorry, it's about the project."

I have some ideas for the plot on East Hanover. Tomorrow? We should look together.

Okay. I'll be at the Pantry early. About 8, she texted.

"That's what I'll call it then, shall I? Your project?" Deedee chuckled.

Angela put the phone on silent, just to show Deedee she could. "Okay. I have a crush on him. I admit that."

"So have a crush. It happens. A girl has no control over that, but may I recommend resisting it? That's the good thing about temptation resisted: you get to go through all the phases, feel all the emotions, learn all the lessons, the way you would if you gave in, but nobody gets hurt, you know what I mean?"

"I don't want anybody to get hurt. Hell, *I* don't want to get hurt. Besides, I don't think he's even interested in anything more than a little flirting. It makes the day go by, is all."

This was another moment of importance. The first lie. She understood she should put a marker there.

"Does, what's his name … Carsten … know you're married?"

"He does."

"Is he married?"

"No. He was. Divorced."

"Uh-huh. So, he knows you're married."

"I said so."

Ten days ago, one afternoon while they worked in the hot sun at the garden plot, he had handed her a bottle of water and as he did, he ran his finger along the inside of her arm. She had shivered. He leaned in and whispered, *I guess your husband would not like that.* She said she didn't think he would. Her skin had flamed. At the end of the day they had gone to a bar with an outside patio. They ordered beer. They talked about earth and fertilizer for a while and then, without smiling, he said, "Enough of this. You know. Do you not know?" Neither did Angela smile. By the end of the hour they were holding hands under the table. Like teenagers. With just that much fire.

Now, Deedee asked, "How are things between you and Philip?"

Angela shrugged. "Philip and me. I don't even know what that means. We're Connor's parents. We live in the same house. That's about it." She massaged her forehead, feeling the beginnings of a headache. "When I think of us twenty, thirty years from now, two wrinkled old people retired to some place like Florida, God help me, or Arizona, playing golf and visiting doctors and going to dinner for the early bird special, without a thing to say to each other, sleeping in separate rooms because his snoring has finally given me an excuse to get out of his bed … when I think of that, Deedee, I'm afraid. It actually terrifies me. What a waste of a life." She had begun to cry and wiped her nose with the back of her hand.

"That bad?"

"He's not a bad guy. He's a good father. He's a good provider — I mean, look at this house. The problem is something deeper, more fundamental. Isn't even that he doesn't listen to me; what man listens?" Angela wouldn't tell her what it meant when Carsten cocked his head, narrowed his eyes and *listened*, listened as though anything she might say was profound, insightful, potentially life-changing.

Deedee rolled her eyes. "Amen to that. Not in the masculine genetic makeup, I suspect. Would be considered multi-tasking, you know, thinking their own great thoughts and listening to yours. Too much for the poor dears."

Angela knew Deedee was trying to lighten the mood, to give her some perspective, but all it did was make Carsten seem even more special.

"Fair enough, but Philip doesn't care. He has no interest whatsoever in anything more than the most surface version of me. Good day, bad day. Chat with teachers. Buy a new dress. Who's coming for dinner? Do I want to go out? Stay in? and I hate to say the lack of depth in our relationship reflects a lack of depth in Philip, but after all these years together, if there's anything deeper I haven't discovered it. He's a nice guy, but nice isn't enough. It just isn't!"

Deedee came around to the side of the island and put her arms around Angela. She smelled of leather and horses and straw and fresh air. Angela thought she probably smelled of the phony, if expensive, scent of her sandalwood shampoo. Nothing true or honest about it. She began to weep in earnest.

"It's okay, darling. All marriages go through bogs. Some more mucky than others, but that doesn't mean it's hopeless. What made you fall in love with Philip in the first place? Come on, girl, you can bring the romance back. A little lingerie and a vacation to St. Bart's, just the two of you?"

Angela drew back, stood up and walked to the fridge. It was only when she opened it that she realized she was looking for a bottle of wine. She wanted something to stop her from feeling the way she was feeling. Which was what? Hopeless, yes, just like Deedee had said. She'd spotted that when Angela hadn't even been able to name it. She wanted to feel … nothing. Just not feel trapped; not feel like she was buried alive. There was a bottle of wine in the door rack, half-full, or half-empty, depending. Now, it looked half-empty. She grabbed it, yanked out the cork, pulled two glasses from the shelf, and poured them to the rim.

She turned and handed one to Deedee while she gulped at hers. Deedee took it, her freckled face, those brown eyes, looking almost comically worried.

Something bitter rose up in Angela, a kind of heat she couldn't help but fan. Why did Deedee, with her Southern romanticism, want to fix her marriage? Angela wanted someone on her side. She wanted someone to tell her she could have the life she wanted, that she should do whatever she had to not to end up a bitter old woman in a loveless marriage.

"Lingerie isn't going to fix this, Deedee. You want to know the truth? Should I tell you?"

"You can tell me anything."

Deedee's voice wasn't eager, precisely; Deedee would never be so transparent, but there was the faintest trace of willingness, Angela could tell, and she realized she was expected to admit to having cheated on Philip. Well, perhaps she had, but not in the way Deedee assumed.

"Okay, the truth is I was never in love with Philip. Never. Not even a little bit."

Deedee pulled back, with a disbelieving expression on her face. "Come on, now …"

"No, I'm serious. I hated the way I was living, and I figured I'd go on working in a crappy office, living in a dingy shared apartment, getting older and fatter. Philip was a way out. I wanted the way out. I thought I did, anyway. And it worked, right? Here I am," she raised her glass and drank, "living the life!" Her nose was running. She had worked herself up to a good snot-flying cry. She pulled a tissue out of a silver box on the counter and blew her nose. "It's not just my marriage. It's me. You think I don't know how awful this is? You think I don't know what an awful person I am for doing this to Philip? He doesn't deserve it."

"Have you thought of going to counselling?"

"Philip wants to go. I don't."

"Why not?"

She threw a tissue in the garbage under the sink and pulled a clean one from the box. She blew her nose. "I don't know. Maybe I'm afraid it will work. Maybe I'm afraid I'll have to stay with him. Or not. That I'll have to leave. Oh, Christ. I don't know."

"Baby, you have one hard road ahead of you. You're really thinking about leaving him?"

"I want it to work." And she did. She wanted to love him. She wanted to love her life. It would make everything so easy.

Deedee looked at her watch. "I hate to leave you like this, but I have to go. Miles to go before I sleep." She stood and put her arms around Angela, who could have rested her chin on the top of her friend's head. "Promise me you won't do anything rash. Think it through, darling."

"I promise. I have no intention of doing anything stupid."

And really, she didn't.

AS SOON AS DEEDEE LEFT, she switched on her phone, to find a message from Carsten.

Cannot go early. Can go late in the day. Cannot be at the Pantry. Have to be on paying job site until maybe 4.

She wrote. *OK. I can go late in the day. Where should we meet?* She waited.

I would meet you anywhere.

How easy it was for her heart rate to rise. She imagined his expression as he waited for her to text him back. Slightly sardonic, teasing, amused. She didn't know what to say. She had planned to work at the Pantry garden in the morning. Three volunteers were to work with her. The boxes were built, the earth was in, and they'd planted peas, radishes, spinach, and the first crop of lettuce; carrots and beets were up next. They were working on the pathways, spreading gravel, and raking. Some local artists were painting murals on the surrounding walls. She supposed she could stay the whole day, and have him meet her there, but she didn't want to. She didn't want to arrive at their meeting all sweaty and stinky. She wanted to look pretty. For Carsten. Also, she wasn't sure she wanted Sister Eileen to see them going off somewhere, business or not. She might have imagined it, but she'd detected a question in her eyes of late.

I have to go home first, and I don't want to leave my car in that neighbourhood after dark. What if we meet in the Artworks parking lot? Artworks was housed in the old Sears warehouse and provided studio space to artists, had a gallery, and gave classes. The parking lot was large and well-lit. Apart from a shooting at the Art All Night event last year, it was considered a safe neighbourhood.

He texted back a few minutes later. He would meet her there. She could leave her car there. He'd drive and then they could have dinner in Mill Hill, the historic section of the city. He knew a place. Besides, he wanted to show her something.

Sister Eileen

Eileen had suggested she and Angela grab lunch together. They sat on black metal chairs at a small table at the Simply Delicious Grill. The plain white walls, acoustic ceiling tiles, and fluorescent lighting looked more suited to one of the many cheap fast food joints littering the city, but the decor was deceptive. The Grill was known mostly as a catering company but served lunch during the week for an incredibly reasonable $8.99. Eileen was enjoying the spicy citrus chicken, and Angela had ordered the chipotle tilapia. They'd both been so hungry they'd been eating for a few minutes without saying much.

"So, Angela," said Eileen, "other than the fact you like to garden, and are so very good at it, I don't know that much about you."

Angela patted her mouth with her paper napkin. "Ah, not much to tell, really. Mother to Connor, seventeen, about to go off to university, wife … not much at all."

"What's your husband's name?"

"Philip."

"How did you meet?"

"We used to work together in the city. A workplace romance. He wanted to move here. He's from here originally. There's something about Princeton that makes people return. I can't imagine wanting to live in the town where I grew up."

"Where was that?"

"Cold Spring, up the Hudson."

"Pretty place."

"I suppose. I didn't grow up in the pretty section. What about you, where are you from?"

"The Jersey Shore." Eileen laughed. "Not the pretty section."

Angela's head did a quick little tilted jerk. "Really? What was that like?"

"Being by the sea is always good for the soul. But we were poor, as were all our neighbours or, if not poor, then only slightly above. Good Catholics all, with lots of kids. Life centred around the church. Too much drinking. Petty crime. We loved hard and worked hard and played hard. Much to admire and much to overcome." Eileen scooped up some of her jasmine rice and broccoli. "The food is so good, isn't it?"

"Did you always want to be a nun?"

"Not always. But close enough. There were a number of people surprised I wanted to become a nun."

"Why?"

Eileen put her fork down. How much to tell, she wondered? How much to share. Sharing built bonds, didn't it? "I was abused by a priest," she said. "Several kids in my family were. My aunt, you see, she was a housekeeper at the rectory. She would bring us kids over to meet the fathers."

"She *knew*?"

"She more than knew."

"Holy shit. Pardon me. So … why the hell did you want to become a nun after that?" Angela had stopped eating.

Eileen raised her chin and said, "I wasn't going to let those bastards take my faith away from me. I'm not going to say it didn't take a long time to learn to forgive and let it go. Frankly, without God, I don't think I ever would have been able to do it. I think I would have ended up bitter and dissatisfied and angry my whole life."

Angela pushed her fish around the plate with the tines of her fork for a moment. "Wow. Well, you have my admiration. Truly."

The restaurant was crowded with people now, buzzing with the noise of conversation and dinnerware, Eileen felt as though she and Angela were in the centre of a hushed vortex, making a chapel of their table. She let the pause between them lengthen, and with her breath she tried to inhale the presence of the holy.

Angela said, "I wish I had that sort of clarity. I've been plagued with bitterness and dissatisfaction and anger with myself from time to time." Her eyes flickered to Eileen's face and then away again. She straightened, smoothed her napkin across her knees, and chuckled. "Pay no attention to me. Probably hormones. Isn't it always?"

"No," said Eileen, "I don't think so, not always. I think sometimes our discomfort is a kind of guide, pointing out places where unhealed old wounds still lurk."

Angela's eyebrows twitched up and back. She took a bite of her fish. Chewed and swallowed. "Oh, who isn't a mass of wounds, lurking or otherwise?"

"My faith teaches me to go to God for healing."

"I'd like to believe that, Sister, but I admit I'm not sure I do. I mean yes, of course, faith heals, or it can, but if I know what I need … to be healed, or happy or whatever … isn't the same as what God wants, well, what's a girl to do? What do you do if you know, I mean deep down in your gut, that the way you're living is just wrong, that it will ... you know ... crush you?"

"Is that the way you feel?"

Angela checked her watch, trying unsuccessfully to make it look as though she were adjusting it on her wrist. "No, not really. I'm just speaking hypothetically, I guess. Everyone feels like that from time to time, don't they?"

"Yes, they sure do." Eileen put her hands in her lap, clasped them. She sensed Angela was close to a fork in the road. Which would she choose? How could Eileen help bring the clarity of Christ's love to her, especially when she wasn't exactly basking in it herself?

"What our tradition tells us," she said, "is that we are most at peace when we are in a state of non-resistance, of pure trust in God's will for us because, being in relationship with God means we know the only thing at stake is our well-being."

"So, even nuns balk now and then, huh?"

"Like mules, now and again." Eileen grinned.

Angela laughed, and then so did Eileen, and for that moment they were simply two women sharing a joke and it felt right.

"Ornery old mules," Eileen said, who understood the time was not quite right, that Angela was not quite ready for whatever God had in mind for her. "Still, guess who wins every time? It's just a question of how long it takes and how much pain I want to put myself through."

The door opened and closed as the customers began to leave. The clock on the wall said after two. It was quieter in the restaurant now, most of the sounds coming from the kitchen, the muffled clank of pots and pans and running water.

Eileen said, "Is there anything you'd like to talk about? I'm here to help."

With a short, sharp motion, Angela pulled in her chin and frowned. "You want to help me?"

"Do you want a coffee? Do you have time?"

"Why would you think I need help? Help with what?"

"Everyone needs someone to listen occasionally."

Angela folded her napkin and placed it on top of the scraps left on her plate. She looked at her watch again and her skin was flushed. Her laugh sounded forced. "Listen, Sister, I'm fine. There are lots of women who come into the Pantry who need help. You know how hard their lives are — often raising kids by themselves; or working two jobs for little money, and their husbands as well; lousy schools, mass incarceration of their men — I don't have to tell you."

"Oh, no, it is hard. Poverty might be no great shame, but it sure isn't a great honour either, as Tevye, the great Jewish philosopher once said."

"Well, I'm sure there are lots of people who'd love to have you help them. God, is it two-thirty already? I've got to run."

"I feel I've said something I shouldn't have."

"Not at all. Of course not. This has been fun. We should do it again."

"I'd like that, very much. You're such a bright light, Angela. People are attracted to you and you just seem to put them at ease. It's a lovely gift to have."

"Don't be silly." Angela was gathering her things. The meals had been paid for before they sat down — one ordered at the counter and settled the bill before sitting down — so there was nothing keeping them. Angela said, "Are you going back to the Pantry? We'll walk back together? I've got to get home and shower and change. I've got a dinner tonight and I really need to freshen up. Can't go to dinner looking like this, can I? I mean, it's nothing special, just dinner, but still. I look like a farmhand. What am I saying, nothing wrong with being a farmhand, for heaven's sake."

They left and walked the short walk back to the Pantry, where Angela had parked her car in the lot across the street. Eileen nattered on about how wonderful the garden was. Finally, Eileen said, “Can we plan on another lunch, then? When are you here next? Early next week, maybe?”

Angela blinked and for a moment looked puzzled. “I’m not sure. I know I’m here Tuesday.”

“Tuesday it is, then.”

“Let’s leave it loose. Can we do that? I’ll have to see how much work needs to be done. I’m on the intake that day and should do a bit in the garden after, I’m sure … but sure, you know, I’d like that. Sure.”

And with that, Angela hugged her and crossed the street to her car.

Eileen watched her go. Such a pretty woman. True, the first bloom of youth’s beauty had begun to fade, but it was replaced by something ripe and, yes, urgent. Beauty was not necessarily a gift. It came with its own temptations. Whereas a plain woman might struggle with feeling worthy or fearing she might never find love, she might be envious and bitter; a beautiful woman often struggled with self-centredness and a certain lack of empathy, not having had to deal with rejection the same as a plain woman would. It could make you blind, such beauty, such urgency. And blindness was dangerous.

Angela

Angela left the car in the driveway. As she walked to the house, something caught her eye, something small, an animal, lying at the side of the walkway. A kitten? No, a squirrel. Dead? Hit by a car most likely or picked up by a hawk and then dropped. She stopped to look, and as she did the animal twitched. It was lying on its side, and there was a gash in its shoulder. It raised a front paw just slightly. Perhaps it was all it could do, in its weakened state, to fend off what must seem like enormous, hulking danger. Could it be merely stunned, not too badly injured?

As a little girl, Angela had rescued three baby squirrels whose mother the boy next door had killed with a BB gun. She'd fed them Pablum from dolls' bottles and built a box cage with towels for them to nestle in. They had sat on her shoulders and on her head and she had loved them fiercely. She kept them all over the winter until the next spring when her mother said she really should let them go. They were wild things, her mother said, and deserved to live freely outside. And so, she had begun releasing them. She took them outside in the day and let them play in the trees in the back of the house. At the end of the day they followed her inside to sleep. And then, one by one, they stayed out for the night, coming back to be fed every morning, and then running off again. By the end of a month they came back only now and then, although they always chattered at her from the trees when she saw them, and she swore she could always tell her squirrels from any others.

And now, here was this broken little creature. A flickering handkerchief of bright green blowflies had arrived, ready to lay their eggs. Angela waved her hand over the squirrel. Couldn't they wait? It wasn't even dead yet. The thought of these creatures, necessary to nature though they might be, burrowing in while the squirrel was still alive made her want to swat them away, to reprimand them. Foolish thoughts. The squirrel's jaw moved. Its teeth were long and muddy. Its eye was still bright, staring at her as she fanned away the relentless blanket of flickering emeralds.

Without making any clear decision about it, she reached into her tote and pulled out a couple of tissues. As gently as she could, she lifted the squirrel. The paw moved again. The eyes looked at her. There was no blood. Only that shoulder gash, which didn't seem too terrible. Perhaps he (she thought of it as "he" now) could be saved. She would put him in a box lined with towels. She would see if he would take food and water. In the morning, if he lived, she could take him to a vet.

A car slowed. She turned. Her neighbour, Diane, rolled down the window.

"You okay, Angie?"

"Yes. It's a squirrel. It's been hurt."

"Oh, you don't want to pick that dirty thing up. Rats with fluffy tails is all." The woman laughed.

Angela thought she might look demented. The tiny animal was curled and warm in her hands. She didn't care if she looked mad.

"I don't mind. I can't leave it here to suffer."

"Okay then. Long as you're all right."

She walked up the walk to the door as quickly as she could, trying not to jostle her tiny charge. Inside the door she stood for a moment, not sure what to do. Should she leave the squirrel alone while she got a box and towels? What if it suddenly woke up? She looked down at it. Yes, still breathing. Maybe sleeping. She carried the creature into the kitchen. Irina, her cleaning lady stood at the sink, cleaning the oven grill.

"I have a little problem," said Angela. Irina was from Poland. What did Poles think about squirrels?

"What have you got there?" Irina came over, wiping her hands and blowing a damp tendril of grey-blond hair out of her eyes. "Oh, poor thing. What happen?"

"I don't know. I found it near the walk."

"Huh. Maybe best to leave outside? Or you want to drown it? Might be kind. Give to me. I do it."

"No! I thought it might get better. Maybe. I don't know. If we let it rest, fed it or something."

Irina rubbed her arm. "Okay then. Well. Do we have shoebox?"

"There's a plastic storage bin in the broom closet. The vacuum attachments are in it. That would do. And maybe some towels?"

"I go get."

Angela shrugged off her tote and sat, placing the squirrel on the table.

The squirrel's sides moved, but only ever so slightly. *Oh, don't die, don't die. God, protector of the small creatures, of all the wild wood, don't let this little one suffer.* With two fingers she caressed its back, stroking gently, whispering reassurances that all would be well, that he was safe now. The fur was so soft, like eiderdown.

Feathers. Angels. Oh, of course he was going to die. There was nothing she could do. A little water. She did not want a creature in her care to die thirsty, and who knew how long it had lain out there in the hot sun. A tea towel. She ran it under cool water and rolled it up. Dripped a little into the animal's mouth. Did the jaw move? Perhaps slightly.

Irina came in with towels and the plastic box. "How it doing?"

"Oh, Irina, I don't think he's going to make it."

Irina looked at it and pressed her lips together. "No, dear. Probably not."

"Do you think I could pick him up?"

Irina put her arm around her. "I don't think it hurt."

Angela slid her hands under the little body and cradled it, watching its chest move, almost imperceptibly.

Irina, a devoted Catholic, said, "I say little prayer." She spoke some words in Polish and then, "Amen."

"Amen," said Angela.

Angela's throat was tight. She recognized the sensitivity of the older woman, and it surprised her and loosened something in her heart. With the loosening came tears. Tears for all the small things, for all the fragile things, for all the things broken beyond repair. The squirrel twitched. *Oh, little one, are you dying?* The paws seemed to reach out for something, and then, the eyes, they became liquid first, and then still. And it was over. Gone. "He's died, I think. I think he's dead."

Irina's hand lay on Angela's shoulder. "There is a power," she said, "a grace in witnessing."

The kitchen was quiet but for the ticking of the wall clock. Outside the window, in the garden, one of the wrens who had come to nest in the blue ceramic egg-shaped house hanging from the porch roof, as they did every spring, began to sing. Trilling, loud, exultant, celebratory. Such a big voice from such a tiny body.

It never ceased to amaze Angela. She chose now to think it was singing for the soul of the squirrel, singing it on its journey, for she believed in such things, and believed that animals, too, were welcomed home at death. After all, St. Francis had raised his pet lamb and pet trout from the dead and called them by their names after they died. Only the most arrogant humans would think God cared more for them than for the other creatures with whom they shared the world. The wren stopped singing.

Irina asked, "You want to bury him? You can't just put him in garbage."

"No, of course not. Yes, I'll bury him. I'll do it."

"I'll help," said Irina. "And then we will have tea, tea with lots of sugar."

They buried the squirrel, and Angela left him in the care of the God of the Wild Wood, as she thought of it, although of course it was just a corner of the garden, between an old rhododendron and a butterfly bush. But it was a pretty place, shaded and sheltered. When they were done, she sat on the deck drinking the well-sweetened tea Irina brought her.

She hoped she hadn't frightened the squirrel more. What must it have felt, in such a strange world, surrounded by giants, if it was even aware? It had seemed to settle in her hands, and although perhaps it was only giving up, she hoped it had been able to tell it would be, for those last minutes, cared for, loved even. Nature was red of tooth and claw and the lion was forever at the neck of the antelope. What was one to glean from that?

THE RESTAURANT WAS ITALIAN, an old, well-known spot. The tables were covered in linen, and the candlelight softened everyone's faces. Angela and Carsten sat in a corner. Carsten had told the waiter they wanted a table where they could talk undisturbed, which was a moment when she could have turned around and changed everything that came after, but she did no such thing. Instead, she ducked her head like a shy virgin and blushed.

A waitress arrived, no more than twenty-five, with a skirt the size of a belt and legs longer than all Angela's insecurities laid end to end. She brought a bottle of wine, of good vintage, and poured them each a glass.

Carsten drank deeply. "Oh, yes," he said. Like Angela, he had taken a shower after work, and must have splashed some cologne on, because she could smell it, the scent of wood and spice and chocolate. "Good," he said. "Like you. Better than good."

Angela picked up her glass and then put it down. She would not tell him about the squirrel. She was afraid he might laugh at her or think her too sentimental. She ran her finger around the wineglass rim, knowing it was a foolish and staged gesture. She asked, "What are we doing here?"

"What do you *want* to do?"

"What do *you* want to do?"

Emphasis was everything. It was the knife edge that allowed her, for the moment, to absolve herself of responsibility.

"You know what I want to do," he said. And these words contained the memory of every touch, every look, every whispered word over the past weeks. They carried the remembered scent of earth and lumber and heated skin and sweat.

It occurred to Angela she might say, *I think you are mistaken, sir. I am a gardener, and the only soil I wish to till is that of a vegetable patch.* She looked at his hands. They were strong hands. The wrists, too, were strong, and the forearms, downed with golden hair. She considered playing the ingénue, and then thought about those arms around her waist. Would she be a girl? Or a woman, full of passion and blood and heat?

"I do," she said. "I know what you want to do."

"I do not wish to complicate your life."

"I don't want my life as it is."

She watched the glass approach his lips, the liquid the colour of garnets. She watched the way he held it in his mouth, so tenderly. He swallowed. She thought soon she would taste that same wine, suck it in on his breath, savour it as she ran her tongue over his teeth. He noticed her watching his mouth and smiled.

She raised her own glass but was lightheaded even before the alcohol took effect. This was another world from any of the worlds in which she lived — not wife, not mother, not friend, not good community citizen, not funeral director to squirrels. Just this circle of light. This sacred ritual of wine. Whatever she was entering, it was separate. It was a *temenos*, a sanctuary, dedicated to the god of … of what? Passion. She chose that.

She was aware of her motions, the articulation of her wrist, the deliberateness of it, aware of the cool glass on her lower lip, aware of the molten jewel flowing in. A part of her expected bitterness, wormwood and ash, by way of warning, but it was ruby honey, smooth as syrup and sweet as dew. It tasted like the answer to everything.

Carsten picked up his knife and fork and cut into the meat, bloody, black and red. Her meat (her flesh?) was not so raw. A pleasing pink and grey. It tasted like an eraser. She added salt and pepper.

Carsten repeated, "I do not want to complicate your life."

She drank again. With the second mouthful, the river of electric warmth flowed along her limbs, her arms, her legs. Her muscles relaxed. The world was as golden as the hairs on Carsten's forearm.

Later, she would understand how in that moment that her vision was distorted; she would understand how, faced with the lava flow into her belly, that her soul, her sanity, her better self, if you wanted to call it that, put its face in its hands and scuttled off to higher ground. But just then, in the glow and heat of that lava, she put her fork down and said, "Something is happening between us. I admit that, and I admit more. I want it to happen."

He put his fork down as well, said, "I must be clear, Angela. I do not want a family."

"Getting a bit ahead of yourself, aren't you? I have a son who's off to college soon. Me being his mother will never change, and he already has a father. He doesn't need another."

As she spoke, her mind, in turn, took notes. So, Carsten was not a family man. In a strange way, it gave her power. Being a mother was a formidable thing and being a man who did not want a family was a juvenile thing. She saw her Viking wearing, for the first time, the clothes of Peter Pan. Wendy was always the one in charge. She said, "What happens between us, or doesn't, has nothing to do with my son."

"And does it have nothing to do with your husband?"

He had her there. The husband was on her side of the ledger sheet, but differently than a son. A son was forever. A husband was, it shamed her to realize, perhaps only a chapter in her life. Carsten waited. His hands rested on either side of his plate, but he made no move to pick up knife and fork. In Carsten's face, Angela saw, in that wide-open stare, in the way his features arranged themselves so definitively, so professionally, in sophisticated amusement, that whatever a husband was or was not, the responsibility for him, for the consequences of … whatever it was they would have, would be entirely hers.

How still this moment was. One of the enchantments of alcohol was the deceitful pseudo-clarity, the sudden conviction that one was finally seeing things as they were. Angela understood that the veil she'd been looking through had been lifted. She saw, high on Carsten's cheek, two small red lines. They marred the skin where the double blade of his razor had nipped him. She looked at it and thought how skin was thin, for all of us, and we all had our defences.

A candle on the table offered a buttery glow. Garnet wine. Ruby razor cut. Amber of flame. She trapped that image in her memory and even as she trapped it, she knew she was trapping it. This would be the moment she remembered, when she saw Carsten as imperfect, as someone who would not rescue her from her numbing life, but someone who would force her to be responsible for her decisions, her hunger, her passions, come what may.

"Why don't you leave my son, my husband, my family to me? All I ask is that you be honest. If you want me, say so. If you think we have something between us, then say so." She was Wendy, demanding Peter admit the real reason he taught her to fly.

Carsten smiled and took her right hand. "Beautiful Angela. Be careful what you ask for." He brought her fingers to his mouth and kissed them.

Her left hand lay on her thigh. Her engagement ring with its big square-cut diamond and the pavé band gleamed, but dully. How enamoured of that diamond she was when Philip first presented it to her, on bended knee by firelight in a cabin in the Adirondacks on New Year's Eve. She had waved her hand about like a symphony conductor for days, but by this time she rarely even cleaned it.

"I don't want to be the one to do the asking," she said.

"An old-fashioned girl?" He chuckled. "Angela. The angel. Messenger of God. Carrying a burning sword, perhaps?"

She thought how dangerous she was. An angel. A bright flame. She thought how he knew her; he saw her in a way Philip never had. To Philip, Angela … Angie, was a name as ordinary as milk and toast. *She* was as ordinary as milk and toast.

Carsten held her hand now in both of his and they had to lean toward each other as he put his elbows on the table. The table was small. He filled her sight. Their faces were near.

"I am Viking, you know. We have a habit of invading the lands of other men."

This sounded slightly theatrical, and she was not sure if she was meant to laugh, to take it as a joke, but his eyes did not look like the eyes of a man trying to be funny. The wry amusement had been replaced with something darker. She stiffened, pulled back, or tried to, but he did not permit that. Her hand was captive.

A long time later she would acknowledge that, had she been entirely sober, she would have seen how ridiculous it all was, but by then such perspective would be entirely useless.

"You are not happy, Angela. If you were happy with your life, we would not be here. I would not set foot inside the boundary, yes? So maybe — no, not maybe — definitely, I am thinking you want me as I want you. I want to see you flame-bright. I believe I can make you burn again." His lips were on her knuckles.

And so, the game was no longer a game. Angela could no longer hide behind flirting, behind play. The coal was already alive in her. She was incandescent. She thought of what would come next. Of where.

She said, "I don't even know where you live."

He moved the plates, his with its bloody remains, so that they could hold hands more easily.

"We know very little about those things in each other's lives." He squeezed her hand. "We must remedy that."

He told her something about coming to America and about Nancy, his ex-wife, an architect. They lived in her house, all renovated in glass and metal, with grey walls and abstract paintings that to Carsten looked like exploding poppies. She was, he said, very firm in her ideas of what was beautiful and what was not. She was, he said, very firm in all her ideas. He felt as though he was living in a beautiful but chilly hotel, with a concierge who did not appreciate him dragging messy, leaf-dropping, dirt-trailing plants into every room.

"We were different elements," he said. "Where she was air, I was earth."

He worked at a nursery, but the work was unfulfilling. When their marriage ended, he couldn't afford to stay in Hoboken, not even with the small income he had from his house in Denmark, which he had rented out. He found a job, a better one, as a designer for a nursery in Hamilton, and had a small apartment there. Two years later the owner decided to retire and put the business up for sale. Carsten went all in. He took out loans and bought the business. That was five years ago. He had done well enough, with a few high-profile projects and the university, the Philadelphia Flower Show, and residential developments.

Angela's wine was finished. Carsten raised the carafe, which was somehow empty, and asked the waitress for another. She brought it and he filled Angela's glass.

"I *still* don't know where you live." She giggled. "You do live somewhere, right?"

He shrugged. "That's what I'm telling you. I put everything into the business. There's a shower, a fold-out couch, a fridge. I have an excellent coffee maker."

Angela couldn't help it. She laughed. She pictured him among rows of Japanese maple, hydrangeas, gerbera daisies, pots of pansies, marigold, and nasturtiums, with spider plants, birdhouses, and wind chimes hanging from the rafters, and everywhere the hothouse smells of earth and growing things.

"You're telling me you live in your garden centre? How bohemian. Do you keep your books on shelves made from bricks? Bead curtains?" She saw his puzzled look. "It's a university student thing. Never mind."

"Does this shock you? Do you think less of me because I do not have a lot of money?"

There was, perhaps, a little defensiveness in his voice. She said, "I know men with money. They don't impress me."

"What does?"

"Intelligence. Passion. Involvement in the world. Someone who stands up and fights for what he believes."

"What? Nothing about muscular thighs?"

She slapped him lightly on the hand, picked up her glass and drank. "Thighs, certainly, but I'm more drawn to a broad set of shoulders."

"This is good to know. I myself am attracted to the long curve of a beautiful neck."

He reached over and ran his finger from the line of hair behind her ear to her shoulder. It sent a shiver up her spine and she shuddered, which made him laugh and he withdrew his hand, leaving a trail of icy heat.

"But I will not always live in this place. Perhaps you have made me want more, getting to know you. You have inspired me. I have made a change, and that is what I want to show you. I have bought a house." The expression on his face was like Philip's when he gave the new car to Connor.

Angela settled her hands in her lap for a moment and then reached for her glass. This talk of changes, brick and mortar ones, was unsettling. It occurred to her she did not know what she wanted at all. This feeling, yes. This talk, yes. This shiver and shudder, yes. Perhaps it was the wine. She shouldn't have drank so much. But it was part of the thrill, too. The danger, the climb and fall, the twist and turn. The being out of control. All at once the ground felt slippery under her chair. The men at the table behind her laughed too loudly and she sensed their jokes were vulgar. The congealing meat on her plate seemed obscene. She scrambled for a way to slow things down. What kind of fool, she thought, didn't ask where she might end up until she was already chug, chug, chugging up the rickety rails? Her kind of fool. The wine tasted sour, but still she wanted it. Fool she may be, she thought, with a sort of nihilistic delight, but she wanted what she wanted, and didn't she have a right to it? Didn't she have a right to be fully herself? It was amazing how quickly the wine in a glass disappeared. She vowed there would be no more tonight. She had to drive home. She would be responsible.

"Don't change your life for me, Carsten."

His smirk returned. "Not *for* you, but perhaps because of you. Look, it is quite simple. I see a woman I want. She belongs to another man —"

"I belong to no man."

"No matter which way you define it, it is." He held up his hand to stop her speaking. "But it does start me to think of what I want, what kind of life. And what I decide is that I do not want to be the old man living alone without a proper kitchen and bedroom and garden. One cannot say what tomorrow will bring, let alone five years from now. Look at me. Did I think I would be living one day in New Jersey? I did not. You would be surprised at how few people in Denmark dream of living one day in New Jersey."

That made her laugh, and she saw it pleased him.

"This is absurd," she said.

"Too soon? Ah! Too much. But still, there it is." He clapped his palms on the table. "Come on. We need a change of scene."

AND SO, A SHORT TIME LATER, Angela found herself pressed up against a wall, his mouth on hers.

What was there to say about a first kiss that hasn't already been said? Was there a new word for the sensation of breath against cheek, for the scent in the hollow of a man's neck, for the tug of his fingers in a woman's hair, or how a woman felt when claimed by the power in a man's hands? And what of those sensations, the thrill when lip first grazed lip, and then when mouths grew urgent, when hips pressed into each other, bemoaning (you'll pardon the word) the clothes between? Shallow breathing. The hint of the dinner they'd eaten, the steak and salad and wine that lingered on his tongue?

They were on Jackson Street, a leafy, lamplit lane of Victorian houses in the old Mill Hill section of Trenton. One might imagine it was the 1910s, not the 2010s, or was she being too romantic? He had taken the key from his pocket with a flourish and ushered Angela up the stone steps of the house into which he would move in two weeks. Red-brick with a towered, patterned mansard roof, hooded windows, and wrought-iron railings, and standing proud beside the more modest cottages on either side. Inside the double-door vestibule, a graceful oak staircase led to the second floor. To the right was a large formal room with a cast-iron fireplace and a bay window. There was no furniture. A cheap fake-gold chandelier hung from an ornate plaster medallion in the ceiling. The light was bright, bouncing off the white walls. Before them the hallway led to the kitchen at the back of the house. Angela caught a glimpse of white cabinets and noticed the wide-plank flooring of the entrance way and living room didn't continue into the kitchen but was replaced by ill-matched laminate. She thought about renovations done on a shoestring, and about how much it cost to add the greenhouse onto her house in Princeton. It probably would have paid for this entire house twice over. Their footsteps echoed, and the air was slightly musty. She imagined ghosts.

"What do you think?" Carsten asked. He worried the keys in his hands.

"What great bones," she said, and it was true. The ceilings were high, the proportions graceful. She wandered into what must have been the dining room, situated between the kitchen and the living room. The walls, showing all the old plaster imperfections beneath, were painted the colour of dark clay. She opened a double cupboard and found a small butler's pantry, with grooved shelves for plates. She moved into the kitchen and Carsten followed her.

"It has a good garden," he said. "And because I have been living in the office for these years, I have saved. The house is not expensive. Very cheap. I have money to fix things. If I am careful."

"If you put in French doors, then, here, it will bring the garden in, don't you think?" Angela started making plans. "Gut the kitchen, knock out the wall between the dining and living room. Fix the floors and stain them dark, lighten the walls. Marble countertops. Built-in bookshelves around the fireplace and a seat in the bay window." She chattered about this and that, subway tiles on the back splash, and wouldn't a big blue Viking stove be wonderful? She meandered back into the other rooms. She opened a door, found a half-bath with a stained white toilet and cracked sink. She closed the door, said, "That will have to go." She reached the stairs, eager to see what was above, whether the bedrooms kept the fireplaces they were sure to have had once.

Her hand was on the newel post, her foot on the first step, and then his hand was on hers. She turned, and his hands were on her shoulders and her back was against the wall, her feet on different steps. And of course, this would happen, why else was she there?

She thought, *This is just a kiss. I can have this kiss.*

In a sweep of vertiginous memory, she relived all the kisses she had endured, not wanting any of them as she wanted this one. Didn't she deserve to feel Carsten's lips against hers, if for no other reason than she so desperately hungered for it, craved it with every nerve on every inch of her skin? Yet, even then she knew she was unkind.

But it was just a kiss, wasn't it? With the traces of meat and wine on their breath, about which nothing new could be said.

Like all things, it had to either recede into nothingness or transition to something else. She pushed him away. He groaned, hung his head, and then looked up at her, his face flushed. She had crossed so many lines, and her head was beginning to clear from the wine. She checked to see if she had regrets and found only a hard nut of defiance in her chest. She took the lapels of his leather jacket in her fists and jostled him a little, laughing. His hands went to her hips, but she shook her head, no. He nodded. She saw in his face what she realized in herself: there was sweetness in what one couldn't have, what one delayed. Never having been one for delayed gratification, this surprised her, and she wanted to let it build. Foreplay, of course, of the most intense sort. She told herself there were still lines she might not cross.

"So," he said, "you'll help me decorate?"

And at that she burst out laughing.

Angela

On the drive home, she stopped at an all-night drugstore and bought Listerine. In the car she took a swig and swished it around her mouth, banishing the scent of wine. She didn't want to spit it out the window and so she swallowed. Other than a slight headache and a desire to lie down, she told herself there were no ill effects. It had begun to rain, gently, and the streets were darkly glazed. She thought she'd pass a breathalyzer but didn't want to take the chance. The streets grew wider, the houses more suburban. She passed schools, and then Rider University and her grip on the steering wheel relaxed. The sensation of Carsten's mouth, his hips, his hands, rose up and she giggled. She should have been ashamed of what she'd done, but she tingled from head to toe. She was alive again. She had been awoken by a kiss, she told herself, even as a quieter voice, somewhere in the back of her mind, begged her to reconsider.

No. She wasn't going to give him up. The very idea was like acid on her skin.

She turned on her windshield wipers. They swish-swooshed across the glass, and the raindrops dazzled like crystal under the streetlamps. The road ahead was clear, in more ways than one. She was not, she now understood, a woman who would ever be happy living a quiet, passionless, cossetted life. She needed fire, and Philip was water. With Carsten she would burn, and he would consume her. She wanted immolation and saw herself as the phoenix, rising from the ash.

When Angela got home, Philip was in his office, hunched over the computer. The only light came from the brass desk lamp. In the gloom, the burgundy walls, tartan couch and leather chair were studies in black and grey. She kissed him on the top of his head. His hair was thin, and his scalp smelled oily.

"You're late," he said. "Everything okay? I was getting worried. Just about to call you."

"I went out for dinner with Sister Eileen, can you believe it?"

"Who?"

"The nun I told you about. The one who runs the Pantry. We talked a long time. I should have called."

How easy it was to lie.

"How was your day?" she asked.

"Same. Markets are a mess. We're diversifying. Just not the time to take big risks and clients are skittish, especially after the crash." He squinted at the screen and began typing. "You don't want to hear about all that."

He was correct. "Did you eat?"

"Yeah, I ate the leftover chicken. Oh, and Deedee called. Said she tried calling your cell, but you didn't answer."

Angela's heart fluttered. "I'll call her."

Philip put his arm around her waist and squeezed. "I'm going to be another hour or so."

"I'll see you in bed."

"Going to wait up for me?" He grinned.

"I'll try." She gave him a peck on the lips.

"You smell of mouthwash."

"Had garlic for dinner. Nobody likes garlic breath."

He turned back to the screen. She doubted he even heard her. She went upstairs, flicked on the switch that lit up the silver reading lamps on the bedside tables, kicked off her shoes onto the Persian carpet and climbed onto the bed, pushing aside the pale blue raw silk pillows, which served no practical purpose. She wondered if it was too late to call Deedee. It was just ten. Deedee was a night owl.

There was a text on her phone from Carsten. *Did you get home safe?*

Safe and sound. Where are u?

A moment later … *Back in my lair of flowers. Thinking of u here, surrounded by peonies and tulips.*

His knowledge of words like *lair* surprised her. His grammar was so formal, and not always perfect, and these odd words crept in.

She didn't know what to say back. She would have to be careful about the phone. Erase texts. Not leave it lying around. She didn't think Philip would go through her phone, but he might, were he to become suspicious. *Am I cheating on my husband?* It felt like she was, even without the final consummation.

Bloop. Message. *Until Thursday?*

She had agreed to go furniture shopping with him.

Until then. Pottery Barn. 2pm. Night.

At night??

No, I mean "goodnight"!

Ah. Night.

They had agreed to meet at the store in Cherry Hill, not the one in Princeton, which had suddenly become an even smaller town in her mind. She imagined bumping into one of her neighbours,

Janet, say, who sent notes around to everyone telling them they should water their trees more in summer heatwaves, or suggesting garbage bins be secured against raccoons. Angela could just see the arch of one of her painted-on brows. *And who's this? Have you gone into the decorating business now? Helping? Aren't you kind? Such a helpful person.* No, Cherry Hill was a better bet.

She went into the bathroom and found a bottle of aspirin in the cabinet. A bottle of Xanax stood next to it. Her doctor had given it to her for anxiety and sleeplessness. She didn't take it often, but now, the headache, which had been merely a slight band of tension across her forehead as she drove home, was throbbing. She didn't think she'd sleep, not with images of Carsten's face and hands playing behind her closed lids. She took three aspirins, a Xanax, and drank two large glasses of water.

She called Deedee as she walked back to bed, shedding clothes as she went.

"Angela!"

"Hi, Deedee. Sorry I missed your call. Not too late, is it?"

"No, it's fine. Just watching a movie. I haven't heard from you in a while and I just wanted to check in, see how it's going."

"I had to sit down with the planning committee for the new neighbourhood garden," she said.

It was, in a way, true. It's what she should have said to Philip. Why hadn't she? Sister Eileen's face popped into her mind. Her almost aggressive compassion. Oh, she sensed something, that one. She was guessing, but still.

"Are you all right?"

"Fine. Sure. Fine."

A pause. "How's Philip?"

"Fine. How's Ed?"

They talked about the beginning of golf season and being golf widows and horses and the kids and the upcoming prom, and then there didn't seem to be much else to say and so, with promises to see each other soon, they hung up.

Angela lay back in bed, slipped her feet under the covers, and waited for the Xanax to help her drift away from the aching, the longing, and that one tendril of guilt: she'd forgotten all about Connor's prom.

"MOM. *MOM!*"

She looked up from her phone. Connor, home for the weekend, stood in the doorway from the kitchen into the greenhouse, where Angela was supposed to be tending to the orchids. The midday sun was too warm, and she'd opened the windows, but it was still steamy and earthy, and she noted a dusting of pollen on the workbench. No wonder she'd been sniffing and sneezing.

"I'm right here. There's no need to yell."

"Really? You're worse than me with that phone these days. Who are you texting all the time?"

"What is it, Connor?"

"I have to get my tux. Prom's like, two weeks away. All the good ones will be gone, and I'll end up with some shitty thing."

"Don't be ridiculous. They don't run out. Do you know what colour Emily's dress is?"

He frowned, and looked very much like his father, all bristle and entitlement. "Am I supposed to know that?"

"Well, if her dress is going to be purple, you don't want to get a tux with an orange cummerbund, do you?"

He snorted. "Like I would. Jesus. Orange." He was typing into his phone now, his thumbs a blur.

Angela went back to her own texting. *I'm not sure I can get away. Connor's prom. It's a big deal.*

I want you to see the bedroom & bath now that the painting is finished.

I bet you do.

I want to see how you look there. In the bath. I have candles. I have wine.

They had painted the bedroom walls white, but not a bright white. In some light it looked almost violet, in others the palest stone. The floors were stained dark brown, and the bathroom was white, too, with tile the colour of a stormy sky. They'd been able to save the old claw-foot tub. It was big enough for two, even when one of them was Carsten's size. Angela knew this for certain, which is how things had progressed. It was in that bath where they had first made love. And then in the bed. And then on the floor. And then in the bath again, when she leaned against his chest and he read the poems of Inger Christensen and Morten Nielsen by candlelight. They drank wine, although it was Carsten who intoxicated Angela. She pictured them in a snow globe, a state beyond the rules, beyond time and consequences, beyond outside influence and profane things like grocery shopping and laundry and zoning issues (for the gardens) and renewing one's driver's licence. Carsten read poetry to her. Philip couldn't tell e.e. cummings from Elizabeth Bishop. Philip quoted stock tips. She tried to remember a single time she'd talked about literature with Philip, or art, or anything she considered meaningful. She and Philip talked about Connor. They talked about dinner with the neighbours. They talked — or he did, she merely listened — about how Wall Street made the world go around. Honestly, she had nothing to say to that, but Philip loved her, she knew, and he loved Connor and he worked hard, at least in part to try and make her happy. He would never intentionally hurt her. Why wasn't that enough?

Carsten read to her from a Nielsen poem, "Death": "As I fell and fell in a coldness without space/from holding a stranger's cold hand in my hand ..."

And yes, she thought, yes, her marriage felt like that.

"Black," said Connor.

"What? What's black?"

"Oh, for fuck's sake!"

"Hey! Don't talk to me like that. Just who do you think you are?"

Connor whipped around and disappeared back into the kitchen. "I'm your son, but you seem to have forgotten that!"

I have to go. Will get back to u later.

She found Connor with his head in the refrigerator, the natural habitat for boys his age. He didn't appear to be actually looking for anything and she assumed he'd chosen the stance for its ability to project indifference.

"I'm sorry," she said to his back. "I've been preoccupied with this project, which is important, you know. It's about feeding people and so forth."

"You might try feeding Dad now and then." Head still in the fridge.

She blinked. "What's that supposed to mean? Dad's not even home and won't be till Thursday. You know that. He's in Chicago with clients. Connor, turn around. Do you want something in there or not?"

He slammed the door and turned to face her, arms crossed against his chest, over a dark blue T-shirt. How large his biceps were. She wondered if he was lifting weights. Gone was the gangly, all-elbows-and-knees boy of just a few months ago, or so it seemed. He towered over her.

"You just never seem to be around these days."

"Connor, I'm here now, in case you hadn't noticed, and besides, you're in boarding school. And, not that when I'm here or when I'm not is any of your business, but how do you know what I do when you're not here?" She went to the cupboard and took down a glass. "I'm having lemonade. Do you want some?"

"I guess."

She grabbed a second glass. Connor moved aside so she could get into the fridge. Lemonade was such a normal, homey thing. Cookies and lemonade.

"You're never home when I call."

"When? When haven't I taken your call?"

"I'm not saying you don't take my calls, *ever*. I'm saying you're never home. But okay, at least twice last week. Dad said you were out at meetings. You're always at meetings."

"Yes, okay, I turn my phone off in meetings. Did you leave a message? I didn't get a message."

"You can see I called. Why leave a message? What's the point?"

"Don't be so dramatic. If you can't get hold of me leave a message and I'll call you right back."

She put the ice in the glasses and poured the lemonade from the glass pitcher. What could be more nonchalant than pouring lemonade? "What was so urgent?"

That produced a storm cloud on his face. "It doesn't matter now. That's kind of the point of urgent, isn't it? That if it can wait it isn't urgent."

"Smartass. But really, what was it?"

"I talked to Dad. It's handled. Nothing for you to worry about, Mom." He took the lemonade and drank a little, then stared into the glass. "I don't think Dad's happy."

"He's under a lot of pressure from work is all. He'll be fine. Why, what did he say to you?"

"It's not work. It's you." Her son's eyes were lit coals.

"I beg your pardon?"

"Dad says you're never home. He says he never sees you."

"I'm here. I'm not the one in Chicago. I don't know what you're talking about."

"He says he's worried about you."

"This is not a conversation you should be having with your father. This is not a conversation you and I should be having."

"Well, then, maybe you better have a talk with Dad."

"Oh, I will, believe me."

"Don't tell him I told you, okay? I think he'd had a couple."

"Was it Wednesday?" She shook her ice cubes in the otherwise empty glass.

Connor drained his glass. Like his mother, he never sipped, he guzzled. "Yeah. Like, about nine-thirty."

Wednesday. She had come home just before ten. With the corrosive lie on her lips. Another meeting, another squabble with the planning council, another chat with Sister Eileen. Whatever she'd said. She found Philip sitting in the dark, drinking Scotch, getting morose and unmovable in his leather chair. *Nice of you to come home*, he'd said, and she'd told him he should be happy she'd found something to give her life meaning. He should be supportive. That had brought a bitter laugh. He opened his arms wide, to take in the house, the garden, the cars, the greenhouse, all the techy gadgets, and the clothes on her back, she supposed.

"I wouldn't mind a little support myself," he said, raising his glass. "Here's to my wonderful, supportive, devoted, loving wife."

She turned on her heel and went to bed. Two Xanax ensured she didn't hear him when he came up.

Now, she tried to keep her face passive as she looked at her son. It was a terrible thing to make a child worry about his parents.

"Sweetheart, don't worry about anything, okay?" She came to him and put her hands on either side of his face. Children turned into adults as you watched, quick as a turning tide racing up the Bay of Fundy, and nothing could stop it. She said, "This is the best time of your life. You're about to graduate, you've done brilliantly, you've been accepted to the college of your choice, you're seeing the nicest girl … the only thing I want you to think about is whether you want a pale blue tux with ruffles, or a purple one with stripes, okay?"

He smiled. "I was thinking of going Goth. You know, white makeup and purple lipstick, all black with a few chains. Maybe a raven on my shoulder."

"Sounds brilliant. I'm sure Emily will be thrilled." Angela tucked her arm through his and bumped him with her shoulder. "Dad and I are fine. Everybody goes through ups and downs, it's normal. You let me take care of Dad, okay?"

He agreed, although Angela wasn't sure he believed her. Smart boy.

She didn't see Carsten that night. She texted him and said things were complicated with Connor and he needed her attention. She'd call him when Connor left for school. The conversation with her son had shaken her. As the kids said, this shit was getting real.

IT WAS AFTER NINE on Sunday night when Connor went back to school and Angela crawled into bed and called Carsten.

"Are you coming over?" he asked.

"I can't." How boring her bedroom looked. How bluely bland or blandly blue. The room of a woman who thought buying a new duvet and matching curtains would fix her life.

"I thought your husband was out of town, no?"

"He is, but, look, Carsten, I'm not sure … I'm not sure I can do this."

"Ah?"

She told him what Connor had said about Philip. She said she was confused and guilty. "Maybe we should just stop this while we can. I don't want to hurt anyone."

"No, of course not." A tiny barb buried in the words.

"I don't want to hurt my husband, or my son, but I don't want to hurt you, either."

"I did not begin with you thinking this would happen, intending to make your life unhappy. I just thought how smart you were, and yes, okay, you are beautiful, this is not new to you. But you are perhaps, right. We might be friends. I want you to be happy. If I do not make you happy, you should of course not see me."

Tears. "You do make me happy."

"Always I told you, I do not want to be trouble in your life. You have had a different path than me. You are a mother. Your family, house, friends, your life as a lady of Princeton —"

"Oh, fuck off. I'm not some suburban soccer mom." How the flames flared at the idea of this. In the pause, she imagined him shrugging. She was practically wailing. "It's not how I am; that's not *who* I am at all."

"It is the life you are living, my *musling*." His little mouse. "I cannot interfere."

"That's a bit rich, isn't it? I mean don't you think you've already *interfered*, as you put it?"

"I understand that if we agree I seduced you, if we agree I stole you away, you will be able to believe you are innocent."

She slammed her hand down on the bed. "I know I'm not innocent!"

He chuckled and if he had been in front of her, she would have slapped him. "Are we having our first fight?"

"Don't be a jackass, Carsten."

"Then, you must be a grown-up, Angela. You must be a woman, not a little girl standing in front of a broken vase pointing the finger at your little brother. What we have, what we have been doing, is as much because you wish it as because I do. You cannot deny this, is that true or not? Because if not, if it is only me ..."

"You know it's not." She drew her legs up and rested her forehead on her knees. "You know that. I am alive with you. I'm dead here."

"And so?"

"I have to think. I need time."

"Remember, I do not ask you to leave your husband."

How could she forget? How much she wanted him to ask precisely that. "Which means what? That we're supposed to carry on an affair indefinitely?"

"People do. Until they no longer wish to. Americans have a great need, I see, to talk about everything, to bring everything out into the open, as you say. But why? Can we not just see where this goes? It is your business, not your husband's. Do you think that, travelling as much as he does, there are no other women now and then? You cannot be so naive, can you? But it does not interfere with your life together. These can be separate things."

Philip? Sleeping with other women? Oddly, although it was easy for her to picture it, given how important sex was to Philip, until that moment she hadn't really considered it. She knew, since now and then she packed his bags for him, that he kept condoms in his shaving kit. She had assumed they were just there, always, so he wouldn't forget them when they travelled together. Or had she? Well, possibly not. Could it be that she was the tiniest bit relieved to think he was getting sex outside the marriage, hoping he would ask less of her? And, did she mind?

She suddenly remembered a young man she'd had a brief relationship with in her early twenties. A blond Venezuelan named Carlos. Very fiery and dramatic and always wanting to have long make-out sessions at parties, which she didn't like. It felt like a public display of his prowess more than real passion. His possessiveness and proclamations of devotion, the (bad) poetry stuffed in her mailbox, and demands for her declaration of undying love rang false after a while and smothered her. She pulled away. But one night he came over to the crappy Hell's Kitchen sublet that she shared with two nurses she hardly ever saw, over a loud Brazilian restaurant where the music and smells of *feijoada* and fried yucca seeped up through the floorboards. There was a bathtub in the kitchen and the window in her bedroom looked into the airshaft. They ended up on her futon for a few minutes of inglorious coitus. When he got up, she noticed long, angry-looking scratches on his back and buttocks. Not the sort of thing she did.

She giggled, hand over her mouth, pointing. "What's on your butt?"

He grabbed his ass, swore, and then turned and threw himself on her, begging her forgiveness while she tried hard, and without much success, to quell her laughter. It had been a ploy, she understood, to make her jealous, part of the game he so loved to play. The fact she found the whole thing hilarious told her more than anything else that the relationship was over and even poor Carlos had to agree.

So, now, did she feel the same way about the idea of Philip sleeping with someone else? Well, she was annoyed, certainly, in this more complicated era of sexual diseases, but since she hadn't been all that concerned with catching anything herself now that she and Carsten were intimate, it was impossible to fault him. Other than that, and what felt like hypocrisy, since she knew, or thought she knew, how Philip would react if he found out about Carsten, the fact remained: she didn't care.

"I know what you're saying, Carsten, but I just don't think that's me. It feels like I'd just be compartmentalizing my life into bits, none of which would feel satisfying. I want more from my life than that. I want, I'm sorry to spout clichés, but I want to be authentic, in all I do, everywhere, with everyone. God, my head hurts."

"I have a remedy for that. Are you in bed?"

"Yes." He was beginning to know her well. "But this isn't the time. I have to think. I have to make some decisions."

"Are you naked?"

"Carsten, please."

"Get naked. You will think better when you are relaxed."

She was uncertain whether he was right about the thinking part, but by the time they got off the phone, at least she was sleepy, and her headache was gone.

SHE DIDN'T SEE CARSTEN for the rest of that week (although the texts never stopped), and when Philip came home, they had sex and talked. Of course, she said nothing about Carsten. She told Philip she loved him, which was true, as a father to Connor and even as a friend — a distinction she didn't articulate. She didn't mention it was Carsten she fantasized about as he pumped into her. Philip whispered into her ear, "I've missed you. I feel close to you." She smiled and hugged him. He was so easily confused by sex, mistaking it for something, on her part, more than the physical release it was, more than the guilty gesture it was. When he was done and snoring on his side of the bed she got up and took a shower, where the hot water hid her tears.

The next night, she was back at Carsten's. He took her against the stairs, not even giving her time to remove her dress. This was what she wanted, she thought as she moaned beneath him, mindless of the bruises she'd have on her back — bruises she'd have to hide from Philip. After that, they bathed and drank champagne in the bath, and he took her again, on the bed, with her arms pinned over her head. It was almost violent, the stuff of porn flicks. She loved it.

When she got home, Philip was already in bed, laptop on his knees, glass of Scotch on the bedside table. She could smell the Scotch fumes. When she came out of the bathroom his light was off and his back was to her. She noticed the glass of Scotch was empty, but the smell lingered. That smell. Full of heather and amber. She was hardly aware of her footsteps. She turned and walked downstairs, directly to Philip's den, directly to the drinks cabinet. Three quarters of a bottle of Chivas. She picked it up and drank.

THE SNOW-GLOBE WORLD she'd created for her life with Carsten was cracking. Hadn't she promised herself she would put an end to the relationship, or at least put it on hold? She couldn't. A day. Two days. After that initial break, when Philip was in Chicago, she never managed to get past three days without diving into Carsten's arms again. At night she dreamed of him, of being together, completely free; the two of them swimming in a great, sometimes turbulent ocean, diving deep, naked as fish; of kneeling on the ground next to him, clawing at the dirt, trying to unearth something. She dreamed of making love with him, of course. She began keeping a dream journal, transcribing these images, referring to him as *V* for Viking, in case Philip found the book. She wasn't seeing friends, hadn't seen Deedee in weeks and weeks. She went to Connor's graduation and dinner at Elements afterward, but she went to the bathroom three times to text her lover. She took Connor to the airport when he and Emily set off for a vacation to France, and from there she drove directly to Carsten's.

Her thoughts were full of Carsten's clove-and-leather smell, the mole on the inside of his upper arm, the raven tattoo on his left shoulder, the taste of him, the strength in his arms, the muscles in his stomach … Connor slid into the shade cast by her desire. She could barely make him out in the shadows. She told herself he was a grown-up now, with a life of his own, that this was *her* time. She had earned it. Connor flew away to France with a pretty girl, and Angela barely kissed him goodbye. She left him at the security gate with nary a backward glance. And where was Philip? At work. As always.

Later, she would remember only the broadest details of saying goodbye to her son but recall exactly what Carsten was wearing when she reached his house: jeans and a white T-shirt with smudges of earth across his chest, because he was working in the garden. He was barefoot. She would remember how he dusted off his hands and wiped them on his thighs before he embraced her, and that she brushed an ant from his neck. She would not remember what Connor wore that day. Later, it would occur to her that she hadn't taken a photo of Connor and Emily, even though they were embarking on such an important journey. It didn't even occur to her. Evidence, she would understand eventually, of the strength of her obsession.

Deedee was concerned. She'd been sending emails and texts, which Angela answered as briefly as she could. *I'm fine. Really busy. See you soon!* She kept catching Sister Eileen looking at her. One day the nun patted Angela's hand and said she was keeping her in her prayers. Angela laughed, and said, "Always happy to have more prayers, Sister, but whatever for?"

"That we don't lose you," the nun said.

"I'm not going anywhere. The Pantry and the garden mean a lot to me."

"Yes, well," said Sister Eileen, "I'm happy to hear it."

Angela

Angela finally gave in to Deedee, who called and said they were overdue for a long chat and she wasn't taking no for an answer.

Lunch at a local restaurant in town. College kids as servers, with their glossy locks and blue nails and high heels. Four different kinds of kale salad and a dozen sorts of toast. Toast with salted cod. Toast with pickled beef tongue. Toast with goat cheese and fig marmalade.

"When did toast become a thing?" asked Deedee.

"Well, it is artisanal," Angela said.

"Ah, that explains eight dollars for a slice of bread and Nutella."

They ordered kale salads and grilled-cheese sandwiches. Fontina with sage-accented sautéed mushrooms. Nothing so plebeian as cheddar.

Deedee ate her sandwich with a knife and fork, cutting it into tiny, bite-sized pieces.

"So, darling, I haven't seen you in ever so long. What on earth is going on, and don't you tell me 'nothing.'"

Angela wasn't so dainty. Two hands. Too big a mouthful. She chewed, swallowed. "Lots," she said. "Connor's prom took up a ton of time."

She told Deedee about the shopping, and Connor's anxiety over getting his look just right, getting Emily's wrist corsage just right. They talked about the prom buses and how only a few kids ended up drunk and puking — not Connor, thank God. They talked about Annecy, the town in France where Connor and Emily had gone, and the family of the nanny who'd practically raised Emily with whom they'd stay before heading off with train tickets through Italy, Switzerland, and back to Paris. A last careless, responsibility-free vacation before going to college.

"Are he and Emily going to stay together when the fall comes?"

"I think they're going to try, but you know how that goes. She's in one city, he's in another … things happen."

Deedee put her elbows on the table and tucked her hair behind her ears. She looked about fourteen. She said, "Speaking of things happening … I can't help but ask … What's up with the Viking?"

Angela considered lying. She had never felt so bonded to someone. She had never felt so alone. She had never felt so free, so sparkling with life. She had never felt so caged. It was the best of times, it was the most terrifying of times, to paraphrase, but even terror was a kind of thrill.

Deedee, she realized, was looking at her as though she'd begun to spit frogs.

"Oh my God! I can tell by looking at your face." Deedee glanced quickly around to make sure no one they knew was within earshot and dropped her voice to a near whisper. "Honey, what are you doing?"

Angela put her elbows on the table and rubbed her forehead with her fingertips. "I don't have any idea." She looked up at her friend, met her eyes, which took considerable effort. “I’m not proud of myself. I don’t want you to think this is easy.”

Deedee took her hand. “Angela, I’m not judging you. I’m worried.”

“So am I.”

“So, you’re actually …”

“Yes. I’m having an affair.”

“Is it a fling, or is it, I don’t know … serious?”

Was it serious? What did *serious* mean? Carsten was a force. Her submission to him was her power. The desire never waned, and just thinking about it aroused her, made her flush. She pressed her lips together, trying to hide the involuntary smile. She raised her eyebrows, shook her head.

I want you. I need you. I love you. He had said these words. They had stopped her breath. She had told him she wanted him, but nothing more. Did she love him? Maybe, but she wasn’t ready to say so. Was it serious? It was. Did that mean she would leave Philip?

“I don’t know.”

“Does he suspect?”

“I don’t think so, but he’s miserable. Even more miserable than usual, so I don’t know. He’s always been droopy. He knows something’s wrong, but no, I don’t think he has any idea there’s another man.”

They had stopped eating.

“Okay, Angela, I’m going to give you the only piece of advice I will ever give you on this subject. Well, two pieces. The first is that if you’re going to leave Philip, and I have no opinion on whether you should or not — you’re on your own with that one — but if you do, leave him clean, meaning you all go ahead and separate and do what you have to, but give yourself a year, a full year, four lovely long seasons all by yourself before you take up with the Viking. Let yourself end one relationship before you start another.

Give yourself time to grieve and figure out who you are all by yourself before starting up as another couple. I have learned that, by the way, from any number of family members who seem to think marriage is something you do as a kind of amusement ride, like you stay on it as long as it's exciting and doesn't cause tummy upset, but once it does you dash off to the next one … and then the next one … without ever giving yourself a chance to stop getting dizzy. Did I tell you about my aunt Millie? She's on her sixth, honey, her *sixth* marriage. Bless her heart." Deedee screwed up her lips, as though willing herself not to speak, but then went on. "But I understand you probably won't take that advice. No one ever does, although I have offered it on so many occasions it might just surprise you, and it is very good advice. However, if you, like most everyone else in the midst of it, can't manage to keep your hands off each other, let me offer the other piece of advice. And that is, if you want to have any sort of self-respect by the time this is all over, and if you want your relationships with Connor and Philip to be even partially intact, try to be kind, darling. Kind to Philip, kind to yourself, and kind to your Viking."

She looked like a tiny, slightly sun-wizened oracle, someone who'd already seen behind the veil of time, to the blood on the asphalt and the tears on the pillows. Angela wanted her to stop talking, but she didn't.

"It is bound to get all sorts of messy and unpleasant, and people say harmful things that just can't be rescinded." Deedee held her hands up. "I have to repeat that no one has ever taken my advice."

"So, outside your family, I mean, you've known other women who've been through this sort of thing?"

"Honey, you would be surprised what goes on in a Southern town, and even what goes on in buttoned-up Yankee Princeton. I seem to recall F. Scott Fitzgerald had all sorts of fun writing about this town."

"I feel like everything I've believed about myself, everything I thought I wanted, was just a lie, but, at the same time, I feel like I'm finally myself." Angela started to cry. "How can this be happening to me?"

"I don't know. But it isn't happening *to* you, Angela. You're making choices. And Philip's not such a bad guy, is he? I mean he really does love you."

"You're taking Philip's side?"

"Is there a side? I didn't think there was. I'm not judging you, Angela. I'm just saying maybe don't be so hasty. This might be an infatuation. It might pass. Philip and you … you've been together a long time. There's Connor. You're a mother first and foremost."

"Am I? Is that what I am. A mother? A wife?" Were they, she wondered, really having this conversation, in the twenty-first century? "When do I stop being a mother? Connor's gone. He's away, then off to college. I doubt he'll ever live with us again."

"Don't be so sure. They come back these days. But even if he doesn't, your behaviour will still affect him, you know. You don't ever stop being the boy's mother."

So, after all that talk about how Deedee wasn't judging her, she was. Well, who wouldn't? Angela thought. She judged herself. But she needed a friend, and not a conscience. The choice was hers, Deedee had said, but was it? Angela assumed Deedee meant the choice to be moral or not. To behave in a "kind" way or not. And just like that, Angela slammed the door. That was the choice she made. Either Deedee was with her or she wasn't.

She pulled back in her chair. She bit into her sandwich, chewed, and swallowed. "Choices? Yes, that's obvious, isn't it?" she said. "I'm making choices. All mine for better or worse, as they say." She picked up her fork. "I really don't want to talk about this anymore. Tell me about you. What's happening with the horses? Are you in competition this summer?"

Deedee said nothing. She just looked at Angela, her eyes blue as a clear but distant sky. She blinked, and for a moment something flashed over her face, and Angela knew she had hurt her, but Deedee, mistress of manners and discretion, only picked up her fork and cut into her now-cold artisanal grilled-cheese sandwich. The lines around her mouth were slightly more rigid than usual, but her tone was cheery, and her back was so straight one would think she wore a corset. Angela listened to her babble on about horses and barns, feed and farriers, and the upcoming dressage tournament, and all she wanted to do was run out of there and drive to Carsten's house.

IT WAS EARLY JULY. The gardens were finished. The plants were in. The volunteers — some clients of the Pantry, some from churches in the areas — were working well together. The Pantry's refrigerators were filling up with fresh lettuce, beets, radishes, cucumber, carrots, and the first tomatoes. Sister Eileen had started cooking classes in the basement of the Catholic church on Broad Street. There was no longer any need for Carsten to come by, and for that Angela was grateful. It was easier to keep their relationship hidden from people at the Pantry if they weren't trying to tamp down their hormones in front of others. Even Sophia and Gladys, two of the regulars, had started teasing Angela about having a crush on the big handsome Dane.

One day they'd been out weeding, and Carsten had popped in to see how the boxes were holding up and to plant a maple tree. Angela was bent over a bunch of radish plants and he'd touched her shoulder as he went by.

Sophia, on the other side of the box, noticed. "That's one pretty man," she said.

Gladys sat in the shade of the building's wall, on an overturned milk crate, her bulk hanging over the sides. She raised the can of Diet Coke she was drinking and winked. "Damn shame to let that go to waste, ain't that right, Angela?" And then she and Sophia broke into cackles and leg slaps, while Angela blushed furiously and tried to laugh along.

Despite the teasing, and how obvious it was she didn't live in Trenton; she was there more than ever. Her house felt sepulchral. She didn't want to see her friends, not even Deedee. She felt more at home with Sophia, Gladys, Sister Caroline, Roland, Sister Eileen, and Isobe. Isobe, a tall man from Liberia, with small eyes that never gave away what he was thinking, had done a long stint in prison. Now he worked trying to keep young kids from going into the gangs and helped them get out if they wanted to. It was dangerous work, and he knew it. Angela asked him once if he wasn't afraid he'd get killed. He'd just shrugged and said death wasn't so hard, but living without hope was agony.

People at the Pantry knew not to ask too many questions. Prying was impolite, since almost everyone had family troubles of one kind or another. A pregnant daughter, a drug-addicted son, a kid who came home sporting gang tats, another involved in street-corner enterprises. Everyone knew someone in jail. Everyone was struggling to find work and to make ends meet. Angela bought fresh, whole-grain bread, and fruit and cheese, and they ate lunch together. Sister Eileen joined them, bringing her own offerings of homemade brownies or lemon squares. Sophia and Gladys, sometimes other women, brought chicken and pasta salad. Isobe, Roland, and the other men around brought their appetites, and sometimes a case of soda. Angela beckoned to Byron one day, as he sat on a bench by the front door, eating a hamburger.

"Come join us!" she called.

Byron saluted and said, politely, "Thanks, but I don't socialize with white people. No offence."

"Manners, boy!" said Gladys.

Byron ignored her. Angela had been taken aback, but she also understood it. He didn't mean the white people who lived on his block; he meant the white lady from Princeton. Fair enough.

Carsten had moved on to other jobs now and they met at the end of the day. She had a key to his house. The neighbours — Norman Cody, a quite-famous photographer who had captured some of the early graffiti artists in New York City on one side; on the other, Glenn and Derrick, both lawyers — had introduced themselves and were frequent visitors. Angela would sometimes find one or more of them in the garden with Carsten when she arrived, sitting under the wisteria, sipping cold beers. Their enchanted garden. They asked few questions, beyond inquiring as to how Carsten and she had met. If they noticed her wedding ring, they were too polite to ask about it, and they were also too polite to stay long after she arrived, intuiting their desire to be alone, and naked.

They developed a habit, a rhythm. She began to feel it could go on forever. Why shouldn't it? Other people had long-term affairs. What was that movie about the couple who met once a year on the same weekend, year after year, for decades? Of course, *Same Time, Next Year.* Alan Alda. Ellen Burstyn. They had been good for each other, helping each other through difficulties, no strings attached. It hadn't affected their marriages.

But one weekend a year wasn't what she was doing. Still, she could, she decided, manage this compartmentalization of the men in her life. She told herself Carsten was helping her marriage. She could be kinder to Philip when she had a real life, something meaningful and important, even if it wasn't with him. She could be more patient, and even enjoy sex with her husband now and again, especially with a couple of drinks in her.

Sister Eileen

Eileen and Angela sat across from each other at a table covered with a checkered cloth, on which was centred a small arrangement of flowers. Angela wore a sleeveless blush-toned tunic over skinny black pants and heels. Her fingernails were painted the colour of pinkish pearls and her hair gleamed. She looked, Eileen thought, like the sort of woman who had come from a job at a fashion magazine, or maybe an advertising agency, something chic and a little edgy. Her perfume smelled of jasmine.

"You look awfully pretty," said Eileen.

Angela picked up her glass of white wine and held it out for Eileen to clink with her own. "Rough day?"

"Ruth was feeling under the weather, so I took her place at the prison."

"She works in a prison?"

"Yup. Chaplain at the men's prison down in Bordentown."

"I don't know how you do that. How do you get used to it?"

"I hope I never do. That would mean a hardening of my heart, I think. The chaplain at the women's prison in Clinton is a Sister of Saint Joseph, as well. Sister Brigid. I don't know why, but the women's prison … look, the men's stories are just heartbreaking, but they somehow don't leave me with such a sense of … not despair, despair is a sin against my understanding of a compassionate God … but perhaps weariness. These women, mothers, so many of them addicted, often abused, sometimes taking the rap for the men in their lives, their sons and lovers and brothers … and sometimes mentally ill."

"Really?" Angela flicked her eyebrows upward. "Mentally ill? I didn't realize."

"Oh, yes. They go off their meds. Things happen. They end up on the street as prostitutes, drug addicts. Babies. Children left behind." Eileen dropped her head for a moment, sniffed, then raised her head and smiled. "Well, let's just say that Sister Ruth and Sister Brigid have found their callings. God chose rightly, as always."

"He chose rightly with you as well, Sister. The Pantry. The cooking classes, the garden … you do have the gift of making people comfortable."

"Well, I'm just glad you asked me to dinner." Their salads arrived and Eileen said, "I was delighted you called. So nice to have a dinner with someone so smart and full of life. The work you've been doing at the Pantry is wonderful. We are in your debt."

"Don't be silly," said Angela.

Someone at the table behind them snorted with laughter and Angela flinched, as if they were laughing at her.

Eileen poured oil and vinegar on her salad. "I did think, though, and forgive me if I'm wrong, but was there something in particular you wanted to talk about?"

Angela cocked her head and absently dragged her fork around her plate. "Why did you want to become a nun?"

Eileen smiled. She didn't think that was what Angela really wanted to talk about, but the truth would come out when she was ready. "That's a good question." She clapped her hands like a child. "It started when I was thirteen with a dream one night of sweeping, flying, down a green and lavender hillside to a silver and crystal cave and finding a statue of Mother Mary inside, her dress all blue and white, with stars on a crown around her head. She came alive and reached out to me. I woke up crying and laughing at the same time and knowing I would never again be happy until I found that woman in that sacred place and rested forever in her arms. The wonder and terror, the reassurance from the woman that all would be well, and that I was safe and understood completely and loved all the more for it — it was amazing.

"It didn't last," she continued, "not in the same intense way, but I never forgot it. It's like she was near me. Inside me. I know it sounds odd, but it's like she's my most important relationship. And the more I learned about her, the more I had the sense she, like Christ, has always been with us, in one guise or another, since the beginning of time."

"Really?" Angela dabbed delicately at her lips with her napkin. "Is that Church doctrine?"

Eileen shrugged. "Doctrine or not, it's a sense I have. I prefer to focus on that, rather than the patriarchy in the Church and the erasure of the female. The truth is that the hierarchy of the Church wasn't what drew me to this life. It was the miracle. It was the grace. It was the wonder and miracle of deep, deep, and eternal life. But," she said, "maybe there was something. Women have always been a bit underground, haven't we? At least in modern history. There's a lot of evidence that women had a much more powerful and equal role in the early Church. But perhaps that's why nuns are at the forefront of so much social activism in the Church. Why we try to help the forgotten, the marginalized, the hungry, the homeless, those without a voice. I'm not saying priests and brothers don't, of course. I'm not saying that."

Angela said, "The priests have a lot to account for, and the Vatican, too, for that matter. All that child abuse and now the rape of nuns, and no one doing much about it, if you don't mind me saying."

"I don't mind," Eileen said. "The structures of the Church have to change."

The waiter came, bringing a simple linguini with olive oil and garlic for Eileen, and branzino, grilled, with roast vegetables for Angela.

"That looks lovely," Eileen said to the waiter. "Thank you." The waiter sprinkled grated parmesan on the pasta, and ground pepper on the fish.

Angela looked up and said, "So, your order. About that. Why Saint Joseph?"

Eileen chuckled. "Because he wasn't the main event. We believe in doing what needs to be done. We honour the beloved neighbour without distinction."

"Devil's advocate here … even the divorced? Even women who have abortions?"

"Well, let me be clear." Eileen chewed, swallowed, and dabbed at her lips. "I believe all life is sacred. Firmly pro-life. Of course, that also means education, housing, healthcare, all that. Otherwise you're just pro-birth. There are terrible decisions humans must make sometimes, and life is complicated. Extremely so. I would want a woman who's had, or is going to have, a termination to know that God loves her even then, even there, and that she is still precious, and that I love her, as well. I might even admit to accompanying one or two women on that journey, were that admission not so easy to misconstrue."

Angela's chewed her lip for a moment. "Life is complicated, isn't it? It's hard to know what people go through, why they have to make the choices they make."

"It is indeed."

They ate in silence for a moment, the sounds of the restaurant — the espresso machine, the conversation, the clink of glass and silverware, the pop music coming over the speakers — creating a sort of white noise. Finally, Angela drank deeply from her glass of wine and said, "Not ever having a father, I find it hard to relate to a male god."

"I don't think God has a gender."

"But you refer to God as Him. The Father and all that."

"It's what most people are used to. I tend to try and avoid pronouns and so forth. But, maybe because of the way I feel about Mary, I think of God in more feminine terms, honestly. I don't think it matters. What matters is that we are in relationship with God, that we know God loves us."

"No matter what?" Angela put her fork down. She plucked her napkin from her lap and began folding it into a triangle on the tabletop. "Doesn't God get angry with us? I mean if we do something we shouldn't … if we behave badly?"

Eileen put down her knife and fork, as well. She entwined her fingers and held Angela's gaze. "God always loves us. I think God grieves when we do something that will hurt us, and others, because … she … wants so much more for us than we could possibly imagine, so much more joy and peace."

"And if doing the right thing means we're in pain? If doing the right thing, the selfless and kind thing, the thing everyone expects of you, makes you feel like you're dying?"

"That's not what God wants for anyone. Is that the way you feel?"

Angela looked up from the napkin. "Yes. It is. When I think about having to spend the rest of my life with a man I don't love. When I think about having to give up the man I do love."

Eileen opened her mouth to speak, but Angela stopped her. "Oh, come on, you can't say you didn't guess."

"No, I can't say that." She smiled. "You haven't been all that good at hiding it."

"So, I suppose you think I'm sinning." Angela picked up her wineglass and drained what was left in it.

"I'm afraid you're going to end up in pain, and that other people will, too."

"I don't want to hurt anyone. But I'm not going to give him up."

"Does your husband know?"

"No."

"Are you going to divorce?"

"I don't know. Another sin." She widened her eyes and feigned horror.

"You must be lying to him. Are you?"

"Yes. Of course, I'm lying to him, and I hate that. It makes me feel awful."

"Can you break if off with Carsten, at least for a while, until you decide what you're going to do? How you're going to do it? It's so important for you, for everyone involved, that whatever happens, you don't do things now you'll regret later."

"You're saying the same thing my friend Deedee says. You haven't been talking to her, have you? Sorry. Paranoid." Angela's lip began to tremble. "I regret so many things. What's a few more?" She began to cry.

"Oh, Angela. I'm so sorry you're in this pain. How can I help?"

"Be on my side." She took the tissue Eileen offered and dabbed at her eyes, being careful not to smudge her makeup.

"I *am* on your side, but because I want the very best for you, I must tell you I think you're making a mistake if you keep on seeing Carsten, as things now stand."

"I probably am. People keep telling me that." Angela looked up and her eyes narrowed with defiance. "And I don't care. I won't give him up. I don't know if I'm going to leave Philip, but I'm not leaving Carsten."

"The world doesn't work like that. We don't get to have our cake and eat it, too. Cliché, but no less true."

Angela bristled. Her eyes narrowed, went darker. "It doesn't sound like you're on my side."

"I'm sorry for that. But I am. I think you're smart and kind and so full of life. You're such a flame, you've got such spark. You bubble with it; you glow with it. That's God's love. Big and bright and bold."

Angela didn't answer, but hung her head, shook it and busied herself with the tissue, blowing her nose. It was a messy sound.

A family sat at the table next to them. Parents and two children, a boy of perhaps seven, and a girl maybe twelve. He wore a blue-and-yellow soccer shirt and held something on his lap. He was petting it, Eileen realized. A turtle? Tortoise. The boy pulled a piece of lettuce from his plate and fed it to the animal. The parents were talking, something about an upcoming vacation, and the girl was staring at her and Angela, eyes full of curiosity. She wore a pink long-sleeved T-shirt and her hair was wrapped in the kind of bun ballet dancers wore. It accentuated her long, thin neck, just as it was meant to do. Perhaps she had just come from a barre class? Angela followed Eileen's gaze and seeing the girl, smiled at her. The girl blushed, picked up her pink bedazzled phone and began texting furiously.

"So why," Angela said, "does God punish me so?" She was soggy and snuffling now.

"God doesn't punish you. God loves you."

"He feels punishing to me."

"What I'm hearing is shame. I've felt that. I was terribly shamed as a child, and I kept asking, 'What is the Truth?' A question intellectual answers didn't help. Intellectual answers don't touch that feeling of shame. For me, it was the irresistible image of Jesus and his love for the least and the lost that pulled me back from the edge. The healing took a long time, and, to be honest, I had a difficult time being patient with God, understanding that God isn't mean or punishing, but painstakingly thorough in the healing. Yes, I fail. I do things wrong, but Christ's desire is to heal the wounds that tempt me to sin. Shame, hiding, they have no place. Soul-corroding secrets have no place. Angela, shame is a limiting, constricting prison. Its windows into reality are small and smeared."

"Yes, it sure is … and you know what? I'm going to leave here now and I'm going to see Carsten."

"I know."

Angela stood up. "Dinner's on me."

"You don't have to do that, and you don't have to rush off, either." Eileen took her hand. The girl at the next table looked over again and sneered.

"Yes, I do. I shouldn't have told you all this, anyway."

"I'm glad you did." She patted Angela's hand with her other and said, "Will you call me tomorrow and let me know how you are? I want to be sure you know I *am* on your side, that I'm here for you."

"Sure. Sure. I'll call." Angela bent down and kissed Eileen's cheek. "Thanks," she said, and then she dashed off, leaving a trail of perfume behind her.

THE NEXT MORNING, Eileen stood at the kitchen counter, chopping onions. It was Saturday, and so the Pantry wasn't open, and it was her turn to cook. Peel back the papery skin. *Onion skin*, she thought, *that's what we used to call airmail letter paper.* Pale blue and fine, nearly transparent. The idea was that the onion-skin paper was lighter than regular paper and therefore less expensive to mail. One didn't need an envelope; one merely folded the paper over, wrote the address on the front. Didn't even need a stamp. The onion skins came pre-stamped. She would write birthday letters to her great-aunt Kate way off in County Sligo on such paper. Aunt Kate was something of a rebel in the family, more pagan than Catholic. She was her father's aunt, and would write much longer letters back to Eileen, filled with strange stories about the Great Worm, warriors and druids, banshees, Balor of the Evil Eye, and the Cailleach, the Old Woman of Winter. The Cailleach was a wild and willful woman, who made the stones and storms. The Cailleach was that force of nature that shaped the world and still did, said Aunt Kate.

The letters would arrive from Ireland in packages with tins of shortbread and loaves of soda bread wrapped in tea towels Aunt Kate had embroidered herself. Eileen's mother would keep the shortbread and tea towels, toss out the soda bread (for of course it was stale and hard as the rocks created by the Cailleach, Aunt Kate having no sense of the great distance from County Sligo to New Jersey), scan the letters and then, with a snort of derision, toss them away as well, muttering about godless pagans. Eileen, however, would pluck them out of the trash, ferret them away, and read them when she could. A child of twelve or thirteen, she found no sacrilege in the old tales and the spirits of the sky and earth. She didn't then, and she didn't now. What was all the world and everything in it, after all, except a metaphor for God, who spoke in the language of whomever God sought, and didn't God seek us all?

The onions were potent and made her eyes water. She reached over the soda bread she'd made earlier, pulled off a small piece and popped it in her mouth. Holding a piece of bread in your mouth as you chopped onions was supposed to stop the tears, and she always tried it, with mixed results. Another tale from the old country. Wild women and forces of nature, and letters on blue, nearly transparent paper, but no one sent letters any longer, did they? They texted. They emailed. Hardly even called.

Texts. Yes, there was Angela's face floating in front of her. Angela texting Carsten, even though he was only a few yards away, working in the same once-blasted plot of land. Carsten, with his back turned to Angela, texting back to her … and then the smile, the giggle and the blush.

Angela. There was a force of nature. A texting force of nature.

Eileen scraped the onions into the pot with a dab of olive oil and set to chopping the carrots and celery. A soup needed to have a good base, something homey and solid, seemingly plain, but without which the soup was thin as gruel. Then the cauliflower, the thyme and sage, the smoked paprika, a little butternut squash, a few peas, homemade vegetable broth Eileen had made a few days earlier. Oh, it was so simple, and such a prayer, this cooking business. She remembered her mother saying you had to always stir the soup clockwise, for that brought good things to you, and you had to pray as you cooked, for that put Christ into the food. A little bit of kitchen witchery there, handed down from her mother's own County Mayo ancestors.

Keeping Angela in mind, texting and smiling, touching her lips to hide her smile, touching her breast to … what? Feel the wild beating of a wild heart? Perhaps. Eileen had always known, of course, that it was Carsten she texted, Carsten she dreamed of. And so, she stirred the pot clockwise and prayed, unsure God was even listening, that God's plan for the good of all might be made reality. She noted the pang of guilt she felt for having been the one to introduce them, and sent that into the soup and so to God, with a pinch of salt. Guilt was not useful. It was too self-absorbed. It was now in the hands of the God she trusted — even now, even so — and for whom she would do whatever was required of her.

She did this in the hopes of feeling that wonderful and terrible awe she had felt as a child, dreaming the dream of Mary. How long had it been since she'd felt the actual Presence? The Companion? Months? Certainly. Years? Yes. Now all she felt was the terrible, agonizing Silence. A woman could let tears drop into the soup to salt it. But that would bring sorrow to those who ate it, wouldn't it?

And so, no tears, just the same prayer: *Speak, oh speak to me my Beloved. My soul yearns for you so. I wait, dying of thirst in the burning desert of your absence. Amen.*

Angela

Angela bolted awake and turned to the clock. 3:10 a.m. Philip lay snoring beside her, the sound wet and thick. She could smell his stale breath. His soft bulk was like that of an elephant seal, a larded creature who might be graceful and fierce in the sea but here was out of its habitat, slightly deflated under its own weight. His arm, the red T-shirt pushed up to his shoulder, was heavy and marked with moles. She squirmed at the idea of touching it, knowing it would be moist and hot. The air conditioning cut in and out. She could never get it quite cold enough in the room, especially since she'd taken to wearing men's pajamas to bed. The digital readout on the clock changed from 3:10 to 3:11. Time away from Carsten moved at a glacial rate, and when she was with him it fled like birds before a storm.

She reached for water from the decanter beside the bed and drank a tall glass. Then she had to pee and rose as quietly as possible. In the dark bathroom, she sat on the toilet, leaned on her elbows, and put her head in her hands. She was drinking far too much. She knew it, and that, coupled with her infidelity and all the lying, combined into an odious stew of self-loathing. She finished peeing, wiped, flushed, and moved from the toilet to the floor, her back up against the bath. She pulled a towel down from the rack and buried her face in it, weeping.

She wept, in self-flagellating torrents, because she was having an affair. A long-term affair. Not a one-night stand that could, in a pinch, be swept into a dark corner of forgetfulness. On top of the smarmy truth that she was an adulterer, there was the fact she had married Philip in much the same way a prostitute leaves the streets so a rich man can set her up in a nice midtown apartment. She'd been clever enough to get him to marry her, though, securing her financial health. A regular little conniver was she. A liar. A selfish tramp. And no heart of gold for this hooker. She was cheating on the man who'd saved her from her fears of dead-end jobs and cockroach-infested shared apartments, like the one she was living in when she met Philip. She had to admit, if only to herself, that she was an opportunist, a carrion crow, swooping down on some new blood-bright piece of flesh for no other reason that she didn't like the nest she'd built for herself and didn't want to sleep in it anymore.

She thought of Connor, off in the mountains of France with his Emily. If he found out she was cheating on his father, what would he think of her? What would he think of women in general? Would he ever be able to trust? And if she left Philip?

She stopped crying.

Left Philip?

Left Philip.

This wasn't the first time the idea had floated past, obviously, but it was the first time she'd reached out and snagged it. People did it. They divorced. They found other partners, lived better lives. And after all, if she wasn't in love with Philip, didn't she owe it to him to let him go, to find someone who would love him as he deserved?

She let her dreams spool out like murmurating starlings, swirling into the ether of possibilities … She would move into Carsten's house. They would toil side by side. She would plan community projects in Trenton. Maybe get a degree in landscape architecture. The work would be useful. She would be contributing to the world. And although she was drawn to the goodness and meaning of such a life, in every image whirling across the sky of her mind it was Carsten's presence that kept forming and reforming. They would be cooking in the kitchen with Chet Baker's trumpet drifting like smoke through the air. Carsten would take her in his arms. Slow dance across the wooden floor. They would shop at a farmer's market. They would eat croissants and drink strong coffee from a French press in the morning. They would wake up next to each other. They would talk about poetry, read aloud to each other late at night — Neruda and Donne, Shakespeare and Austen, Sappho and Joyce.

Was it so wrong to want this? To want a life in which she was true to herself, a life lush with love and elegance and passion?

She dried her face. She didn't want to go back to bed. She crept through the house, down the stairs. She got a mug from the kitchen, went to Philip's office, and poured brandy into the mug. She padded into the greenhouse and sat in the dark on a wrought-iron chair next to a matching circular table where she sometimes took tea, just like the English ladies in the books she'd devoured as a child. Roman Kaiser's book on the scent of orchids lay atop it, as did Dr. Henry Oakeley's books on orchids, and a couple of others.

Building this conservatory had been like prestidigitation, like conjuring. She'd dreamed it into being. For months she had studied architectural and gardening magazines, looking for precisely the right design. And then she'd found it. A glass cupola, leaded copper roof, and trimmed on the inside with mahogany bead board. She had worked with the designer for another three months, going over every detail of pattern and structure. It took nearly a year to complete. She had measured every shelf, every window panel. She'd drawn the designs she wanted on the stained glass surrounding the cupola and the half-moons where wall met ceiling — delicate flowers in red, blue and gold with oval leaves and silver leaf patterns along the frame. She'd insisted the roof be left clear so that the sky would always be visible … sun and moon and stars and clouds. Philip had given her free rein, paid every outlandish bill without complaint. Called it a ten-year anniversary present. She had cried the day it was finished. Cried again when her first orchids arrived, delicate as lace, lush as velvet.

Philip had sat with her at the wrought-iron bistro table and poured them champagne. "To the beauty you bring to our home," he'd said. She cried again then.

Now, the ghostly flowers surrounded her on the wooden slatted tabletop. Palest of pink, yellow, lavender, shadowed red and burgundy as well as white. Bone-white. Under the tables rested bags of earth, and, on the shelf next to the coffee maker, the trowel and fork, green gloves, and spray bottle were tucked neatly into baskets. The air smelled of loam and the flowers' scent, faint at night — notes of cinnamon, raspberry, coconut, vanilla, roses. Angela could pick them out, each one, after all these years of cultivating not only the flowers, but her senses. She stretched her legs and rested her head on the back of the chair, looking up through the glass panes. She sipped the brandy and watched the waxing moon and stars move across the blue-black velvet sky. This place was her Eden and her observatory, her church and her sanctuary. She would have to give it up if she was to have a new life. It would hurt like being skinned, but she'd have to do it, have to sacrifice, she told herself, on the altar of love.

How slowly the stars and moon moved. *We are all just hurtling through unforgiving space*, she thought. Tiny, minuscule dots of light, of no consequence whatsoever, and she found that oddly comforting.

The brandy sang its sweet song along her neurons. Whatever it was that hung the stars in the sky was all part of a cosmic intricacy far too complex for her to figure out. She was less than the speck in the eye of a dead ant. She didn't have to figure it out. All that could possibly be required of her was to do what she thought right, what *felt* right in her gut. Why couldn't people like Sister Eileen see how simple it all was? Let the rest of the universe take care of itself, and that included Philip. Life, she reasoned, was so short, so bizarrely brief, that not following one's heart was tantamount to sacrilege, since the heart was surely the human seat of God.

She downed the brandy and decided she wouldn't go back to bed. She'd sit there and wait for the dawn. Tomorrow she would speak to Carsten. They'd make plans. She would tell Philip. The sooner the better. By the time Connor came back from France at the end of the summer, they'd be well on their way to sorting out the details. He'd be off at college, anyway. He'd be upset, of course, but not terribly. He'd be busy with his own life. Hell, it was quite possible the majority of his friends' parents were divorced.

She decided she needed a little more brandy, just to keep her nerves from getting the better of her.

"ANGELA! WAKE UP!"

Philip was shaking her shoulder. He stood over her, dressed in his red T-shirt and pajama bottoms. She was staring at his bare feet.

"What are you doing here? Did you sleep here?"

Angela moved, and as she did a pain shot up her neck into her head. She must have fallen asleep with her head at an awkward angle. She scrunched her shoulders, turtlelike, trying to pull away from both Philip's hand and the pain. She massaged the spot and managed to straighten her back.

"I was watching the stars," she said. Croaked. Her throat was dry as plaster.

"The stars. Really?" He picked up her cup, smelled it, and then put it down again. He folded his arms over his chest. "Do you think I don't know, Angela? Do you really think I don't know?"

Her head was muzzy. What did he know? She blinked, trying to clear her thoughts, her vision. Carsten?

"What are you talking about? You know. Know what?" She stood up and tried not to let Philip see how painful her back was, how cramped her neck.

"You've been drinking every day. You're drinking like a longshoreman."

He followed her into the kitchen. She rinsed out the cup and put it in the dishwasher. Had she brought the bottle of brandy into the greenhouse? How much had she drunk? She had a vague memory of several more trips to Philip's office.

"My drinking's none of your business."

"Is that so? Well, I disagree. I'm starting to think you have a real problem."

She wanted water so badly but didn't take any. Downing a glass of water would only confirm his suspicions. "I don't know what you're talking about. I'm fine."

He glared at her, leaning straight-armed on the island. His mouth was ugly, contorted. Would it be so bad if he did know about Carsten? Maybe that would simplify everything. She tried to meet his eyes, to be dignified in her truth. Philip's arms were trembling. He looked as though if she said the wrong thing he'd crack and crumble to dust.

"I'm too fucking old for this shit, and so are you. Holding a girl's head while she pukes might be tolerable when she's in her twenties, but not at your age."

So, drinking, then. Not Carsten.

"You're a fine one to talk about drinking. Have you gone to bed sober once in the past I don't know how long?"

"Living with you would make anyone drink."

The morning light coming in from the eastern-facing windows made Angela feel like a vampire. She couldn't hold off any longer. She grabbed a glass and filled it with tap water. Drank half of it.

"Piss off, Philip."

He shook his head. "You get your shit together Angela. If you don't care about me, at least give some thought to how what you do affects your son."

She reminded her husband that Connor was in France, with his girlfriend, and upon his return would embark on a new life in which his parents would be only peripheral figures. As she talked, however, it was as though the person speaking was doing so without Angela's involvement. While this woman — and a shrewish-sounding person she was, too — waffled on, Angela tried to figure out what Philip meant. She hadn't hurt Connor. He had no idea what she did or didn't do, and as far as Angela could tell, he didn't care all that much. What teenager did?

"My son loves me," she said. "And I love him."

Philip said, "Don't make him feel about you the way you felt about your mother."

She wanted to rake her nails across his cheek for that one.

Isabelle. Her mother, dressed in witchy, black flowing dresses and high-heeled boots, bosom like a ship's maidenhead; long, tangled, dyed-blond hair. She'd had her greatest year, reached her peak, in 1968 and never descended. She clung to the side of that hippie mountain like a pot-infused barnacle.

In 1980, Angela overhead her grade five teacher speaking to the school nurse after Isabelle had flounced into a Christmas pageant, pausing at the door so everyone was sure to see her. *Who does she think she is, some flower child? A little wilted, I'd say*. And they laughed.

How old would Isabelle have been when Angela was ten? Thirty-two? Thirty-three? That seemed young to her now. Isabelle never gave up on her vision of herself as a black-lace-clad seductress, though. She showed up at Angela's senior prom, saying she didn't get enough pictures of her and Steve, her date. She'd put on a lot of weight by that time and the clothes that had looked silly on her at thirty-three looked frightening and pathetic on a woman over forty. She pawed Steve, saying how pretty he was, prettier than Angela, she said. She tried to kiss him, leaving a smear of lipstick across his mouth. He pulled back, pushing her away, wiping his mouth. The mirror ball whirled, House of Pain sang "Jump Around" and everyone laughed and pointed.

Angela left the prom in tears. She never spoke to Steve again. She left home a month later and rarely spoke to her mother after that. Saw her only on holidays, out of a sense of guilt and obligation. Philip was always kinder to Isabelle than Angela was. Angela thought he got a kick out of her. She died skeletal and angry and — between coughing fits that left her near-drowning in phlegm — telling Philip that Angela wasn't nearly good enough for a big old handsome man like him. When Angela buried her ashes in a municipal plot, she cried for the life she might have had, if she had just accepted things the way they were.

And her father? Angela never knew him. He left Isabelle, to whom he wasn't married, when Angela was six months old, to be a musician in California, Isabelle told her. She hadn't even kept a photo.

Angela was nothing like her. Nothing. Nothing at all.

Now, Philip cocked an eyebrow, and smirked, knowing he'd hit a nerve.

The rage Angela had felt a moment before splintered. Instead, she rather enjoyed Philip's cruelty. It justified her own.

"Well, if Connor felt about me the way you feel about *your* mother, would you like that better, Philip?"

Three months after Philip's father had died, his mother, Evelyn, had moved to Taos with her "best friend," Edna. Philip was furious, saying she was disrespecting his father, which was about as serious an insult as Philip could imagine. Evelyn told Philip to like it or lump it — her words exactly. She said she'd lived her whole life for other people and now she was done. She was going to love whom she wished to and live how she wished to and that was that. Philip never forgave her. He felt she'd lied to his father the whole of their married life, let him work himself to death and had probably been "carrying on," as he put it, with Edna since they'd gone to Sarah Lawrence together back in the day. He was probably right. Angela admired her. In fact, at this moment she admired Evelyn enormously.

She cocked her head and smiled sweetly. "You know, because you're just so proud of her, right? Of how she reached out and took what she wanted, even if what she wanted had nothing to do with you? At least Connor knows I'd never move away and not care if I ever saw him again, right?"

As soon as she heard them, she wanted to stuff the words back in her mouth. It was too much. She wanted to chew them up and swallow them, bitter as they were. Philip's eyes widened for a second, as though he couldn't believe what he'd just heard.

"You bitch."

"Yes. I probably am. I'm one unhappy bitch and one mean bitch and I wouldn't blame you at all if you wanted out of this marriage."

Philip straightened and crossed his arms. He looked big and, Angela thought, like some feudal lord about to hand down an edict.

"Me? Want out of this marriage? And give you all the money I've worked my ass off for? No way, sweetheart. And you'd come after me for it, wouldn't you? I'll make sure Connor gets every cent and you get nothing. Am I clear? Nothing. You're not going anywhere."

"I don't want your money."

"You never wanted anything else."

Oh, his eyes were like scalpels, stripping away every layer of skin and muscle, down to the cold hard bone truth of who she was.

"That isn't true." She had to say that. It was what one had to say. "You're wrong," she said.

"I wish I was. You don't know how much. You think you're such a fucking mystery, don't you? You and your Danish bastard."

Wasn't it odd how time slowed down in such moments, how it crystalized and thickened, at once drawing outlines around everything, like chalk marks at a crime scene, and holding one in place, forcing one to look and not avert the gaze?

"Philip … look …" Oh, there was no point in denying it. She didn't want to, although there was no defiance, no pride, no relief, which she thought there might have been, when considering this moment. None of that. Only a desire to hide, as though she were in one of those dreams when one suddenly realized one was in the midst of a crowd, completely naked. "It can't come as a surprise to you. We haven't been happy."

"I was happy."

"How did you find out?"

"You mean did Deedee tell me? Yes, she did. We had a little chat. Quite a few, actually. She's got heart, that woman, which is more than I can say for you."

Rage sparked then. Exploded like a landmine beneath the suddenly unstable earth. Deedee? Why hadn't Deedee told her? Warned her? She'd had *quite a few* chats with Philip? *Betrayal*, a word she shouldn't have been able to use, given who she knew herself to be, but still, a flesh-searing brand of a word.

Philip's stance had widened, and his hands had gone to his hips. He looked like a cartoon version of a cop or a football coach and in other circumstances Angela might have laughed at him.

"I thought she was my friend. Wrong about that, I guess."

He laughed, and the bitterness sprayed from his mouth. "What the hell would you know about friendship? About loyalty? Nothing. I've watched you, my girl."

Girl? *His* girl. No time for that. The idea he had been lurking around, following her and Carsten, sent an electric shock up her arms. What had he seen? Them kissing? Embracing? Did Philip know where Carsten lived? Would there be violence? A shooting, a stabbing, a fistfight in Trenton?

"You're wondering, aren't you," he said, "how much I know. Well, I know it all. I know about the house in Mill Hill. You should close the fucking curtains. I know about his business. I know how much he's worth, or not worth, to be accurate. You want me to go on?"

"No."

"Look, I really think you're having some pre-menopause breakdown or something. It's hormones, and I don't mean to be condescending when I say that. I've read up on this. It skews the perceptions. I'm not condescending, okay? I'm trying to understand you." He pulled out one of the stools and sat down. He motioned for her to do the same.

"Is that what you think? That I've lost my mind? How very Victorian of you," she said, not moving.

He clasped his hands in front of him. Calm. Controlled, in charge. He was the principal at the school, the vicar in the refectory, the vice-president of human resources, so full of understanding, but clear about the rules. She considered how much she hated him.

"Suit yourself," he said. "But we are going to talk about this. We are going to come to an agreement. To an understanding. I think you need help and I want to be that help for you. Even now, Angela. Even so. Understand that."

Oh, how she understood what he wanted, what he expected. She should be humbled by her guilt. Lowered. Debased. And then he would be magnanimous.

"Philip, I'm sorry. This isn't going to turn out the way you want it to."

His chin raised up an inch, but his eyes were steady. "Honey, it's not going to turn out the way you want it to, either."

"Well, I guess that's up to me."

"Don't do this, Angela. Don't let a few minutes of stupidity ruin your whole life."

"I'm done. I'm just done." Saying that was like dunking her face in cool water. It cleared up everything. It silenced the doubt. It was as if she was writing the phrase on a concrete wall in indelible marker. *I'm done, I'm done, I'm done.* "I'm sorry, Philip. I really am."

And as she said it she was already walking out of the kitchen, her mind on her suitcase, and on what she would take (lingerie and photos of Connor and cosmetics) or leave behind (books and cookware and bedding), knowing that whether she took them or left them, each thing would be a fishhook in her skin, pulling her back into the life she wanted to leave behind, and that the pain of the tug and skin-split would be enough to keep her from ever coming back.

His cry was sharp. Like a wolf in a trap. Like the bear who has fallen into the staked pit when he might have so easily stepped around it. It might have been different. It was a screech, high-pitched and ragged, and two things at once: acceptance and refusal. *It cannot be. I cannot lose this. I am lost.* And at the end of the yowl: *I will die from this. I will die from love.* Wordless. But no less eloquent for that.

With this sound in her head she ascended the stairs and entered the bedroom and opened the closet and took out her suitcase, the small one, not the big one. It all felt terribly formal, composed, scripted, even. *There ought to be a soundtrack*, she thought.

Something sweetly sad but with a note of urgency. Her only obligation now was to see the story through to its inevitable conclusion. She'd come back for the rest of her things later, and a part of her considered calling Carsten now and telling him what had happened and that he was no longer unknown to her husband, but that none of that mattered and she would be with him and they would be together forever now. She ripped off her pajamas and pulled on leggings and a denim tunic. Thrust her feel into sandals. She threw things into the case … underwear and jeans and a pair of sneakers and T-shirts and toothbrush and what did it matter? She would be with Carsten, and that was all she could think of, even while the sounds of her husband's mourning clawed up the stairs and clung to her clothes.

She was a monster. She was a monster broken free.

As suddenly as it began, the yowling from below stopped and was replaced by the sound of his heavy body moving quickly, in full charge. She slammed the case closed and held it up in front of her as though it would stop a bullet or a knife blade and only then did she realize she was afraid of Philip, and then he was in the doorway, filling it, leaving no space for her to slip by. His hands were on either side of the jamb and he was panting, his face red and wet. In a small part of her mind she wondered if he'd have a heart attack. An attack of the heart. A dreadful choice of words.

"That's it?" he said, the words clogged with his huffing. "Just like that? You think you can just pack a bag and leave?"

"That's exactly what I think. It's what I'm doing." She took a step toward him, but he didn't move, and she stopped. "Philip, let me out."

"And what if I don't? I'm not finished talking. We're not finished."

She shifted the suitcase to the ground, pulling up the handle so she could roll it before her, use it like a plow to break ground if she must. She grabbed her purse from the bed and slung it over her shoulder.

"I don't want to talk any more right now. We can talk later."

"You're going to his fucking house."

"I don't know where I'm going."

"Liar. Lying bitch." He moved toward her; fists clenched.

He hated to lose. Philip did not lose. Philip got what he wanted. Well, not this time.

"Are you going to hit me? Lock me in the house? Do you think that will help?" Her heart pressed up into her throat and felt almost like hands around her windpipe.

"I should hit you. I should knock this stupid shit right out of you, you ungrateful bitch."

"Let me out, Philip. Don't make this into more of a cliché than it already is. You'll only look more foolish."

He blinked, frowned, opened his mouth, and then closed it. "Jesus," he said, "you really are as heartless as that, aren't you? You just don't have a scrap of heart in you. All these fucking years I made excuses for you, for how hungry you always were, wanting more, more, more. And there was me, thinking I could change you."

He had gone soft in the midst of his speech, deflated, wilted, and he let her push past him. His voice followed her down the stairs, but he stayed where he was.

"You're nothing but a starving ghost, Angela. Hollow inside. You're going to be miserable. Mark my words."

She was pulling out of the driveway when she looked up and saw Philip watching her from the upstairs window. His face was as closed as a drawn curtain.

Her hands were shaking. She drove a few minutes, toward Trenton and Carsten. Would he even be there? He'd be on a job. It was morning. That's right. It was morning. Early morning. How was it possible that so much had happened and it wasn't even …

what? She glanced at the clock on the dashboard … 9:00 a.m. That explained the traffic. Rush hour. People dashing off to their jobs, their desks, their obligations, their to-do lists, and inboxes as though nothing had changed at all, when only everything had changed. A school bus was stopped in front of her and she had to brake more forcefully than normal. The car behind beeped at her. She waved an apology in the rear-view. Yes, her fault. Sorry.

She pulled into a drugstore parking lot and called Carsten.

"Hello, beautiful."

"Something's happened. Philip knows. I've left him."

"What? What do you mean you left him?"

"Deedee told him. I can't believe she did that. I've left him."

"Where are you? Where's your husband?"

"I'm on my way to your house. I left Philip at the house. Where are you?"

"Driving to that job in Far Hills. My God, Angela, are you all right? What are you going to do?"

The parking lot was nearly empty, since the drugstore wasn't yet open. Three turkey buzzards were pecking at something next to the big metal dumpsters at the side of the building. Pizza crust? Bread? One of them clacked its beak and regarded her with its bright black eye amidst the red flesh of its face.

"What do you mean, what am I going to do? Aren't you going to come back? I have to see you." She was dangerously close to tears.

"I will see you, yes, of course. But I must go to work."

"Call them. Tell them you're sick."

He sighed. She heard it, the held breath. She could imagine so easily the look on his face. The patience he was trying to muster.

"I will try to be back midafternoon."

"I, I, what should I do? I can make dinner. For us."

"Yes, to eat is good when there is trouble. There is food. Steaks, I think. We will talk then, tonight."

"This afternoon, if you can."

"When I can, yes."

He was gone. Angela sat in the car and stared out at the trash bins and the buzzards and the worn-down little businesses on the street next to the drug store, the nail salon and dry cleaner, the Dunkin' Donuts and Baskin Robbins. She stared and stared, while in her mind the scene with Philip played over and over and over again. She heard a car door slam. A couple of cars must have pulled into the lot while she was sitting there stunned and were parked near the door to the now-open drugstore. She hadn't even noticed. People went about their business, their errands, their obligations, they went between the rooms of their houses and the shopping malls and their offices and schools and talked of what? Michelangelo? Reality stars? A man with his jeans slung low beneath his belly exited the drug store carrying a small bag. He walked over to a rust-scarred red car with duct tape holding on the side mirror. He glanced at her and nodded as he got into it. She turned away.

It was important to get to Carsten's. She rephrased that in her mind. It was important to get to her new home. She was not a homeless woman sitting in a parking lot, albeit in an SUV. She was a woman on the way to starting her new life with a man who understood her, enlivened her, enflamed her.

The last thing she wanted was to be alone right now. But what was she going to do? Call Deedee? Oh, yes, she'd call Deedee, but not from the car. Stores were open. She'd pick up a few things. She'd forgotten her tampons and she'd have her period in a day or two. Jesus. Did she have her birth control? Yes, she remembered tossing her diaphragm in her bag. She pulled into traffic. She mustn't let her mind run riot. One thing at a time.

Why had she pulled out of the parking lot? If she needed tampons, why not get them at the drugstore. Fuck it. She'd go to the grocery store. They had everything a girl could need, right? She turned around, hit the highway, and headed to the big box store.

A place like this was always packed. Already the lot was nearly full. This had been a mistake. She should have gone directly to the house. She'd think of it that way, as The House. Simpler. But she was here now. Out of the car. Lock the door. Nod at the woman thoughtfully returning her cart to the corral. Try not to judge the woman with the Juicy sweatpants straining across her mammoth rump. Wait for a car to pass so as not to get run down entering the store. Simple things, the sort of things one would do on any day. Inside the store the air was icy. She grabbed a small cart and realized she wanted special things, goat cheese with fig and cognac, lamb chops, plump raspberries, Devon cream. Rich and fatty. Sweet and decadent. She would begin her new life with a seduction of the senses. The tongue. The nose. The lips. Licking off the fingertips. Oil and pine nuts.

She went from one aisle to another, picking up things by intuition. She tried not to make eye contact. She refused to. She was a thing skirting shadows in the brightly lit bastion to suburban gastronomy. Scurry. Scurry. She made her way quickly to the back of the store, where the alcohol was sold. Champagne. They needed champagne. At the cash register, she handed her identification, a requirement for the purchase of alcohol, to the clerk, a girl with what Angela thought of as a rather alarming architectural hairdo.

"I'm having a celebration," Angela said.

"That's nice." The clerk looked past her, to the clerk at the next register. No, not past her. Through her. She might as well have been a screen door.

"I was in at five," the girl said.

"You stocking?" said the other girl, this one tiny, with painted brows arched high above her eyes.

"But they said I could move off the register, right?" The clerk put Angela's purchases in bags, a special sectioned one for the champagne bottles. "You okay," she said, pointing at the credit card reader. "Darryl says I should try to move to the bakery, you know. But that's getting up at four every day."

Angela opened her mouth to ask, who? But thankfully realized her mistake before she spoke.

While the girl kept talking to her friend, Angela left, wondering if the world had always been like this, a place in which she had so little solidity. Perhaps, or perhaps it was merely a question of transformation. She was vanishing from one life and hadn't quite appeared in her new one.

She would be at the house in twenty minutes, and then it would begin.

THE HOUSE WAS QUIET. She plopped the bag of groceries on the counter and checked her phone. No messages. Not from anyone. This felt wrong. Surely a crisis like this warranted phone calls and conversations and someone — Carsten — should race to her side. Something clicked. She jumped, and then realized it was the dishwasher shutting off. He must have run it before leaving.

This was fine. This was her home now. She would begin as she meant to continue. She would begin living the life she envisioned. An elegant house in an edgy, up-and-coming neighbourhood full of artists like Carsten, who certainly qualified as a landscape *artist*. She would work with him and side by side they would help create a new Trenton. The light shone in from the back garden, dappled by the trumpet vine, the fleshy orange blossoms hanging heavy and bee-laden beyond the window over the farmhouse sink.

She pushed aside the silver fruit bowl on the counter and emptied her shopping bags. She put the champagne in the fridge. A bottle of Chablis, three-quarters full, stood in the door shelf. She pulled it out and poured herself a generous portion, admiring as she did the pretty, etched Depression glass, and its colour, like a lake in fog. She had found six of them in a vintage shop in Lambertville and bought them for Carsten as a gift. They were perfect, special, unique, nothing like the fancy, but blandly respectable, Bavarian crystal handed down from Philip's mother.

She didn't care it wasn't yet noon. On this day, there was no noon, no night. It was a day unlike all other days and all the rules were gone, blown up in the explosion that had ended her old life. She drank, and the wine tingled on her tongue. She unpacked the making of this evening's meal, the lamb chops and mint and goat cheese and pistachios, the Bibb lettuce, grapes and pomegranate seeds (figs were out of season, alas), the blackberries and brie and frozen pastry (she'd make tiny tarts). She drank her wine and poured more.

By the time she finished her second glass of wine, and checked her phone several more times, she had made up her mind. She pressed Deedee's number.

"Angela? Oh my God, honey, where are you?"

"Hello, Deedee."

"I'm so sorry."

"So, you've spoken to Philip."

"Ed's with him now."

"I'm surprised you aren't."

A sigh from Deedee. "He said he knew, honey. I thought he did."

"You didn't think you should tell me? You're supposed to be my friend."

"I thought I was your friend, but since all this started, it's not like you've reached out to me, either, is it? I can't say I'm sorry he came to me. He sure needed somebody to talk to."

"You're going to justify this? You can't be serious. And what about me? Your *friend.* Didn't I need someone to talk to?"

"Darling, I'm worried about you. We all are. Philip is worried about you."

"Fuck off, Deedee, and if you call me darling or honey or sweetheart one more time, I swear I'll reach through this goddamn phone and strangle you!"

"Have you been drinking?"

"Well, can you blame me if I am? Betrayed by my best friend?"

Deedee's voice was low. "I'm not the one doing the betraying, am I? Not really. I'm sorry, I don't mean to hurt you, Angela, but I think you ought to turn that mirror around, I really do."

The rage was like burning coals held to the tips of her fingers. Peel back her skin and there'd be nothing but red.

"My God," she said, "you never knew me at all. All these years I thought you knew me, and you didn't, you're just like every other fucking Princeton matron with her head stuck up her hairless ass. To think I confided in you and you're nothing but a —"

"You take care, honey. You take care of yourself."

And with that, Deedee was gone.

Angela thought of throwing the phone and the satisfaction there would be in the heave and shatter of it, but she could not throw the phone. She thought of throwing the wineglass and the delightful shriek it would make as it exploded in splinters against the wall. She put both the phone and the glass on the counter, carefully, softly, as if afraid they might fling themselves into oblivion. Her hands were shaking. She slapped them flat-palmed against the granite, hard enough to make her palms sting. Twice she slapped them and cried out each time — short, amputated, guttural noises.

She picked up the phone again and picked up the glass and drained it.

"Yes, hello?"

"Carsten, I just talked to Deedee. You wouldn't believe what she said to me."

"Can I call you back please, in a few minutes? I am with a client just now."

"Fuck." She had started to cry. "Call me right back, okay?"

"Yes, yes, in just a small while."

She needed music. That would help. She went into the living room, picked up the Bluetooth speaker from the bookshelf and brought it back to the kitchen. The press of a playlist and Annie Lennox's voice filled the room, begging for the world to make it rain. Better. Angela would start to cook until Carsten called back. She opened a cupboard, meaning to find a mini-tart pan, but remembered there was no such thing in this kitchen. It was still, for the moment, a man's kitchen, with only the basics. She would buy more cooking utensils. But for now, what to do, if she wanted to make these blackberry-and-brie tarts. The short answer was that she wouldn't. She could make little galettes. She grabbed a cookie sheet. The dough was still frozen. She'd have to wait.

She had nothing to do. Why didn't he call back?

She poured another glass of wine and went out the back door, carrying the speaker with her, to sit on the porch beneath the trumpet vine on one of the cast-iron chairs. The music changed. Patty Griffin. *Let him fly*, she sang. It was lovely here, in the shade. A hummingbird hovered above her head, dipping into the long, nectar-filled flower of the trumpet vine. She wondered if she could talk Carsten into putting in a small pond. A water feature would be wonderful.

Why didn't he call back?

Maybe he was on his way home.

She texted him. *When are you coming back?*

Fifteen minutes later he had not texted back.

Something told her she mustn't bother him too much. He was, she knew, a man who did not enjoy drama. He enjoyed pleasure.

She would join him in that. Take a bath. Unpack. Back in the kitchen, speaker tucked under her arm, she emptied the bottle of wine into her glass, took another from the under-counter rack and popped it in the fridge.

Upstairs, in the bathroom she had designed, she lounged in the tub. Opera arias spilled from the speaker. The air was scented with ylang-ylang and jasmine, from the bath salts she had bought. She noticed her toothbrush hanging in the holder beside the bevel-edged mirror over the sink and thought how silly it had been to bring her own. Of course she had a toothbrush here already. This was the home she had been making with Carsten, even if they hadn't come right out and said such a thing to each other. Her taste. The furniture, the tiles, the bedding, even, that she'd picked out. She sank her head beneath the water and listened to the nothingness, besides the faint bass from the speaker (like a heartbeat). Her eyes were closed. She floated for a moment … then, broke the surface again like a mermaid, hair slicked back. Her hand ran along her thighs from knee to groin. Softly, feather touches in the water. No, she would not masturbate. She would save herself, her energy, for Carsten tonight. She imagined herself astride him, his cock deep inside her, rocking, his hands on her ass, her breasts …

Oh, she had better get out of this water, and keep busy.

She had left her suitcase in the bedroom. Now she berated herself for not having packed something sexy. Never mind. She drew on her jeans (no underwear) and pulled one of Carsten's shirts from the armoire, holding it to her nose first to breathe in his scent. What, after all, was sexier than a woman in a man's shirt with nothing underneath. It was best not to try too hard. She would be casual, a little bed-rumpled, and completely at ease. She flung herself across the sturdy oak bed, rolling, luxuriating on the top of the fluffy, white comforter. The fireplace with the original mirror above it on the mantelpiece made her wish it was winter. A fire, and her lying naked before it, would be the perfect way to welcome Carsten to their new life.

Kathleen Battle's voice came on the speaker, singing, *Hush, hush, somebody's calling my name …* slow, swampy, sexy. She remembered being at one of her concerts at the Lincoln Center years ago with Philip. Battle sauntered onto stage in a curve-defining gossamer dress of peach silk. Philip, sitting next to Angela, whistled low and said, "Man, does she sing, too?" Angela had been younger then, and had laughed, not at all threatened by the beautiful, talented woman, secure as she was in her own allure. Now? At her age? She knew Philip was an ass to have said such a thing, but an ass she wouldn't have to worry about any longer.

She wanted more wine, rose from the bed, and noticed she was just the teeniest bit unsteady as she descended the stairs. Why not? Why not dance with foolishness and joy?

Why hadn't he called?

She wasn't halfway down the stairs. Back up. Phone, please. And speaker. Music was essential to the New Life.

Down again … down, down. Kitchen. Wine. No. Why open a new bottle of wine when champagne was waiting? Fuck this cork. Thumbs and thumbs and pressure and … fuck this cork. Try again. Twist and turn and thumbs and POW! Oh, God! It left a mark on the ceiling. Just a small brown smudge, so surely no one would notice. Carsten wouldn't notice. Forget it. She considered finding a champagne flute, but it was too much trouble. The wineglass, oh, such a pretty glass, would be excellent.

And now, what music? She looked at the iTunes playlist possibilities. Tried hip-hop. Jesus. No. Tried "Sexy This Second," a playlist by Victoria's Secret of all things. She knew that one would be laughable. Then … "Sexy Smooth Voices." Sade. Erykah Badu. Corrine Bailey Rae. Women, sexy women. "Paradise." Yes, that was it. She swayed around the kitchen as "Paradise" morphed into Badu's "Window Seat." Sway and roll.

She checked her phone again. *Come on, Carsten.*

She had to talk to someone sympathetic, and who was left? Which friend? Deedee? Ha. She could call her back, but for what reason? Would she humble herself? She would not. Champagne bubbles fizzled against her nose. Who? Who? Who?

Sister Eileen. A mad idea? Perhaps. But hadn't the nun practically begged her to confide? She had. And she was a nun. Spiritual guidance.

She called.

Voice mail. "Um, Sister Eileen? This is Angela. Look, I'm having a pretty scary day. I'd really love to talk. It looks like my life is breaking open. I've left Philip. Can you call me as soon as possible? Thanks. Really. Thanks."

On the Find My Friends app, it looked like Carsten wasn't any closer to coming home. What the hell was wrong with him?

She checked to see where Connor was. It took a minute to load. Yes, there he was, in some town called Menthon St. Bernard, beside Lac d'Annecy. She wanted to see pictures. It dawned on her she hadn't packed her laptop. This was a jolt to her gut. What was on the computer? Had she left emails for Carsten? She didn't think so. Everything was on her phone. But she wanted to see where Connor was. Not on the small screen of the phone. Where was Carsten's computer?

Her phone rang and her heart leapt, but no, not Carsten. Sister Eileen.

"Hello?"

"It's Eileen. What's happening? Are you all right?"

She picked up the champagne and drank. "No, I don't think I am, or yes, maybe I'm exactly as I should be, but it's a mess and I'm alone."

"Where are you? I'm at the Pantry, but if you wanted to come over later, I'd love to see you."

"No, no. But it's been a hell of a day and what time is it now? Barely after two."

"Tell me."

"Philip and I had a fight this morning and he knows about Carsten. I left him."

"You left him?"

"I sure did."

"So where are you now?"

"At Carsten's." That sounded wrong. It wasn't just Carsten's, it was hers, too. It was. "I have my things here. I'm going to stay here."

"But are you all right? You sound …"

"How should I be? This is so confusing. I should be happy, right, but Carsten won't come home, and he should, don't you think? I mean this is big. It changes everything."

"It does. I agree. Where's Carsten?"

"He says he's at work."

"Do you have reason to doubt that?"

"No, I don't mean that. Of course, he's at work, but if it was me, I'd come right away. I mean, I'm hurt. I am. I know it was me who was having the affair, but it's a big deal and I want support. He should understand that. I checked on my phone, you know that friend-finder thing, and he's where he said he would be, but why doesn't he come back?"

"I'm worried about you."

It was possible she wasn't making a great deal of sense. It was possible she was slurring just a little. She wondered if she might ask Eileen to come over, but then what if Carsten came home, would he want a nun sitting around consoling her? Judgment, oh, judgment, how it scalded. The wren sang from her nest and the song was so exultant, so carefree.

"You don't have to worry about me. Or you do. But I mean, I didn't have anyone to call and did I tell you it was my friend, Deedee, who told Philip? How does anyone deal with that kind of betrayal?"

Even as she said this, she had a stab of insight. It was stupid, the betrayer complaining about being betrayed. What Deedee had said.

"No, Eileen, that's not what I mean. Well, I do, but it's separate, isn't it? I mean, I couldn't live with Philip anymore; it wasn't fair to him or me, but I don't know what's going to happen now. There will be so much paperwork and lawyers and I know it's going to be awful."

"Aren't you getting a bit ahead of yourself. Can you calm down a little?"

"I am calm. More or less." She held the champagne glass to her forehead. The bath had made her hot, and she felt flushed. The glass was cool.

"You'll have to take things one at a time, won't you? You're by yourself now, and maybe that's not a bad thing. I think you need to be still. To centre yourself. You know the contemplative prayer practice, don't you?"

"I don't know. Meditation? I did meditation at yoga."

"You sit, open yourself to God, consenting to whatever God has in mind."

The idea of sitting still for twenty minutes made Angela squirm. She drank more champagne.

"That's a good idea," she said. "I should do that now." The nun wasn't going to help her, with her talk of God. She got it, she got it. God in our hour of need, the guidance of God, the solace of God … but right now Angela was about ready to jump out of her skin.

"Do you think you can do that, then? Connect with God and ask how you can best serve God's plan for your good and the good of all? Pray for the freedom to choose God's will?"

Was there a hint in Eileen's suggestion that perhaps prayer would cause her to return to Philip, to be the dutiful, self-sacrificing wife?

"I was really hoping you'd be on my side here, you know? I mean, I was hoping you of all people wouldn't judge me, would just support me."

"Angela, I do support you, of course, and I'm not trying to tell you what you should or shouldn't do, only that, well, can you give some space and consideration to what God might want for you? What God wants is always so much more wonderful than what we want for ourselves."

"Okay, sure. I'm going to go pray now. Honestly. No problem. Look, I'll call you back later, how about that? Tonight, or tomorrow." *Or never*, Angela thought.

"Are you sure you're all right?"

"Completely. I'm actually quite excited about my new life. I hope you're excited for me."

"I love you, Angela."

Angela hung up. What had she been thinking calling a nun for support with something like this? Surely Carsten would be on his way home by now. She checked the friend-finder app. He hadn't moved. What the hell was he doing up there? An image of Carsten flirting with another woman popped into her mind. The way he ran his finger along his lower lip when he listened, his head tilted. Was that something he did only with her, or with other women, as well?

She finished the champagne. She was being ridiculous. She was the one with her extra toothbrush in the bathroom holder. She was the one who'd picked out the furniture, who'd helped him renovate the place that was now theirs.

Suddenly she felt quite tired, which was understandable. She looked around the kitchen, noting the pastry dough was thawed. It felt soft and cool and a little sticky under her fingers as she prodded it. No rolling pin, of course. Something else for the list. She fished the empty wine bottle out of the recycling bin and used it to shape the dough on the granite counter. She forgotten to sprinkle flour on the counter first, so it stuck. Didn't matter. She took a drinking glass out of the cupboard and used it to cut the dough into rounds, then folded an overlapping edge around each one, trying to make them look pretty. She turned the oven on and waited for it to heat up. While she did, she poured herself another glass of champagne, knowing she shouldn't, but the waiting was making her crazy and it calmed her. She unwrapped the lamb chops, put them in a pan and mixed a marinade of red wine and mint and garlic, then put the meat in the fridge.

She called Carsten.

"Angela, I am just about leaving."

"I can't wait to see you."

"I'll be there in about an hour or so, depending on traffic. You are okay?"

"I will be when you get here. I'm making a fancy dinner. I'm drinking champagne."

"Ah, champagne. Well, save some for me."

"I love you."

"I will be there soon."

And he was gone. Okay. Perhaps she should take a little nap before he got home. She had drunk quite a bit and she should eat something. A peach yoghurt and some bread would do it. She ate and finished the glass of champagne. The oven was ready for the pastry and she popped it in. She would take a nap. Halfway up the stairs she realized she'd forgotten to turn on the timer. Jesus, that would be bad. Burn the house down on the first day she moved in. No way to start their new life. She set the timer on the phone, but it wasn't long enough for a nap. She'd finish the tarts and then nap.

Back downstairs. She'd left the back door open, too. Couldn't do that in this neighbourhood, even if it was the nicest neighbourhood in Trenton, it was still Trenton! She was, she thought, probably more upset that she realized. She closed and locked the door, set the timer, and took it with her into the living room where she lay back on the white tufted sofa and admired the red Beljik rug, which they'd found in a second-hand shop. A simple room, clean and yet already with a lived-in look, a bit wabi-sabi. The rooms of her new life. She would be happy here. She began to drift away but the alarm pinged, and she rose, reluctantly, and returned to the kitchen to finish the tarts.

Cool the pastry, add the bits of brie, the dab of blackberry jam. Oh, they were pretty things. According to her phone, Carsten was about half an hour away, maybe less. No time for a nap, then. It was midafternoon. The sun had shifted to the west, but the kitchen was still bright and now smelled delicious from the pastry. She realized she had to eat more as her stomach rolled and she quickly fixed some granola and milk. Something to sop up the booze. She should have bought flowers, she thought, and went into the back garden to pick some hydrangeas. Oh, beautiful things! Some blue, some pink. She gathered an armful and put them into a big old ceramic vase, setting it on the island. She realized she'd drank more than half the bottle of champagne. Well, that was all right, but she wasn't sure she wanted Carsten to know she'd also drunk the partial bottle of wine in the fridge. She took the bottle out to the recycling bin standing in the laneway.

Derrick, one of the lawyers from next door, was just coming home. He poked his head around the side of the house from his porch.

"Hello, darling, how are you?"

"Excellent," she said. "Just great."

Derrick was the younger of the two men and had apparently been something of a beauty when in his prime, but had now gone jowly and thick-thighed. He wore a rumpled shirt and had his jacket slung over his shoulder and carried a heavy-looking briefcase.

"Air conditioning broke down in the office again and I cannot cope. I am not made for hot weather. A child of the Outer Hebrides. How do you manage to look so cool and composed?"

"Clever disguise."

He nodded. "Into the air conditioning and a shower for me. See you later."

"You'll be seeing a lot more of me!" She giggled, then felt silly and shrugged. She remembered then that she wasn't wearing a bra under Carsten's shirt. Seeing more of her indeed.

"I'm moving in," she said.

"Are you? Well, that's lovely. We should get together for dinner soon."

"We'd like that."

She went back inside thinking how good it felt to say "we."

She set out the champagne flutes, plates, and napkins. She arranged the grapes next to the brie-and-blackberry tarts. She rolled the goat cheese in crushed pistachios and found some water crackers to go alongside. She made the salad and sprinkled pomegranates on the top, popping a few in her mouth and revelling in the sweet acid spark. Carsten would surely be home any second. She checked his progress. Almost home. She poured the champagne, drinking some in anticipation, and then dashed to the powder room with her lipstick.

Yes, that was the sound of his truck door slamming. She was sure. She looked okay, a bit flushed, but why shouldn't she be? Pity about the nap, but never mind, they'd be in bed soon enough. She tousled her hair and reapplied lipstick, unbuttoned another button on the shirt. Yes, let him see that deep cleft between her breasts. Her feet were bare, and she liked the way the red nail polish looked against her sun-browned skin.

The front door.

"Hello?"

She ran to him, this big, beautiful Viking of hers, and she threw herself at him, loving the fact he was a bit dirty and smelly and hot.

"My God, such a welcome," he said between kisses.

"I've been crazy, waiting for you," she said.

"I am here now." He held her at arm's length, considering her face. "You must tell me what has happened."

She hooked her arm through his. "Come into the kitchen. I have champagne and food and I'll tell you everything."

"Champagne?"

"To celebrate!"

"You have already started, I think."

"I am in a celebratory mood. I feel like my real life has just been waiting to begin, and now it has."

His arms were thick beneath her hand, his body a tower, an oak, next to her. He was solidity and surety made flesh.

In the kitchen she poured him champagne, and herself, as well. She held the glass out to him from across the expanse of the marble island. He took it and was about to drink.

"No! We have to toast. To us, to our love, and our future," she said.

He raised his glass.

But his eyes were downcast. "No," she said, "you've taught me we must look each other in the eye and pledge our toast or else it means nothing. Eyes on mine, Sir Carsten!"

He smiled, and his eyes locked on hers.

"To the future," he said. And then, "Okay, we have had our toast. Now you must tell me what happened."

And so, she told him what had happened and who had said what and how stupid and unfair, but maybe not, maybe how inevitable it all was and for the best and how it had to happen sometime and how it was better even for Philip, or would be, in the long run. She came around the island to where Carsten stood and hopped up on the counter and spread her legs and she pulled him in, close between her thighs. "Philip will find himself another wife," she said. That was inevitable; men like Philip couldn't be alone for long, they needed someone to take care of them, but it wasn't going to be her. "I only want to take care of you, of us." She wrapped her legs around his, tucking her ankles around the back of his knees. Then she leaned back so her spine was arched and reached for one of the tarts she'd made. She nearly upset the plate and then felt dizzy but pulled herself up against the strength of Carsten's arms.

"Try it, I made them for you."

He dutifully opened his mouth, his hands on her hips. He chewed. "Delicious," he said. "You are as good a cook as you are a gardener."

"I want you to fuck me," she said, and she poured what remained of the champagne in her glass down the front of the shirt she wore. "Lick it off me," she said.

He lifted her off the counter and stood her facing away from him. He took her that way, with her still wearing his shirt and her jeans in a loop around one ankle. It wasn't what she wanted, although it aroused her, and she came in a spasm that made her hips bang against the counter and she knew would leave bruises.

He pulled away from her and tugged his pants back up. She turned and kicked her jeans away. She plucked a tart from the tray and popped it in his mouth.

"Good, right?"

"Very good. I'm going to take a shower. Want to join me?"

She did.

LATER, WHEN THEY WERE CLEAN and freshly dressed, she in a T-shirt and a pair of sweatpants she'd thought to throw in her bag, he in jeans and a shirt, they went to the back porch, where he would grill the lamb. There was a small table there at which they'd eat, and Angela had brought out the champagne and cheese and plates.

They were on the second bottle of champagne now, and by rights she should have felt intoxicated, and perhaps she did, but she could hardly tell where the high from the sex and all that had happened that day ended, and that from the alcohol began. She was dizzy with possibility and only wanted it not to end.

Carsten put the lamb on the grill and closed the lid. He sat down on the wrought-iron chair on the other side of the table, picked up a grape and sucked on it a moment before chewing it, and then said, "So, a great deal has happened today."

"That's an understatement."

"He knows everything, then."

"Yes. Everything."

"He knows where I live?"

She didn't want Carsten to panic. "I think so."

"Will he come here, do you think?"

"I doubt it. It's not Philip's style to fight or anything like that."

"Good. I do not want to fight him. I have nothing against him."

"Well, no."

A catbird flew into the yard, and landed on the birdbath, flicking its tail and flying off again without drinking.

"I mean, I guess you'll have to meet him sometime," she said. "It's bound to happen. It's not like he just disappears now. He'll always be Connor's father."

"I do not want to meet him."

"You might not want to, but I don't see how you can avoid it." She reached out for his hand, but it was awkward, holding it across the table with the plates and the cheese in the way. She let it go.

"Why should it be necessary?" said Carsten. "What is between us is between us. It has nothing to do with your relationship with your husband."

She drank, considering Carsten over the rim of the glass. "Philip's not going to be my husband much longer."

"You do not think?"

"What are you talking about? Of course not. We'll divorce."

He stood and checked the meat. "Almost done," he said. He liked it rare. He reached out for a plate and she handed it to him. He put the meat on the plate and tented a piece of tin foil over it. "We will let it rest for a moment."

"Carsten, why would you question whether I'll divorce or not?"

He shrugged. "It is not required because of an infidelity. It is not pleasant, of course, but not all couples end their marriages over it. My father and mother were married fifty-three years, and were happy, I believe, despite the fact my father took other lovers. My mother might have, as well. I do not know this for certain, though."

Parents? Infidelities? It occurred to Angela how little she really knew about Carsten. Did he have brothers and sisters? It also occurred to her they had never really spelled out what would happen in their future. She knew he didn't want a family, but she had never asked him to define what he meant by "family." She had assumed it meant children, a suburban life. She finished her champagne, took the bottle from the ice bucket and poured herself another glass.

It was hard to think. Hard to put everything that had happened, was happening, together in a reasonable, logical fashion. She was here. They were having a celebratory dinner. They had made love like starving people, and … what? It felt as though she was expected to ask a particular question. Something specific. Something definitive. She didn't want to. The smell of the meat was thick and made her a little queasy. It was cooler now in the garden, and the sun was a flame through the pine tree at the back. It was a great yellow ball of fire through the branches, just the sort of thing one might confuse with a burning bush, if one was so inclined. The sort of sign — big and bright and impossible to ignore — that pointed to a crystal moment. *Oh, pay attention*, it said. *Pay great attention.*

Carsten sat across from her and picked up his glass, taking a small sip. She caught him glancing at her from the corner of his eye, as though checking on her, as though waiting for something.

She would not ask anything. Not now. Not this minute. She had to catch her breath.

After a moment, he rose and cut the chops with quick efficiency, the blood pooling on the white plates.

"I do not think I want champagne with this. There is a bottle of Merlot. I will have that. Do you want some as well? I'll get glasses."

"Sure," she said. "Fine."

He disappeared into the house. He'd changed the music to play the blues music he loved. Howlin' Wolf was singing about evil going on, and brother, something ain't right at home. Jesus. Carsten had said, more than once, that he loved her. She was being an idiot.

He returned with an opened bottle of wine and two glasses. He poured them both good measures. He grinned at her. "This is good," he said. "And a good meal, too. Thank you for all this preparation you did on such a difficult day."

"I wanted to do it."

She served them salad on separate plates. That's the way he liked it. The European way, he said, to eat one's salad after the meal, which was good for digestion. She felt the urge to put hers on the same plate with the lamb, to cover up the blood, but didn't.

They ate for a moment in silence and then Carsten said, "So, we must talk, I think. I know you are happy this has happened, but tell me, do you know what you want to do now?"

And there it was. Oh, that burning sun through the trees. It might as well have been a flame-thrower. Carsten had his eyes on his plate, on the meat he was cutting. She understood he was deliberately avoiding her gaze. She wanted to believe this was because he was afraid she was going to reject him, that he was concerned she would say she was going to go off and start a new life in Bora Bora or someplace without him. The mouthful of lamb in her mouth was fatty and slimy and salty and she wanted to spit it out. She swallowed it, not without difficulty, taking a drink of wine so it wouldn't choke her.

She put her knife and fork down. She dabbed her lips with her napkin. She put her hands in her lap and sat up straight, just like a good girl. Howlin' Wolf sang about being built for comfort, not for speed, and she wanted to go into the kitchen and throw the speaker in the garburator. She wanted to listen to it grind and shatter and scream.

Oh, how still the world became when it teetered like the sun on the apex of a mountain peak, just before it tumbled down the other side. What a long and silent moment it was. And yet tumble it would. The world was designed that way, with a before and an after. She thought, with some tiny part of her brain still capable of objectivity, *I'm going to remember this moment forever, aren't I? It's going to change everything. It's going to be a tattoo on my heart.*

"I don't know what you mean," she said. "At least I hope I don't. What I want to do is what I've wanted to do for months. I want to live here. I want to live with you. I want my life to be entwined with yours in every way — in work, in our bed, in our garden, in the kitchen — I want to be with you."

Carsten put his fork down as well now. He ran a hand over his face. "Angela," he said, "you know I care for you deeply."

"I believe you've used the word *love*."

"Yes, this is true. I have said that, and I do love you."

She waited. She would not, she would *not* help him.

He hitched up in his seat. "I also said I do not want a family, that I was happy with the way things are between us."

She had become as cold as frozen steel. She was regal, she hoped, in her frigid fury. "I don't believe you put it quite that way. Not when I was helping you renovate this place. Not when I was picking out your furniture and your bedding and your dishes and fucking you. No, certainly not then."

"There is no reason things should change, Angela." He reached for her, but she would not meet him halfway and so he got up and came to her side of the table, squatting beside her. She pushed him back, so he had to reach out behind to catch himself from falling. She stood and, picking up her glass, went into the kitchen. She stood leaning against the sink, shaking. She was an idiot. She was a fucking idiot.

He came in and stood near her but did not touch her.

"Come on," he said. "You can stay here for a while, of course. But you must know I am not good at living with others. I like to live alone. We will find you a place somewhere. And you and I can still see each other. But I must be clear, Angela. I must be. And I hope you will forgive me if in any way I misled you ..."

"Misled me? Are you fucking kidding me? Misled me? You seduced me."

He ran his thumb and index finger around his lips. "That is not the way I remember it. You cannot say you were innocent. You wanted me, as well. And what, now that I turn out not to be the same man as the one you married, someone who will take care of you, because I want my independence and assume a woman of your age —"

"My age?"

"You are not a child, Angela."

How she wished he would stop saying her name. The kitchen, which that afternoon had seemed the heart of her new home, full of light and space and cleanliness, full of possibilities, now seemed stark and cold and, if she were being honest, a little shoddy. The renovations had been done so quickly, and not with the best of materials. Corners didn't quite meet. The cabinets were only veneer. It was entirely possible she was a child; possible she was a child just playing house.

"No, I'm not, am I?" She began to cry.

Carsten tried to put his arms around her, but she pushed him away. "Don't, don't, for God's sake, don't hug me."

"Angela, you are making things far more dramatic than they need be." His voice was calm and measured. So deliberate and adult. Some girl was singing now about chills and fever.

"Turn that goddamn thing off," she said. "I can't believe this. I mean, I have no one but myself to blame, obviously, but you couldn't let me have even one night, even a week, thinking I was home and safe with you, when all I am to you is a convenience that has now become inconvenient?"

"You are talking nonsense."

"Am I? Nonsense. You fuck me and eat my dinner and then say you're throwing me out —"

"I am doing no such thing."

"After I got champagne? Made this dinner?" She finished the last of her wine, knowing how idiotic it would be to insist that because she made him tarts, he should want to live with her. But he should. He should.

"Look," he said, "we will eat the rest of our dinner, which is lovely, and we will talk and then sleep and in the morning things will look much better and not so awful, yes? We will make plans. It is late. We are both tired."

Every nerve in her body ignited in white-blue flashes to the ends of her fingers and toes. Stay? Eat? Sleep? Talk? Make plans that didn't include them as a couple? Although that wasn't exactly what he'd said, she understood what he meant. Oh, yes, she could plainly see where they would be in a few months. She would be in an apartment somewhere, looking for a job, and he would be getting on with his life, letting her come over maybe on weekends, if he hadn't found someone else by then. She couldn't. Every second spent in this house would only be another reminder that she was wanted only when it suited him.

She could go back to Philip. Beg his forgiveness. She pictured herself prostrate on the stone steps of their house, begging him to let her in, while Deedee and Ed peeked out from the windows, their faces full of pity. She let out a strangled noise.

"I have to get out of here." She pushed past him.

"Do not be ridiculous," he said, but didn't go after her.

There were so few things to gather. Had she not been blinded by tears, it would have been a matter of seconds, but she had to stop twice to wipe her face and blow her nose. She threw the wadded, mucous-covered toilet paper on the bathroom floor and left it there.

Leaving two houses in one day? Quite an accomplishment, wasn't it? She had wanted freedom and a life of passion? *Well*, she thought bitterly, *I'm getting freedom at least. Free as a fucking bird.*

Carsten was standing at the bottom of the stairs.

"Angela, come on, don't leave. I do not want you to leave."

"What you want doesn't matter."

"All this because I said I don't want you to move in? My God." He was in front of the door. "I think you are hysterical."

"I'm furious. There's a difference."

"But I don't understand why. Is it so strange you should have your own place, if you are really leaving your husband?"

"If?"

"Yes, who knows, you might change your mind. But either way, nothing has to change between us."

"Too late, Carsten. It's already changed. Fuck it. It was never what I thought it was, anyway." Her voice cracked. "You said you loved me!"

"And I do. But," and here he had the good grace to look slightly ashamed, "perhaps there are more ways to love than just one and —"

"Get out of my way!" She thumped his shoulder.

"You cannot leave, Angela, you have had too much to drink, for one thing."

"Get *out* of my way! *Move!*"

He simply stood there and so she turned and ran through the hall, into the kitchen and out the back door. She was in her car. He stood in the now-open doorway, his hands in his pockets. She started the engine and pulled away into the darkness.

Where would she go? Where *would* she go?

Not back to Carsten.

Not back to Philip.

Not to Deedee.

A hotel. She could go to the Westin. It was outside of town on the highway. No one would know her there. Staying in Princeton would mean bumping into people she knew. Staying in Trenton was unthinkable. Maybe Philadelphia? She didn't even know hotels in Trenton and envisioned human trafficking and drug deals. There were the long-term stay places on Route 1, but they scared her for the same reasons. She had her own credit card, and a bank account with enough money in it for now, her sham nod to a woman's independence. Oh, sure, she was going to live the bohemian life, was she? She wiped away tears.

She screamed, banging her palms on the steering wheel. It needed to be released, this scream. It would explode inside her if she didn't let it out. She screamed and screamed. A right turn … a one-way street … another turn. All that mattered was she keep driving, keep moving, keep putting distance between her and …

She didn't see the man. She didn't see him until it was too late.

His eyes. Wide eyes. Open mouth. Hands up.

Hands up, it flashed through Angela's mind. The gesture, the chant of protestors. Michael Brown. Hands up. Don't shoot. The spark of metal against metal as … what? A shopping cart hit the grill? Things flying through the air. A running shoe. The man's body, strangely limp, as though disarticulated, dislocated. And her foot on the brake, but it meant nothing, her effort, and nothing stopped. Oh, but it wasn't a shopping cart, was it? No, not unless the man was sitting in it. It registered in Angela's mind that time had stopped working because she shouldn't have had enough time in the midst of this horror to think about time at all. But here she was. Wheels in the air now. A wheelchair? A man in a wheelchair? She'd hit a man in a wheelchair? Bang. *SCREEEE* …

Silence.

Her fists clutched the wheel, her arms out straight, pushed into the shoulder sockets. She blinked. And just like that, whatever had happened was no longer happening. Whatever had been happening had *happened*. Was over. Done. Unchangeable. Absolute. Immutable. All creation held its breath with her. She did not want to breathe again. Ever. She did not want to see anything. Did not want to hear anything. And her wish was granted. Only the huffing of the car engine. And she then thought that hearing screams would be better than this silence. She sucked in air. She looked.

The man was on the ground, between a grocery store and a small white church, with his head against the curb. His legs were grotesquely bent. His wheelchair, for a wheelchair it was, lay some feet away.

She thought, where on earth was he going at this time of night? In a wheelchair? Why was he here at all? Her fist went to her mouth. She wasn't blaming him. She wasn't, was she? The street was commercial on one side, houses with chain-link fences on the other. Lights were on, but no one was coming out. There were no faces in windows. The sound of televisions and the bass of rap music leaking from somewhere.

She was going to vomit. She might have wet herself. It seemed she had. Dark stains along the inside of her jeans. She got out of the car. As she stepped to the weeds by the sidewalk, she noticed a movement. The man. His arm moved. She swallowed back the bile that had risen in her throat and walked closer to him.

He had sunken, stubbled cheeks, white hairs against the brown skin, and his hair was speckled with grey and his mouth was loose, and she realized his dentures had been knocked askew. She reached out and, with one hand on his forehead, used the other hand to reposition the plates between his gums. The man's eyes flicked and opened and again she cried out. He looked at her as though he had never seen a human face before, and she could not tell if his expression held hope or horror. She understood that whatever happened to her from this moment on, this man's brown eyes would be the first thing she saw when she woke in the morning and the last thing she saw when she fell asleep at night (if ever she was to sleep again) and they would haunt her dreams.

But he was alive. *Thank you, God. Oh, thank you for that.*

She ran back to the car to get her phone. She would call an ambulance. She saw the dents in the front and the hood of the car. But no blood on the car. She didn't think so. Hard to tell in the dark. But no, nothing. She got into the car. Looked through her purse. Found her phone. She would call an ambulance.

She meant to. It had been her intention. The phone was in her hand. Just three small numbers to press: 9-1-1. And then so many things would happen. Police and handcuffs and jail and Philip and Carsten and, oh, God, *Connor* would know what she had done. A drunk madwoman mowing down innocent people. *Princeton woman, charged with drunk driving causing …* what? He might still die, the man. She would go to prison. She couldn't do that.

There is no one else here, she thought. *There is no one on this street. No one to help. No one to hinder. No one has seen me.*

A security camera hung off the back of the grocery store, but it was pointed to the parking lot, not to the street.

And then she was driving. But would anyone find him? In time? Whatever that meant. She hit the horn. A long, loud blast. Again. Again. In the rear-view mirror she saw lights come on at two houses. Doors opened. She was gone, though. Just a car on a street. She was turning down a street. It was a one-way street, going the wrong way. She turned onto another and another, her heart erratic in its cage of bones, panicked now that she would somehow end up driving past the man again, and people would be there now, and they would drag her out of the car and kill her, which she might well deserve, or maybe this was some *Twilight Zone* loop where she would just keep hitting the man over and over again. And then, another turn, and yes, there was the way out … onto Route 1. She was signalling. She was moving into traffic. She was not sober. Not exactly. Not close. But enough adrenaline pumped through her veins to keep her more or less alert. She was going where? She was going to Philadelphia.

TO DRIVE ALONG A HIGHWAY at night after having committed a hit and run was a tricky business. First, there was the problem of shaking hands. Second, there was the problem of the mind, which refused to be where it needed to be. The windshield was not broken, and yet it no longer functioned as a windshield, or more precisely, it now insisted on a dual function; the first being a normal pane of glass allowing Angela to see what was in front of her, the second being a dream screen, showing her a repetitive and grisly loop of what was behind her, of what she had done.

Within a few minutes, as her heart began to slow, and her cheeks became wet with tears, she understood she would not be able to drive for long. Shock might be setting in. She was trembling. Her teeth were chattering. She smelled of urine and alcohol. She had to get off the road. She had to find a place to think, to hide, until she could figure out what to do. She looked at the signs as she drove. That little bed with a roof over it. A hotel. Any kind. Yes, there. Remembering to turn on her blinker, she took the exit to Langhorne. She would change her pants in the car. She would get a room. She would find a cave to crawl into.

Sister Eileen

Later, Eileen would wonder if she'd been expecting the call. At the time it seemed to come out of the blue, but of course these things never come out of the blue and she had felt the nagging twinges of fear for Angela for months, hadn't she? Nevertheless, the aforementioned notwithstanding (a silly phrase her mother used to say when she was arguing with Eileen's father, meant to downgrade the seriousness of whatever it was), when the phone rang and she heard Angela's choked gargle of a cry she had the wind knocked out of her. It was just before her alarm was set to go off at five-thirty. The room was barely light, just a wash of pale not-darkness. No phone call received at such an hour meant good news. Angela, barely coherent, something about an accident, and help, she needed help. Eileen hadn't heard from Angela since the day she'd called from Carsten's, the day she left her husband, which was what? The day before yesterday? It took some minutes for Eileen to understand

Angela wasn't at Carsten's, and wasn't at home, but was at a hotel over the river in Langhorne.

Sweet Jesus, prayed Eileen, *guide me through this*. Another mess made by someone else that she would now be expected to clean up. *Really, God? Really? Really.*

It was a short drive and at this time of the morning no one was on the roads. She arrived before she really had time to wake up. She had prayed all the way but felt as though she could use another hour or two. And coffee. She needed coffee. She parked and walked into the garish lobby. Turquoise carpet, fuchsia curved couches, a daffodil-coloured medallion on the ceiling, beyond that a bar area with high black stools and a good deal of chrome on the walls. Blue tables and chairs. Meant to be cheerful, probably. A man sat reading the paper and eating eggs at one table, and at another a woman was texting with one hand, drinking orange juice with the other. Thankfully, the coffee service was set up. She grabbed two large paper cups and filled them with the Breakfast Blend, stuffing little creamers and sugar packets in her pockets. She smiled good morning to the young woman behind the reception desk and headed to the elevators.

Angela opened the door. Oh, dear. Her face was bloated, her eyes red and a little wild. Her hair was in tangles. She wore jeans, a black T-shirt. Her feet were bare. She reached for Eileen's embrace, and as the two women stood holding each other — Eileen still holding the coffee cups — Eileen couldn't ignore the smell of alcohol seeping from Angela's pores.

"All right, all right," said Eileen, herding her into the room and closing the door behind them.

Angela pulled away and began pacing the room, which was clearly designed for the business traveller. A tiny pantry area with a little refrigerator and microwave, cluttered now with evidence of room service — a couple of plates with remnants of wilted salad greens and a half-eaten sandwich. Two wine bottles and a glass. A desk acted as a partition between the entry and the bedroom. Dark green carpet, pale green curtains, white walls, a mirrored armoire in the corner, the wood a cheap veneer. Angela had walked around the bed and stood looking out the window for a moment and then turned and backed herself into the corner. The only chair in the room was the one at the desk, a black thing with wheels. It looked like a metallic spider in this otherwise washed-out room.

Eileen walked over and put the coffee in Angela's hands, wrapping Angela's fingers around the cup with her own. She then rolled the chair around the partition, near the bed. She gestured toward the bed. "Sit," she said. "Tell me what's going on."

Angela sat, and put the coffee on the bedside table. She hid her face in her hands. She sobbed.

Oh, thought, Eileen, *if she slides into hysteria this will go very poorly indeed.* "Come on now," she said. "That's not going to help. Sit. Speak." She used her teaching-teenagers voice, perfected from years of doing exactly that. *I can't help if you don't calm down and tell me what's happened.*

Angela emitted a strangled sound, pressed the heels of her hands into her eyes, then dropped her hands and sighed with a deep shudder. She sat at the end of the bed. She looked hollowed-out, faintly green. Eileen had seen it often enough on her father to know the signs. Hungover. She rolled her chair closer. "Come on. Let's have it."

The story began to trickle out. Rage at Carsten, the need to escape, the impact … and then Angela went stock-still, her mouth open, eyes wide, seeing something not in the room. She convulsed, clapped her hand over her mouth and ran to the bathroom, retching. Eileen followed her, lips moving in prayer, and stroked the woman's back while she vomited thin strings of bile and little else. The nun shut her eyes, begging God to tamp down the fires of her disapproval. *Selfish Angela. Selfish. Childish. Selfish woman. So careless.*

Would there never be an end to the ways one must learn to love? Would there never be a time when she might arrive at that place of peace, the vantage point from which all things were seen through the shield of Christ's love? The shield, the light, that transformed one's personal distaste to healing? No, of course not, no more than there would be an end to broken people, difficult people, to love, just as they are. Right now. Right here. Angela. Angela, who was only going to feel God's love in this terrible moment if Eileen let Christ work through her.

"All right, dear. It's going to be all right. Everything will be all right. You are not alone."

Angela slumped onto the floor, her back against the tub. Drops of vomit stained the front of her T-shirt. She held her head in her hands.

"Oh, Eileen. What have I done? What if I've killed a man? What if he's dead?"

"What man?" Eileen sat on the floor so she would be eye to eye with Angela. She felt a warmth course through her, which was surely love, but she felt something else, as well, something like a held breath. The air had become still and the silence tangible.

As she raised her head, Angela let out a shuddering sigh. Her eyes were less wild, but now they revealed a sort of blankness. "I hit a man, with my car. I hit a man in a wheelchair. When I left Carsten's the other night."

"You hit a man in a wheelchair with your car."

"Yes." Angela paused, but her eyes held Eileen's. "And then …"

"And then?"

"I drove away." Her hands flew to her mouth as though trying to catch whatever bloody, vile thing was trying to exit. "I left him there. On the ground."

"Oh, Angela."

This was bad. It was worse that Eileen had imagined. She had thought of Angela's husband, of her son. She had envisioned arguments and accusations and dreadful shame and self-loathing. But this? No.

Angela was talking. "He was alive then. I know he was. I saw him move. And I honked my horn really long, so people would come out and help him. Somebody came. I saw. I'm sure I did. I panicked. I was drunk. I was. Oh, shit. There is that. I was drunk, drunk, drunk." Her voice rose with each repetition.

Fat, oily tears glazed her cheeks and she wiped them away so harshly Eileen feared Angela would begin slapping herself. She reached out and took the younger woman's hands.

"And you've been holed up here since then?"

Angela nodded.

"You will get through this. Yes. Yes, you will. Even this. But now, I want you to get up, can you do that? Good. I want you to get up and clean yourself up. Wash your face. Brush your teeth. I am going to order some food. And more coffee. And then you and I will sit down and talk about all of this and determine what you want to do."

Eileen left her in the bathroom and called the Pantry, leaving a message on the machine. They could get along without her for a day.

By the time the food arrived, Angela was sitting on the end of the bed. She had changed into a clean T-shirt and with her teeth brushed and her face washed she still looked drawn and exhausted. She had been shivering, although the room wasn't cold, and Eileen had found a sweatshirt for her to put on, and socks. It was shock. And a hangover. And grief. And fear. So many things that all reinforced the knowledge that what Angela had done she could not now undo, no matter how much she might wish it to be different. She was quiet and defeated. Her hands lay like dead birds in her lap. Telling Eileen what she had done had calmed her, but also made it real in a different way. This was a dangerous moment, and Eileen, well-trained, well-educated in not only the ways of the soul, but the ways of the heart and mind, understood thoughts of suicide probably swept across Angela's mind like snow clouds. She understood that if Angela was to survive this, there needed to be not only reality, but acceptance, and the peace that comes from surrender, unconditional and complete. But first …

The food was on a tray on the desk. Poached eggs and toast. Orange juice. Eileen brought them to Angela. "Come on. You have to eat."

"I don't want any."

"That doesn't matter. You will eat. The coming days are going to be difficult, to say the least. You're going to need your strength. Eat. Do as you're told." Eileen rolled the black chair over and sat down, watching.

Mechanically, Angela nibbled the toast. She ate the egg.

It was a start. "Have you talked to your husband since you left?"

"No. I haven't talked to anyone. No one. I don't ever want to talk to Carsten again, and Philip? No. I couldn't think of anyone to call. Except you." All those acquaintances she had, and yet so few friends.

"I'm glad you called."

Finally, her hands around a large cup of hot coffee with plenty of sugar in it, Angela looked up at Eileen and said, "I have to know if he's dead or not." Tears filled her eyes again.

"Yes, you do." Eileen held her hands out, palms up, as though willing Angela to receive what was being offered. You realize whether or not this man died —"

"You think I don't know I left the scene of an accident? Of course, I know that. You think I don't know that?"

A flare of anger there. Well, of course there would be. Angela was still Angela.

Angela frowned. "Are you going to turn me in? Are you bound, like, is there a rule about this sort of thing?"

"I am not required to report. And I won't. I will hold this with you. That's a promise, but it depends on this: you can't hurt yourself and you can't go out and hurt anyone else. That's the bottom line."

Eileen knew the power of shame. Even after all these years, every time the memory lurched back into her head it was the same. She saw the look on little Jack's face in the second after she cracked him one in the mouth because he wouldn't stop crying. He was only eighteen months. Oh, the shock on his tiny face, and the red mark. His eyes so wide, and his mouth … that terrible silent moment, and then the screaming, shrieking outrage and horror from the little child who, up until that moment, hadn't known that someone who was supposed to love him could betray him so. This was Eileen's shame. Murder? No. Grand larceny? No. Rape? No. Just the destruction of a child's world with one selfish, violent act. Child abuse? Yes. And the years of trying to forget, to pack it away, to say it wasn't such a big deal. And her years of desperate need to rescue everyone else to make up for it.

And to make up for being unable to save her father, too. All those years learning to detach with love. *I thought we were done, Lord. I thought we were done.*

"Angela, I'm not going to turn you in, but I can't do anything that takes you further away from the one God created you to be. My prayer for you is that you find the rest of your self, not just the part of you that's done this awful thing, because that part is not the whole of you. And when you are whole, everything will look different."

Angela doubled over and dropped her head into her hands. "I want to kill myself. I want to die."

"I hope you don't. It's not a solution."

"Isn't it? At least the pain would stop."

"Maybe. Maybe not."

"Connor will never speak to me again. I can't go to jail. I can't!"

"Let's take this one step at a time. You've told me what you did. Now what?"

"What do you mean?" Angela looked up and frowned.

"How can I help you?"

"I don't know. You'll find out if the man's okay?"

"Yes, but you could probably do that yourself."

"I can't."

"Because?"

"I'm too afraid."

"I understand, but I think it's better to know, don't you? Isn't that partly why you called me?"

Angela closed her eyes and took a deep breath. "Yes, I guess it is. Will you do it now? Please. I don't think I can take this not knowing much longer."

Eileen took her phone from her bag and tapped in a query for hit-and-run accidents in Trenton. There it was.

> TRENTON – Police are investigating a hit-and-run accident that has landed a Trenton resident in hospital.
>
> According to Trenton police, around 10:00 p.m. Tuesday, 47-year-old George Clarence, who is wheelchair-bound, was crossing Brunswick Street when he was hit by an unknown black SUV travelling north. The vehicle then fled the scene.
>
> Clarence was later transported to Capital Health Regional Medical Center where he remains in serious condition.
>
> Police believe the vehicle involved in the accident has a broken right front headlight and possible hood damage. Detective Keith Danburg is investigating the case. Witnesses are asked to contact Trenton Police at 609-989-4170.

George Clarence? Sweet Christ. Eileen knew George Clarence. He used the Pantry. Angela might even know him. He had lost the use of his legs as a child. He had been eleven, racing his bicycle down a hill with some friends. They saw the construction on the bridge before them, but he didn't, or perhaps he did and couldn't stop in time. He didn't remember. He was impaled on a piece of rebar and it took four hours to get him down. He lived with his twenty-two-year-old autistic sister, Darlene.

"What, what is it? Is he dead?" Angela stood and backed up toward the bureau.

"No, no. He's not dead."

"Oh, thank God." Angela crumpled into a squat.

"I know him. George Clarence. You might have met him at the Pantry."

"What?" Angela's eyes darted about. She looked like an animal backed into a corner, about to dash for escape. "You know him? I don't know him. I never met him. I've never …"

"Well. He's at Capital Health. He's quite … well, fragile. I mean, his health has never been terribly good."

"You're saying he might still die?"

"I don't know, Angela. I'll go and see him."

"You're leaving? You're going to see him?"

"You'll be fine. I'll come back. Will you do something for me?"

"What?"

"Do you have any alcohol here?"

"Not anymore." Angela face reddened. "I got a couple of bottles of wine from the bar, you know, yesterday, I guess. I drank them. I just wanted to black out."

"Can you not drink any more today?"

"I won't. I promise. I couldn't."

"Good. Here's what I want you to do. I want you to consider going to an Alcoholics Anonymous meeting."

"AA? I'm not an alcoholic." She rose from the squat and sat on the bed, on leg tucked up underneath her.

"To me the definition of an alcoholic is someone who drinks in spite of the consequences. I would say you've been doing that, wouldn't you?"

"Well, that night. Yes. I guess. But it was an accident."

"Do you think it would have happened if you'd been sober?"

Eileen could see the resistance, the defiance, the defining characteristics of the alcoholic. Angela's jaw worked as she ground her teeth. Her lips were a hard line. Beautiful Angela wasn't so beautiful any longer. How often had she seen this defiance on her father's face? On the face of all those people, a few nuns included, over the years? Too often. *Enough, God, enough.*

"Angela," she said, "a person without an alcohol problem does not drink all day, drive drunk, have a hit-and-run accident, and then keep drinking all the next day."

"But I don't drink every day. I don't have consequences, not in the way you're making it sound. It was just this awful accident. And I've been out of my mind with … I just needed a drink to keep from killing myself. Why are you making me to do this? And why today, of all fucking days? Haven't I got enough to deal with?"

"I'm not making you do anything. You must make your own decisions. I can't make them for you. I'm going to leave and find out what I can —"

"Can't you just make some calls from here?"

"I could, but I want you to have some time with God. I want you to pray and think."

"I don't want to be alone. I don't know what I want!" She was on the edge of wailing again.

Eileen made her voice firm. Not unkind. But it must be clear she wasn't going to baby this woman. That wouldn't help. "God is with you," she said. "Remember, God loves you. That has never changed, and it never will. I'll only be a few hours. If I'm going to be longer, I'll call you. You'll be fine. Sit. Do you have some paper and pen? There's some on the desk. Talk to God. Write it down. Be still. Listen."

"What am I supposed to listen for? That's why I called you! I need help."

Eileen moved to the bed and put her arms around the shuddering, tearful woman. "And I'm going to help you. I am committed to your freedom, your freedom from shame, from guilt. It's going to take some time, but this is the only way I know."

They sat for a few minutes this way until Angela's tears subsided.

As Eileen left, she looked back at Angela. She sat on the side of the bed, one leg bent beneath her, her profile to Eileen, staring out the window. The light was harsh, and made the room look cold, as though there wasn't a single shadow to hide in. Angela looked small and thin and brittle. She looked, for the first time since Eileen had known her, old, like a woman closer to seventy than forty-five. Her fingers plucked at her sweatshirt. Would she pray? Eileen didn't know.

Angela

When the hotel door clicked closed, Angela felt it like a whip-crack. As though it was a signal to an unseen mechanical device, the air in the room was instantly hard to breathe. The room was a tomb. If she was lucky, she would die here and never have to go out into the world again. Oh. Not the room. Her. She was holding her breath. She opened her mouth and gulped in the recycled air, and then stood, stumbled to the breakfast tray, and poured a cup of coffee from the Thermos. It was so bitter. Wormwood. Gall and wormwood. Appropriate.

She thought she would feel better, lighter, once she told someone, but didn't.

Her shame was out in the world now. Dragged out from under the rock. Dug out from the earth. It was no longer the Man. It was George Clarence. A man with a family, with a history, with a life. Perhaps she had been a fool to tell Sister Eileen. She might have got away with it. A broken headlight and a scratch or two on the SUV. A deer would account for that. She might still get away with it. Sister Eileen had said she wouldn't tell anyone, and Angela believed her. It was sacred, wasn't it, for nuns, this keeping of secrets? And maybe she'd come back and say the man wasn't badly hurt at all. Just some bumps and bruises. What was the point then, of taking things any further?

Was this prayer? She thought not. Angela drained the last of the coffee. Her head was clearing, but in the clearing, in that absence of muddle, her thoughts sped up. Contradictory and sharp as flying glass. She curled up on the bed and pulled the covers over her, suddenly cold again. She closed her eyes but the instant she did, the man's face was in front of her. *No!* She opened them again and pressed her thumbs into her temples. Stop it! Get away with it? Was she the sort of woman who could live the rest of her life with a secret such as this? Was she? Maybe she was. She'd been rather good at carrying on a secret affair. More or less. Then again, maybe that's why she told Sister Eileen — to make sure she wouldn't get away with it. Some twisted instinct at self-punishment. If she was going to hide this away, then she'd never be able to see Eileen again. She couldn't bear that; couldn't bear the look she knew she'd see in the woman's eyes.

Her phone rang. She cried out. A mouse-like squeak. An image of police in the parking lot, surrounding the building, flashed through her mind. Had she been found? Did Sister Eileen lie to her? Bring the cops to arrest her? It could only be Eileen who would turn her in, because only Eileen knew where she was. She had been lucid enough the night of the accident to block the friend-finder app. Thank God. She supposed, if she was going to go on the run, she'd need a burner phone, or no phone at all. Whom would she call?

Who thinks like this? She does, apparently.

She picked up the phone from the bedside table. It was Carsten. Angela cradled the phone in her palms and looked at his name. She kept looking at it until the phone stopped ringing. It was as though she were two Angelas. One screamed at her to answer the phone, and flashed visions of reconciliation before her. This Angela said Carsten had realized what a fool he'd been. He would hold her and love her and see her through whatever this was going to be. But the second Angela. Ah. How dispassionate she was. She looked at the name of her lover as though it were some robocall, some charity she didn't believe in trying to solicit funds. It was something from another life, this name, this Carsten, and it was a life to which she would not, could not, return. He was a page already turned.

The phone showed a message. Should she listen? What was the point? Still, still, even so, she wanted to hear his voice.

Angela. It is me. If you don't wish to talk, that is fine, but I do not like the way you … the way we left things. I think we should talk. Please call me. A pause. *At least let me know you are all right and where you are. Perhaps you have become more calm now. I hope so. I do care, you know that.*

Ah, he cared, did he? There was no urge to call him, no desire at all. Carsten had become merely a space where someone had once stood. In fact, the space was large enough to include this Angela person, whoever she had been. For surely, she was dead, too.

Dead. Oh, God. What if the man dies? Eileen seemed to imply that was possible. *Please, no.* Maybe that was a prayer. *Oh, God.* She slipped from the bed to her knees, in the very pose she had prayed in as a child, asking this distant God to bless her mother, and her teacher, and her hamster. The hamster had died, anyway, of course, as hamsters do. Why remember that now? Must she remember that God, whatever that was, didn't fix things? What did Sister Eileen always say? God is with us.

Is that enough?

God, be with me.

God, show me what you want me to do.

The tears again. And yet, in crying them now she felt somehow as though she wasn't crying for the right reasons, or for the right person, even.

God, let that man, George, be all right.

What kind of prayer was that? Why did she want the man to be all right? Because it would be better for her, or for him? She couldn't answer that, she realized.

God, don't let Connor hate me.

An honest prayer there, at least. Would Connor love her, no matter what? Had she loved her mother, no matter what? She had not. And what had her mother done that had been so terrible? Embarrassing, yes, and unmotherly in various ways, but at least she'd never killed anyone. At this thought Angela feared she might suffocate. Her throat constricted, and only by uttering a cry, bestial and low, could she open it again. She got up and began pacing, hoping the movement would stop her mind from ricocheting around inside the garbage can of her skull, banging and clanking like a demented rat trying to escape. *God save me.*

How convenient it was, her mind told her, all this calling out to God when you needed God, when you were looking for a lifeline.

She crumpled to the floor. The room was darker now. Clouds had moved in outside and the previously harsh white had become murky and grey. Angela fancied she could smell a whiff of vomit wafting from the bathroom. Is this what prison would be like? Or jail? What was the difference between them? Jail for under a year, she thought, remembering conversations she'd had with people at the Pantry. Prison for more serious crimes with longer sentences.

For a moment she found this hideously amusing. All those times she'd sat, serene and kind as milk, listening to mothers talk about their sons and daughters, women talk about their husbands, daughters talk about their mothers. Robbery. Assault. Concealed weapons. Drugs. Domestic violence. How non-judgmental she'd been. Why not? It was nothing to her to be sympathetic to those unfortunates. Poor things.

She was one of them now. The criminal class.

Or she could just get back in the SUV and drive like hell until she landed somewhere in the west. Wyoming, maybe, or Alaska. Hadn't she read that half the people in Alaska washed up there because they didn't want to be found and no one asked questions? She could be a bartender. No, bad idea. She could be a waitress. Live in a little house with a wood-burning stove, and she could have a dog. She would be the sad-eyed woman with the mysterious past.

Oh, God, she prayed. *How I hate myself.*

She wished she had Deedee to talk to. But Deedee was on Philip's side now. Not hers. Another image flashed into her mind. From a book of photos called *The Family of Man* she had once owned. It was a black-and-white photo of a woman, in the 1940s maybe, in a courtroom witness box. She wore a tweed suit and a little beret. She was leaning forward, her face a haggard mask of fear. Her hands were open, reaching. Her mouth was open, and from her expression it was clear she was pleading. Underneath, the caption read: *Who is on my side? Who?* She had looked up the quote. The story of Jezebel, the desperate, pagan queen of Israel, Ahab's wife. After Jehu killed her husband and son, he came for Jezebel herself, who defiantly dressed in her finest to meet what she must have known was certain death. Jehu called up to the eunuchs in Jezebel's service. *Who is on my side? Who?* And with that they defenestrated their queen, her blood splashing on the stones, her body trampled by Jehu's horse, her flesh eaten by dogs.

It had shocked Angela. She had thought, surely, given the photo, it would have been Jezebel who cried out this plea. But if she had, the answer would have been clear. *Who is on your side? No one, my dear.*

Perhaps she should call Philip. Would he take the call? She imagined his voice. The fury, the heartless assessment. No more than she deserved, but what did she hope to accomplish by calling him? If the positions were reversed, she would not take him back. And, she realized, envisioning herself in her greenhouse, surrounded by orchids, dressing for a dinner with friends, sitting on the board of the counselling centre in town (oh, the irony!), that all that life, with its polish and sheen and luxury, was also over for her. Even if nothing happened, even if she was spared having to pay for what she'd done, she could no more go back to Philip than she could sprout gills and breathe underwater.

The canal popped into her head. The tow-path, where once mules pulled barges throughout Pennsylvania and New Jersey, carrying goods before the highways were built, now a place where people walked their dogs, rode their bikes, and went for long strolls. Sometimes people drowned themselves in the muddy waters. That was still an option.

Sister Eileen had said there was no guarantee the pain would stop if she killed herself. Wouldn't that be just her luck. Hell, after all, would be real and she'd find herself there, a chestnut roasting over an eternal fire.

"I can't go to prison. I can't. Make it different," she moaned, "make it not so."

If Sister Eileen didn't come back soon, Angela didn't know what she'd do. She couldn't very well throw herself out the window. She was only on the second floor and besides, the windows only opened a fraction. Had that been planned by the architects?

Oh, God. She wanted a drink. Or did she? No, she didn't. She just wanted it all to go away, to not have been. She didn't want to be Angela. She remembered an old joke: Why do you drink so much, asked Bill of Bob. To augment my personality, answered Bob. But, said Bill, what if you're an asshole?

And therein lay the problem.

Sister Eileen

Eileen sat in her somewhat battered Toyota in the parking lot. She closed her eyes and prayed. *This is the last one I want to deal with, okay? I thought we were through with this.* Years ago, when forgiving the people who had harmed her seemed both essential and yet impossible, she had felt the way she did now. It had taken a very long time for her to let go of the anger and disgust toward the priest who had done to her what he had done, and to her aunt, who had facilitated it. It had taken a long time to let go of her father's drunken carelessness and occasional violence, of her mother's inability to shield her children … all the usual and unusual pains of a life. She thought of the day she'd sat by the ocean, written the name of each of the people she needed to release on rocks she'd found on the shore and then hurled them into the waves, shouting, "I don't want them anymore! Take them back!" And that, the ritualization of so many months, years, even, of working with her spiritual director, of prayer, of meditation, had freed her. And yet, here she was with another messy, careless, selfish person. Another glitteringly beautiful soul hidden under the mire of misplaced desire and narcissism.

Eileen did not want to forgive Angela. And yet, that was what God required. And so, she sighed, and so, she and Angela would walk this path together. *But, let's be clear, God, I'm not happy about this and although I recognize things come around and around again in different form, just to make sure everyone's growing as they should, I think this sucks. Last time. Make it the last time.*

What to do first? She didn't want to leave Angela alone for too long, since she recognized the woman's precarious state of mind, but she had needed to get out of there for a little while. She needed to centre herself. She had been shocked, and she didn't shock easily. It was a combination of things. The drunken accident was a shock, but that might have been predicted. She had not, however, considered Angela someone who would leave a man lying in the street, with or without a wheelchair. Oh, she was in more spiritual trouble than Eileen had thought. She was also somewhat surprised Angela had chosen to call her. But she knew she shouldn't be. That was surely the hand of God reaching down in a last-ditch (although, of course, there was never really a last-ditch when it came to God) attempt to bring Angela home, back to the place of her soul's healing.

Fine.

First things first. She had to check on George Clarence.

AFTER LEARNING WHAT floor of the hospital George was on, Eileen stopped at the nurses' desk to see what she could find out before seeing him. The head nurse didn't want to say much at first, but when Eileen explained who she was, and that she knew George from the Pantry, that he was a member of her community, she relaxed a little.

"You people doing some all right work down there," the short, round woman said. "I know people come to you. You don't get all preachy and holier-than-thou like some of those folks who give out food at the soup kitchen do. Coming in from Princeton, thinking people should be grateful." She snorted. "Like they don't think they could ever end up in the line."

"You never know what's going on with people, do you?" said Eileen. "And George? How's he doing?"

"You know what he was doing out there that night? He was going to the corner store for cereal, for Froot Loops. His sister, you know his sister?"

"Darlene, yes. I know her."

"I guess she with some cousin for the time being. Anyway, she don't like to eat much and when she gets her mind set, well, you know, she's special like. So that night all she wants is Froot Loops and George going to get them when he gets hit. The accident fractured his pelvis, broke his left femur, left arm, and three ribs."

"That sounds terribly serious."

"Not good. And there were complications due to his previous injuries and problems with blood flow. A blood clot developed in his leg."

"Oh, no." Eileen's heart fell to her stomach.

"Yeah. They had to amputate."

Tears sprang to the nun's eyes. And she reached out to the counter to steady herself.

The nurse patted her hand. "Won't make much difference, really, you know. And I think he gonna be fine, given some time, you know. You go on and see him. Just know he on some pretty good pain meds."

George was in a private room. White walls, linoleum floor that had seen better days, brown veneer closet and shelving, a television on a metal arm, a fake-leather recliner, a window overlooking the parking lot, the various pings and dings and ringing phones, busy hallways and ubiquitous smell of disinfectant … in short, a hospital room in an older hospital.

He lay on his back with his head tilted to face the window, the bed raised slightly. The television was on, turned to a news program, but the sound was low. He was a thin man. His curly salt-and-pepper hair was flattened on one side. An IV line was taped to the back of his right hand, a white clothes-peg-like device monitored his heartbeat, and an oxygen line ran into his nostrils. One arm was in a cast and rested on a pillow by his side. A tent had been placed over the lower part of his body. His chest was bare, and bright white bandages swaddled his ribs. Various tags and wires were affixed around his heart and sides. A bag containing fluids and pain meds hung on a silver stand next to the bed. Would those drugs cause more problems in the future? Possibly. A computer screen on a metal table reacted to his heart rate and other vitals.

There seemed to be more equipment than man.

"Hello, Mr. Clarence? George?"

He turned his head to her, the whites of his eyes reddish, the lower lids dropping slightly. There was a crust in the corner of his mouth. He licked his lips. "Can you pass me that water there?" he asked.

She picked up the blue plastic water glass with the straw and handed it to him. He shook his hands slightly, and she took this to mean she should put the straw in his mouth, which she did. He drank long and deep.

"Thanks. Who you? I know you, right?"

"I'm Sister Eileen. I work at the Pantry."

"Ah, right."

"I hope I'm not intruding."

"I look like I got anything to do but lie here?" His eyebrow twitched.

He must have been handsome once, Eileen thought. Those cheekbones, that strong jaw. The shadow remained, but time and care and pain had had their way with him.

"I'm so sorry for what's happened to you."

"Yeah, sure. Thanks. Bitch left me in the street to die like a damn dog."

"That must have been horrible."

"And I bet even if they find that woman, she be white, so she don't do time."

"Tell me what you need, George. Tell me how I can help you."

"You want to help? You see Darlene's okay, right? And maybe see we don't lose our place. Hard to find a place got a working elevator around here like I need, and we lose that, I don't know what we'll do."

"Where is Darlene now?"

George's eyes had closed, but they fluttered open again. "Damn, man, these drugs. See why people like 'em. What you say?"

"Where is Darlene? The nurse said she was with a cousin."

"Yeah, but that ain't so good. Tiffany don't like her all that much and Darlene need her routines right. She don't do change so good. She be okay on her own in the apartment, if somebody bring in food for her, check in. She just sit in front of the television or read. She like to read. But she can take care of herself. Keep herself clean and dressed and all like that. Don't bother anyone. Just don't like to eat but certain things."

"Like Froot Loops?" Eileen smiled.

"That be Tuesday food. Ran out. My bad."

He was starting to doze again.

"George? George? If you can tell me the address where she is, and what her food preferences are, I will try to get her back into the apartment, and I'll see to it someone comes by two or three times a day to make sure she's all right until you come home."

She had to wake him up twice, but finally she got the information she needed, and he trusted her with the keys to the apartment.

"I'll leave you now to get your rest. I'll come back tomorrow, if that's all right."

"Always good to see you, Sister." And with that he was asleep.

Eileen stepped out into the hall. A policeman was talking to the same nurse she'd spoken with.

"What's she doing here?" he was asking. A large man, the kind who kept hitching up his pants, who kept his hand on his gun.

"She say she know him. She's okay. She's the nun who runs that Our Daily Bread Pantry."

"We'll see," he said.

"Good afternoon, Officer," said Eileen.

"Sister." He turned to her, looked down. "I'm Detective Danburg. What do you know about what happened to that guy?"

"I know he was the victim of a hit and run and that he needs support."

"You going to support him, are you?"

Eileen could see in his face that he was not a man who had much respect or affection for the Church. A lapsed Catholic? Many police were. And since the abuse scandals in the church had become public knowledge, and along with the decades-long cover-up, ensuring law enforcement weren't informed, well … she understood why so many felt the way they did.

"I'm going to try," she said.

"Well, good for you. That's just great. You know," he widened his stance and folded his arms, "It's my experience that people like you know a lot about what's going on in the community."

Eileen thought it best to ignore the "people like you" remark.

He continued. "Know anything about who hit him? Left him lying in the street?"

She had been expecting the question, but still, her heart beat a little erratically. "It's awful, isn't it? Hard to imagine anyone doing something like that."

"So, you don't have any idea who might have done it?" He was practically sneering at her. He had good instincts this one. Pity.

"Bad things happen in Trenton, Detective. I see it all the time, as I know you do. But we're both trying to help, in our way, aren't we?"

"Sister, do you know who hit Mr. Clarence?"

"Detective, honestly." She sighed. Oh, these men with power. Priests and police. "I certainly know that whoever did such a thing must be in terrible pain."

"Where were you Wednesday night?"

"I was at home. I live with several other Sisters. You're welcome to talk to them, if you like."

"I think I might just do that. Why don't you write down your information for me, Sister?"

"Of course." Eileen took the paper and pen the nurse, with a slightly embarrassed look on her face, her lips pursed in disapproval, passed across the counter. She wrote down her cellphone number, as well as her address and the names of her housemates. Handing it to him, she looked at his name badge. "There you go, Detective Danberg. Call anytime. Come by for coffee. We'd love to get to know you."

"Or maybe you'll come down to the station for a little chat."

"Whatever you like. And now, forgive me, but I have to run. I want to arrange someone to help with Mr. Clarence's sister's living arrangements."

As she walked away, she felt the police officer's eyes on her.

This was going to be tricky. She would not lie, and so at a certain point, if it came to that, she was simply going to have to refuse to answer questions. She sighed. *Oh, God. This is a fine pickle you've gotten me into.*

And yet, even so, as she stepped onto the elevator and then through the cool, institutional entrance and back to her car, she felt the peace descend. It had been Eileen's experience that life was only truly difficult when you didn't surrender to it. Once one discerned which path contributed to the highest good for all, including the self, and committed to it, things became simple. She supposed there were a number of things the police might do to try and persuade her to reveal Angela's name to them, if they did believe she knew more than she was telling them, and she thought they might. They might threaten her with withholding information, with impeding an investigation. Whatever the right terms were. But they could not compel her to speak. She would have the right to remain silent, and she would use that if she must.

Oh, she hoped it wouldn't come to that. Angela was in charge there, however.

One thing at a time. She sat in her car, called the Pantry and talked to Caroline. She started explaining that George Clarence had been in a hit and run, but Caroline broke in and said she'd already heard. George was a known figure around town, both at the soup kitchen and the Pantry and other social service places.

"He's going to need help caring for his sister." She relayed what George had told her. "Can I leave this with you, Caroline?" She gave her the address and phone number where Darlene was staying. "You'll have to go gently. Darlene is very capable, but this has been traumatic for her."

"Don't worry, we'll figure something out and get her home. Any idea how long George will be in hospital?"

"Well, I think it will be some time. The amputation's one thing. But the pelvis, the ribs, the arm … he can't use his wheelchair until he's much better. They may transfer him to a rehab, but I don't think it's going to be quick, even if there are no complications."

"Yikes. All right. I'm on it. Are you coming in?"

"Not today."

There was a short silence. "Are you okay? Related stuff?"

"I'm fine. Could use your prayers."

"Praying. Bless you, Sister Eileen. With you in spirit."

"Bless you, Caroline."

ANGELA OPENED THE DOOR so quickly Eileen wondered if she'd been standing by the door, waiting.

"Did you see him?"

"Yes. I saw him." Eileen urged Angela back into the room so she could close the door. "He's pretty banged up, and they had to amputate his leg."

Angela groaned. "Oh, God."

Eileen rubbed her arm. "He's going to be okay. I believe that, but it's going to be a long and, I suspect, difficult journey. We're sorting out help for his sister."

"His sister?"

"I told you, she's autistic. She'll need someone to keep an eye on her until George is home again."

"I can help with that."

Eileen's heart leapt. This was, perhaps, the first step. "Would you?"

"I'll hire a caregiver. Sure. I can do that anonymously."

"Ah, well, that might be useful, yes. Sorry. For a moment there I thought you were offering to be the caregiver yourself."

"I would, but I don't know anything about that sort of thing, autism, you know?"

"Of course. Come, sit."

They sat on the bed together. Eileen said, "Did you manage to pray?"

Angela dropped her eyes and plucked at a thread on the bedspread. "Yes, I mean, I think I did, but my head's just going around and round. I thought about calling Philip."

"And?"

"I can't. What's the point? Especially now. I don't want anyone to know where I am."

"You don't want to stay here, do you? In this hotel?"

"I hadn't given it much thought." She got up and went to the window. She looked into the parking lot. "I might leave. Just go."

"What about going to a meeting? Did you think about that?"

"I'm not going to a meeting."

"That's certainly your decision to make, but I am sorry. I think it would do you good."

"Not now."

Eileen let the silence build, knowing Angela would interpret it in ways that might reveal what she was thinking. A moment. Another. Angela's shoulders rose and twitched as though she was shadow-boxing in a dream.

Finally, she said, "Do you know an apartment for rent, anything like that?"

Good, thought Eileen, *she isn't planning on skipping out at least.*

"I think we can find you something, but do you want to live in Trenton? Most of the people I know are in Trenton."

"I don't care, really. Or, maybe I do. Maybe I don't feel like I belong in Princeton any more. Maybe I never did. Maybe this has happened just to show me that."

"You think God would hurt George in order to teach you something?"

"You're the one always telling me how everything's connected, how everything happens for a reason."

"I believe what I've said is that God will make good come from all things, even from something awful. I don't actually believe that old saw about everything happening for a reason, or rather I do, but sometimes the reason is that we've made really crappy decisions."

Angela made a sound, a little snort, that might be interpreted as a chuckle.

"I guess that sounded pretty self-centred, didn't it?"

"Maybe just a tad."

Angela began massaging her temples. "Look. I can't think straight. I don't know what I'm saying. I don't know what to do. Where to go. Who to talk to. I just need some time to figure it out. A place. Somewhere safe. Will you help me?"

"Yes. But you have to enter into this with me. You have to be committed to healing, to figuring out why you ended up here, and what the best way out is, what your new life, your resurrection, if you will, will be. You have to be as committed as I am. Because let's be clear, Angela, you can't go on the way you have been — not if you want to be whole."

"I'm never going to be happy, am I? I just have to accept that, I guess. I've ruined everything. My life, that man's life, probably my son's life. Philip's." She put her hands over her eyes. "I feel like I'm suffocating." She moaned.

"God wants you to be happy. He wants more for you than you can imagine. And I want that for you, as well. So. Here's who I can be for you. You're not going to change immediately, not perfectly; no one does. But I will ride hard on you. I will affirm you. I will call you out when you're not being your best self. I will walk through the pain with you and accompany you as long as you tell me you want it, and as long as I see you doing the work. That means, I'm afraid, going to meetings and praying and doing journal work and being accountable for what you've done, Angela."

"I can't go to jail. I can't do that. I can't stand the idea of everyone knowing … Eileen, it's too much! You're asking too much. You say you're on my side, but then only if I do what you want. What kind of a friend is that?"

"I love you. I care for you. And this is the only way I know to help you. But before we run down that road to jail, let's take it one day at a time, yes? Will you agree to go to a meeting? You don't have to say a word, but you have to go, if you want my company on this journey. Now, I'm going to leave you to think about that, and I'm going to go down to the lobby and make a few calls about getting you somewhere to live. I also think you should consider calling Philip and at least letting him know where you are. Will you do that? Think while I'm gone?"

Angela flopped down on the bed, making the frame creak. "Yes. I'll think. I'll think. I'll think. I'll think until I go mad." Tears were leaking out of her eyes, rolling toward her ears.

Good lord, thought Eileen, *this is like dealing with a teenager. How dramatic.*

Angela

By the beginning of the next week, thanks to Sister Eileen, Angela was ensconced on the top floor of a small house owned by Mrs. Simonofsky, the elderly Polish lady who lived downstairs. Just two rooms and a bath, but she didn't need any more than that. An old house in a quiet neighbourhood. A kitchen/living-room space with oak cabinets and a small wooden table with two chairs under the window, through which a maple tree was visible, a television, and a somewhat worn couch. The bedroom had a double bed with a blue chenille spread, a bureau, and a side table with a matchbook under one leg to level it. A gooseneck lamp on the table waited for her, in case she ever read a book again. Bathroom through the bedroom. She didn't feel she deserved even this. She still thought of running. There was something, though, about the nearly monastic room that she admitted calmed her. There was even a crucifix over the bed. Starving, suffering Jesus.

"Mrs. Simonofsky had the same tenant for years, an older woman who went to live with her kids in Chicago last month," said Sister Eileen when she brought Angela here yesterday. "I think God wants this for you. It's a safe place, and quiet. And Mrs. Simonofsky will leave you alone, but she's there if you need her."

Mrs. Simonofsky, a widow in her seventies, hair dyed an improbable blond, said she was glad to have Angela in her home. "I would," she said, as she handed over the keys, "be happy with almost anyone, because Jesus told us to give comfort to the homeless." That made Angela wince. Was she homeless? Hardly. Well, technically yes, she was, she supposed, although not in the way that her new landlady seemed to think she was. At least that meant Sister Eileen had told her very little. She was just a piece of human flotsam washed up on the shore of this little blue house in Trenton. She could hide here for a while. The only people Mrs. Simonofsky would not rent to were homosexuals, she said. They were not good people, she could tell you, because Mrs. Simonofsky, who still cleaned houses to make extra money, had seen inside their houses. "Oh," she said, shaking her jowly face in revulsion, "the things I have seen. I don't clean there no more." She said, "Making home is my gift from God. It is my prayer."

At any other time, Angela might have launched into a spirited defence of the LGBTQIA community, but not right now. She simply regarded Mrs. Simonofsky as another person of her kind — the people who hurt others. At least Mrs. Simonofsky was up front about it.

Yesterday she had driven the SUV, following Sister Eileen to this address. She still hadn't fixed the dents and headlight, and wondered a bit absently why that might be? Did she want to be caught? Possibly. At least then she wouldn't have to make any decisions, a responsibility-free state that appealed to her. They had stopped at Target on the way so Angela could pick up some things she needed: hygiene products and pajamas. No other clothes. She didn't care about clothes anymore. The few items she had in her bag were fine. She didn't care about makeup, either, since she had no interest in the male gaze. She didn't know if she would ever again. Then they stopped at the grocery store to pick up a few essentials, but mostly it was Eileen who chose. Angela found eating a kind of agony, like stuffing a foie gras–destined goose. Sickening and bloat-inducing. She had diarrhea often. All she wanted to eat were crackers and, somewhat surprisingly having lost her taste for alcohol, all she wanted to drink was seltzer.

Had she gone to a meeting? She had. Although she didn't think this accounted for her sobriety. What Happened (which was how she thought of the accident), had knocked the desire for a drink out of her. True, she had been drunk the day after What Happened, but that wasn't really *after*, or so she justified. That was still part of What Happened. What Happened ended only when Sister Eileen appeared. Since that moment she hadn't really wanted booze, although she certainly wanted to forget. Still, she went to a meeting, and Eileen went with her. Angela was surprised to find some of the people in the badly lit church basement room knew Eileen, greeted her warmly.

"I didn't know you were an alcoholic," said Angela.

"I'm not. We know each other from Adult Children of Alcoholics meetings." She laughed. "Some of us call that the graduate program."

Eileen encouraged her to get a sponsor, but Angela certainly wasn't ready for all that steps-and-salvation stuff.

It was fine. She sat with Eileen in the back, drinking coffee that tasted like a combination of prune juice and battery acid, and listened as a woman at least ten years younger than Angela, with piercings in her nose and lip and eyebrow, with tattoos completely covering both arms, talked about how awful life had been, how she got fat and ugly and foul-mouthed and fought in bars, physical fights resulting in black eyes and knocked-out teeth. "See," she said, pulling her lip back with her forefinger and revealing a gap. She said she woke up one morning in a pool of blood and vomit and accepted she was an alcoholic right then and there, and now was sober, living a terrific, serenity-filled life and working in a hair salon. For this she got applause, and then other people responded, saying how much they identified, because they'd been there, too. Well, most did. There were a few who complained about spouses and bosses and health and how even after all these years they wanted a drink and Angela thought, *Oh, great. Years of sitting in rooms like this and you still want a drink? Just kill me now.* Then they all stood, held hands and prayed. Oddly, that part was all right. She'd closed her eyes and felt Eileen's warm hand in hers and pictured blueish-white energy swirling around and around over the heads of all these poor people. If asked, she wouldn't have been able to say if she'd made the image up or actually experienced … something. It was disturbing.

As they were leaving, Eileen wanted to know when her next meeting would be.

"Soon," said Angela. "I'll go back. I promise."

So, she'd have to go back. But not today.

Today, she had promised Sister Eileen she would do something else, and she *would* do it. And she supposed the time had come. It was after 7:00 p.m. He'd be home now. She realized she was biting her thumbnail. She torn a hangnail and now it was bleeding. She sucked on it, willing her breathing to slow down. She picked up her phone and he answered on the third ring.

"What do you want?" said Philip, his voice like a hollow log.

"I thought we should talk," she said.

"I presume you won't be contesting the divorce?"

Oh, she thought, are we *there* already? Yes, of course they were.

"No," she said. "I won't contest."

Did she want to? No, she didn't. It was foolish to think Philip, always so on top of details, so proud of his ability to be one step ahead of anyone else, wouldn't have already contacted a lawyer.

"So, give me your lawyer's name and address."

"I don't have a lawyer."

"Too busy fucking to get one?"

She heard what sounded like ice cubes rattling into a glass. She could picture him standing in the kitchen, filling up the space. It would be spotless, that kitchen. Cleaner than when she'd lived there. Philip hated even a spoon left out on the counter. Yes, there was the sound of water from the filter spout in the refrigerator door glugging over the cubes. In a moment he'd be chewing an ice cube. The sharp crunching setting her teeth on edge. He knew she loathed this habit of his.

"I'll find somebody."

"Well, don't expect a recommendation from me."

"I'll give you my address —"

"I know where you are, remember?"

Surely there was a wild, wicked ocean between them, swirling with the million details of the past days. Days? Eons.

"I'm not at Carsten's house. I have an apartment."

"What? Oh, don't tell me!" Silence for a moment and then the shattering sound of him chewing ice. He was chewing, she thought, as if on her bones, and winced. "Oh," he said, "that is rich. Come on, spill. Why aren't you in the love nest? He threw you out?"

"I'm not going to talk to you about this, Philip."

"Wait. You weren't calling to see if you could come back, were you? Because I'm here to tell you that if I have my way you will never set foot in this house again. In fact, I'm going to put it up on the market, throw all your stuff into a big bonfire, and buy a place in the city like I've always wanted."

It seemed pointless to tell him he had never mentioned wanting to live in New York, that buying the place in Princeton had been his idea, not hers. Her heart jumped a little, to think she'd never sit in the greenhouse again, never have her fingers in the loamy soil she used for the orchids, never smell their intoxicating scent again.

Voices snuck into the room from the street. She looked out the window. Teenaged boys, with wafts of vape-smoke around their heads, laughing and punching each other on the shoulders.

"Fuck."

"Motherfucker. Fuck him."

"You would!"

She never heard street noises when she lived in Princeton. What a small, contained world that had been. Is this what Connor was like when she hadn't been watching? So much of his life, she now understood, probably happened when she hadn't been watching. Oh, Connor.

She must have made a noise.

"What? What did you say?"

"Nothing. Just someone outside."

"So, where are you?"

She gave him the address. For a second afterward there was this odd, full-of-electricity silence, and then he said, "What the hell are you doing there, in that neighbourhood? What sort of dramatic shit is this? You don't have to live like some Trenton rat. Listen, Angela …" Ah, she imagined him bending over the counter, leaning on his elbows, resting his forehead in one hand. She smiled a little. How well she knew him, even now. The difference between their environments struck her like a ringing bell. The stairs to her apartment led directly into the kitchen, such as it was. No granite counters here. No Sub-Zero refrigerator. No dishwasher. Just a metal sink, with two oak-veneer cupboards above, a small, impossible-to-clean oven. An under-the-counter fridge. For the first time, she thought how lonely Philip must feel, all alone in that huge house, so full of her, her imprint on every surface and fabric and colour and lampshade. She wondered if her smell lingered.

"I'm fine, Philip. I'll be fine."

"Whether or not you're fine isn't my worry any longer. However, I'll set up a bank account in your name, so you'll have funds until this all shakes out. I don't want anyone saying I put you out on the street, you understand? I'll email you the details. Don't be a martyr. It makes you ridiculous. More ridiculous."

"I may need some more money, like a lump sum."

"What for? You want to buy a place?"

"Something like that."

"We'll see. Get a lawyer. Have him call my lawyer."

Of course, he would never think her lawyer could be a woman. He gave her the information, and, after taking a moment to search for a pen, she wrote the name and number down on the back of an old magazine cover.

"Have you called Connor?" he asked.

She thought, *Reach right in and rip out my heart, why don't you?*

"He doesn't pick up," she said. "Have you told him?"

"Yes, Angela. I told him. I told him everything. If you didn't want me to do that, you should have acted better. Frankly, I don't think he's going to want to talk to you for a long time."

Tears, of course. "I know." In the silence that followed she wondered if he, too, might be crying. Had she been a different woman entirely, who had not done what she had done, she might have been tempted to ask to see him, to see what might be salvaged from the wreckage she had created of so many lives. But she was not another person. "I'm sorry, Philip. I really am. More than you know. But —"

"Goodbye, Angela. Good luck." He made those last words sound like a cosmic joke, and probably it was.

She looked at the phone. She wanted to try and call Connor again, but it was far too late in France now. He'd be asleep. She would try again tomorrow, and the day after that, and she knew somewhere deep inside that he would not pick up, and that continuing to call would only make it worse. She took out her laptop and wrote him an email.

> My darling Connor. I know your father has told you we are no longer together and will be getting a divorce. I also know he's told you this is all my fault. It's true, I have been an enormous idiot and have behaved very badly, and it is also true that I haven't been happy for a very long time, although now I've just made everything worse. You don't want to talk to me. I understand. All I can do now is tell you I love you, very much.

She had been about to write, *more than my own life,* but she had proven that wasn't entirely true, hadn't she? Besides, she wasn't sure that was the best thing to say. It smacked of guilt's noose, didn't it? No, *very much* was fine.

We will all be fine. We will get through this.

Did she believe that? No, not really, but it was the only thing she could say to her son, so far away, with a girl he loved.

> I am living in a sweet little apartment and will be here for the foreseeable future. You have my number. You have my email. Call, write ... whenever you want. Do what is right for you. Just know I love you and that I'm sorry and that I'll always love you, my darling boy.

She hesitated. There was so much to say and so much she absolutely would not say. She would not tell him What Happened.

How could anyone tell their child they'd done such a thing? And the man was going to be all right. That was why she'd asked Philip for a lump sum, wasn't it? At the time she'd said it the words coming out of her mouth sort of surprised her. Something, she supposed, was swirling around in her head about how to help the man. How to assuage her guilt.

She would go to bed. She would not look at her phone again until tomorrow. She considered hanging herself from the bathroom door. But that seemed like it would take a lot of energy and would leave a mess for someone — Mrs. Simonofsky, probably — and she didn't want to be any more trouble to anyone. And so she sat. She read a bit from the book on alcoholics the people at the meeting had given her. The stories were depressing and formulaic. And all that stuff about wives being understanding of their husbands because the men were cranky during early sobriety. It was written during the 1940s or something, but still. Hadn't they thought to update it, not even now, in light of the #MeToo movement? She nibbled crackers and drank a cup of decaf, not that it mattered. Sleep? A joke.

She turned on the old television and something on the local channel caught her attention. It was the story of a local woman, Annie Bright, who had been in a widely watched television show back in the early eighties. She had been driving drunk a few years back and had rear-ended someone at a stop sign. The woman she hit realized right away that Annie Bright was drunk and tried to take her car keys away, but Annie Bright fled the scene in her SUV and some minutes later slammed into the side of a car as the driver turned into his driveway. The man, Mr. Sampal, survived, but the passenger, his wife, did not. Ms. Bright had been sentenced to three years in prison, two years less than the mandatory minimum, which a lot of people thought was a travesty and that the judge had been influenced by how pretty she was, and by her modest fame.

She served less than half of her sentence and was now speaking out about the dangers of drunk driving to high school students.

Angela gazed at the images on the television. She watched the woman, roughly her own age, with hair the colour of wheat and big blue eyes and expensive-looking clothing, smiling and talking.

How was it possible she could go on with her life, after what she'd done? Did she really think talking to a few high school kids would make a difference? Understanding this was imperative. This woman, who had done what Angela had almost done, had paid for it, had gone to jail (no matter how short the sentence), and was now out again in the world, living a useful life, wasn't she? And Angela hadn't killed anyone, so surely there was hope for her, wasn't there?

Annie Bright flicked her hair off her shoulders and said being in prison was like witnessing your own death, and that most of her friends had deserted her. But she was sober now, had been since the accident, and that's what mattered. She tilted her head, her smile radiant.

Yes, thought Angela, *that is what matters*. Friends deserting her? Oh, now here was something she could relate to.

"So, have you had any contact with Mr. Sampal," asked the journalist, moving the microphone closer to Ms. Bright's glossy lips, "since your release from prison?"

A flash of annoyance crossed Annie Bright's face. "Well, no. I haven't spoken to him."

"Do you think you might? That you might make a public apology?"

Annie Bright was obviously trying to compose her features into a pleasant expression, open and caring, but she wasn't doing very well. She looked livid. Angela thought she must not have been a very good actress. *Like witnessing your own death? What about the other person's death? Jesus.* Angela leaned closer to the television.

"I apologized the day I was sentenced," the actress said. "I said it directly to Mr. Sampal. So, I've apologized, I just don't think I should have to keep doing it."

Angela snorted. *Really? She didn't? How bizarre. How could she do anything but spend the rest of her life apologizing?*

She turned off the television and sat staring at her hands, and at the plate of mostly untouched food.

That woman, she thought, *is going to be miserable the rest of her life, and so is everyone associated with her*. It was so crystal clear. She was the sort of person, Angela presumed, who would say going to prison might be interesting for her *narrative*. Annie Bright probably fancied herself another Robert Downey Jr. Anything that interfered with that take on events was, well, *annoying*.

Was this who Angela was doomed to become? Or was this what she already was? Some privileged woman, some Martha Stewart who might have made, you know, a *mistake*, but really, life had to go on? Feeling sorry for herself. Trying to justify herself? What good did that do anyone? Was that why she was having this furious reaction to this has-been television actor? Because she saw so much of herself there? Because they were no different? Not really?

Her phone rang. Carsten again. This was the third time he'd called. She hadn't answered the others but now, something about her anger at Annie Bright, and at herself; something about her sorrow over Connor and whatever one called her confused emotions about Philip made her want to hear Carsten's voice, if for no other reason than to snip away that final barb stuck in her skin, to simplify just a bit.

"Hello."

"My God, Angela! I have been trying to contact you. Why have you not returned my calls? Are you all right?"

"What do you want, Carsten? Didn't we say it all?"

"I know that you had certain expectations, and yes, I may be guilty of not being clear, but you knew who I am."

"I do."

"And now you sound very cold."

"I'm tired."

"My feelings have not changed. I want to see you. I care for you. There is no need to end things."

Oh, but there was. So many reasons.

"No, I'm not going to see you. There just isn't any point. Things are different. They've changed."

"What do you mean changed? Ah, you are going back to your husband, yes?"

"Sure," she said, since that would be the easiest explanation. "That's it."

"Will you keep my number? And I will maybe see you at the Pantry, yes?"

"Take care of yourself, Carsten. I have to go."

"You are not being altogether reasonable, to ignore what is between us."

Jesus. Did he really think she'd continue as his mistress? Even without What Happened, that certainly wasn't the life she'd wanted. It was never for her to be alone, with him floating on the periphery of her life. It didn't matter, though. What Happened had happened. It was not a bell one could unring.

"Goodbye, Carsten."

She hung up before he could say anything else. She doubted he would call again. *Snip. Snip.* Another thread attaching her to the old life gone.

She stood and went into the bedroom, although she wasn't sure why. One room was no better than the other. Nothing changed. The double bed. The floor lamp. The rickety bedside table. The rag rug on the floor. A full-length mirror hung on the back of the closet door. She saw herself. Skeletal. Dirty. Her skin grey. The sweatpants and T-shirt and cardigan all baggy and unwashed. She was useless. A liability to the world.

Without family. Without a home. Without her son. *Oh, Connor.* Without friends, none of whom she blamed, except Sister Eileen, who couldn't keep the disapproval out of her eyes, no matter how hard she tried. Without Carsten. Carsten. Carsten. Oh. Oh.

Angela fell onto the bed, face buried in the pillow, crying until her eyes hurt too much to cry anymore and then she fell into something like sleep.

Sister Eileen

She was finishing up some bookkeeping at the Pantry when the phone rang.

"Our Daily Bread Pantry. How may I help you?"

"Is this Sister Eileen?" asked a male voice, one she recognized.

"It is."

"This is Detective Danberg. I'd like to ask you a few more questions and I think it would be best if you came into the station."

"If you like, Detective."

"I like. Tomorrow, shall we say, if it's convenient for you."

She ignored the sarcasm in his voice. "I'd like to be here to open the Pantry and get through the busy hours."

"I was thinking two o'clock."

"I'll see you then."

She hung up and stared out the window to the litter-clogged metal fence surrounding the parking lot behind the Pantry. She tried to imagine Angela in prison and found it difficult. The women's prisons were, of course, less hideous in some ways than the men's prisons, but then again, they were more depressing. Mothers without their children. Women doing time for the men in their lives. Drugs. Despair. Gossip and fights. Fights and gossip. Well, it was as yet unclear if Angela would take accountability for the accident. Eileen might be in jail before Angela. This was the third time Detective Danberg had called her. The previous times he'd been polite enough, even though the hostility she'd noted at their first meeting lingered. When she'd said, during one conversation, that as a nun she was duty bound to try her best to do the right thing, he'd said, "I wish the nuns in Catholic school beating the crap out of us had felt that way, or maybe your idea of what's *best* and mine aren't the same." She had tried to apologize for any pain he'd experienced at the hands of the Sisters, but he shut her down, and she didn't blame him. It explained a lot, however, about his dislike of nuns. He'd gone on to ask, as he did in every conversation, if she remembered anything yet that might help the investigation. She said she hadn't, and she'd understood that part of his reason for calling her was to remind her she was still on his radar. George Clarence was still in hospital, but Darlene was back in the apartment, and the Sisters were checking on her. She was doing remarkably well, really, but part of that might be the result of her not engaging with the world emotionally. *Sometimes*, thought Eileen, *such emotional isolation might be a blessing. Angela, Angela.* Well, all Eileen could do was to keep praying, and keep the relationship with Angela alive. No matter how much the police might pressure her, she would keep Angela's secret until Angela came to the right decision herself. *Let it*, she prayed, *be soon.*

Things kept changing. And yet some things didn't change. God, ever constant, even while the world danced and tilted and struggled. Even when God wasn't speaking to her. Even then, yes …

The river of faith flowed on, sometimes wild and white-capped, sometimes placid and calm, but always itself. The trick was to get your feet up off the bottom, not to try to swim against the current but to let the water carry you where it would, trusting in the destination and the water's fidelity to you, to the weight of your body. Even in the rapids? Yes, even there.

EILEEN NEEDED TO SPEAK with her spiritual director, Sister Felida. She drove to the Mother House, praying as she drove for discernment and guidance.

She believed God was with Angela, but still … when she thought of Angela two things came into her head: the woman's nonchalant way of moving through the world, as though she expected things to flow around her, always showing her in the best light and making allowances, her utter selfishness and self-serving, even now, post-accident; and the physicality of her, the languid way she moved, the … oh, there was no other word for it … the sexuality of the woman.

These two things, combined with her inability to be satisfied, to sit still, to reflect, had led her to this terrible place. And, oh, how the circle of people adversely affected by her kept widening. It was infuriating. Enraging, almost, if Eileen were someone so inclined. Which she wasn't, she thought, not anymore. Or was she?

If she was to love the neighbour without distinction, she must do so here. She mustn't judge Angela, only try to see her as God saw her.

With gratitude, and a loosening of her grip on the wheel, she pulled into the parking lot of the grey stone house where Felida lived with six other Sisters, just down the road from the Mother House. As she walked up the path, it began to rain, and the stone beneath her feet turned from being the colour of a pigeon's wing to shiny charcoal. Thunder rumbled in the distance over Philadelphia.

Felida waited for her in the hallway and within a few moments they were sitting in the living room, which was largely unused except for these sorts of meetings. The house had been very grand at one time, a place of servants and formal dinners, built by a Philadelphia financier in the 1920s. When he had lost his money in the Great Depression, it had, like its owner, fallen on hard times, going from hand to hand, even housing orphan boys at one point, before the Sisters of Saint Joseph bought it in the 1980s.

The Sisters who lived there cared for the old place, but felt it was all a bit too grand for them, with the butler's pantry and high-ceilinged salons, which they used mostly for seminars open to the public, on subjects like contemplative prayer and how to be of service in the community. But this one rather cozy room, the leaded-glass windows, the bookshelves, the huge old fireplace, the window seat and low, coffered ceiling, gave the impression of, perhaps, an idealized convent setting, nestled and cloistered and hushed. Talks of importance and intimacy were held here, over cups of tea and biscuits.

Now, Felida sat in an old burgundy horsehair chair near the fireplace. She wore navy blue slacks and a cotton-candy-pink T-shirt. Eileen sat on the other side of the fireplace in a chair meant to be tufted red leather, but was irrefutably imitation, and it creaked when she moved. The room was dark, as it would have been even had it not been raining. The moderate shower that had begun as Eileen arrived was now alternating with raging torrents that made her feel as if she were crouched in a cave behind a waterfall, perhaps the hermitage of one of the Desert Mothers who sought nothing but silence and communion with God.

Laughter came from somewhere in the house. Someone was playing classical music, something by Mozart? Chopin? A piano something. Someone was talking on the phone in the hall.

Felida's intonation rose. She was asking Eileen something …

"What do you fear will happen to this woman?" Felida's head was cocked to the side, her eyes earnest.

"I fear she'll never come to terms with herself, with God. I fear she'll spend the rest of her life running and fighting and never realizing what she wants is her own soul, in God's hands."

"You care about her deeply; I can see that. How does it make you feel that you are offering your hand, your help, and she doesn't seem to want to take it?"

"She takes the material things, but not the spiritual. It breaks my heart. I feel helpless."

Felida nodded. "Imagine how God feels. Imagine how Christ felt, with this wonderful gift just waiting to be claimed. This is the grief of God."

Sorrow swelled in Eileen. Yes. The vastness of God, and the loneliness. Yes, the loneliness of God, of Christ in the garden, knowing something awful must come, knowing it and having to accept it. She had her own dark nights of the soul. Had thought they were over, more fool she.

"But more, too. I also feel something else. I feel a kind of anger."

Felida nodded, which encouraged Eileen to continue.

"There's something careless about her." She struggled for the words. "I can't go into all the details, but she's hurt people, a number of them, in a number of ways. She has certainly misused her sexuality."

"Hmm. Well, let's talk about female sexuality." Felida ran her finger around the rim of her teacup. "There's nothing wrong with sexuality, with enjoying one's body. But anything taken to the extreme will hurt people. It's an archetype, isn't it? The *femme fatale*. The woman whose worth is measured by her allure. It's a delightful persona to explore when appropriate, but like any archetype, one can become trapped in it."

It dawned on Eileen, not for the first time, how incredibly lucky she was to have someone like Felida in her life. Or, *Dr.* Felida, as she might be called. With multiple degrees in theology and psychology and literature to her name, she was one of the most widely read people Eileen knew, and reminded her a good deal of Sister Elizabeth Johnson, Eileen's mentor in college, who had taught her so much about the theology of Mary. Like Elizabeth, Felida never judged, although she sometimes mirrored, as Eileen suspected she was doing now.

"Consider the enchantress Circe," she was saying. "She's one of the symbols of this archetype, and what did she do in the *Odyssey*? She turned men into pigs. While it's true the *femme fatale* can be interpreted as the embodied rebellion against traditional gender roles, Jung saw it, rightly I think, as the lowest manifestation of the *anima.* Such a woman is irresistible on a certain level, and extremely dangerous, but what about the danger she presents not only to those around her, but to her own soul?

"Which bring us to your soul, of course." She smiled softly and tilted her head to the side. "Being subjected to someone's insatiable sexual desires has blocked you from your own rage, don't you think? Angela, in this way, serves you. She enables you to access that rage and in accessing that rage you come home to your own self, where …"

"Where God waits," said Eileen.

There was a great crack of thunder and flash of light, and then the power went out.

Felida laughed. "Oh, for heaven's sake," she said, "God certainly isn't being very subtle today, is She?"

Eileen had almost spilled her tea. "Did the house get hit, do you think?"

"I doubt it." Felida cocked her head, listening. There was silence, nothing but the rain falling, and then someone laughed again, and the piano music began again. "No, I don't think so." The older sister rose and took some matches from beside the fireplace. She struck one and lit three candles, two on the mantel and one on the table between them. "Power goes out all the time here. Never for long, though, thank goodness." She sat down again. "Where was I? Oh, yes …" Felida shook her head. "I would think that's a terrifically painful space to occupy. I always remember poor Lilith, Adam's first wife, according to Jewish legend. His equal, we're told, powerful and sexual. Adam wanted to rule over her — and from what you've told me, that's what Angela's husband wanted to do, be it through negligent kindness and the sort of false security that demands servitude, or through outright cruelty, and the discounting of her personality. That's what those men, I can't call them priests, did to you, isn't it? Servitude, cruelty, a discounting of self. When Lilith could take no more, she fled the garden. After that there are a lot of stories about her being a savage seductress who killed her children. Useful stories if you want to study the reinforcing legends of the patriarchy."

Felida chuckled. "But more to the point, her rage, such a potent force, rose up in her and forced her to freedom outside the garden, which certainly wasn't a paradise for her. My point is, this archetype is wonderful if it isn't repressed, but if one makes peace with it, and acknowledges the wound."

The storm, having made its point, was moving away, and the rain against the windows was softening.

"I see that. Seems God's inviting me to do some soul-work around that." It rattled her to see so clearly what she hadn't seen, but it made sense. What bothered us about the *other* was always what bothered us about the *self*. "I'll bring it to God. It feels right. One more thing, though. I'm holding space for Angela, and for her wounds, her pain, and that may lead to certain, um, complications.

There are things she has told me I've promised I would keep safe insofar as I can. Quite serious things."

"Let me ask you, Sister, are these things of a legal nature?"

"I can't say."

"I see. Well, you have been in discernment, I assume, and feel you are taking the path God wishes you to take?"

"Yes."

"So, this helplessness you're feeling, and your fear, which I share, that Angela may be headed for a difficult time … has there been another time in your life when you've felt that?"

Eileen made a small sound that might have been a laugh. Oh, how breath was hard to get into the lungs at such a time. "There is. Something I've never told anyone."

"Would you like to talk about it now?"

"No. The opposite, but I have to." She brought her fingertips to her forehead and massaged it, as though trying to erase the memories there. No such luck. "When I was twelve, I babysat for a neighbour. A little boy, a year and a half old, named Jack. He, he wouldn't stop crying. I was at my wits' end. Well, no excuses." Breathe. Breathe. "I hit him. Hard. I slapped his face. I still remember his face in front of me, like he's sitting right there. It took a second, you know. He was in shock, I think; he'd never been hit before, I'm sure. He just looked at me, mouth open, and then the wailing started. And the red mark showed up. There was so much despair." Eileen was crying herself now and Felida passed her a box of tissues. "So much anguish in that cry. I felt, feel, like I ruined the world for him. I can't even now, I can't …" She made a sound and then couldn't go on.

Felida let her cry for a moment and then said, "You can't get out from under the guilt, just like Angela can't, and you recognize that fear, just as you recognize the anger. She's quite a gift to you, and a reminder that God makes good things come, even from bad things."

"I try to believe that."

"Slapping a baby, like causing whatever harm Anglea has caused, is a bad thing. It's a sin. We can't soften that."

"No, we can't."

"But neither can we martyr ourselves on that cross; we can't keep self-flagellating, provided we are truly remorseful and willing to make amends. Do you know what became of Jack?"

"He's a pediatrician in Newark, family, three kids."

"Well, who knows. God might have taken that very moment to plant a seed so that Jack grew up wanting to protect and heal children. It's all very mysterious, this great weaving, isn't it?"

"Trust God, you're saying."

"Clever woman. Now, this brings me to something else. I wonder if these feelings might not be about your own lack of connection with God. Is that possible? Do you feel deeply connected to God? What's your personal prayer life like these days?"

Eileen was about to say it was fine, but as she opened her mouth, she realized it wasn't. She said, "I don't know. I thought it was all right, but I don't know. Maybe I don't feel" — she was surprised to realize her hands were trembling — "like I've ever really been in God's presence." She put her hand over her mouth. "Is that possible? I mean, after all these years?"

Felida reached out and took her hand. "The silence of God. Oh, this is a terrible place to be. Full of fear and helplessness. We all experience it at one time or another. Even Mother Teresa suffered unspeakably, and for decades, with a sense of being left in the darkness without God's presence."

Eileen plucked another tissue from the nearby box.

"Remember that the longing you feel right now, this great hole in your soul, if you will, is God's longing for you."

"I should know all this, at my age, shouldn't I?"

"Oh, you do know it. But life, as you also know, is cyclical. A spiral dance, as some call it. We go around and round, coming back to familiar spiritual territory, although never in precisely the same way. As Heraclitus put it, 'No man ever steps in the same river twice, for it's not the same river and he's not the same man.' Perhaps now the invitation is for you to rest there for a while. It's not as though you have much choice, is it? But you can rail against it —"

"Like Angela's doing — railing against her dark feelings."

"Well, we don't know what God wants for her, do we? Not every marriage should survive."

"I've said that to her, I even said it before she destroyed her marriage, but she's just so hell-bent, you'll pardon the expression, on having her own way. I fear she'll run before she learns, before she realizes."

"And that's what frustrates you? That she discounts God's will, seeking only her own?"

She hated to say it, because even as Felida asked the question, she knew not only what the answer was, but what it meant. "Yes, I think so."

"And so, I might suggest, you are feeling some frustration with yourself. If you are experiencing God's silence, and this guilt, and this anger, it's very difficult to know what God wishes for us, and we're uncomfortable experiencing the silence fully, uncomfortable accepting it. Have you ever heard the story of the Hassidic Jews who were imprisoned in a terrible jail? All of them struggled to rise above their suffering and keep a gentle and joyful outlook, except for one Rabbi, who wept. When his followers asked why he didn't accept these hardships as signs of God's love he replied, 'When God sends bitterness, the least I can do is to feel it.'"

Eileen was able to smile through her tears.

"So, perhaps all that you feel is as much for your own soul as for that of Angela's or even little Jack, who may be grown now, but still lives as that little boy in your heart. I think, when you come to terms with that, Eileen, when you bring even this despair to God and let God heal it, you will also be able to trust that God holds not only you in a loving embrace, but also everyone else, always."

Felida let go of Eileen's hand and poured her more tea. "Drink that. It's the British in me. I believe in tea *and* prayer. Spend some time with St. John of the Cross, and his dark night of the soul. 'Endurance of darkness is preparation for great light.' The gift of tears. The gift of holy desperation. And remember, my dear, even Jesus wept."

An hour later, as Eileen was leaving, the lights came back on and the sky cleared, showing stars and a full moon. The air smelled washed and rinsed with rosewater, the scent rising up from the plants that edged the walkway. She drove back to Trenton feeling that perhaps all would be well after all and perhaps she didn't have to hold the reins of life quite so tightly. As Felida said, it wasn't her job to control life, but to be of service to God's will that the world be filled with good. All she needed to do was her own small part and to trust.

Angela

It was just before ten in the morning. Angela turned into the driveway and parked. Getting out, she looked at the headlight, all fixed now, shiny and new. The scratches and dents to the bumper and hood were gone. Not a sign of anything wrong with the car at all. The man at the body shop had even been solicitous when she told him she'd hit a deer.

"You're lucky," he'd said, whistling through his bottom teeth, his square jaw jutting out. "My neighbour hit a buck a couple of years back. Head and antlers came right in through the window and stuck him through the shoulder."

"Oh my God!"

"He's all right," said the man, who smelled like cigarettes and gasoline, which was surely a dangerous combination. "Doesn't like driving at night anymore, though."

"I'm with him."

And that was all.

Philip, true to his word, had set up a bank account in her name. He'd cancelled the credit card she'd been using, but it hadn't been much trouble getting another. He'd told her to keep the car, for now, whatever that meant. When she went back to the garage a few days later to pick it up, she decided she'd pay cash. It made her flush, this covering of her tracks, but she had nightmares about being dragged away in handcuffs, being locked in a small room with an angry mob outside. She handed the money over and if the mechanic noticed her fingers were trembling, he said nothing except that since she was paying cash, he'd knock off the tax.

So, with the SUV all bright and shiny in the driveway, which she hoped was the last of all this, she climbed up to her little apartment. Three weeks. That's all. And yet her mark was on the place now. Philip had refused to let her come by the house, which was fine with her. Going back there, to that now-foreign land of dinner parties and charity boards, seemed far too wide a chasm to cross. Neither did Philip have any interest in seeing her, so he had sent a UPS delivery with some of her things. Sweaters and dresses (she couldn't imagine wearing them again) and shoes and pants and shorts and workout gear, all tossed into boxes without being folded, her toiletries (including a bottle of Coco that had broken in transit, the perfume infusing an acrid reek on her pajamas and slippers), yoga mat, and some old DVDs; a few books: *Eat, Pray, Love* and *The Life-Changing Magic of Tidying Up* and *The Handmaid's Tale* and *Under the Tuscan Sun.* She couldn't help but believe Philip had chosen them for irony's sake. Well, let him. And so, these things were strewn about the place. Clothes on chairs, books on the table, next to her laptop and a half-eaten bowl of chicken soup. The place had an undernote of stale Coco.

She had gone, at Sister Eileen's urging, to a few more meetings, but doubted she'd go again. She didn't want a drink. Never craved one like the poor people in those rooms. She wanted only to be left alone.

Her phone rang. She looked at the ID. Apparently, Sister Eileen didn't want her to be alone.

"Hi, Eileen."

"How are you?"

"I'm fine."

"I wondered if you'd given any thought to seeing George Clarence?"

"I've thought about it nonstop. And I want to. I do."

"I'm glad to hear that."

"But if I do, well, that's an admission, isn't it? I still want to set up a fund for him, you know, for his care and his sister and all that, but I think it's best I do it through a lawyer, you know, anonymously. And it will have to wait until the divorce, I suppose. But I have access to money. You got the PayPal transfer for him, right?"

"I did. And he's most grateful. I didn't tell him who it was from, of course. But I know he'd like to thank you in person."

"I wouldn't have to tell him?"

"Not if you don't want to."

What was this weariness in Eileen's voice? It was unlike her.

"I'll give it some more thought."

There was a pause. A waiting. Angela could practically hear Eileen putting her thoughts in order. "Are you okay? Is everything okay?" The room looked darker. Clouds moving in outside, rain on the way.

"Angela, I think you should also know that I've been asked to go to the police station this afternoon at two and answer a few questions about the accident."

Angela, who had been standing by the table, now sat, hard, on the chair. "Oh God."

"As I said, I'm not going to implicate you. You know you can trust me, but I also will not lie."

"What are you going to say, then?" She had been an idiot to trust this nun. Why should a nun be any more trustworthy than anyone else? "I'd think you would have had some experience in the church with lying and keeping things covered up." She balled her hand up into a fist and rapped her index finger on her forehead. "No, sorry. I shouldn't have said that. It's just a shock, you know. I'm scared. I know you won't, I mean, you promised."

"And I will keep the promise." A deep intake of breath. "But you must be prepared, Angela."

"For what? You think they know? Then why aren't they coming for me? Why are they asking you questions?"

"I met a detective when I first visited George. He was curious about my interest in the case and I don't think he believed, at least not entirely, that I didn't have some information. I'm also, well, I'm also wondering if he doesn't think I was somehow more directly involved."

Angela was chewing the side of her thumb. "He thinks you might have been driving?"

"It's possible. I really don't know. I'll call you afterward. Angela, do this for me, will you? Consider what your life will be like if you keep this secret, even if you do get away with it. Even if you have no legal repercussions from this, you will still have to live with it. Of course, if the police investigation does eventually lead to you, the fact you haven't come in willingly will make things worse, I suspect, but let's for a moment assume it does not, and that you are never held accountable … do you think you can live with that, or will it haunt you? That in fact you will be doing yourself a disservice? It may seem as though being found out would be the worst thing, and it would be very hard; your friends and family would know, and you may even do a little time in jail."

Angela sobbed, and it was all she could do not to cut off the call and throw the phone across the room. She should never, ever, have told Eileen. A moment of weakness. Shock-induced. She would leave now. Never see Eileen again. Why not? What was holding her here? She had to rouse herself from this lethargy.

"Angela, please don't panic. Breathe. Breathe. Are you there? Can you hear me? All right, just consider, please, that the invitation from God in this terrible moment may be to claim yourself more fully, good and bad, as we all are. I envision this awful time as an open door, a threshold to cross, into a new house where you needn't drag all the old things that no longer serve you. Remember that what God wants for you is so much more wonderful than you could ever imagine. Can you remember that?"

The rain had started. Thick, fat drops slapping on the roof and the windows like jellyfish. God wanted wonders for her? Nothing looked like wonder. Abandonment. Rejection. Connor. Carsten. Philip. Deedee. All those empty chairs. Wheelchairs. The sound of metal against metal. A row of tiny black ants marched along the floor at the base of the kitchen cabinets, disappearing into a crack on the quarter-round. She wanted to smash them, to smear their bodies into black mush.

"Yes," she managed. "Call me when you know more, okay? I have to go now."

They ended the call and Angela wobbled into the bathroom. Her stomach was sloshing, roiling. She bent over the sink and spit a couple of times, breathing through her mouth. No, she wasn't going to vomit. She sat down on the toilet and began to cry.

The small apartment seemed full of dark corners. It would never be clean enough. There, behind the bathroom door, was a patch of greyish, sticky buildup of something. Old soap. Hair. Flakes of skin, no doubt. Wasn't there some nonsense about all the world, even, or maybe even especially, the dust floating in the air being made out of the same stuff as stars? Well, if so, the stars were disgusting. The world was disgusting. Animals, insects, humans, all disgusting, with their fluids and smells and wrinkles and flaps and folds, their clacking teeth and beaks. Stars gave the impression of something serene and coldly clean, something noble, even. Humans were anything but. Selfish and cruel and untrustworthy. Vile, really. She had read somewhere once that you could think of the very worst possible thing a human could do to another human being — boiling alive, flaying, rape of children, burning, knives in eyeballs — whatever it was that haunted your darkest nightmares, and you could rest assured that at that very same moment someone, somewhere, was doing precisely that thing to someone else.

Snot was dripping from her nose. Her eyes were wet and red and sore. Her mouth tasted like bile. Dry skin flaked around her fingernails and a hangnail had ripped, blood rimming the cuticle. The inside of her left wrist showed bluish-green veins through the pale skin. She ran her finger over them, and they moved slightly, like worms on wet pavement. The skin was thin as onion peel. The veins so vulnerable.

It wasn't the world and all that was in it she found so revolting, she realized, it was her own appalling self. Liar and cheat. Coward and selfish pig. Criminal. A person who, even now, would let a friend walk into a police station so she didn't have to.

"No," she said and stood up. She pushed her not-exactly-clean hair off her forehead and looked at herself in the mirror. Jesus, but she was a mess. From an emotional remove, she wondered if she cared enough to do something about it. Shower? Makeup? Hairdresser? Laughable, all that. No, she did not care.

She had said *no*, but she wasn't sure what it referred to. No, she wasn't that repulsed by herself? She was that repulsed. No, she wouldn't let Sister Eileen walk into the police station alone? She would. No, she would be different, a different person, almost resurrected, almost, she snorted, born again? Certainly no.

No. Just no. No to every fucking thing and every fucking person and that was all. No. She would prefer not to, all things considered.

She wandered out of the bathroom into the bedroom and curled up on the bed, listening to the rain, harder, sharper now, against the windows. The light in the apartment was dim, watery itself. Angela's throat constricted, and her stomach lurched, but it was not bile that rose, it was something else, something not quite physical, but rather a cloud, a fog, shadow … and like brown churning water crashing through a dam, frothing and full of buried debris and hidden currents, ready to crush bone and suck everything under, despair convulsed her. It wrapped around her like an ice-water-soaked blanket. It covered her eyes and ears and nose and mouth, and she felt as though she were drowning under the frigid weight of it and didn't mind. She didn't mind one bit. It would be a relief. To die. To sleep. For it all to be done.

She spasmed with the force, groaning. She slithered to the side of the bed, onto her knees, shaking and sobbing.

She had to move, to act, to run. Something.

Angela snatched up her purse. She stood still. Where was she going? Somewhere.

The sound of Mrs. Simonofsky's vacuum cleaner rose up through the floorboards and then went silent. If the landlady was home, she'd have to sneak out. Acknowledging she didn't want Mrs. Simonofsky to know she was leaving made Angela admit she was thinking of running out on all this. The eagle-eyed old lady would see her with a suitcase and then what? Fine. No suitcase. Rain jacket. Stuff a couple of pairs of underwear and a T-shirt in a shopping tote. Toothbrush. Jesus, every time she did this she took less and less.

Sure enough, Mrs. Simonofsky must have heard her feet on the stairs. Angela waved, and kept walking to the car. She imagined Mrs. Simonofsky being questioned by the police. "No, Officer, I don't know where she went, but she looked suspicious, I will tell you that!" But by then Angela would be halfway to … where? She'd know when she got there.

SHE WAS NEARLY AT BELMAR by the time she realized that was where she was headed. The beach. She parked, stowing her tote in the trunk, walked to the grey booth on the boardwalk and paid the freckled, red-haired girl inside nine dollars for a beach badge. The rain was a fine drizzle, the sky a moody pewter.

"Not much of a day for a swim," said the girl as she handed Angela the turquoise badge.

Angela pinned it to her rain jacket. "I'm not swimming."

"Some surfers out there," the girl said, pointing.

"Thanks."

Angela walked up the beach, away from the surfers. A woman jogged by. An elderly couple held hands and strolled, wearing American flag windbreakers. They looked happy. The air smelled of salt and iodine and the sand was hard-packed under her feet. A family had set up under a large green umbrella, and two little round-bellied boys ran back and forth at the edge of the waves, shrieking like the gulls whirling above them, oblivious in their joy to the inclement weather. One waved a yellow plastic shovel. A flock of sanderlings, legs flying, dashed into and out of the foam. The misty rain soaked her hair and forced her to wipe her eyes. Another jogger, this one a tattooed male with a bushy black beard glinting in the rain, and earbuds. He nodded at her.

Angela walked until she came to a jetty. She climbed up and walked to the end, where the only thing she could see before her was the sea and sky. The clouds were low and heavy, and the horizon shrouded. A foghorn lowed. She sat and drew her knees up, wrapping her arms around them. She was damp all through, below the hem of her jacket, but the day was warm and she didn't care. The jacket was long enough to cover her behind at least.

Where would she go from here? Maybe New York City. A person could get reasonably lost there. Or was it too obvious? Would there be a warrant out for her arrest one day soon? Maybe she'd go south, work on a travelling carnival, one of those ones that set up in parking lots and agricultural fairs and paid you in cash and didn't ask questions. Or there was Alaska. A person could surely get lost in all that wilderness.

Offshore, something bobbed up in the water. A harbour seal, its doglike eyes so curious and soft. A selkie, maybe, come to lure her, come to play, come to save her.

There was always the possibility of swimming away from land. Swimming until you couldn't see shore. No one would even see her slipping into the water. A plan? It felt just as plausible and sensible as dreaming of running a Ferris wheel at the Iowa State Fair. She watched the seal until it disappeared under the surface again. She waited to see if it would resurface, but it seemed to have moved on. She inched down on the rocks, so her foot touched the water. She couldn't walk in. She'd have to jump.

She looked up. Yes, there was the seal again. Just for a moment and then gone. Florida? Alaska? Iowa? Davy Jones's locker?

More damn tears. She prayed, knowing it was a fucking cliché, but she prayed anyway. *Take it. Take the whole damn thing. I can't do it. I can't go through another day like this. I can't do it. I can't. Take it take it take it take it.* She had no name for whatever, whomever, she prayed to. She had no form for it. She had only the abyss, the void, the darkness.

After some moments she felt her chest loosen ever so slightly, as though a belt had been undone, or a rope untied. It occurred to her she could, in fact, die without dying. She shook her head. *What a ridiculous, sappy, religious concept*, she thought, embarrassed at the idea, even as her breathing slowed. Resurrection? Really? How absurd.

Or was it? What was she saying? She imagined a cicada scraping out of an old husk, a snake sloughing off its tired old skin.

Suddenly, she was thinking of her mother. *Really? My mother? Now?* She remembered being at the beach when she was perhaps eight or nine. A sun-bright, eye-dazzling day. She and her mother were walking when they came across a sharp, hard pinkish thing on the sand, gritty and broken.

"A dead crab," said Angela.

"Is it, though?" Her mother had turned it over and looked inside. "I'll tell you about crabs." Angela's mother was like that. She knew things other people didn't, odd informational scraps of flotsam and jetsam.

"Crabs are crustaceans," she said.

"Crustaceans," Angela repeated.

"Right. So are lobsters and shrimps. They have a hard shell called an exoskeleton or a carapace."

"*Carapace*. I like that word."

"Me, too. This means they wear their skeleton outside their body."

"Yuck," said Angela.

Her mother laughed, and the light caught the silver of her dangling earrings and made it look for a moment as though she had stars on her ears. "Think of it like a suit of armor, like in King Arthur, the ones the knights wore. Except that crabs keep growing and so they need a new suit of armor when they outgrow the old one. So, every now and again they start to grow a new soft carapace under the old one. The old shell splits and cracks open —"

"Does it hurt?"

"Huh. I don't know. Probably not. But maybe. But I'm sure it's not comfortable, only necessary. Anyway, when that happens the crab climbs out and drinks a whole lot of water so that it gets all plump before the new carapace sets hard. Then it can grow into the new shell until it has to repeat things all over again. So, see, inside this carapace," she held out the shell to Angela, who wiped her hands off on her tummy before taking it, because it seemed like a fragile, almost holy thing now, "there's nothing at all. If it was a dead crab, you'd see bits of it, but there's nothing at all here, so this is just an old suit of clothes."

"Can we take it home?"

"Sure, I guess." Angela's mother put it in the pouch she wore slung over her shoulder, in which she put their found things, shells and stones and whatnots.

They walked some more, and then Angela asked, "Isn't it dangerous for the crab, when he doesn't have a hard shell, when he's all soft like that?"

"It is a scary time," said her mother. "Good thinking. It has no protection then and so it needs to hide away under a rock or coral, so nothing comes along and tries to eat it. But it doesn't have a choice if it's to live."

Cicadas. Snakes. Crabs. Shedding old skin. *Well, thanks, Mom.*

What was stopping her from doing the same?

Nothing.

She made a little noise that sounded almost like a laugh. Nothing. Exactly what she had. A big mountain of nothing at all. And that nothingness became a clean thing, a sheet washed of blood, a countertop swept of crumbs, a sky without clouds, a sea without waves, blue and pure as crystal. She felt as though she'd lived her whole life in small spaces, in apartments and towns and tree-cluttered gardens, and now, all of a sudden, in a lightning flash, a ripped-away veil, a sudden blast, it was all gone, and she let herself drift into the nothingness. She let it carry her, for it was a thing, this nothingness, it was solid in some metaphysical way. No thing. What would save her? No thing. Nothing. Everything. A kind of eerie freedom, in which all things were unfamiliar and uncharted.

Sister Eileen

The room Detective Danberg had ushered her into was small and grey and windowless. Eileen sat on a metal chair with her back to the wall, facing the detective across a small desk as he sat with his back to the door. He was a restless man, fidgeting. One minute he leaned back on his chair, balancing it on the two back legs, and the next he plunked forward, elbows on the desk, neck jutting toward her. He picked up his pen and clicked it over and over. He drummed it on the table. He scratched his head. Moved his shoulders around and cracked his neck.

Eileen sat still, with her hands in her lap. She understood the detective's display was intended to annoy her, to make her ill at ease, and it did. Although the half-smile she kept on her face betrayed little sign of her discomfort, she very much wanted to tell him to cut it out, to sit up straight, to be still.

"So," he said, not for the first time, "what are we gonna do here, Sister?"

She remained passive, which she suspected annoyed him as much as he annoyed her. She didn't necessarily wish to annoy him, but short of saying things she had no intention of saying, she didn't know how to stop. "We've been here for over two hours, Detective. Do you think much will change if we talk for another two?"

"What I wonder —" he put the forefinger of his left hand in the middle of the manila folder in front of him, and spun it around with his other hand "— is what it is you're hiding. I mean, we've got two possibilities, right?"

"You've mentioned that. Several times."

He flattened his hand on the folder and it stopped spinning. He opened it and tapped at the page with his pen. "But I guess we should go over it again. Now, where were you the night of the accident?"

She sighed. "At home, with the other Sisters who live with me."

"Yup, yup, yup, and they were all home, right … Sister Ruth, Sister Caroline, Sister Anne?"

"They were."

"That's cozy." He played his index fingers like drumsticks on the edge of the desk. "Okay, so let's say, just for the moment, that I believe you."

"That would be nice. I am not the lying sort."

"Why? Because you're a nun? Listen, Sister, I know plenty of religious people who lie, don't you? I mean, come on, all those priests and little kids? You can't tell me you people don't lie like dogs in front of a warm fire."

"Are you speaking from personal experience?"

He glared. "No. I'm not."

"Are we here to talk about church scandals? Because if so, you might be surprised to find you and I are more like-minded than not."

"That would be something. Yup. But no, maybe we'll save that for another time. Like I was saying, let's say I believe that you and your roommates were all tucked in for the evening. So, it wasn't you, or them, who ran George Clarence down and left him in the street like a piece of trash." He folded his hands and rested them on his not-insubstantial middle. "But you know who did it, don't you? Oh, yes, I think you do." He leaned in now. "Come on, Sister, where's your sense of justice? That poor guy. Lost a leg. In a goddamn wheelchair. A wheelchair. Somebody hit him. A guy in a wheelchair."

"We've been over and over this, Detective, and I am aware of George's circumstances."

"Yup. You've been taking pretty good care of him and his sister, haven't you?"

"We do what we can."

"And it costs some, too, doesn't it? Well, doesn't it? Where'd you get the money from?"

"People donate to us, in order that we might help others."

"Yup. But in this particular case, who gave you money for George Clarence?"

And this is where things got tricky. Phrasing was important. She did not lie, after all. "I'm not always aware where specific money comes from."

"You aware in this case?"

"I'm not able to say."

He puffed out his cheeks and held his nose, as though from a bad smell. "You see, that's just the sort of non-answer that makes me awfully suspicious, Sister. You're not able to say. You could, but you won't, is more like it, and I bet you keep records, so I could, I guess, go to all the trouble of getting a warrant to look at the books I'm sure you keep down at that Pantry place and all that. Charitable donations earmarked for Mr. Clarence donated by … who? You know, like you see on the television — a bunch of guys in full gear stomping through the Pantry, opening drawers, letting people see us. I don't suppose that would be good for your, what do you call them, your clients' sense of safety, would it?"

"An anonymous donor is just that. You wouldn't find anything useful to your case." She would not say that, should such a thing happen, it was likely their clients' sympathy would be fully with the Sisters and not with the men and women in blue. She sighed and used the gesture as a distraction as she stole a glance at her watch. It was after four. Enough. "Are you holding me? Or am I free to go?"

"I'll ask directly, Sister. Do you, or do you not, know who is responsible?"

"And I will answer you as best I can. Responsibility is a vast term and there may be any number of people responsible."

Bam! The detective slammed his palm on the table, and she jumped.

"Stop dicking around. You know who's responsible and you're damn well gonna tell me. You Catholics, always half-truthing and dodging responsibility for the crap that happens under your watch. Well, I'm not going to have it, you understand? What the hell is wrong with you? That poor man — you don't give a shit about him. So pious, but what's that good for? He still gets no justice, right?"

It was difficult for Eileen not to point out the number of times the police department had failed the very man for whom the detective now feigned such concern. Three times over the years George had fallen out of his chair on ice or uneven sidewalks and the police had never come to help. Once he had lain in the cold for almost an hour before someone driving by stopped to help him. Or perhaps she should remind him of the times — twice — he had been stopped and frisked, with the police assuming he was dealing drugs hidden somewhere on his chair simply because he occasionally liked to hang out on the corner and chat. Poor man? Yes, indeed.

Of course, she said none of this. Detective Danberg was as damaged a man as any other, and surely there was a wound down there that had never been properly healed. She tried to picture him as a boy, one who had been wronged in some way, a boy before all the layers of anger and cynicism grew over his heart.

She put Christ between them and tried to speak to Him instead.

Just as she was about to speak of justice for everyone involved, even this angry policeman, the door opened and a female officer with thickly painted-on eyebrows asked him to come outside for a moment. He shot her a look of something very close to disgust, snapped, "Stay," and left Eileen alone.

It was surprising how fast her heart was beating. Christ or no Christ, no one enjoyed being interrogated by the police. She knew she could leave. She was not under arrest, but he had told her to stay. It was difficult not to be obedient to such a command. What must it be like for young people who had been taught to mistrust the police entirely to sit alone in small rooms like this? Well, now she knew, at least a little of the helplessness and the humiliation it entailed. The way things were going, she might well learn more.

She closed her eyes and prayed.

After a while the door opened. It was the female officer.

"You can go," she said.

"The detective said I should stay."

"Well, now he says you should go." She shrugged, arched one of those rather alarming brows, and gestured with her hand that Eileen should get up.

The hall was brightly lit and through a window in the wall she saw uniformed men and women hunched over desks, busy with paperwork and phones. Farther along was a steel bench to which a young man she didn't know was shackled. He didn't return her smile.

They were right at the exit door when she saw Angela. She was being ushered by the detective to a counter, next to which hung a height chart — a backdrop for photos. She looked frighteningly thin next to the policeman. Her hair, which looked wet, was pulled back in a ponytail and she wore a sweatshirt, pants, and running shoes. If she'd come with a purse, she didn't have it now. Oh, wait, the detective was carrying it, making him look like a reluctant husband on a shopping trip.

Eileen's heart flipped, as if she had just jumped into the cold, cold sea. "Angela," she called. "Angela."

Angela turned, looking for her, but the policewoman was ushering her, with a hand on her shoulder, out the door into the reception area. Eileen couldn't tell if Angela had seen her or not.

"That woman," she said, "may I see her? May I talk to her?"

"You know her?"

"I do."

The woman smirked. "Huh, so Danberg was right." She snorted. "You people are something. You could be charged with impeding an investigation, you know."

"May I talk with her?"

"She'll get a phone call after processing. If she wants to talk to you, she'll call."

THE CALL CAME THAT EVENING just before seven. Eileen sat in the living room with Caroline, Ruth, and Anne.

"Sister Eileen. It's me."

She nodded, her hand held up, letting the other women know who it was. Ruth bowed her head in prayer, Anne nodded smiled a little. Caroline looked heavenward with her hands, palms, together at her lips. Since Angela had turned herself in, Eileen felt able to share the outline of events with her housemates.

"Oh, Angela. Tell me what's happening."

"I'm being charged with third-degree something or other. Knowingly leaving the scene of an accident causing serious bodily harm. I think. Whatever. I'll stay here tonight, and then be transferred to Mercer County Jail until I'm arraigned, or preliminary arraignment, I think."

Her voice sounded tired, and small, but was steady.

"Do you know when that will be?"

"I'm not sure. Maybe tomorrow."

"What made you do this?"

"Sister Eileen, you've done so much. You stood by me. I just wanted to thank you. I'm okay. I'm kind of surprised, but I am. I'm sorry I put you through all this. Really sorry."

"You sound calm."

"I feel calm. Or I guess it's calm. Numb, you know. Really, really tired. I'm going to jail. I told them everything. Even about drinking, so I guess they'll charge me with that, too. I'll find out at the preliminary hearing, or whatever."

"Do you have a lawyer? They did say you need a lawyer, didn't they?"

"I don't want one."

This surprised Eileen. To be accountable was one thing … "Are you sure that's wise?"

"Wise? I don't know. I'm going to plead guilty. I already confessed and everything."

"I see. This is quite a turnaround."

"I'll tell you the story of a crab one day. But I don't have much time. Could I ask you a favour?"

"Yes, of course."

"Will you call Philip and tell him what's happened? There's stuff I've been thinking about, insurance and so forth. He's going to have to be involved, I'm afraid, legally. I don't know …"

"Take it one step at a time." Eileen realized her cheeks were wet. "I can't tell you how amazed I am, watching you come home to yourself. Things will unfold."

"Will they? Well, I don't know. Even if —"

There was some noise in the background.

"I have to go. Maybe you'll be in court?"

"I'll be there."

"Thanks."

And then she was gone.

Eileen explained things, and Anne came over to the couch, sat next to Eileen, and hugged her. "That's the God we know," she said, and the other women agreed. Caroline, who had a rather dumbfounded look on her face, said, "Wow. That's kind of a miracle." And then she stood and went to get Eileen a cup of tea.

Eileen said, "I wondered about that girl, but I think she's going to make a fine nun after all."

Sister Eileen

The visitors were herded into a concrete-block room. Tables with round-seated stools attached to them were bolted to the floor. A wall of meshed windows let in a little light, but not much, since it looked out onto another wall. A play area in the back of the room boasted a small bookcase, some old colouring and storybooks and a stained, purple carpet. Three vending machines stood against the wall. Soft drinks. Chips. Chocolate bars and candy. Guards assigned visitors seats at different tables, the empty places a testament to loss and hope in equal measure. It was quiet in the room. Tension was a slithery thing in the corners, creeping up walls. Eileen realized every muscle in her back was stiff, and her hands were clutched so tight the knuckles were white.

A buzzer rang, and a door clanged somewhere and then, at the other end of the room, another door opened, and the prisoners entered. Eileen's heartbeat increased, and her stomach gurgled.

And then, there she was, in the prison's orange jumpsuit. Angela was still skeletal-thin. Her hair was pulled back and she wasn't wearing any makeup. She looked pale, and wan, and her hair was no longer the shining auburn it had once been. It was growing out and there was a duller, greyish tinge about an inch or so from her scalp. Her hands were held, fingers entwined, at her waist. She might have been walking into the choir stalls at church. Sleeplessness shadowed her red, sore-looking eyes.

Angela spotted Eileen and smiled. Something of the dazzle and beauty Eileen associated with Angela reappeared, but only a fraction. She sat down. "It's good to see you."

"How are you?"

"'I don't know." Angela tried unsuccessfully to smile.

"Do you want something from the vending machine?"

"No, no, thank you." Angela spoke softly, carefully, and kept blinking.

"Well, I'd like a drink. Maybe a Coke? Come on."

"Sure, then. A Coke."

Eileen got up and fed the dollar bills visitors were permitted to bring with them for this purpose into the machine. Next to her, other people were buying crackers and cheese, chips, soft drinks. She bought crackers and cheese, too. A little girl sat on the floor with a young woman, her mother, presumably, playing with a contraption on which one slid wooden circles and squares along a winding piece of plastic wire.

Eileen came back to the table carrying the drinks, snacks, and two paper cups. They poured out the fizzy drinks.

"Are your eyes all right?"

Blink. Blink. "Dumb, right? Cried myself into conjunctivitis."

"Did they give you anything for it?"

"Some drops, but they didn't do much."

"You need to see the doctor again." Eileen opened both packages of crackers and cheese and slid one over to Angela.

"Okay." Angela kept her eyes on the Coke.

"I sent you some cash through JPay," Eileen said, meaning the self-contained e-messaging service inmates, as well as their friends and family, relied upon for email, money transfers, or to request appointments with any of the internal services provided by the Corrections Department. Of course, there was a cost for every message sent. At the moment the charge was forty-seven cents a page, but it went up from time to time. To send money to an incarcerated person cost somewhere around ten dollars.

"I got it, thank you. But you don't have to. My lawyer sends me money every month, so I'm fine." Philip had insisted she have a lawyer, Richard McBride, and she had finally acquiesced, although he couldn't change her mind about pleading guilty. "You use the money another way, okay? Lots of people can use that money. Actually" — Angela winced — "I wanted to give it to one of the other women who doesn't have anyone on the outside, but we're not allowed."

"No, you can't do that. I learned that through Sister Ruth. And speaking of chaplains, have you met Sister Brigid yet?"

"Yeah, I think. She and someone from Educational Services came into Reception and gave a little talk. I don't remember much."

"I'm not surprised you don't. This is all traumatic. Have you made an appointment to see her?"

"What would I even say?" The note of irritation in Angela's voice was, possibly, an improvement on the previous flatness. "Anyway, she's booked up. And I have to figure out that JPay thingy. There's a kiosk in the unit, but I don't know how to use it."

The inmates lined up at JPay terminals and could use them for no more than fifteen minutes at a time, less, if someone else was waiting and impatient.

"Eat something. Okay?"

Angela nibbled at the cheese.

Eileen said, "I'm sorry I couldn't get here sooner. I was in Florida at a conference." Angela had been at Edna Mahan for nearly a month. Eileen hadn't seen her since that day in court.

Angela shrugged. "Reception was hell. Just a big room with these bunk beds stacked up in threes. I can't get used to it. I just can't." She put her hands over her eyes, as though trying to block out the visions. "Going to the bathroom in front of people. The food." She dropped her hands into her lap. "It comes in these big plastic bags and it's like, I don't know. Dog food or something. I can't eat it. The smell. And the noises. Crying. Shouting. Laughing like maniacs. It's never quiet. I hate the noise. I feel like my skin's coming off. I'm afraid all the time."

"Of what?" Eileen took Angela's hand, lying on the table like a dead thing, cold and damp.

"Myself. Mostly myself. That I'll freak out and hit someone, or start screaming and never stop. I can't sleep. I just can't sleep. I wish I could talk to Connor. Every time I close my eyes, I see his face."

"You haven't heard from him, then?"

"No. I tried calling. He won't pick up. I write letters. Maybe he's just throwing them in the trash."

"But maybe not. He might be reading them. Give him time. He's in my prayers, as you are. Do you want me to call him?"

Angela looked up. "No. Yes. No." Tears fell again. "I don't know."

"Tell you what? Give me his number and you think about it. Let me know."

"Okay," she said, and Eileen repeated it three times so as to commit the number to memory.

Angela shook her head as though to shake out the thoughts. "I'm in a unit now. They moved me three days ago. Bravo Unit. They call everything by military names. It's so strange."

"That has to be better than Reception."

She shrugged again. "It is. There's a common space with a microwave, cups and things. A washing machine and dryer. Metal furniture all bolted down. This guard, or officer, as I'm supposed to call her, sits at a desk and reads mostly."

"What about the women?"

"A couple are okay. I have a roommate. A 'bunky,' if you can believe it." She didn't quite sneer, but Eileen thought she might have, had she not been so exhausted. "Diane. She's tried to help me."

There was something bitter in that last phrase, and Eileen suspected Angela was not faring at all well with women she would consider, in her old life, somewhat beneath her in education, class, experience. Hard lessons here.

"She's all right. A little younger than I am, but she's been here for nine years. She was in maximum, but they transferred her to minimum a few months ago. I don't know what she did. I understand it's best not to ask."

"Probably wise. She'd tell you if she wanted you to know."

"Nobody asks what I did." For a moment they were quiet and then Angela made a sound that might be interpreted as a laugh. "You know, I thought there'd be something noble in 'fessing up to what I did, to making sure you weren't in trouble, to trying to help that man." Her eyes were very wide now, the swollen lids puffy and flaking. "I set up a trust for him with the lawyer. From the divorce settlement. It's a whack of money. It'll last a long time. What a fool, right? Thinking I could buy my way out?"

"The trust is a good thing. A wonderful thing. It's going to make an enormous difference in their lives."

"Well, good for me. Noble me. But there's nothing noble about being here. It's a coffin. It's nothing. And okay, it's just what I deserve, I get that, I do, but what's the point? What good does it do anyone to have me here? Diane has a tattoo on her face! Her face. She has *anarchy* tattooed on her *face.*" She leaned in and half-whispered, "What do I have in common with someone like that?"

"Angela, she's just a woman, and someone trying to be kind to you —"

"I know, I know. I'm trying, okay, but it's not easy. I don't know, it's not what I expected. I thought I'd be better. I imagined I'd be the one helping. I'd be doing, I don't know, leading yoga classes or some crap like that. I spend my time scrubbing toilets and mopping the floor." She crushed the package of crackers. "I wish I'd kept on driving or thrown myself into the fucking sea."

"Well, I'm glad you didn't. You'll get through this, Angela. And I know it feels as though you're all alone. But you're not. And it's not forever. Five years."

"Five and a half."

"You won't serve it all. Eighty-five percent max."

"I don't think I'm ever going to get out of here."

"Give it time. Reach out to Sister Brigid. Promise me."

Angela pushed back. "Sure. Why not?"

There was silence between them for a moment. The conversations went on around the room, with some voices pleading, some women crying, others laughing, children occasionally shrieking the way nervous children do. They drank their Cokes. The sweetness, with no ice and rapidly warming in the too-close room, set Eileen's teeth on edge.

Finally, Angela said, "Can I ask you something?"

"Yes, of course."

"You're angry with me, aren't you?"

"No, of course not."

"Don't lie, Sister Eileen. You're a nun. Not supposed to, right? I mean, not supposed to be angry. However … nevertheless … you're furious and disappointed with me. I know. I could tell right off, as soon as I called you from that hotel. It's okay. I don't blame you."

"Angela —"

"No, seriously, I'm furious with myself. And horrified and, to be honest …" Angela looked out the wall of windows and chewed her lower lip for a moment. "I mean, it all seems like madness now. Such a crazy dream. If it wasn't for me being in here, I'd wonder if any of it ever happened at all."

Eileen felt a red worm of judgment rise up in her. After all these years, all this prayer, all this incense and flame … *Oh, settle, settle, oh, breathe, breathe.* She thought it wasn't that easy for other people — the man who'd lost his leg, Philip, Connor — to relegate Angela's appalling behaviour into some convenient back room of the mind. "That's one way of looking at it," she said.

Angela kept her eyes on the milky light coming through the window. "You know, you once told me you believe we're all intertwined, like a spiderweb, each thread attached to the other. Not a new image, of course, but the way you talked about it …"

She turned back to Eileen, eyes full, nose running. Tears for herself, for her son, for the people she'd harmed?

Angela continued, "It's a question of letting God take the messes we've made, all those tangled bits of thread, and believing they can be sorted, spun, woven into something useful, a pattern, maybe one that's even there by design."

"I don't believe the accident was destined, Angela."

"Yeah, I know.

Eileen said, "There's nothing, however bad, that God can't transform into something good, though, if you let God. Look, Angela, you didn't run. You stood up and held yourself accountable. That counts for something. I know that right now, in this place, awful as it is, it can appear as though only more awful stuff is in your future, but we don't know what the future will bring, only that whatever God has in mind for you is more wonderful than you could imagine."

Angela looked hard into Eileen's face. "I'll have to take your word for that," she said, and then looked away. "There was this one woman in Reception, right? She left her seven-year-old daughter, who had Down's syndrome and cerebral palsy and was on a feeding tube, alone in the apartment while she went out to some bar. When she got back, the police were in the apartment, waiting for her. I don't know exactly what went wrong, but the child was dead. How do you live with that guilt? She wouldn't stop screaming, yelling about what she'd done. They took her away. What's God going to do with that?"

"I don't know. I only know the story's not over."

"Isn't it? Well, at least I still have a chance with Connor."

A harsh buzz came over the P.A. system. The guard pushed forward from the wall against which he'd been leaning. Their time was up. Eileen's eyes stung. "I'll come back."

"If you want. I don't mean to sound, oh, I don't know what I mean. You take care."

Eileen hugged Angela, as she was allowed to do, once upon seeing her, and once upon leaving her. "Time, Angela. Time and trust. Bless you."

At the door, Angela passed through the metal detector and kept on walking without turning back.

Not good, thought Eileen, *not good at all.*

EILEEN COLLECTED HER JACKET, car keys, phone, and wallet from the locker in which she'd left them before entering the visiting room. She quickly jotted down Connor's number on the back of a grocery receipt. She waited as some of the other visitors cleared the metal detector and stepped out into the bright, chill September Saturday.

She called Brigid.

"Brigid Kenney here."

"Hey, Brigid, it's Eileen."

"How did it go?"

Eileen pictured Brigid, short shock of white hair, gold-framed glasses, probably wearing one of the bright-coloured sweaters she favoured. She'd be at home in the red-brick house next to Our Lady of Mount Virgin Church she shared with five other sisters in Middlesex, maybe looking out her bedroom window at the front of the house onto the statue of Mary surrounded by a circle of flowers in the front garden.

"Not great. She's not doing well."

"No surprise there."

"She's got some awful eye infection, and I suspect she needs antidepressants."

"Has she asked for medical services?"

A number of people were walking down to the bus stop. Others getting into cars. Everyone was quiet, sombre. The post-visit letdown. Several children were crying. And Angela would be back in her unit. Doing what? Eileen couldn't imagine her chatting with the other women, couldn't imagine her doing much other than curling up in her bed and crying. "Not yet."

"There's not a great deal I can do unless she requests a visit."

Eileen told Brigid that Angela had a roommate recently transferred from maximum, someone with an *anarchy* tattoo on her face.

"Oh, I know her. Diane. She'll be good for Angela. Knows her way around. Has the respect of the other women. Good heart."

"I'm not sure Angela sees it quite that way. Not yet, anyway."

"I told you it would be a shock for someone like Angela. For some of these women, the structure and discipline are the making of them. They need it and thrive, believe it or not, but for someone like your friend, with her background, being used to doing pretty much what she wants when she wants, wow. She's got quite a road. You emailing her?"

Eileen said she was, a couple of times a week at least.

"Good. Keep trying to get her to ask for me. I'll come running. And, speaking of running, I've got to. A pile of things to get done before the 'Journey Through Grief' session in about half an hour. Let's keep in touch on this, though, okay? And we'll keep praying. Blessings."

And praying was precisely what Eileen did on the forty-five-minute drive back to Trenton. Angela, Eileen noted, had not asked about Carsten, and so she had not told her that Carsten had come to see her, to apologize, and to say he did not think, for a while at least, that it would be good for him to help out at the Pantry. She had told him he would always be welcome to come back, but perhaps it would be good to take a little break and reflect. She prayed for him as well.

Angela

Prison was a horrible mixture of boredom and revulsion and fear and exhaustion.

First there was the boredom, exacerbated by the fact nearly everything was not only metaphorically drab, but literally. The doors, the cement-block walls, the concrete floors. The metal beds. The black plastic mattresses, no more comfortable than sleeping on a napkin over stone. The white(ish) pillowcases and sheets and brown blankets. The white socks and T-shirts and running shoes. The plastic tub at the end of the cot for personal possessions. The high-schoolesque grey locker (the actual lock was an additional fee). The food was brown with bits of less brown. The bread was white. The plastic trays were grey. The toilets stainless steel. The common area in Bravo was at least a very faint yellow, one might even say urine yellow. Certainly not daffodil. There were, however, those orange jumpsuits, unless you were in maximum, and then they were khaki.

The cell Angela shared with Diane was the same as every other cell. It had a small window. She had to stand to see out, and mostly all she saw was the wall of the other wing of Bravo Unit, but if she looked a little to the left, she could see a tree, a large oak. She was allowed in the yard three times a week for an hour and had seen the trees there and the grass, remnants from when the land had been a farm. So, if she stared at that tree, she could imagine a rolling farm just out of sight and hills and more trees and no people, just earth and sky and the sea somewhere beyond.

6:00 a.m.: Wake up.
7:00 a.m.: Breakfast.
8:00 a.m.–10:00 a.m.: Work or education. Medical.
10:00 a.m.: Return to housing unit for count.
11:00 a.m.–12:00 p.m.: Lunch.
12:00 p.m.–3:00 p.m.: Work. Visitors on Saturday: 1:00 p.m.–3:30 p.m.
3:00 p.m.: Back to housing unit for count.
4:00 p.m.: Off duty/time in yard. Chaplin. Medical.
5:00 p.m.: Dinner.
6:00 p.m.–7:00 p.m.: Religious and specialized programing. NA. AA. Anger Management. Visitors on Tuesday and Thursday: 6:30 p.m.–7:30 p.m.
8:00 p.m.: Return to housing unit for count.
11:00 p.m.: Lights out.

Everyone worked. The pay was $1.40 a day.

You might mow lawns, or shovel snow, or work in the kitchen, or the laundry. You might work in the commissary or the library. You might pick up trash from the roadsides.

Weekends? Work your job. Visitors 1:00 p.m. to 3:30 p.m. Saturdays. Sunday church services if you liked that sort of thing.

Repeat. Repeat. Repeat. Repeat. Repeat until you're nothing *but* repeat, no self, no return, no hope.

The revulsion: the smells of women who at times couldn't afford deodorant or toothpaste, and awful coffee, and women's bodies and the bones and sags and rolls of fat, the varicose veins and dirty nails, the missing teeth, the tattoos, the farts (the louder, the more amusing), and the phlegmy throats and coughs, the raucous laughs, the loud voices. There was the exhibitionist, all four hundred pounds of her, who flashed the officers and mooned the other women and bared her enormous, thick brush of pubic hair whenever the urge took her. The bathrooms. The stains in the bowls. The unflushed toilets. The mould on the walls. The leftover spittle in the sinks. The food: unending unidentifiable stews that smelled only charnel, with bits of what was probably bone that crunched between her teeth before she gagged. Realizing Diane was masturbating just across that narrow room.

Fear came from screams in the night and a tray thrown and sudden, horrible threats, and officers barrelling in with nightsticks and dragging women away to lockup, their orange jumpsuits torn, revealing white and brown and black skin, sometimes smeared with blood. Did this happen often? No. Did it have to? No. The threat was always there. Fear came from not knowing what was expected of her and if she could trust anyone. She had learned not to trust Marilla, for example, because Marilla went from sullen silence to fury in no time at all and it was impossible to tell what would set her off.

"Do you want some?" asked Angela one day, while making herself a cup of microwaved tea. "Hell, no," said Marilla. She had then followed Angela into the showers, pushed her up against the wall and said, "You fucking think I need your charity tea, Princeton? Fuck you." She shoved her hard enough to bang Angela's head on the wall and then left as though nothing had happened. Fear came from the officer who sometimes stood just a little too close, smirking. Diane said there wasn't much fear of sexual assault these days, but a couple of years ago it had been "every fucking night and half the days." Then an investigation and people went to jail, one officer for sixteen years. Could it start up again? Angela didn't know. Not knowing was also a kind of fear.

Who could sleep in this place, on this hard, cold bunk? Diane could, and she snored like a dying rhino. So, exhaustion. Like bags of bricks strapped to Angela's legs, to her back, to her arms.

The days passed, though, as days will, dripping from the limb of a life, and it was a miracle the things a person could grow accustomed to, could endure.

ANGELA'S FIRST MEETING with Sister Brigid was on a Tuesday morning, two and a half months into her sentence. She was in the shower room, swabbing the floor when the officer called her. She rang out the mop in the aluminum bucket and leaned the mop against the wall.

Sister Brigid, tiny and trim and tidy in grey flannel slacks, white running shoes, a raspberry-coloured sweater, a badge and a whistle (in case of inclement prisoners) around her neck on a lanyard. Her blue eyes shone clear and bright behind wire-rimmed glasses. Her hair was white as baby powder. She carried a Bible.

The nun reached out her hand. "Angela? Hello? I'm Brigid. So glad you asked to see me. I've heard such lovely things about you from Eileen. She thinks the world of you, you know."

Angela considered that Sister Brigid might be exaggerating just a bit. "She's great."

"Okay, let's see." Brigid looked around the room. "Are you okay talking here?" There were roughly eighty women in Bravo Unit, but most were at programs or jobs and only three women sat at a table playing cards. "Or do we need somewhere more private?"

Sister Brigid was brisk, and so very neat. Angela realized how little time she might have with her, and still wasn't sure what she wanted. Best not to waste it. "I'm good. Do you want tea? I can make us tea?"

"No, that's fine. Let's just talk."

Brigid ushered her to a table as far away from the officer and the other women as possible.

"I brought you this. Don't know if you have one." She grinned. "Or want one."

Angela picked it up, held it in both hands, looking at the gold lettering on the cover.

"I don't think I've ever really read the Bible."

"Well, you'll have time for that now, if you like. And there's a Bible study group."

"Okay."

"So, how are you getting along?"

"How much do you know about me?"

"Eileen's been candid, not only about the cause of your incarceration, but also about what you've done for George Clarence."

Angela's hands smelled of bleach. She looked at the cracked skin and ragged nails. Only two months, and this is what she had become? Ragged-haired, a bathroom-cleaning skeleton whose son despised her, whom no man would ever love again, who had ruined every chance she had, all that great, great privilege. "Well, that's great," she said.

"Is it? You don't look like it's great."

"I wish I were dead."

Sister Brigid leaned forward, elbows on the table. She was so short she might as well have put her chin on the table. "And yet you're not, and because I'm hopelessly Catholic, might I suggest there is some use for you in the world yet, that God has not abandoned you?"

Although she were ashamed of it, Angela couldn't deny the spark of defiance that crackled under her ribs, talking to this woman who would go home at the end of the day. "What if I've abandoned God?"

Sister Brigid chuckled. "You think God cares about that? As my mother used to say, 'pish.' God is a whole lot bigger, Horatio, than is dreamt of in your philosophy. And I don't use that quote with everyone, you understand, but I know you'll get it, right?" She poked Angela in the shoulder. "I know you do."

Who was this woman?

"Listen, Angela," she continued, "I'm not going to sugar-coat this. There's a rough road ahead and living with a bunch of other women isn't easy — as a nun, I can tell you that. I remember, years ago, when I was sitting on a balcony talking to my spiritual director and complaining mightily about someone, and my spiritual director looked at me and said, 'You don't think on some other balcony somewhere someone's complaining about *you*?' Bit of a reality check, I can tell you.

"Now, here's yours, Angela. You got time in this place. Not as much as a lot of women, and you haven't done anything nearly as bad as some of these women, and you're going to get out eventually, which some of these women aren't. And you've got a chance at a real life after this, a real, you'll pardon the expression, 'resurrection,' which some of these women don't. Bottom line? If you blow it, then, that's on you, not on God. Despair, Angela, is boring."

Angela's back straightened, in a way she hadn't known it could straighten before she came to prison, if she admitted it. It was a kind of anger and defiance and challenge all at once. "You're a bit different than Sister Eileen, aren't you?"

Sister Brigid grinned. "Hell, yes. I'm here to tell you that you've got work to do, my friend, and it's about forgiveness. It's about forgiving yourself and getting that lovely little ego out of the way and letting the light shine on through."

"Easy as that?" Angela was not sure whether she wanted to walk away or turn her battered and fragile soul over to the care of this woman, who was so damn *sure.*

With a laugh, Sister Brigid said, "Not in any way. But you want to walk that road, I'm here with you, and so is Eileen, but you already know that."

"And my son?"

"Hey, miracles take time. Give it a chance."

The clarity in Sister Brigid's face came close to seducing her. "Pretty sure of yourself."

"I'm sure of God."

And it started like that.

Intermission

What is there to be said about the endless days and weeks and months and years of prison life?

What about outside those razor-wire-topped walls?

Time passes, as time does. There is one season … spring-green, and then another … furnace-hot … and another, full of colour and wind, and another … when the snow softens and silences the land and then melts into memory. And they repeat, as patterns do. And people do terrible things, and people have terrible things done to them. Some die. Some go to hospital. Some go to jail. And people do marvellous things. They catch babies dropped from burning buildings. They discover new stars. Lives are shattered and lives are repaired. Hearts are broken and hearts are mended. Couples divorce. Couples marry. Children are born. Wars begin. Wars end. Times of famine and plenty.

Philip remarries. He marries Ginny, a woman from the golf club, also divorced. They wed in the clubhouse and Connor is the best man. Deedee is the matron of honor. Connor is dating Deedee's daughter, Harper, and everyone hopes they'll marry one day.

Carston has a new love. Actually, he has two, and the women have yet to find out about each other, but when they do for a while they will all three be together, but that won't last and Carston will find himself alone while the women will go off and hike the glaciers of Iceland together.

Sister Brigid and Sister Ruth go to the prisons every day and hold the hearts of the men and the women as high above the turbulent waves of life as they can. And the men and the women have endured terrible things and done terrible things, and will learn, not because prison is a good place for them, but in spite of it, that they still matter. And Sister Caroline goes to the school and teaches young people about literature, because that is her vocation, and she believes, rightly, as it happens, that at least two of these children will go on and write great literature of their own. And Sister Anne retires from teaching. She lives in Camden and teaches English to newcomers at the Sisters of Saint Joseph Neighborhood Centre. And Sister Eileen still goes to the Pantry every day and she feeds those who have nothing, and there are more and more of them every day because the government does not wish to, or cannot, care for them — the poor who will always be with us. And so, as the seasons spiral, this net of nuns and others like them minister in a vast web to those who are the dear neighbours.

Wheels and wheels and wheels, and so they turn.

Angela

Three years, four months, two weeks, and three days later. Angela sat on the metal stool at the JPay kiosk. The light in the hallway was harsh. There wasn't a single skin tone it flattered and Julie, who was next in line, looked much the way Angela knew she, too, must look: washed out, hard furrows around her mouth, blotchy. She remembered paying a fortune for creams promising velvet skin, Ayurvedic oils, and Korean serums. A lifetime ago. Some of the women wore makeup. She had a cell of her own now, but her last bunky, Chelsea, has used a lipstick so purple her mouth reminded Angela of a grape popsicle. Angela couldn't be bothered. In fact, she didn't want to be attractive. The less attention one garnered here, the better.

Angela nodded at Julie, who nodded back and chewed her index fingernail, spitting what she pulled off onto the floor. Angela hardly noticed it.

She had fifteen minutes to read her messages and dash off quick responses. First, notification of money into her account from her lawyer. Good. She needed tampons and toothpaste and was desperate for some chocolate biscuits, if the commissary had any. She needed tuna, too, and some crackers and peanut butter. She had learned ways of eating as little of the prison food as possible. A note from Sister Eileen, saying she'd seen Connor. And a note from Connor! *Joy, joy!* Connor still refused to come and visit her, but after talking to Sister Eileen on a number of occasions, he did write, not frequently, but he wrote. It was something.

> Hey, Mom. Not much new. New semester starting. Doing okay. Don't hate my roommate. Lots of work, though, so got to run to the library. Take care of yourself. Connor.

She wrote back. Told him she loved him. Told him she was proud of him. Told him she was okay. Any harder conversations? No, no one was ready for that. Sister Eileen and Sister Brigid both told her to take it slow. She was trying.

What was this? *G. Clarence.* Sudden vertigo.

"Fuck. Oh, fuck!" She glanced over at Julie, but she didn't notice and if she had she wouldn't even care. One learned to keep out of other people's troubles in prison. Julie was talking to Mercedes, a tiny young woman with her hair in box braids. Something about their kids. "My mom don't think they need no vaccines," said Mercedes and shrugged. "Yeah, I say, let 'em get all the chicken pox and measles and shit while they're with her, not me." The women laughed.

Angela turned back to the screen and read.

> Dear Ms. Morrison, I think you will recognize my name. Sister Eileen gave me the address to find

you. She and me have been talking and she suggested I write to you to say thank you for making sure Darlene and me are taken care of. So that's what I'm doing. I'm not going to say it wasn't awful what you did but I guess I don't have to tell you that. You're paying for it and you are making amends so that says something. It has been hard for me. I will tell you. But I should also tell you that I forgive you for what you did. You should not have been driving drunk and you know it but it was you leaving me there that was the hard thing. I had a lot of trouble with that. You can thank Sister Eileen for it, I guess, but I have come round to forgiving you, if for no other reason than I got tired of being so mad at you and that was hard when you are paying my rent and food and stuff for Darlene, right? Joke. So there, I said it. I don't know if you want to write back or if I want you to. But you can if you want. There it is. God bless. George Clarence.

Angela quickly signed out, and, without a word, walked back as fast as she could to her cell and closed the door. She stood with her back against it and realized she was trembling from head to toe. Even with the T-shirt, jumpsuit, and sweatshirt on, she was freezing. True, it was always freezing in the prison in winter, just as it was always a furnace in the summer, but this was different. It was soul cold. It was bone-buried-in-ice cold. She feared if she began shaking, she would simply splinter into particles.

George Clarence's face, as it had looked during What Happened, came back to her, as it often did. The eyes, the terror, the grief. The mouth, open in silent screaming. He hadn't been in court, of course. He was still in the hospital. She'd only seen him in that single, frozen-in-amber moment. He had lived in her brain, frozen in exactly that second.

He forgave her.

He forgave her.

She had, she now realized, never considered that. Was this true? She pressed her fingers to her mouth and tried to think. When she had set up the trust, had she not hoped for forgiveness? God, no, she had not. She had set up the trust in the hopes the court would show her mercy, for her goodness, for her great good regret. It had never dawned on her that George Clarence would forgive her. She slid down the door until she sat on the icy floor and wrapped her arms around her legs, burying her head in her knees. George Clarence forgave her.

SISTER BRIGID FINISHED listening to what Angela had to say and smiled.

"How do you feel?"

"I don't think I know."

They were sitting in an empty classroom in the Hall, since Angela had requested a private meeting with Sister Brigid. The room was painted blue with the kind of metal tables that had chairs attached and made a terrible squealing sound if they scraped across the floor. Through the windows the grounds lay covered in snow, the boughs of the trees laden and drooping. The sky was a sharp, almost glassy blue. A group of women in the yard were having a snowball fight.

Angela took a deep breath and let it out. "I feel like I was waiting for it, but I wasn't. Does that make sense."

"Perfectly. I suspect you've been waiting for some external sign that you might forgive yourself. Some sort of approval. If someone else can forgive you, then you are not unforgivable."

Angela pondered this. She clasped her fingers and pressed her thumbs to her chin. It was slightly less cold in this room than in the cells. Her shoulders relaxed just a little. "Maybe." Her voice was choked and her eyes stung. "Probably."

"Are you going to write him back?"

"I've been thinking about that. I'd like to."

"But?" Sister Brigid tucked her chin and looked at Angela over her glasses. "What's stopping you?"

"I don't want to impose."

"He invited you to write, didn't he?"

"Sort of. He didn't sound sure." Angela took the tissue Sister Brigid offered her and dried her eyes. She had learned over the months they'd been talking that the nun was always sympathetic, but not a big fan of tears. Angela suspected she thought they were usually pretty self-indulgent. Angela suspected she might be right.

"Well, you can understand that. He doesn't actually know much about you except that you hit him with a car, left him in the street, and then made his life a hell of a lot better. You can understand the confusion."

For a second, Angela bristled with her old tendency to feel insulted, but then remembering what she'd come to know about Sister Brigid and her often subversive sense of humor, she started to laugh.

THAT EVENING, just before seven, Angela sat in the common area of Bravo Unit, drinking tea and playing Crazy Eights with Janelle, Lynne, and Ellie. Other women were in their cells watching television or their JPay tablets (if they could afford them), gossiping and talking at other tables, a couple reading magazines. Angela had developed a friendship with Janelle, who was smart and witty and who liked to do crossword puzzles. She had an eighteen-year-old son studying economics at Penn State and they talked together about their sons often. Lynne, a freckled blond who looked like a skinny teenager, and who reminded Angela of Deedee, was new, doing five years, and was as nervous as Angela had been when she first arrived. Ellie, who came from up in the Ramapo Mountains, would be getting out soon. She was afraid of getting out. She'd been inside for fifteen years and although her sister said she could stay with her, their relationship was hardly good. She was a rough, motherly sort, all floury and soft in the middle.

Janelle laid down an eight of clubs, looked at Angela and said, "What's going on with you? You got a new boo on the outside, or what?"

Angela chuckled, raised an eyebrow, and throwing down an eight of spades on the eight of clubs, said, "A boyfriend? Hell, no. I don't care if I ever have one of those again, but I think maybe, well, maybe, a new pen pal."

Ellie popped a six of clubs onto the pile. "You don't need a pen pal … you need a man. Yum, yum, yum. Puh-leeeze." She smacked her lips. "Or am I talkin' about me?"

The look on Lynne's face showed how gross she thought it was that a woman of Ellie's age, being over fifty, would want a man.

"Don't give me that look, girl," said Ellie. "You'll see once you been here a while."

"You go to one of them prison pen pal sites?" Janelle asked. "I didn't think you was the type."

"No. Hardly. Just someone I met once. We have a mutual friend.'

"Well, good luck to you," said Janelle. "That's me in!" She tossed her last card onto the table. "I win!"

Epilogue

It is an early October morning, six and a half years since Angela went to prison.

Eileen looks up from her prayer journal and gazes at the maple tree outside her window, vibrant in the apricot light of the rising sun.

She will leave for the Pantry soon, and there she will see her friend Angela.

And it had happened this way: year three of Angela's incarceration. The same metal tables. The same children playing and crying. The same Cokes and cheap snacks. The same officer at the door. Angela in her orange jumpsuit. After all these months of visits, after all the prayers, after all the conversations Eileen had with Brigid, after all the conversations Eileen had with Connor, after Connor began to accept Angela's calls … Angela had been different.

She had leaned across the table toward Eileen, rolling a can of Coke between her palms, and said, "Listen, I know everyone hates being told someone else's dreams, but I'd like to tell you mine. Is that okay?"

"Sure."

"Well, I had this dream, and in it I had died. I was dead. I was in some place without form, and really dark, but not black, more reddish. And next to me was this — I know it sounds corny — *light*." She ran her fingers through her now short hair, more grey than auburn now. "Capital *L* light. In a sort of column. How Biblical, right? And here's the thing — I'm on my knees with grief. Absolute, inconsolable grief, the kind a child has when she's like, accidentally killed her puppy. That grief. It was crippling. And I kept saying, over and over, *if only I'd lived my life differently. It would have been so easy. If only I'd lived my life differently. It would have been so easy.* But it was too late. I'd fucked it all up. Like, I'd damned myself. But here's the thing, that Light, that Light, it knew all this and loved me still. There was no judgment, except the judgment I was passing on myself now that I *knew*, I understood, and it was excruciating. But that Light. It was nothing but mercy." She rolled her eyes. "Well, that sounds cheesy."

Eileen said, "There's nothing God can't forgive. But like you've talked about with Brigid, sometimes forgiving yourself is more difficult."

Angela wiped away tears. "And here's the other thing. I read this book of poems last week — it's here in the library — by a woman who wrote it while she was dying of leukemia. Jane Kenyon. There's a line that says something about how God is like mercy wrapped up in light." Angela shuddered and laughed.

Eileen sat quietly, and then she, too, chuckled. Because God was funny that way. Turning up where you least expected, okay, *her*. But turning up. Playing with time. Even in Angela's heart, it seemed that every vestige of resentment and anger was washed away.

"You've had an encounter with the Sacred."

What a day that was. What a moment of grace.

ANGELA WORKS AT THE PANTRY part-time as a sort of general dogsbody now, doing whatever is required, from stocking shelves, to gardening, to dealing with clients. She is good at her job. Carsten even pops in from time to time to see how the garden plots are faring and to help if needed. He and Angela are friendly now that the initial awkwardness has faded. Eileen credits Angela with the ease between them. Angela had been genuinely happy to see him and had even apologized. There is a new woman in Carsten's life, Pilar, quite young, unmarried, a girl who fancies long flowy skirts, lip piercings, and has a python tattoo slinking up her right arm and shoulder. Angela seems to like her, and if she is in any way envious, it never shows.

Claire, who handles communications and fundraising at the Pantry, plans to leave when her baby is born in three months and Eileen hopes Angela will take over. She also works part-time for an organization that brings literature to marginalized populations. Neither job pays much, and she lives in a little one-bedroom apartment down the street from Eileen, Ruth, and Caroline. Her social circle is comprised of people in the neighbourhood, people who work in the Pantry, and people she's met at church, and one other person: her son, Connor, with whom she is slowly rebuilding a relationship. She missed so much of his life — the whole of his undergraduate and most of his graduate years. He works with his father now, and is engaged to Harper. It's slow going, this rebuilding, but Eileen is more than hopeful. Connor even came to the

Pantry twice to volunteer and Eileen had been concerned Angela might explode from joy and pride.

After months of warily circling each other, a number of emails, telephone conversations, and several coffee dates after Angela was released, with Eileen acting as mediator, and even more with just Angela and George, the two have become unlikely friends. And not merely because of the trust Angela had set up so George and Darlene need no longer worry about making the rent or about health insurance. It turns out George, Darlene, and Angela share a love of popcorn and jigsaw puzzles and old classic movies.

Eileen shakes her head now, and smiles. What a gift Angela is to her. It is easy to love those who have been harmed by life. But not so easy to love and to forgive the ones who have done the harming. It is easy to love the old lady who's been robbed, but how to love the man who robbed her? How do we love the boy who shoots the man waiting at the bus stop in order to steal twenty dollars? How do we love the woman who leaves her children alone for days at a time while she's out getting high? How do we love Angela, who lost herself, became terribly selfish, and hurt people? How does she love herself, a woman who slapped a child?

It is good to have an angel to wrestle with. Angela had been her angel disguised, as angels often are, in the clothes of the sinner, disguised even to herself. Not that Angela is an angel, or even a saint, not even close, but she is full, full of life, of love, of passionate care for others, full of surrender to grace.

Eileen says a prayer of thanks. She opens her eyes and once again looks out the window, thinking how autumn is a lesson in the beauty of letting go, releasing, allowing the good air to take you where it will, and letting the good earth hold you when you got there. In this moment, the leaves shine copper, bronze, and brass. When the wild music of the wind blows, the leaves flurry and swirl in their unrestrained, irrepressible dance, free at last, and joyfully surrendered.

ANGELA SITS ON THE BENCH in Cadwalader Park, a small dog beside her. Prison life has trained her to get up early, very early, and she is grateful for that. She often rises before 5:00 a.m., prays and does a little yoga, and then takes Bailey, the whiskery rescue pup, to the park for a frolic before going to work. (Bailey has become something of a mascot at the Pantry.) Just to sit or walk in the green (safe at this hour of the day) is a blessing after so long in small, noisy, locked spaces. Oh, the gift of quiet. Who knew she would cherish it so? To sit in a quiet room, by herself, or to sit here, with the cathedral of trees, the stained glass of the leaves, is a luxury beyond measure.

She loves the mourning dove who calls with her plaintive song, and the nuthatches, the chickadees, the wrens and sparrows, the robins and wagtails and finches. She loves the pigeons, too, and the mice and rats and foxes and the possum she'd seen once, although Bailey remained unconvinced about the possum. This time of day is good for the creatures, before people come and stake their claims. She loves the squirrels, too, and laughs at their antics, their nerve and irritation. Every creature going about its business, needing nothing but what it is meant to do next. A place without fame, or spotlight, or craving.

She tilts her head back and closes her eyes, letting the sun warm her.

Bailey makes a little noise and then a little yip of greeting. Angela opens her eyes. A woman approaches, pushing a rickety shopping cart filled with plastic bags and cans and some things that might be sweaters or T-shirts. She wears camouflage pants and a black sweatshirt and a red jacket far too large for her. The clothes are soiled and stained. Greasy tendrils of brown hair escape the baseball cap she wears. On her feet are canvas sneakers, but no socks, and her ankles are smeared black and grey.

Bailey's tail wags like crazy. The woman nears Angela and says, "Give me something." It is not a request; it is a demand. She is malodorous, with scabs on her face, one of which she picks at.

Angela wears a small leather pouch across her body, containing a small amount of cash, her keys, a driver's licence (although she doesn't have a car), and a bus pass. There is no makeup; she gave that up in prison. She has a ten-dollar bill, which was supposed to be used for a few groceries later. She hands it to the woman, who takes it without thanks, and it disappears into her coat somewhere. Bailey continues to wiggle and tail-wag.

"Dog looks friendly," the woman says.

"Hasn't met a person yet he doesn't love, in spite of the abuse he suffered as a pup."

The woman reaches out to pet Bailey, who squirms with joy.

"Would you like an orange?" Angela takes the small clementine from a brown paper bag she carries and holds it out.

"Yeah," the woman says and sits down on the bench, her feet hooked around her cart, as though afraid someone will make off with it. She begins hurriedly to eat it, tearing it apart rather than peeling it, and biting into the flesh, the juice running down her chin.

"What are you doing here?" the woman asks.

"I like it here. It's quiet and pretty. What about you?"

"Me?" The woman cackles. "Well, sweetheart, I have a broken heart to heal and a broken soul to save."

"Don't we all."

"True, that is true." The woman chews on the orange peel, her hand on Bailey's head.

"I think I'll take another orange, if you've got one. Or maybe a sandwich. You got a sandwich?"

Acknowledgements

First, I must give my deepest gratitude and love to Sister Rita Woehlcke, SSJ, for her incredible generosity and wisdom. You guided me through the writing of this book, all thirteen drafts, as you guide me through life. I honestly have no idea where, if anywhere, I would be without you. All my love.

I'd also like to thank all the Sisters at the Saint Raphaela Retreat Center in Haverford, Pennsylvania, for letting me come and live as one of you. Special thanks to Sister Kathy Gazie, ACJ, for making me feel so welcome, to Sister Lyan Tri, ACJ, for sharing your own writing with me, and to Sister Jessica Kerber, for the great chat and incredible lunch. You all taught me many wonderful things, including the proper way to use an industrial dishwasher. I don't know where you get your energy!

Thanks as well for nick-of-time guidance to Sister Kathleen Rooney, SSJ, chaplain at the Edna Mahan Correctional Facility for making sure I didn't make too many mistakes. You were a godsend (literally) right when I needed you.

To Lynn Wilson. You got me all the details I needed. Thank you SO much.

David Forrer at Inkwell Management, you believed in this book so much you called me early to tell me! Ha! Thank you for your continuing support. This is our sixth book together. Let's do at least six more. You're the best. I'll try to earn an early call on the next one, too.

Thank you to everyone at Dundurn who shepherded this book through a pandemic! It's a real pleasure working with everyone: Jenny McWha, Scott Fraser, Rachel Spence, Sophie Paas-Lang, Sara D'Agostino, Kathryn Lane, Heather Wood, Kendra Martin, and Lisa Marie Smith. I hope we'll have a long association.

Shannon Whibbs, most excellent editor. Thank you for your patience as I flapped around on the final draft. Your calm, confidence, and willingness to take somewhat panicked phone calls saved me.

Thank you to Heidi von Palleske for urging me to submit to Dundurn. I'm so glad you did! Delighted to be sharing such a fine publishing house with you.

The pleasure of sharing literary pursuits with Sandra Kasturi is considerable, as is my gratitude for her instincts and humor.

Susan Applewhaite, what can I say? Constant as a northern star. My talented friend.

Thanks to Sarah Unger, who provided insight into the workings of a food pantry, and all the wonderful work you and others do at Arm in Arm Trenton.

Ron. I love you. The light in the window still guides me home.

About the Author

Lauren B. Davis's previous books include *The Grimoire of Kensington Market*, *Against a Darkening Sky*, *The Stubborn Season*, and *The Empty Room*, which was named one of the Best Books of the Year by the *National Post* and the *Winnipeg Free Press* and an was Amazon Editors' Pick. Her novel *Our Daily Bread* was longlisted for the Giller Prize and named as one of the Best Books of the Year by the *Globe and Mail* and the *Boston Globe*. She is also the author of the bestselling and critically acclaimed novel *The Radiant City*, a finalist for the Writers' Trust Fiction Prize. Lauren has published two short story collections, *An Unrehearsed Desire* and *Rat Medicine & Other Unlikely Curatives*, and her short fiction has been shortlisted for the CBC Literary Awards and the ReLit Award. She was born in Montreal, lived in France for ten years, and now lives with her husband, Ron, and their dog, Bailey-the-Rescuepoo, in Princeton, New Jersey.